HYMN

HYMN

Huck Fairman

Cover Art by Mara Arakaki.
Library of Congress Number: 2003098296
ISBN :   Softcover   1-4134-2352-3

This book was printed in the United States of America.

To order additional copies of this book, contact:
Xlibris Corporation
1-888-795-4274
www.Xlibris.com
Orders@Xlibris.com
20354

For Pamela

ACKNOWLEDGMENTS

I would like to thank Leita Hamill for her editorial assistance, for her encouragement, and for her friendship.

I want to express my deepest appreciation to Pamela, my wife, for her editorial assistance, her encouragement, and her support.

WINTER

New York City
Early 1990's

March 11th

Somewhere a phone is bleating, yet warm at last under my white wool throw, I'm reluctant to stir. The blank pages of my journal, of my recent life, stare up from my lap, daring me to begin. This last year, this Winter has stretched dark and heavy, has seemed interminable, like the ringing. Yet just as I know at some point my scribbling will begin, I recognize that first I will push myself up through the chill air, to snatch the thing from its cradle.

"Hello!"

"Christine . . . that you?"

"Who's this?"

"Easy gal, it's Josh. How're ya doin'?"

"Oh . . . Josh . . . Sorry."

"I happened to see in the paper that your father died . . . Wanted to say I'm sorry. Sorry for you both."

"Oh, well . . . thanks . . ."

"The notice said it was a long time coming."

"Yes, a long time."

"He wasn't that old . . ."

"Sixty-five."

Low whistle. "His smoking?"

"Yup . . . So, what's up? . . . Guess you're my old man now."

Josh coughed and gracefully changed gears, offering work, his usual travel piece, this time to "the blue skies and limitless vistas of Santa Fe, land of Georgia O'Keefe. And it's warm out there, I hear."

Tempted, need the work, the travel—change. Somehow he gets people, women mostly, at his pathetic rates—women eager for life, adventure, articles to fill their résumés. There was a time when I would have taken it, life on a shoestring, the romance of places and the occasional man. Before my marriage, when I was young. "Can't Josh. Got rent problems. I need more than you pay, unless you're opening your pockets."

He laughed. "Like to, for you, but you know . . ." He was being kind. He knew my rate has climbed beyond what he offers. But we chatted. He carries a fondness from the time we dated, years ago, after college.

Just before hanging up: "Oh Chris, try Kirsten. I heard she's looking for a staff writer, and she pays decently."

Thanked him before skittering back through the chill to my couch. Outside the wind had begun its low mourning moan, and rain railed bitterly against the sliding doors. Though I love this place, my aerie—even as it's bled me dry—warmth has never been its reason why.

Pulled up my throw again, and my pages. Have begun recording, under this blanket of snow, events, thoughts, and reflections in hope they'll tell me something new, and deliver me from these winter storms which never end.

March 12th

Called Kirsten at her office, my appeal carefully assembled on my tongue. Friend or colleague? Together we suffered through our divorces, but her editorship of *Avenue Magazine* rarely leaves her time for me. I've written free-lance articles and stories for her, which she's liked, but months go by without a word.

Today a new voice impatiently informed me she's out of town.

"And taken all civility with her, I see." Left my name.

Thus despite Josh's call, winter does not abate. I remain lost in a snow drift, twenty floors up, embraced by numbing cold, suffocating with interior stillness, pent up here in my penultimate penthouse, hostage to my three-thousand-dollar rent. If I leave,

Richard will have won, and I will have lost my only compensation from the divorce. Although I know I should be out pounding the frigid streets, seeking work and a place I can afford, I do not go. To go would be to concede defeat, not to mention that this is where I work best, where I forget the city and immerse myself in writing. Now, without Richard's stuff, it's clean, airy, and open—my Olympus, in an otherwise unremarkable life.

Feel the wind seeping in through windows and walls. Pull my Irish sweater more tightly up around my neck and stare into my white ceiling, rather than into the back pages of the *Times*, for apartments, jobs. Perhaps the headlines hold me back: violence and victims, the icing of cabbies and bodega pops, the homeless and gangs, kids killing kids and men killing women, drugs and corruption and clan annihilating clan—rage in all colors—men mostly, killing and killing. What's wrong? A miserable design, or genetic flaw? Father, for one, was resigned. This is the way, he said, it's always been.

My landlord gives me to the 31st to pay this month's and last—more money than I can hope to earn. Such are the prospects on the first anniversary of my divorce.

March 13th

Father, is it not *this* month, of extremes in these unnatural, CO_2 times, that is the cruelest? The month when winds howl and men tumble away like leaves, father or husband. Was it not these leonine winds which carried you off, snatched into nothing, your anger, your smoke, streaming up from your cigarettes, signaling your presence and your departure, each puff your signature, each a flag flying a doctor's prediction, accurate to the month. Your suicide.

Isolation is evidently our family affliction, shrouding Mother, Father, the lost one Luke, and me.

Fortunately, Kate rang, lifting me out of it, brimming with startling news—pregnant! Due late November!

"My God . . . Katey!" I knew they'd been trying, but . . . "Well congratulations!" Astonished, thrilled, even as I could hardly picture her with an infant. Yet we baby-talked until the phone blushed: googoo, booboo, doodoo—the essence of life, she laughed, not without ambivalence. Said she wants a boy, but then as that hung on the line between us, she amended it, saying she'd be happy either way. Yet husband Larry told her he wants a girl, like me. Yi-ee, men!

By October Kate will reach thirty-two, a year ahead of me, who's been wondering if she'll ever be a mother.

"Don't worry, Chrissy. A husband's a good first step however."

"Apparently not just any husband."

"Agreed Richard was a mistake, but I don't have to tell you you're fortunate in many ways. Things will turn around for you. I can feel it."

"Oh? Really?"

"Believe me. Larry was beginning to doubt we'd ever have a child, but at some point I just knew we would."

"Well I'm happy for you. And it gives me hope. Or maybe watching you, I'll get it out of my system."

"No, don't, Chrissy. Don't give up. You'll see, it's cycles. Larry says it's true of the market, and most everything else, and for once I agree with him. Wait, you'll get a job, find a guy; even the city will rebound."

"Right. And men will find grace."

"And you'll save your apartment."

Her intentions were kind, even if pie-in-the-sky. Showed me how pessimistic I'd grown. Something Father had noticed last Christmas. "Christine, my girl, cheer up. We all have our ups and downs. You know your mother was deeply affected when she lost her first pregnancy, but I told her it's Nature's way, not everything works out. Yet if one thing fails, something else comes along. The end of one thing is the beginning of another. And you see? Not too long after that, along you came."

No mention, however, of his cruelty to Mother, nor of poor Luke.

"Chrissy, you've read the Greeks. They understood the nature of things, two thousand years ago. What on earth makes us think Nature's changed?"

What indeed? And yet it's change I'd sought, and thought I'd found with Richard. But no . . . Ironic, for Mother and me, both devouring the wisdom of the ages, in books, that we did both marry badly. But ironies sprout like weeds. Our lives are half what we think they are and half the opposite. How often do I listen to friends describing other friends only to realize that they are in fact describing themselves. But then that, perhaps, is all we know. And yet, even there, though we continuously sketch ourselves, we seldom see the patterns.

March 15th

Despite the wind and cold, forced myself out into the park, to let my anxiety settle, or freeze, and to try to think. Can't deny it's foolish to hang onto the apartment, but it's my refuge, and now the only continuity in my life, without which I'd feel rootless.

The crocuses were pushing their tiny purple heads above the gritty, city earth. Myrtle soon will offer its shy blue flowers; forsythia buds about to burst, and fields of daffodils will soon unfold their green shafts and sheen of cream under the trees. Nature is clawing out from under its winter shell. Stopping, looking around, I saw that I was not far from where the woman jogger was raped and beaten to within an inch of her life.

March 16th

Middlenight, cannot sleep. Out of the dark march worries, like soldiers tramping hither and yon. What will I do? How should I live? Questions I thought I'd answered. Mind marches back to Middlemarch, that sleeping village where in an attic Dorothea labors, pondering a worthy life. My ardent heroine who never convincingly finds fulfillment or communion with her own oary-footed kind. Eh, Richard? My Casaubon.

Outside the windows, through half-opened eyes, I watch the

Ides silently coating spires with spears of snow and ice, late winter's spite. Hours pass drifting through shadowy thoughts. Arose in the dark, made coffee and toast—aromas which quicken the cells. So silent is the night, I might be in Maine, in the cabin by the lake, where I am landlord now, with brother Luke.

More questions come: what am I making of my time, my fortune, my mix of joy and loss? Though introduced to much, I linger in the shallows, or hide in my tower above the screaming streets. How to move myself into the possibilities?

Began to fill out a story accumulating in my head: a young woman, Penney from Penobscot—no, Eileen from Deer Isle. Eiley, as in wilely, who flees the damp New England winters and distant—no, abusive father.

> . . . Stepping into the kitchen, she felt hands and arms
> encircle her, jerk her off her feet, shake her violently. His
> voice came grating deep into her ear, "Listen, you try t'turn
> Ma against me, 'n' I'll snap your connivin' neck. You
> hear?" . . .

A swallowed, uneasy laugh. And yet Father had indeed sometimes evoked that fear, when he got angry.

Admist these musings, the lobby buzzed. "Ya brotha's down here, Miss."

Brother? Now? And yet I saw it was nearly eight.

When he stepped into the apartment, uncertain and ragged, it was in his usual cheap, chino jacket over a colorless, thread-bare sweatshirt hanging off his shoulders. His face was sallow and drawn, his hair and teeth thinning and worn. For years, my father and I have tried to help him, but he resists with remarkable agility, eluding each and every effort. His scattered thinking cries out for treatment, but his anxiety and paranoia hold him back. "Morning, Luke. What brings you here at this hour? . . . Been thinking of Father at all?"

A chilling glance, a scowl hidden by his turning head. "Yeah right." The angry sneer, from that familiar skull, whose shape is my sibling/myself. "Uh, listen, sorry to bother you. Just need to sort some papers." His Kafkaesque repetition uttered ad absurdum, after which he goes into my spare room, closes the door, unlocks his trunk, and for hours leafs through pages he's leafed through before.

Money from Father allows him to keep an ever-changing series of apartments, usually studios in the East Village, but he believes the landlords rifle through his belongings when he goes out, and so prefers to keep here what valuables he has, and lists this lofty tower as his legal address. Richard refused to acknowledge his existence, looking through him as if he were air. I offered Luke some toast, cereal, coffee.

"Uh, no, no thank you." The invariable pause before the invariable rejection. Moments rarely connect for him. I considered telling him about my threatened eviction, but decided its only effect would be alarm.

Later, after Luke left, I stepped out onto my terrace to feel the wind, inhale the air, Winter's last breath, I prayed, here high above the distant honking. And then turned to work again, amidst my cloud-like walls, and my two Giacometti-like paintings, two charcoal scars of spine and ribs, the only things I ever produced that Richard liked.

> . . . Through smudged windows, she watched the bleak, brown winter landscape bump by. On the bus she had briefly cried for her mother, with whom she had pleaded to come, to join her, to leave him to his stinking boat and fishing shed with its grimy nets, traps, and tools. But her mother only shook her head and tried to smile. Her eyes seemed to recede from Eiley . . .

Late afternoon, Kirsten finally called, summoning me. Trouble was, so had everyone else discovered she'd returned to her beehive. As I sat across from her at her desk, our conversation buzzed in sound-bites between her calls. I attempted to convey that my free-lance life wasn't paying my rent, and that I'd heard she needed a writer.

Dimly this registered. Her face tightened. She nodded and shook the hair back off her brow. "By the way, sorry to hear about your father." A pained expression creased her face, before she snapped up the phone again. When she'd dispatched another: "Now . . . where were we?"

"Kirsten, you had long ago asked if I might be interested in a staff job, and now I hear you're looking for someone."

"Oh, right . . . Well, yes there are some possibilities," she allowed through a calculating smile.

"If I don't find something, I'm going to lose my apartment."

"One can't expect to hold onto everything, my dear. Surely your father left you something."

Unhappily I stared at her. She blinked in grudging apology.

"You know the apartment was the only thing I got out of Richard. And it's the perfect place to write."

"Is it? Well then, it *would* be a shame to lose it. Maybe *I* should take it." Her cool, grayish eyes lingered on me, then swooped back to her desk and the again-ringing phone at which she swiped.

I pondered asking her for a loan, but something about the way she dismissed her other petitioners discouraged me. Some people, without knowing us, think we look alike and wonder if we're sisters—by which they mean they've noticed we're both blond, northern European types. Now as I watched her, I imagined how I may look when I reach forty, as she recently has—that unforgiving number, popped up on the horizon.

Free once more, she studied me with deliberation. "Now, as to your situation, unfortunately you've landed on me on one of my worst weeks: deadlines, conferences and this weekend, my annual Spring party. So maybe at the end of next week, I can give it some thought. I do need someone."

I stared at her, trying to hold myself in check, wondering if she enjoyed watching me dangle, wondering if I could broach the request for a loan.

"By the way I'm counting on your usual excellent hors d'oeuvres, for the party."

Embarrassed at this leap, this dismissal, I glanced away, then heard her take another call, and realized in this instant she'd forgotten me. Is this the world in which I want to make my way?

Later her secretary, Bill, called with a list. "Ready Christine dear? Got a pencil? Now, she wants those plums in brandy from Grace's, your divine pesto in filo dough, and your endive with roquefort. I'm nearly salivating . . . Oh, and she hopes you'll bring a few bottles of BV Beautour. Shall I spell Beautour?"

"Bill! I told Kirsten I have no money."

"Well surely, love, there must be a cash machine near you."

"Bill! There's no money in the account! Do you want me to spell *that* for *you*?"

Silence. "I see." Audible hemming and hawing. "By the way, I prefer William now. As for the other thing, maybe we can just put it on her little card."

Must be nice to be able to hire someone such as Billiam to take care of billings.

I'd nearly forgotten the party. Maybe it'll be the needed tonic. Wonder who she's set her sights on this time? Which unsuspecting male writer? I never know which ability she selects for first.

And yet I owe her, as many of us do. Her parties are famously festive, swirling, seasonal bacchanalias, drawing flocks of migrating luminaries, interesting people attracted like moths to light by her power and connections which she unhesitatingly exploits and interweaves masterfully. Confess sometimes I stand back in awe. She's got balls—whereas once again I'll be consigned to join the regulars, flinching with faint dismay as we catch sight of one another, lining up to winnow the possibles from the hopeless, seeking that rare, attractive, mature, unattached hetero. Hate the idea, but the alternative's worse. And give Kirsten credit, somehow she does manage to lure them, interesting men, from all over— more than I could ever unearth. Indeed some quite attractive, if too often married or gay—neither of which seems to bother her. Perhaps it shouldn't me.

Later, called Kate. Dear Kate didn't mind that it was late, as Larry's travelling. Said she wants to continue teaching right up until the birth; then will give it all up for at least three years. No problem as Larry's raking it in—never mind that she hardly sees him. Indeed she seems to accept the intrinsic limitations of husbands as part of the natural order. Seems to feel it's women's burden to hold relationships together, through all the charming crap. "Who d' you think would do it, Chris, if it didn't fall into our laps?"

I had no answer. I was recalling that when Larry makes his little sexual comments to me, she treats them as if coming from a little boy, as may essentially be the case. I've never told her about Richard and his little students.

Later began thinking maybe I should give up the apartment and travel . . . travel, work, travel . . . Yet I'm no longer like that, no longer the adventuress, and growing less and less so. These shocks, these losses have, I fear, shaken something out of me.

March 17th

St. Patrick's. In the distance, drummers drumming; their percussive waves come rising through me, as I imagine their legs lifting in lockstep, while before me in my mirror, my face, pale bone, stares out insipidly. 'Classic,' I'm told; 'striking,' I've heard; even 'beautiful, like the moon.' Yet am tired of its surface, and same old stare. How to reach where the drummers do? Within the lunar curve.

Now I hear the horns blaring above the drums. The bagpipes begin their wail, reaching for recumbent hope. Can almost understand

> why men march out to die,
> called by a greater hope to be,
> beyond the ancient Gods who paced the sky,
> jealous of those who died for thee.

Cannot move. Recall the faces of early heartthrobs, boys with features smooth and scrubbed, and gem-like shining eyes. Did they share the lofty visions? The souls I gave them, the ones I loved.

March 18th

I shiver in solitude, motionless, watching my last dollars slip from my hands. Today I dare not step onto my terrace, lest I dance off.

The silver lining is that I have more time, Father, to say goodbye—as we never really said hello . . . Can it be true? Both parents gone? . . . I still do not understand why you didn't stop your smoking, in face of warnings everywhere. You were not so old, had years to fill. Or is that what sent you?

The days drop off. My second year out of marriage meanders aimlessly. Seldom think of him—so odd that we were married. And sadly, Father, your image too begins to fade. I cannot hold on to anything, it seems. Or is it this rhetoric which holds me from myself?

Wind-blown clouds cross a tumultuous sky above my terrace, veiling and unveiling shades of blue. Wrapped mummy-like in three blankets, stare up into the beyond, and beyond the beyond. Who is this? And what have I to give?

Across the street on another terrace, a solid, middle-aged woman in gray dress and white sweater, unmoved by the gusts or sky, sweeps and cleans with never a pause or glance above. Farther south, two window-washers, stick figures in the distance, stuck like bugs to glass, squeegee in tiny strokes their Sisyphean labor. Yet we four are the only visible beings in this giant landscape. I turn away. There must be reasons why I'm no longer married, have no infants, am not working faithfully in an office or not begging on the street, or not writing something new.

SPRING

March 21st

The vernal equinox ushered in its celebratory party—a god-send allowing me to slip the weight of worry for an evening, taking me out of myself, assisted by a tall Belgian, Laurent, with whom I talked and talked, and when Kirsten led him away, he was soon back. We talked of all things: life and love and literature, discovering an easy understanding between us.

Of course eventually confessed he was later catching a flight home to Brussels—not that I'd had any real expectations.

We drifted around Kirsten's huge apartment, gazing out upon the yellow lights, talking of the city and Paris. I was dizzy trying to understand that he would so soon disappear. Someone caught us arms around each other in the bedroom. Painful to have to pull away—a feeling I'd forgotten. Wondered if it was him, or simply 'someone.' Thought of mentioning that my apartment was not so far away, with an even better view of the city. But couldn't quite bring myself.

He asked me if work takes me to Europe and gave me his card.

Then remembering he had to buy presents for his kids, invited me to run out shopping with him . . . No, no. For the wife too, no doubt. No, there were other people there whom I wanted to see. Accompanied him to the elevator, then into the stairwell, for a farewell kiss, which nearly seared the walls, all but consummating . . . What is this magnetism? Like discovering like? Finding light in another's eyes? Pure fantasy?

Said he flies over several times a year. Okay, okay. He knows where to reach me. Stayed alone in the stairwell a few minutes, to cool down. Then slipped into the bathroom to straighten things.

Kirsten of course made a point of mentioning his wife—very smart, very chic. Kind of her.

Yet now I was alight and alive. Met several interesting women, including a mesmerizing poetess from Senegal, who is a mother of six—delightfully sharp and positive. Also one very strange, diminutive androgynous soul from Bombay who oddly is writing about the early Christians and their Jewish precursors. How sad this little man's eyes were, so earnest his tiny dark face, to which I had to bend to hear. He seemed a shipwrecked creature from a nether world, not accustomed the sun, and in whispering his idea to me, he seemed to find shelter, "You see, I am studying, dear lady, the Teacher of Righteousness, founder of a sect which prefigured your Christ."

Possibly it was my own precarious future, or this little man, or the confluence of recent changes, but something got to me, for walking home I noticed, as if for the first time, two of the familiar neighborhood homeless, shadows in the doorways. I thought of the party I'd just come from, of all the money spent, of all the smart, glamorous, fortunate people. I thought of the ridiculous cost of my rent; I pictured my little Indian acquaintance trying to find truth in the shifting, illusory past. I thought of my brother, whose face is too familiarly my own, but whose brain I cannot begin to understand. Something's wrong, out of kilter. I see it everywhere and feel it in myself. I know I must shake myself, rid myself of things . . . and yet my Bombayan acquaintance reminded me that the reach of troubles has been with us from the beginning.

March 22nd

Morning sun lifted hopelessness, and I felt warm and weightless in my bed on this first Spring day—as if he were here. Arose into a fog, deliciously thick, where past was present. Such imaginings were still possible.

After coffee, I danced, to lovely Sati and Borodin on the radio, faintly crazed: pirouettes, arabesques, pliés and prayer, ecstasy-filled tears, over what was and what might be. Replayed last night's goodbyes, in French, taking both parts.

And when at noon the phone rang, held my breath, "Hello?"

"Christine."

Heart pounded, even in the instant I knew it wasn't Laurent.

"It's John . . . Trevelyan . . ."

My mouth opened, but my tongue was held by the past tumbling forth, pieces hurtling end over end. " . . . John?"

"Yes. Sorry I haven't called in a while."

"A while? Try September . . ."

" . . . That long?" I heard his breath expelled.

"Sure you called the right number, John?"

"Yes. Listen, Chris, I wanted to say—Well let's begin by saying I think we both knew we weren't a match made in heaven, heavenly though it sometimes was."

"Running old lines, Johnny?"

"Okay, okay. I owe you an apology, I admit, which is one of the reasons I called."

"John . . ."

He breathed. "The other reason is I'm coming to New York."

"Why, where are you now?"

"The beach, Malibu. But I've got a film coming up in the city and upstate New York. And I thought you might like to do a profile on the director, David Loomis. He's an interesting guy, your type I think. And as I said, I owe you, owe you as well for the profile you did on me, which has turned my career around. The phone's been ringing ever since. My agent loves you.

"So? . . . Chris? You there? . . . What d'ya think? I'll talk to him, set it up. It's worth meeting him. Then you can make your own decision. But I'm sure he'd be interested. *Avenue*'s a prestigious magazine, with national circulation. He couldn't turn down the publicity."

"A deal-maker now, eh? Adapting well. I'll have to talk to the editor first."

"Of course, but let me get the ball rolling. I'm sure your editor will jump. You know Loomis's name. He's big in New York, right? In the cities. He does those . . . thoughtful films."

Did 'thoughtful' nearly gag in his mouth, like 'foreign'?

"And hey, it'd be nice to have a drink, Chris. See you and so forth, when I get there."

My silence elicited the desired response, audible squirming.

"So what, uh, Chris? . . . Chris? . . . Okay, okay, I was wrong for not callin', but, you know—I mean you said yourself that we were night 'n' day; you were rebounding . . . and besides, to be honest, you know the scene out here . . . So listen, really, I'll talk to David, and I'll get back to you. Honest. I'll call you."

And that was that. If nothing else, an augury of things stirring, of change riding in on the March winds wailing through the blocks, moaning round my aerie. Street banshees I called them.

Tried Kirsten, but of course she was out. And so amused myself by turning Loomis over in my mind—what I know of him. His name conjured something uplifting, avian, an eagle, whom I may ask to follow in his flyways. A director of sad, lovely films, tragedies, of men primarily, gone wrong.

The possibility that this could bring Johnny and me back in contact was, well, an ambivalent prospect, representing as he did, impulse over reflection—something I thought good for me, at one point. After academic Richard.

March 26th.

Fools abound, however, closer than I cared to admit. Went out wearing my light suede jacket, thinking it was warm, only to be caught in icy blasts hurtling across the park. Frozen through, each rib individually freeze-dried, leading to the inevitable cold.

In bed, numbed with cold pills, spirits down, I noticed the weeks on my calendar were turning so quickly I'd barely had time to gaze at their art. And in the newspaper, for every uplifting story, glared two of murder and mayhem. 'Eastside man shot walking home.' Naturally Kirsten picked this day to call, but impossible to go out to meet her—a coughing, snot-filled mess. Like the snot-green sea, she quoted, sounding relieved and about to get off.

"But wait, Kirsten, wait . . . Two things."

She inhaled, re-girding her patience.

"First, I have a chance to meet the film director David Loomis, and do a profile. You interested?"

"David Loomis? How on earth did you . . . ?"

"Through a friend."

"He doesn't usually give interviews."

"Well, I'll see."

" . . . Sure, if you can get him. Let me know."

"And Kirsten, one other thing . . . Is there, is there any possibility of borrowing some money, as an advance of some sort, to pay my rent?"

Silence.

"I realize this is an imposition . . . and awkward," I mumbled. "But unfortunately I have no one else really to turn to." The words jangled, as unreal to me as they must've been to her.

"Why didn't we ask Laurent, when we had the chance?" she needled. "And surely your father didn't work all his life in insurance for nothing."

Her harshness stunned me.

"Sorry," she recanted. "How much are we talking about?"

" . . . Two months. Three thousand each."

"Two times three is six. Surely we can still do our tables."

"Thank you, Kirsten."

"Yes . . . Well, as I said, there is something. When you recover, come in and we'll discuss it."

"But Kirsten, in the meantime . . ."

"What's your bank? I'll send William over with a check."

The speed, not to mention the relief, dizzied me. I mumbled the branch and account number, but before I could add thanks, she was gone, the dial tone clicking on. Whether in relief or humiliation, my nose began spewing forth, more than it's possible for me to produce—the one area in which I'm prolific. Kirsten, in her inimitable way, comes through. Have to concede that for all her brusque self-absorption, she gets things done.

March 31st.

Recovered enough to venture out into the warming weather and walk a check over to the landlord's office, which I smugly gave to a secretary who seemed thankful for something to do.

Meandering light-headedly back through my neighborhood, as the dread of eviction slowly lifted, I found myself noticing, and this time pausing near, one of our local homeless souls, a black man, maybe thirty, whom I realized I'd seen before, sleeping on the grates, bent and leaning in doorways. For the first time I saw the real sadness in his eyes held to the ground. And yet, from my experience with Luke, I feared the problems were deep-seeded, the solutions long-term. Heavily I turned away, moving slowly down the block. Yet soon enough passed another, as if Fate thrust them before me. This time an older, large-framed, white woman I'd also seen before, carrying two shopping bags, a distressingly vacant look in her sunken eyes, recalling my poor cancer-ridden mother a decade ago. I forced myself toward her as she stopped and turned, swaying now in a townhouse doorway. Reaching out, I attempted to push five dollars into her hand, saying, "Here, I thought you could use this to get some food." But alarm gripped her; her mouth flapped in rising panic; she spun wildly and pushed through the outer door into the vestibule. Fearing that if I followed she might flip out entirely, I backed away to the sidewalk, stuffing my crumpled bill back into my jacket pocket.

April 1st.

Could not displace these encounters from my mind. They stood in stark contrast to my own improving prospects. And as others have before me, I wondered why I am here and they are there.

Called Kirsten. Away naturally. April fools. But William, perhaps hearing my frustration, stepped beyond his usual role.

"Christine, my dear, don't fret. While her highness is not in today, I can tell you, between you and me, that not only does she have a job for you, but she's selected an office, with real possibilities."

"Oh. Well, thank you. What is it?"

"Corner office, lovely view, a red Persian, and an art deco desk to die for."

" . . . And the job, William?"

"Oh you know, writing. But you might want to begin thinking about colors."

"Colors? . . . Well thank you again, thank you."

How strange and light I felt stepping out onto my terrace to clear my head and gaze. Then back to my couch, to work on Eiley's oily story.

> . . . She had shared an apartment with Cassandra for two months before her father somehow got her number. On their machine, she listened to him sputter, threatening to come down and carry her back. She imagined him red-faced and snarling before two New York cops in her lobby. Other times, he concocted lies about her ma's health—it never occurring to him that they talked when he was out . . .

And later still, scribbled a series of profile proposals to impress and properly nudge Kirsten—all finally culminating in a paroxysm of cleaning, down upon hands and knees, scrubbing with brush and soap my cell—a penitent, even as I felt unshriven.

April 3rd.

Unexpectedly, John called promptly back, delighted in announcing that yes, Loomis will meet with me, and "the rest, Chris, will be up to you and your charm." A West Coast dig, coming from where charm is only a ploy.

When I in turn called William to leave this information, Kirsten hopped on the instant I mentioned it. "Congratulations. That's a real coup. And I'd like to meet him, by the way. I expect you to arrange it . . . As a matter of fact, while I've got you, why don't you come down. I'll explain this idea I have, and I want to introduce you to the people you'll be working with."

In her sun-strewn office, I presented my proposals and a description of Eiley's developing story. Leaning back in her chair, she appeared . . . well, pleased.

On the subsequent tour, she introduced me to Melissa and Benjamin, "your colleagues, if it works out," and showed me my office, instructing William to take my list of needs and colors. Colors? What else but the whites and blues of my skyway?

When I asked her if I might continue writing part of the time at home—only in its solitude do I begin to stretch my brain—she told me to work it out with Melissa and Ben. And then she was off.

This time I didn't neglect to broach the subject of pocket money with William, who, from beneath a condescending, if munificent smile, produced a check signed by herself, rendering me, in stuttering images from my past: apprentice, dependent, daughter.

At home, called Loomis's office, discovering his friendly secretary, Martina, knew my name and would check with him and get back.

April 7th

Thus were patterns shattered. Now daily I have spiraled down, bumping shoulders 'midst the hurly-burly, straining to learn the ropes, writing, writhing, rewriting to find the style she wants— she who doesn't hesitate to criticize. Researching, proof reading, critiquing my drafts and theirs—half journey, half drudgery— mostly with Ben, as Melissa has remained mysteriously aloof, floating along the halls beyond reach. Yet I have liked her writing and told her so. And neither has seemed to mind if sometimes I disappeared in the afternoons, when not collaborating.

Thus it was, at the end of one such afternoon, when the city was once again strangely subdued, as it had been under the last snow, and nothing moved up here in the stratosphere,

where I lay napping,
after hours of tap-tap tapping,
working up my tale of wear and fear,
came a dream a-gently ringing
like a bird a-softly winging
gliding past my reclining ear.
Tried to catch this cool deceiver,
tried to calm my rising fever,
but then came Martina's proclamation
that my year long consternation
will vanish with the wind;
that all I'd hoped heretofore
would soon set foot upon my shore;
that David Loomis and Trevelyan,
and all the other nameless hellion,
would soon be here.

Whereupon I must arise and go
to persuade this man I do not know
that I can bring some special thing
to his world of which he's king,
that though I'm little more than half his age,
I shall summon the wisdom of a sage.

Yet, lest I forget the twists of fate, as I was floating through the lobby late, out for bread and wine, and thence to Kate, Tony took me aside and told me sotto voce that an elderly woman on the tenth floor had been beaten and robbed as she opened her back door to put the garbage out. No one saw the man besides the old woman, and she was in too much shock to describe him. Tony doesn't understand how he got into the building, as he swears he keeps an eagle eye. But he warned me to be careful when using my service door.

It infuriates me how frequently these older women are victims. What kind of scavengers are these men? I could become a real sexist, if I allowed myself to vent my rage.

April 11th.

Did I have everything? Notebook in bag, a fistful of pens, a swatch of clippings and contracts. And most importantly, hoped this outfit was pleasing, for as much as I have resented it, first impressions in this business can be crucial, can persuade one Loomis or another to stay open the door. Is there one who's not a sensualist?

Despite this being end-of-day, and having glanced at my watch seventy times, despite my anticipation, I was somehow late, even before I got out the door. And of course the elevator wouldn't come, tied up by all the little shoppers and poodle-trotters shuffling home. Thankfully Tony was still on the afternoon shift, and not Frank the grump, for dear Tony found me a cab, though pathetically I'm still not sure what to tip him. It lurches from fifty cents (and a terrified smile) to five bucks (and a casual shrug) all for no apparent rhyme or reason. He must wonder, as do I, Tony. As do I.

But the lunacy didn't stop there. My cab driver was some pumped-up Rasta, swaying and driving to the music—". . . No woman, no cry . . ."—barely visible through the safety partition and incense. He made the turn onto 57th Street on two wheels, then let me off in the passing lane—at rush hour. God! One wonders how the city functions. Ran between the screeching cabs, the screaming drivers, the piles of people rushing home. Felt my skirt riding up as I ran, my blouse tugging open. Unraveling at the crucial hour? Maybe not the cool analyst of men of vision. Maybe just a simple country girl.

> Kinda wonder should I ask her,
> if she left her heart out in Nebraska?

Somehow found the office, where kind Martina seemed unconcerned by my tardiness. Down to earth, no pretensions, inner strength, mother of three, I gathered from the carefully posed Kodacolor on her desk. Rather uncommon, I've found, in the precious world of filmmaking, and a good omen about him. Perhaps he would be neither disdainful nor bored.

While Loomis was held captive on the phone, she gave me a publicity blurb on his new film, "The democrat."

> 'Unfolding in the picturesque Adirondack mountain town of Trappers Lake, "The democrat" portrays the struggle of a young man, Stephen Boylan, to save his dying community. Changing economies and recession have left it on the ropes. Most of the young people have fled, for want of jobs or fun. Yet the old guard resists innovation, having seen the promise of the 80's dry up. Divided by these contrasting visions, factions have grown contentious and bitter. And when Stephen proposes a community-owned club as a first step to revive the town, the fears and frustrations on both sides finally erupt . . .'

Land of love . . . though I've seen some of Loomis's films and know of his reputation . . . still, dying, rural town? Whose idea was this? And what was I supposed to do with it? Write its obit? Thank you, John . . . Well, I supposed less auspicious premises have been hewn into compelling shapes before. If John can somehow transform himself into a credible Stephen, given his own less-than-idealistic bent, and if Loomis proves to be the magician John hinted he is, they may mold something. Otherwise the public will shower this tale with yawning inattention.

"David's off the phone, Christine. Why don't you go in."

"Thanks, Martina."

Stepping inside his office, a little shaky from both his eminence and the blurb's infusion of doubt, I found him seated behind a desk at the far end of a long, silvery, green-gray room. Distant though he seemed, I could make him out scribbling busily with a silver pen on blue index cards, his silver-haired head—all so nicely color-coordinated—tilted intently down. When he looked up, the effect was unexpected—evoking, and it's the only thing that comes to mind, Spielberg's mother spaceship, all light and transcendence, a sublime, floating cathedral.

His eyes, the center of this effect, were large and embracing, within the airy blond frames of his glasses. They seemed, as I approached, to take me in, and I found myself, even experienced old me, transported, slightly dizzy, as if encountering an extra-terrestrial.

With some effort I managed, "David, Christine Howth."

Peering over top of his glasses, his attention apparently tugged in several directions, he rose smiling, extended a hand, and murmured, "Delighted." We shook hands. His was cool, bony, not soft, and from the other, the dim glow of a wedding band solemnly winked at me. He smiled again with a radiance arising, it seemed, from contemplation of his own greeting. And somehow I shared his bemusement.

Under his silver hair, his face was sharply sculpted, its outline and planes still youthful, his skin still relatively smooth. There was a delicacy to him, and yet his features were not quite harmonious, not all of a piece, but composed regions, across which the overarching impression was . . . luminous.

"Glad you could come, Christine. I apologize for keeping you waiting. The phone, as it probably is for you, is both boon and bane of this business. Have a seat, there. Please."

Half-turning, I found the suggested chair occupied by a pile of 8 x 10 glossies, topped by a too-glamorous, ever-smiling actress—your basic nightmare, to borrow a line. No matter, I settled down upon her anyway (incubator, incubus) peering cautiously back at David, who, descending into his chair, didn't notice. Despite loftier admonitions, I found myself gauging with some relief that he was close to six feet—important to me at 5'9" in bare feet, maybe even 5'9 and 1/2". His gray cotton pants and blue denim shirt produced an effect both younger, in styling, and older, in their slightly starchy weightlessness, than his years. But without question, the focal point was his dancing, yellow-green eyes—bright, blinding filaments.

"So, I understand John Trevelyan has sent you."

"Well yes," I squinted back. "He's thrilled to be working with you. But before that, I'd seen two of your films, "The Kestrel" and "The Rise and Fall of Daniel Morrone," which I thoroughly enjoyed."

His eyes laughed; his mouth began to, silently enjoying, I surmised, my attempt to cover the bases. But he composed himself, so as not to offend me, nodded graciously and waited patiently. His warmth encouraged me onward.

"I am, by the way, as John must have told you, a free-lance writer, who has done, among other things, a piece on John which appeared last Fall in *Avenue Magazine.*"

"Oh? Well yes, I remember . . ."

"I have a copy with me."

"Yes, I'd love to read it. Thank you." His blinking eyes dispensed discreet flashes.

"As for why I'm here, I would like, if I can interest you, to write a profile on you, in which I would focus on you and your new film, but would weave into it some of the themes of your earlier ones." Bravely I maintained my gaze, as he scrutinized me. Fearful of some telltale twitch, I tried to relax.

"My goodness," he exclaimed, and unexpectedly I detected a flush of embarrassment. "I'm flattered . . . I guess John had mentioned something of that too, but so many things are mentioned; one never knows." And he bowed to me Japanese style, from which he did not altogether rise, remaining bent in pondering. I saw concern etch tiny dark lines at the corners of his eyes, which moved slowly, carefully, over the papers on his desk, until he looked up. "While I generally don't give interviews, tell me what you have in mind."

Remembering to breathe, I began to explain, "I find, David— Do you mind if I call you David?"

"Not at all, it's my handle."

Amusement mingled with amusement, smile released smile.

"I thought, David, that if possible, I would like to draw from a series of conversations with you, and from your rehearsals and naturally the filming itself, an understanding of how a good film is put together. And for this, my editor has promised me generous space in the September edition."

Eyebrows rising, he studied me, touched his chin thoughtfully. "Well yes, and how would you like to write a little publicity for us as well? We need a little alchemy."

Had I been too glib? I felt myself tense.

Perhaps he saw I needed rescuing. "As kind as your proposal is, I wonder if there's much interest these days in filmmakers. I know the era, if not the error, of auteurs has passed, with the passing or retirement of many of the great directors. I've read we're living through a pared-down decade, paying for the excesses of the past, facing another fin de siècle."

Faint panic rose. Rejection? What should I do? How to save it? Without thinking, I replied, "Surely, David, there must be a sizable audience out there which is interested in serious films and their makers."

"In films yes, but who, these days, wants to meet their maker?" (Fleeting grimace, both.) "For one thing, people have come to recognize that we, in this business, are the usual flawed souls, at best." His eyes have narrowed into a speculative glint. "And, Christine—Do you mind if I call you Christine?"

"I don't know what else to suggest."

Eyes danced.

"I won't presume to tell you about your medium, of which I know little, but I was going to say that the period for great, innovative films seems to have passed . . . as it has, it seems, for novels, symphonies, painting, rock music, statesmen. These flourishings, I've read, come in clumps. Then things stop, fall fallow for a time."

"My goodness, David, are you really so pessimistic?"

His eyes widened as he summoned his explanation. "It's not pessimism, merely cyclical reality. No? Look around. Isn't the evidence staring us starkly in the face?"

Unwilling to look, my eyes fell to my notes. Could not fit together his darkness and light. When, however, I found his face again, it had darkened noticeably—casting a pall over my idea?

"But David, surely you don't accept that for yourself. Where would that leave you? How would you continue?"

He twisted his mouth as he looked away, jaw working. "The nimbly avoided question—because I have no satisfactory answer. What keeps me going? Inertia perhaps, or some faint ray of hope."

"Are you serious? "The democrat" sounds like a hopeful, even idealistic story."

Faintly he nodded. "I guess my point is that I'm not sure this is the best time to be following me around."

"I needn't do it literally."

A flicker of appreciation briefly animated his face. "Still, personally, it may not be a good time."

"But I needn't make it excessively personal. I wouldn't intrude. I'm flexible."

Again he sought out my gaze, yet I could not tell whether he was annoyed at my persistence or weighing my concessions. "But you see, Christine, that unless I solve some things, I'm likely to grow increasingly irritable and uncooperative, and why would I want to give audience to that?"

"But if directing were easy, what value would it have? If every hurdle were cleared with ease, if every film were a gem? . . . And David, the other argument I can make is that quite clearly you've solved these problems before, in your earlier films."

His eyes looked down and sightlessly floated over his desk with all its papers, until his expression sharpened, and he found my gaze again, producing in me a mild, and I hoped imperceptible, tremor.

"Don't think me ungrateful, Christine. I appreciate your offer. Indeed it's exactly what we need, so please don't misread me on that." And truly he seemed to wrestle with his own conflicting inclinations.

As I waited, I was startled by the sound of wings flapping—some waterfowl slapping the surface to lift free. Turning slightly, I scanned the room, but saw nothing. Did his silence make me mad?

Loomis stared out the window, drumming his pen on his notes. Finally he looked back. "May I propose this? . . . If I agree to go ahead, you must keep away from the details of my personal life, keep the focus on this film and earlier ones if you want—at least until such time as I have seen how several things are going to develop."

"Well, why yes . . . although I hope you will allow some account of what drew you into filmmaking, and directing."

He tilted his head to one side as he looked at me. "Limited to that, that would be fine."

"A deal, then?"

His face relaxed, softened. "A deal."

"Terrific. Thank you."

"And I'd like to read your piece on John."

I pulled a copy from out of my briefcase and reached forward to hand it to him. "David, I also have a letter of agreement, which you could look at and tell me if it seems reasonable. I'm glad to make changes. Then assuming we can reach agreement, we can begin." And this too I handed him, stretching forward across his desk. As I did, I could not help notice that his eyes fell to my blouse, then lurched further down, to the pile upon which I sat, whereupon they widened in distress.

"Good God, Christine, by all means move those photos off the chair. I'm sorry. Just throw them on the floor." And he shook his head, as I turned, stood, and bent to affect this little improvement, smiling superiorly at the ever-smiling, dark-haired beauty on the top of the pile whom I now placed face-down on the floor.

More comfortable, I asked, "Do you have some idea when I might sit in on your rehearsals, or when we might begin our chats?"

He looked down to his desk and calendar. "Of course I'd like to go over this agreement . . . but uh, . . . God, how the weeks fly. What's today . . . Tuesday? Give me a few days. How about chat Friday, observe Saturday, something like that?"

"You're already working on weekends?"

"Have to. Your man Trevelyan has other projects breathing down our lean and hungry necks." His furrowed eyebrows expressed distinct displeasure.

Yet as we gazed at one another, I told myself that for once Johnny may have been right. Here was an intriguing man, someone I looked forward to getting to know. And with that hopeful gaze, our meeting ended, and my little project took flight.

Buoyed by renewed hope, released by relief, I strode back out of his office, thanking Martina and exchanging a few words in anticipation of seeing each other again.

Out on the sidewalk, now less crowded, the thought that I will once again be engaged, solvent, excited lifted me off the pavement. Floating home up Madison Avenue, I found Loomis's face drifting balloon-like ahead of me, younger in my recollection, with the radiance of an angel, the beatitude of a saint—or some such phosphorescence.

Is it not these moments which lift life above mere existence? Does not occasionally the Sun rise bright, bathing the land, softening the views? Father, you see, there can be happiness in my life. It is not all drift and error. I hope that this will lift the disappointment which dulled your eyes.

As I walked, as my eyes floated into the Madison windows, wonderfully alive and bright, if obscenely priced, I reminded myself to enjoy it, Miss Chris, enjoy each moment, for this last year has all too clearly etched the lesson that things are ever turning.

Evening, April 12th

Spring unfolding has supplanted my famine with a feast. The pattern of my life has come half-circle, as Kate predicted. Thus arriving home electrified by Loomis's dancing light, I heard the phone ringing and found Trevelyan calling breathlessly from his midtown hotel, "Haven't eaten, Chrissy. How about a meal? What d'ya say? I'll come pick you up."

The pulse of life, the throb of blood, seemed to sweep all ambivalence away. He would come at eight.

Yet the clock struck eight, and John was late. Patterns indeed. Fidgeting, then fuming as I strode between bedroom and bath, passing the mirror's embarrassed image twenty times, neither of us able to smile. Attempted to work on Eiley's story.

> . . . Fiona, the editor she'd been hired to assist, wound
> slowly among the desks, acknowledging the others with a
> word or stiff smile, until her raven eyes locked on Eiley . . .

But Loomis's brightness blotted this out. Consumed a glass of wine and threw myself onto my sofa, breathing deeply—only to hear the buzzer buzz. Oh buzz off! It was nearly nine.

Waiting the final moments, tried to remember what he looked like. Then opening the door, saw it was a wasted effort. He'd changed, nearly into someone else: smoother, more tanned, more Hollywood. Brief pause, as feet and expectations shifted. Then an ushering in, midst garbled words, a hurried hug. "How great you're looking," he gamely tried, followed by a gaze of mild interest around my Spartan walls, before I lead him to the kitchen through a cloud of weightless thoughts. A beer I poured him. Cheese and crackers were slid under his nose. Watched him gobble, as I refilled my wine full up.

Don't know, maybe it was the tiny kitchen, the wine, the long solitary winter, the recognition that all is transitory—or maybe it was unfounded hope—but hands were soon alighting, playing over shoulders, curls and collars, and I had somehow mislaid months of fury.

And yet, in no mood to rush things, and as he was plainly famished, I took his hand and lead him out onto the terrace, where the cold wind buffeted us together—gazing into the firmament of city lights. And soon thereafter, we were in a taxi heading south to Soho, to a new French bistro, high on the in-crowd's list, his choice, not mine, where quite unexpectedly, we discovered things to talk about. He described excitedly his new role and working with Loomis, and I retold the saga of desperation that lead to my new job. But though he didn't notice the mention of Father momentarily subdued me, he did react to my excited account of meeting Loomis. His enthusiasm dimmed, his face fell slack, his eyes avoided mine. Poor man. Yet it is at just these moments, when John loses his too-confident glow, and exhibits a little despondency, a little vulnerability, that I find him most endearing. A humanness creeps in. His feelings feel almost real.

At some point, when he buried his face in the menu, I took the opportunity to glance around, and encountered the gazes of several women at other tables studying him—I had forgotten his celebrity. But faced with my counter-gaze, they shied away. Yet hey girls, no need to, not on my account. I have no proprietary feelings toward the man; in fact felt airily detached, perfectly content. Indeed the ambience, the thick white tablecloth, the heavy silverware, a single yellow rose in the slim-necked vase, the live piano music, the attentive staff—all suggested an order to life and Nature's forces. Whereas in fact it is to veneer the warts and rot and quiet desperations.

Asking Johnny about the cast, was surprised to see his face twitch uncomfortably. Hurrying a sip of wine, shaking his head, he explained he thought David was going to cast a Stephanie someone, but instead chose Pat Eliot. "Who's, uh, very good, but well . . . we just don't have the same—I mean I don't know her yet. I guess I should give it some time." He glanced at me, jaw clenched. "I mean she's fine, very good . . . but she's a little older, and strong, very strong . . . I don't know . . . Of course I can see David's point. An older Teresa makes her decision to throw in with Stephen . . . heavier, I guess."

Thoughtful John gazed thoughtfully at me, as if he were considering my age and suitability for this very role. But then he caught himself, swallowed, and in a nervous gesture ran his fingers through his dark hair. I imagined I could understand the anxiety he felt. How would he bring Stephen roundly into life? What would he draw from in his former existence, an Indiana farm hand's son, Johnny Trubinski?

Seeing that he needed a little support, I reminded him that David obviously believed in him, and without thinking, I reached for Johnny's hand and squeezed it—which he returned briefly, until the waiter swept up to take our orders, and ogle him.

When the fellow left, John reached for his glass and threw down his wine, shivered, and sent an unhappy look out across the room. Possibly he thought I was being condescending, and possibly he was right. But my intentions were honorable, for I hope things will work out, for David, and him.

Unexpectedly the wine loosened him, relaxed him, so that he began reciting Stephen Boylan's lines from the screenplay:

"Listen, Teresa, let's not forget . . . I mean I've been down there now, t' the city, and seen the hardness, where money rules, and little lasts . . . But here, somethin's thrown us together . . . to help each other maybe. Somethin's tied us . . . So let's not let it slip."

I wondered, as he said these lines to me, staring into my eyes with feeling, what he was thinking. I know John's quite a different fellow with someone else's lines in his head. As for me, I recognized that I needed something of what he has to give, even as I felt myself reaching for the brake.

Nonetheless our evening proceeded talky, tasty, occasionally catty, unexpectedly playful, until we found ourselves among the last patrons to unsteadily rise and sway out onto Prince Street to find a cab.

Slouched against each other, we went to his hotel and the dénouement, which yes, lived up to its billing, semblance of flings past.

I will say this much for John: as he tends to be mercurial, one needn't suffer any one mood too terribly long. And he does have his points of interest, beyond his God-given looks. Perhaps this fluidity of character is right for an actor, and in the right hands, just might develop into something.

As night crept into dawn, as I lay unable to return to sleep next to the heavily-breathing—nay, snoring—John, I wondered where this time it would go. I watched, it seemed, two smoke figures writhing in the dark above the bed.

But then my thoughts turned once more to Loomis. In my half-awake, pre-dawn state, in which I could not distinguish the city light from Loomis's aura, I thought of the worlds spun out by his movies, of the protagonists reaching, exceeding their grasps. At the same time, from somewhere in the neighborhood—we were not far from Carnegie Hall—I thought I heard faint strains of "La Traviata," its sadness and beauty, and I savored it, real or imagined.

Across the ceiling, reflections of cabs, headlights, buses edged then slid to the corners and dissolved. Loomis's face, faintly

Lincolnesque in its sharp features, and sadness, floated for an instant before me, winking, making me smile.

April 15th

Yesterday along Fifth, people were carrying their coats under their arms at lunchtime—heads up, eyes wide, drinking in the faces flowing by. The sun now presses through one's clothing and into one's skin, and crossing the avenues one need no longer lean into the headwinds. Within the park, fresh fragrances fill the breezes and a soft flickering effulgence dances on the new leaves.

Today will see my first official chat with Loomis, where I go, notebook in hand, to begin to sketch this man. I have fantasized my portrait may reveal him as the next Truffaut or Bergman, or that my critique of his themes will uncover some new interpretation. I laughed—Richard's dwindling influence, I suppose.

But what do I actually know of Loomis? An experienced director, who, despite what I believe are several quite good, intelligent, even moving movies, is not considered among the masters, however depleted they are these days. This may be more a matter of 'box office' than 'artifice.' Anyway, I shall see.

He's fifty, said John. Too bad not a bit younger.

But, on the plus side, he's a New Yorker.

Alas on the negative side, he's married, with two daughters.

Yet again on the positive side, some hint of trouble with the wife . . . And the oldest daughter's away at college.

Alas on the negative side, this turns out to be only up at Columbia, having recently transferred down from Smith. Grave mistake, said I, but 'no,' purred John. "She's something *special*." What does this mean, and how does he know? Alas how else? Nonetheless, John lauds Loomis, as after all, Loomis cast John. And John maintains I'll be pleasantly surprised.

Opening the door, I greeted Martina, who looked striking today with her dark hair pulled tightly back. We chatted about the weather, the movie, the city, Loehmann's—in short, the world. And then David was ready. As I gathered my things, I couldn't help but wonder if Martina works for him out of love, for when she talks of him, her face takes on a soft luster.

Holding my breath, I stepped in, as if entering a darkened theatre, play in progress. Indeed his office was darker this time, and he was again on the phone. Thus I had time to notice he wore an old, brown, suede jacket, having arrived from rehearsal not long before me. Holding up a finger, he indicated he'd be right off. Have a seat. And yes—brief smile—this time the chair was clear.

I sat, swiveled, and peered around. Along the wall facing the windows, away from his modern, cluttered desk, skylights bent and blended twilight with citylight into an unearthly glow. Photographs from his productions, tinted magenta by the glow, hung in two rows, and the actors' poses seem oddly discordant with one another, as if they might flicker and flee out of frame. I recognized tragic Horton Keswick from "The Kestrel" and haggard Daniel of "The Rise and Fall of Daniel Morrone," and the portrait of mid-American townspeople from "Terre Haute." It occurred to me that both Horton and Daniel attempt to bend the world to their visions, but stumble as they press and force things, whereas Stephen Boylan adapts to the realities. What does this theme sung over and over tell me of David?

My gaze crawled over piles of scripts, film cans, industry magazines and papers, piles of 8 x 10 glossies and résumés, videos, shipping cases, and even a few miniature model sets—the shavings and sawdust of his work. To be in the presence of all this, to recall those movies, gave me an indescribably rich feeling; I could smell the resin.

"Christine! Sorry. How're you doing?"

I turned to find him, though smiling, looking tired, bag-eyed, with dark patches marring the planes of his face. His glasses sat slightly down his nose; his hair, which had appeared silver when I entered, now seemed almost white, at which I could not help but recoil slightly.

"I'm fine, David. How about you? How'd rehearsal go?"

Holding me in his gaze, his attention nonetheless appeared to drift away. "Uh . . . better. Better I think." He blinked. "We were working on some of the early scenes, and John's coming along . . . coming along, coming along." Now even the focus of his eyes seemed to ascend toward the ceiling.

Waiting for their return, I was happy to dwell on his face which grew almost childlike in its absorption.

"You know I read . . ." he resumed, finding me again, "your profile of John, and found it both insightful, and delightful. You saw his potential, even if that movie was on the light side."

As I bowed appreciatively, I saw the lamplight dance in his glasses, reflecting, in their corners, portions of the windows, picture frames, and my own silhouette.

"Perhaps I should not have been surprised that we know two different Trevelyans," he reflected.

Our eyes focused in upon each other. His, softly yellow-green behind his lenses, appeared to have guessed about Johnny and me—something I'm reluctant to acknowledge publicly.

"For one thing," he began, delicately shifting, "while I knew he was from Indiana, I didn't know he was 'Trubinski,' before 'Trevelyan.' In a way I think it's a shame, maybe even a mistake, to detach himself from that fabric of his life. Although maybe not. What do you think, Christine? Do you mind if I ask?"

Alas he knew. I knew he knew from his expression and voice, and I could not help but flush and look away to gather myself.

"Maybe, David, very possibly. Sometimes he seems . . . I don't know, lost, unconnected, despite his recent successes."

David digested this, then leaned back slightly. "It's a difficult split actors are asked to perform, isn't it? To look daringly and unsparingly inward, while impersonating someone quite other to draw from and yet eclipse the solipsistic self."

"Can it be learned?"

"It can be refined, if the ability exists, but that ability to thoroughly inhabit body and mind of different characters is relatively rare."

Although his reply re-stirred doubts about John, it was the face before me which drew me, its particular light, its regions, its thin lips curling into smiles and thoughtfulness. And all of this brightened as he added, "Whether John will develop it, I'm not yet certain, but I'm hopeful, encouraged, even as there's work to do on this delicate task."

"And yet you cast him."

"An educated leap of faith, a calculated roulette Russe. Spin the chamber . . . and yet he has the raw materials for Stephen: mid-American directness, plain-spokenness, an instinctive egalitarian view, and, in the right situation, passion. And perhaps most important, the inexplicable: on the screen he holds one's attention."

"Then what exactly will be your role, if he has all that?"

Faint smile. "To be his mirror, his mentor, his navigator. We are both feeling our way, learning about Stephen and learning about how each other works, neither of which can happen overnight. Stephen is a complex character: simple yet sophisticated, idealistic yet angry. It can be tempting to follow a single tendril. But John, who's never really been pushed before, is ready to be, and I shall oblige him."

In spite of my skepticism, I put on a hopeful face.

"It's an interesting process, for all of us. Working, imagining, synthesizing, a process of filling one's self up with possibilities, and then paring most of them away. It's largely intuitive, which is not to say it doesn't take considerable thought and work. Christine, may I read you something?"

Startled, I wondered had I heard correctly?

I saw that he was searching his desk for something, leaning and finally snatching several sheets of paper. Finding me again, eyes flashing, he repeated, "May I?"

"I haven't been read to in years."

His cheeks creased, then crinkled. "This is from Becker's novel. I'll ask Martina to get you a copy of the script." He cleared his throat.

"For hours Stephen Boylan had been wandering up from the Lower East Side. The prospects for a reasonable job had fallen away over the two weeks, leaving him nearly penniless. Now as he crisscrossed the thirties, the specter of the long bus ride home grew more vivid, and he feared that if he paused to think about it, he might just hop on a bus at the terminal, no longer so many blocks away.

But crossing Forty-second Street at the Avenue of the Americas, he found himself hemmed in, shoulder to shoulder with office workers, shoppers, delivery boys, and salesmen and women. Swept along past other phalanxes surging south, seeing no seam through which to escape, he resigned himself to the multitude, and for a block and more he was carried north. Yet even when the mass began to dissolve, he could not immediately free himself, caught as if by its slipstream. His head, then body, grew light. The motion, the colors, the sunlight intensified. Finally, fearing he might pass out, he managed to thrust out an arm and hook it around a lamp post at 47th Street. Pulling himself to the edge of the stream, he closed his eyes and deeply and repeatedly inhaled.

When he opened them again, things had changed. Gazing west through streaking yellow cars, against canvases of white, the groaning buses, he now felt slightly above and apart, staring down at the humanity flowing around him— darting, striding, veering, like so many corpuscles. At the same time, so varied and vigorous were they, it struck him that this corner must be one of the world's unacknowledged crossroads, where its races, classes, and many of its cultures funneled together: businessmen and bums, Asians, Africans, Middle-Easterners, Middle-Westerners, and Middle Europeans, Hasidim, Muslims, musicians, actors and diamond dealers, panhandlers, students, and secretaries, merchants and shoppers. They and more were here, striding, sliding, and selling, yacking and yammering, begging the dollar and the question, stepping up and down, around and over—in short, acting out the madness of the modern urban matrix. And although now familiar with the city, he felt the scene before him was strange, almost alien. Its otherness chilled him, sent shivers, revealed, more clearly than before, how starkly different was the world from which he'd come.

As he watched, he began to think that for all its apparent energy and order, the city might explode—destabilized by its fundamental weakness: no longer was there much sense of community, with its attendant responsibility and sacrifice. All these individuals were moving faster and faster, each in his own direction, until the thing might come apart. And although money, ambition, and greed had long sustained, had long driven the city, now, in its accelerating fragmentation, it seemed to be reaching a state where it would lose cohesion, splinter, and tumble into chaos.

Standing there, pinned against his lamp post, he felt this fear urging him to flee, back to where forces appeared visible, abiding, and perhaps more tractable.

And yet, his reaction disappointed him for he knew that there were men who could understand, negotiate, even orchestrate things at this level. But not he, he who had been all but defeated by it. If there was one compensation, it was that he'd come to see his limitations more clearly, and accepted them, and now knew this place was not for him. He saw he must escape and return home. Yet he also saw that there were things, ideas and inspiration, he could take with him, things which carried the seeds of possibility.

David looked up, caught perhaps by some glimpse of this scene, before he blinked away whatever it had been and found me again. "A simple scene, essentially, Christine, but one that stirs and lifts him."

Yes, I was thinking, calling myself back from that corner, and wondering what about it specifically had moved David. "It stirred you too."

Our eyes met, although our minds seemed caught back above the avenue. "Yes," he murmured.

"Was this the passage which inspired you to do the movie?"

Tilting his head forward and shaking it slowly, he answered, "No, the book offers several passages of power and poetry . . . but for Stephen, this was the moment that revealed, amid this river of variety, that he might find something to contribute. It changed his perspective, and his life."

"Do you think, David, John will be able to convey that, that spirit?"

David smiled in a detached manner and looked away. "The key for him will be finding those strands in Stephen's life which that scene awakens: the possibilities, his determination rising out of defeat, the necessity of risk . . . If together we can find ways to convey those truthfully, then Stephen's transformation will unfold believably and interestingly." As he spoke, he grew pensive and still.

I could not help but wonder if this arose out of something personal. Yet reluctant to ask directly, I returned, awkwardly, to my list. "David, in your last two movies, you dealt with the dangers of ambition. Is that something encountered in the movie world . . . or is it from your own experience?"

Glancing at me he frowned, concerned that perhaps this had wandered into the personal sector. But then his frown softened, as he appeared to dismiss this difficulty. "Ambition, in my case, was first the naive desire to create scenes, and worlds, as I saw them or wished them to be—improvements upon the real world. Not a single vision or message to deliver, but situations and relationships to explore and solve. Both Horton and Daniel Morrone begin with something of innocent visions, but in their headlong rushing, their lunging, they stir up too many slights and wounds, and allow them to fester. Even Johnny, in "Johnny Be Good," runs afoul of festering."

Yes, I was thinking, bruises, slings, and arrows—the whole hearty crew, dispensed by father, husband, and egos everywhere. "And yet, David, directors and artists, never the easiest of types, have long been given latitude."

"Yes . . . but something wears . . . intrudes . . . limits, distracts from, the best work . . . Whatever one's hopes, it's just damned hard to get everything right. The best films are almost never made at the beginning or end of a career."

Attempting to fit these pieces together, I wondered what precisely troubled him. The path of his own ambition? The difficulties? Some haunting around the current film? "David, should you not take heart from your last two films? It's not only my view that they were stirring and beautiful, even sublime."

His eyes flicked my way, not happily, before a cloudiness suffused them. From some frustration? I couldn't tell.

But then his expression once more relaxed, and his features cleared. "What is directing? But juggling balls in the air . . . imagination and the quotidian, personalities and resolve . . . There are ample opportunities for things to go wrong, in story and character, but there is strength too, and serendipity, and others to help. If we brew rich fantasies, it is in the real world that they must be realized. To our many-ringed circus comes a stream of ideas and contributors, all with balls in the air." Now a sly smile emerged in his eyes. And though unable to quite interpret it, I felt myself joining in. Yet underneath, my question nagged. "But David, though clearly you've learned the director's art, still something concerns you."

His eyebrows reached above the rim of his glasses. "Of course. Nothing's cast in stone. Each production presents its own challenges, its own surprises and problems. There is no path or guideline, nor anyone, really, with an adequate overview to consult. And then one finds, the most implacable, insurmountable obstacle turns out to be oneself."

Inside I heard a chord resound, knell to my own slow-motion apprenticeship, in my trade and life. I fumbled through the notes in my lap, such plodding notes, and decided to alter the next question. "David, do you find at least some of the reactions, reviews, commentaries helpful, insightful . . . redeeming?"

His eyes moved over my face, then slipped again down to his desk. "Letters, the thoughtful letters, are perhaps the best. Some of the reviews, and obscure articles, are helpful, gratifying. But I have no preconceived notion of how people should respond. We tell each other stories. We offer observations. People take pieces or the whole, as they will. They find the threads they want, or those that tug them.

"What *is* disappointing is the superficial discussion in the popular media. I think those publications underestimate people, with their simple opinions, up or down. Moreover, not to discuss where things come from—at least the serious efforts—or what is added, is an historical and intellectual disservice. That was the value of a reviewer like Pauline Kael, who not only critiqued a film, but frequently placed it in context or history."

As a kind of offering, I believe, I said, "It's my intention to place your work within the larger context."

To hide, possibly, his amusement, he bowed, in a courtly manner. I appreciated the performance, and felt a smile warm my cheek. When our eyes again met, he seemed to study me for a moment or two. He then glanced, however, at his watch. "You know, Christine, I have something I usually do at this time each week."

What? I felt my heart skip. Cutting me short? Are my questions disappointing? Has he lost faith?

Perhaps seeing my expression, he smiled reassuringly. "Not to worry . . ." His eyes shone. "I have every intention of continuing our discussion. I was wondering, though, if you would consider accompanying me now. We could chat on the way."

"Why, what is this other appointment? You promised me plenty of time."

"Time, in this business, is the most precious commodity." The gray glint of irony briefly flashed behind his glasses. "But my promise stands. What I do is visit a homeless woman at a shelter, once a week or so."

This took a second to grasp. Had I heard correctly, or was he pulling my leg? I leaned forward, and found his face quite earnest. "A homeless woman?"

"Yes, and on the way, I thought we might walk past Steven's 47th Street before we grab a cab."

Experiencing a kind of mental whiplash—enticed by the prospect of viewing the location with him, recoiling from my own feeble homeless encounters—I tried to avoid his gaze. But standing, he urged, "Come, we'll talk."

I wondered if I must. Why not insist, or refuse? But finding him again, I saw his expression was conciliatory. So what should my response be? I exhaled, releasing annoyance, but then, reminding myself that in this game patience is needed, I pushed myself up.

Passing Martina, he left some instructions for phone calls, and she and I said goodnight. And then we were on the sidewalk, walking east into the deepening lavender canyons. He strode quickly with the urgency of one accustomed to time ever at his back. My feet flashed as I hurried to keep pace. Dodging and swerving around the oncoming crowd made conversation impossible, and I wondered if I'd been misled.

Swinging south onto Sixth, we now flew past clumps of commuters striding home. As we increased our pace, he seemed caught between the passing scene and some inner concern, until we both became aware of someone calling, "Scusa, scusa, Signore."

We slowed, then halted in front of a man, woman, and child, a family of tourists, from their too-stylish outfits.

"Scusa, please, Signore," began the father, "where is the Broadway? And how to find, please?"

Turning to point the way, David began to explain. I bent to smile at the little boy, maybe three, who was staring up at me with black, marble eyes. "Hello . . ."

His mother, pretty and round-faced, urged him to reply, "Giovanni, say 'hello' to the signora, Giovanni . . ." But little Giovanni turned and hid his eyes against his mother's designer jeans. Her manicured hand patted his head as she smiled and shrugged.

Having completed his directions, David now faced mother and son and bowed warmly. All of us shyly took in each other, nodding, smiling, beginning to back away.

When we resumed our march, I found myself delighted. "So, was this it? Have I seen it? The director directing?"

His eyes widened and briefly danced my way.

"Was this the thing which sends you back time and time again?" I pressed. "Sending supplicants along their paths?"

His gaze, now reaching ahead, narrowed then brightened. Accelerating a step ahead, he pushed up upon toes, arched his back, and imperiously gestured right, left, and ahead. I fell behind another step. People swerved out of his path. Head held high, shoulders back, scanning, he cast a cold eye above the passing crowd. I followed more slowly now, not quite sure what to think, before he, as suddenly, folded back to mortal size, and turned to wait.

I came forward, held in uncertain trance. His hand, palm up, asked for mine. A chill rose up my back. My hand went out. He enclosed it, then turned again to our walk.

For some moments we wove along, until ahead I saw 47th Street bobbing into view. Reaching the corner, we halted and stared east. The changing traffic light unleashed a seamless mob, surging across the avenue toward us. Hastily we retreated behind two newspaper vending machines, from where we watched the flood bearing down and parting around us. By his shoulder, I heard him mutter something but could not quite catch it, as the raincoats, overcoats, capes and jackets flowed by, a segmented blur. Surprisingly the faces seemed more homogeneous than Becker described, but the shear unending mass did assume a strange quality, a carapace atop regimented feet. Yet without the blinding noontime sun, the transforming effect that Stephen experienced was missing.

When the traffic light changed again, we stepped out, a part of the east-bound millipede, and crossed the avenue. Upon reaching the far side and continuing a few strides toward Fifth, David abruptly swerved and pulled me with him into the protection of a doorway, from where we looked back. The day's somber rays cut sharp contrasts into the buildings and street. Geometric shadows, interspersed with slashes of yellow light, confused perspective and seemed to subdue the din. In the unnatural quiet, a lumpy, pulsating organism writhed before us, an agonizing beetle. I felt myself start, my legs tingle, so that I checked my shoes. The scene, from this vantage, did seem removed and other-worldly, recalling the undiffused, low-light pictures from the Moon. David glanced at me, eyes glowing with the effect. "This, Christine, although the light is different, captures something of what I want, something of how Steven sees the city, which is so different than his Adirondack world. And I am hoping, praying, that this film will be my best knitting of story, character, and its own visual style."

When he glanced up west again, the dying sunlight bronzed his skin and wrinkles, like some old Achaean, and I, staring as from within a dream, heard him growl—threaten really—"It had better be." Then with an unexpected hardness, his eyes shifted back to me, as if challenging me to penetrate his thoughts. But before I could look more closely, he was swinging around, gently coaxing my elbow, urging me to move on once more.

Evening

Facing out his window, as our cab bounced east to Lex and down, his glasses intermittently filled with the hybrid twilight glow. From behind these changing reflections, he began explaining how this involvement fell upon him unexpectedly one rainy November night. He had passed an older woman rocking slowly along the sidewalk near his building, a woman without umbrella or raincoat, apparently adrift. He had looked back, and then turned and went to her and offered his umbrella. She hesitated, suspicion warring with need, then took it, staring at it strangely. About to set off again, he saw that she didn't move, and so once again approached her, this time noticing that she might be sixty-five (older than my woman) and that her otherwise pleasant face looked forlorn. He asked her if he could help her go somewhere. She didn't reply.

Remembering that he'd read of a women's shelter downtown, he asked her if she would consider accompanying him there. Still she didn't answer, avoiding his eyes. He told her that they could go together, to see if the shelter seemed suitable and safe. But he could see that the idea of the shelter dismayed her, even frightened her, though she said nothing. Only at this point did it occur to him that beyond homelessness, she might be suffering from mental or physical illness, and so he urged a bit more assertively to consider, at least for this night, a shelter. There she could get out of the wet and dry her clothes. But when still she neither responded nor moved away, he hailed a cab, which God improbably provided out of the rain, and she, moving at his gentle urging, got in. And downtown they went—just as we were now.

Arriving that night long after dark, fortune had saved her a bed, yet he saw that she remained hesitant and uncomfortable. An attendant brought her a bathrobe to wear while her clothes were washed and dried. Her stench, David now noticed, was choking. The attendant explained to her that a shower and thorough cleansing were mandatory, but seeing little reaction, the attendant turned to David, whispering that the woman had lice. And so two attendants escorted her to the showers, and David went to the men's room to wash his hands and then to a table where coffee and tea were available. While he was waiting, another attendant brought him a piece of paper from the woman's coat pocket. On it was written, 'Eleanor.'

As he sat wondering, he could not help but picture his wife and daughters in these straits if circumstances conspired to leave them destitute, as some movie disaster and consequent legal action could.

I felt a shiver run through me, recalling the harsh, raging battles long ago between Mother and Dad, between two ill-matched people, with widely differing views of parenting.

At the shelter now, as we stepped inside, David was greeted warmly by an attendant, Marcia, who knew him. But almost immediately her face fell and she became reluctant to look at us. When David asked for Eleanor, Marcia haltingly told him that she had not come back a week ago.

The news, I could see, jarred David. He stared at the floor. Marcia tried to soften the news by telling us that as the weather warmed up, many of the residents stopped coming in at night, preferring to live outside in doorways or some corner of the park, and many, she said, returned to their old neighborhoods.

David thanked Marcia, but he seemed uncertain, as we stood there silently. I imagined he must be leafing through scenarios concerning her fate. Something prodded me to ask him if he would mind waiting while I took a quick tour. A look of mild surprise and curiosity spread out from his eyes, before he nodded. I turned to find Marcia.

Explaining to her that I am a journalist who might like to write something on the homeless, I asked if she would mind briefly showing me the shelter. She hesitated, glancing around nervously, but then, with the other attendant occupied, she decided she could. We entered first what seemed to be the dining room, with several rows of long tables. A few of the residents sat here and there alone. Several others talked in low voices. I was not quite ready for the impact. Some of the women reminded me too much of Mother in her last weeks: emaciated, eyes watering weakly. But most distressing was that, as with my parents, I saw no prospect for improvement in their lives. They were just waiting for the end, living in these joyless, impersonal surroundings. I was also struck by the variety of faces and attitudes: some appeared meek and spiritless, while others brightened with a few words from Marcia, while still others scowled sullenly, avoiding our eyes.

Marcia now lead me into the large room that serves as the sleeping area, a hall filled with narrowly separated, iron-framed beds under a canopy of foul air cut by ammonia fumes. Many of the women were already asleep. Others sat bent on their beds. A few talked with a neighbor. The dull drone of what must be air-conditioning added to the impersonal, distant, dismaying atmosphere. As we turned away, my gaze passed across Marcia's, and I was startled by the dark distress I found there. But, as I walked back, I realized I could not tell whether her reaction was to the forlorn residents, the shelter itself, or what she feared I might write.

When I found David again, I asked him if his wife ever accompanied him. Rather quickly he replied she had her hands full with their two daughters, an assertion contradicted, I thought, by John's telling me the oldest was away, uptown at Columbia.

When we pushed through the heavy doors together, it was a relief to breathe the comparatively cool, fresh air. He asked if he could take me to dinner, in compensation for this digression, and to continue our chat.

While part of me wanted to take the opportunity, part was reluctant. David seemed to guess the reason. "Christine, I should explain that my wife and I have been separated since last Fall, coincidentally around the time I met Eleanor. And while I still have some hope that we can find a way back, I have to face the fact that our ability to talk has gradually eroded. One repercussion has been that my evenings, outside the film, have been glaringly free. Which is one reason why I continue to do this."

I felt my mind bridle a bit, under several difficulties.

"But now, as I've dragged you down here, allow me," he urged, "to take us both for dinner and a drink. It's been a long day."

Still divided, as we moved north along the sidewalk, I heard myself counseling that one of journalism's rules is to seize one's opportunities. And so once again I agreed.

This time our cab took us north to Park and 46th, a few blocks from the restaurant, in order that we might walk a little—something we both needed. There was a soft breeze, and the air felt moist and fresh, and I inhaled deeply, wondering if there was a way to bring those in the shelter somehow closer to this fortunate life, to somehow deal with the basic problems, so that they might be able to walk through Manhattan in the evenings, as we were.

Inhaling, and gazing up Park, I was slowly drawn away from reflections about the shelter, into the grand view extending to the horizon. At night, the dirt and cracks go unseen; the noise and competition diminish; all floats: lights, traffic, fellow-pedestrians. Held by this, one can forget the sadness that underlies so much.

As we waited to cross 48th, I found that David—perhaps lifted away momentarily from the concerns of the movie, and maybe from those for poor Eleanor—seemed younger. Or perhaps having relaxed, his young man's face emerged from under the lines, creases, and soft layers of his silver hair, and I imagined him in his early thirties, and thought how incongruous it is for physical age to superimpose its crags and crust while our minds are still active and our hearts still ardent. My poor parents embodied variations on this, their mismatch draining both of vitality, more rapidly than the years. Ironically my mother's illness drew them back, if only for a short time, before the end. Afterward Father seemed to have forgotten their difficult times. But not Luke, who so nakedly carries the scars of their lovelessness.

Blindly I sought the gentle breeze to clear my eyes.

The restaurant was intimate if unprepossessing. And though sleepily half-full, it was warm, and the staff, knowing David, gave us a handsome table for four in a corner and brought a bottle of white wine which was dry and good. And so we sat and drank and talked, not about filmmaking but about the shelter.

I wondered aloud if I could bring myself to go down there to do what he did on a weekly basis, although part of me wanted to. Exactly why I felt hesitant I couldn't say.

"In my case, Christine, it was only the chance passing by Eleanor. Also, if she had moved on, I would not have returned to her . . . If my marriage had been healthy, I probably would not have continued. If I had not made these movies, parading the weaknesses of Daniel Morrone and Horton, I would not have felt compelled to prove myself not a fraud."

Sipping my wine, I allowed, "It would be easier to do it in a small town like Trapper's Lake."

He agreed, "But in my case, there is another set of circumstances which have also pushed me."

I waited with some foreboding.

"What I should tell you must be off-the-record, although it may affect you, or your piece. Do I have your assurance on that?"

Although I was ready to agree, part of me wondered if this was wise. But unable to think why it might not be, I nodded to him, as I found his expression slipping into shadow. Studying me, he said, "There are several developments in my life which have changed or may change things. It's exasperating, infuriating that they're inserting themselves. I don't think I chose them, but for some reason they seem to have chosen me. And so far, I have found no way to get around them. I guess I have an obligation to tell you, so that you may decide what you should do."

I tried to compose myself as he looked carefully at me.

"Several things, as I said, have been unfolding at the same time, recently. Inevitable change, one might say, is a part of life. Anyway, as I've said, my marriage of nearly twenty years may have irreconcilably ruptured, for reasons I can both understand and not understand. At the same time, and perhaps as a result, my two daughters have increasingly become sources of concern, about which I feel increasingly unable to do anything. And finally, I have been told that within a year, possibly in a matter of months, I may lose my sight."

What? Had I heard right? The percussion, the unreality of it beat at my brow and ears. Time slowed, though I was conscious of him watching me, and though I saw the corner of his mouth pulsating slightly. "My God, David . . ."

"Yes. You see, it raises questions. None of which are easily answered."

"I'm sorry . . . That's horrible."

"Well," he began quite evenly, "it's several different things. And while conceivably some may turn around, generally things don't work quite that way."

With my gaze moving over his face, I felt my mind tumbling. "What's the problem with your eyes?"

He blinked and looked around the restaurant. "Nothing, at the moment. They work fine; I see; I delight." And he looked intensely at me. "They feast on every detail."

Under this scrutiny, with his news breaking over me, I felt hot, queasy—even as I made every effort to clearly see his face.

"Sorry," he murmured. "Sorry to land you with all of this. Particularly before dinner. But obviously this may affect you."

"Never mind me . . ."

"But you have a responsibility to the magazine or your editor."

This, I knew, I could not dismiss so easily, aware of Kirsten's demanding ways.

As he watched, I wanted to touch him, take his arm, maybe even cry for him. But he continued, "Of course for me, there are the obvious obligations, to Kath and the girls, and to the investors here." Watching his expression tighten, I felt an inch from his face.

"Yet the fact is, Christine, I've told no one."

A bell sounded distantly in my head, drowning out all other sounds. I looked around, feeling the reverberations.

"That is, about the eye problem," he added. "The immediate dilemma is that I can't be sure I'll be able to finish the film, which, aside from the production difficulties, puts me, and possibly my family, that is, my resources, at considerable risk. I'm not sure the production insurance would pay up, having kept this a secret . . . I've taken some financial precautions, but . . ." He breathed, frowned, and pressed his lips together. But then surprisingly, to me at least, he allowed a chill, ironic smile to spread across his cheeks. "Fact is, I've taken a chance. The safer course might be to bow out now, try to find another director to take over, rather than leave everyone stranded, should something happen. But that, too, is chancy. I'm not sure we could find a suitable director, and the banks might pull out and demand repayment. So I'm hoping I can complete shooting, at least, and possibly the whole thing. But there's the possibility . . . that I won't see the final print of "The democrat." And his eyes, suddenly darkish-green, stared into mine. Inwardly I winced.

"Unfortunately, none of the doctors can be certain about the course of this thing."

We studied each other for a moment, before he looked down.

"They say it's . . . an infection, which hasn't responded to the usual drugs—a new strain or something. But again, I've told no one. So please don't break my confidence."

God, how could I? I reached for his hand and held it.

For some moments we sat there, eyes moving over the other, but minds wandering God-knows-where. And while he appeared calm, I felt hurled—across my terrace by some overwhelming force.

"Christine, maybe the first thing for you to figure out is how this might affect you, and then what you think you should do. Of course I would have preferred to have told you straight off, but, not knowing you, I couldn't be sure you wouldn't spread it around."

Although slightly dazed, I understood. Only gradually did the possible difficulties present themselves. What if he couldn't finish? What about my piece? What of interest would remain, besides his personal story? Glancing over, my heart went out to him, even as I tried to clear my mind.

Fortunately, our waiter arrived, a dignified, roundish, balding man, probably in his sixties, and who might be from Brussels or Jersey City. He and David exchanged a few words about work, the weather, and the evening's specials, before David asked if I'd like him to order for me. In my preoccupation, and with little appetite now, I indicated I would. "Something light."

As the waiter shuffled away, we looked at each other. My half-formed thoughts were breaking under his revelation. Eventually I realized I had to raise my concerns. "David, while none of this changes my interest in doing the profile, if your circumstances should change, what would I do? How could I not report something of that?"

"Well, in that case, that would become part of the film's story, or, I suppose, my story. But if I can complete the film, if the eye problem doesn't develop as quickly as it could, then to reveal it before completion, or indeed before it brings darkness, would be a deep disservice, not only to me but to my family . . . You see my problem?"

I did. "I wouldn't write anything without consulting you."

His eyes softened in appreciation. Our appetizers were brought, but as I surveyed the rich-looking goat cheese mixed into green salad, I felt no hunger. He, on the other hand, ate ravenously.

In time, we managed to turn to other things. He told me about the actors and about his cameraman, or Director of Photography, Rudi, who shot his recent films. "Despite his all-but-impenetrable accent, Rudi and I communicate well. Which suggests that perhaps it's better not to understand every word, but to rely on intuition."

It was a relief to see David's face reviving. He asked me about myself. But I found myself stammering. What story comparable to his did I have to tell? Not that this was the first time this problem had arisen, for though I appear relatively independent and intelligent, I find I never live up to the interesting things people believe, and expect, I've surely done. How can they understand the terrible waste of time and psychic energy my marriage was, or how my family history of unhappiness and troubles has never found adequate airing or solution.

April 19th.

Ordinarily, I love the early mornings, their optimism, their coolness, which falls away, high up here, as imperceptibly as one's skin. It is then that I am stirred to think of the possibilities, as I move through the air which whispers I'm alive. Today, however, the coolness carried memories of David's dark cloud, which I have not yet fully imagined—save to shut my eyes—and carried the specter of Eleanor, wandering through the dimness of our streets.

After work, John came again, an hour late. However, as I had not called him the evening before, I allowed we were even, and waiting, was happy to rework Eiley's progress at work.

When he wandered in, as I took his raincoat, it seemed we were both absent. Indeed a hint of perfume about him seemed to place him elsewhere. Nonetheless, I sat him down on one end of my black sofa, myself at the other, to watch the twilight fade behind an oncoming storm, which he said had dogged him all the way uptown. Its dark gray clouds closed around us. The wind rose, whistling low in prelude, and the terrace leaves suddenly swept up like a cape against the windows. When the rain came, it hissed and splattered, blurring our view of the lavender buildings and the gray-black sky, and into my vision emerged faces: Father's, David's, Kirsten's, Eiley's, until a thunder clap frightened them away.

Neither of us moved, held by the storm, whose clouds flowed not far above, slowly shifting their placid, staring surfaces, imperceptibly merging, brightening, darkening, taking us in with supreme indifference. When lightening flashed, it lit up the neighboring buildings, bleaching them cartoon white, blinding me. John too was transfixed, though perhaps not by the storm. We talked little and drank steadily, until one particularly close thundering crash drove me deeper into my seat, and glancing at each other, a smile reached out through the room.

In time, the storm moved east over Queens and Long Island, where I watched its filigree of lightning and wisps of dark clouds hugging the skyline. And eventually I arose to cook the fish I'd bought, thinking that with my new salary I should buy one of those gas grills for the terrace. Such are my plans for the future.

John came in, slightly weary, and we talked in subdued forays, then fell silent. He was already unsettled and mumbling about David's techniques. Yet turning and twisting to cook in my tiny kitchen, I couldn't clearly grasp the problem—probably no more than his discomfort with something new.

Later I told him of Eiley's story, but he listened like the wind, there and not there. Yet it didn't matter, for I was envisioning how I would shape the difficulties Eiley inherits and in what manner they would impinge upon those she encounters.

John asked me to read some of it to him, but we never did, distracted by one thing or another. There was, despite his here-and-not-here presence, something wonderful about the evening, with its nothing-in-particular-to-do feeling, like college days, when whole nights stretched on into the darkness, meandering and intimate, without purpose, and it seemed, without end.

We ate surprisingly hungrily, given our initial languor, and, once revived, the other thing followed. On the sofa, he leaned to me, running his hand up along the back of my head, through my hair. A kiss, surprisingly alive, a pressing into one another, a blurring of motion and selves; mind drifting away as senses rose up on toes. Hands peeling layers, and I falling free into his hands, trembling. Standing and tugging his belt—he all but ripping off the rest— his long length hard against me, pressing, touching, prying, and in time, the night clouds rising, then falling away, and I thinking the thunder had returned, crying out, then laughing and falling back. Yes, it's been a long time.

Lying on our backs, chests heaving, listening to the now-distant storm, I felt we were lost children in summer, lost siblings. Some implicit connection. The cynic in me snorted of course, but I know I wished it were so. We're split creatures, women, I think, more so than men, always wondering—while John lay face down, spread eagle, dead to the world, his ass surprisingly round and soft—as my chimerical secondself danced on the terrace in the dark.

Spring has chased away this winter's dread,
and left a satyr in my bed.

April 20th

Awoke to the sound of a shower slowly spattering against the tub, washing all traces away. Remained in bed dreaming, pretending to be sleeping when he tiptoed out. Happy not to speak.

Floated through hopes, past and future, until a cool breeze, brushing aside the blinds, prodded me up. No more Supinia, Queen of Sardinia. Into the bath. No office today. Instead, my first rehearsal.

The studio lay west on 21st Street between Sixth and Seventh, and the appointed hour, nine-thirty, allowed the luxury of busing down Fifth on the coattails of rush hour. Cleared by the storm, a fresh, glorious, blue-skied morning was mirrored in the windows and puddles, and from my bus, I watched the late ones stretching their strides, hurrying over the sidewalks, veering into doorways.

Stepping into the building, I paused before entering the elevator. All senses froze. Before me an airless, urine-reeking, graffiti-marred box, and could-be tomb—I hoped not mine. Prayed no crazed male stepped in after me. And once in, it barely crawled up the three flights—this, in frantic New York—time enough for several bloody scenarios to unwind in my head. Am I a growing hysteric, under my skin, or is it the city?

Urgently, I pushed open the door and stepped with relief back into the rational world: an office recently renovated in wheat and gray, and opening into a larger, white room bordered by a wall mirror and ballet bar at one end, and clusters of chairs below windows running the length. Beyond, a warren of dressing rooms and small offices hop-scotched out of sight.

Arriving just behind me, via the stairs, a striking dark-haired woman, exotically Mediterranean. Introducing myself, I experienced the bump of recognition—Pat Eliot, David's choice for Teresa. We shook hands, and when I mentioned the elevator, her eyes closed, eyebrows trembled. "A nightmare." We chatted for several minutes before she went off to prepare.

I wondered, with her sharpness, what she must think of John. And I understood his trepidation, for she's ever so much more sophisticated. However, at the mention of David, her eyes lit up.

It was he who appeared next, radiating and evidently recharged, as he confided, "Slept like a lamb, thank you ma'am, for letting me run on at the restaurant. Hope I didn't unduly burden you. Hope you didn't have second thoughts?"

"No, David, none."

The smile he sent me was warm and complicitous, before he turned away to organize the day with the young manager.

Mind alight, I turned to find a seat. Out the window, the sunlight had transformed the building across the street into a gleaming, golden temple, which lured me out of my chair. Leaning against the window frame, I gazed down upon the still shadowed street where men stood talking and wrestling heavy boxes onto dollies, and women wove gingerly between them, wobbling on high heels, antennae out.

Behind me, footsteps. Turning with momentary apprehension, I discovered John, cheeks twitching under glances flung out in all directions. Assured we were alone, he tiptoed quickly to me, our smiles replaying last night's lightning strikes. Bodies clasped, blackout for a millisecond. Cool air poured in as he pulled away, toward the back rooms, spinning, smiling slyly.

Turning back to the window, I felt his imprinted heat once again the length of me. Even with all his imperfections, and however fleeting, the moment was electric.

When the three had gathered, David explained the scene: that in which Stephen and Teresa meet by chance in the local laundromat. And while John and Pat knew the scene, and their lines, David nonetheless proceeded to paint it, for my benefit, but equally, he said, to create a mood. He wove in, as well, a reminder of their initial meeting, when Teresa drove to the club to inquire about the jobs advertised in the county paper.

Through all of this, David spoke so softly that we all had to bend forward to hear, and somehow this altered things—our concentration closed in upon this other place.

From the outset, Pat was the more convincing and had more deeply explored her role, although John was not as bad as I had feared. But she became Teresa. Everything she did seemed grounded in that personality and history, and her concentration was seamless. Yet David never criticized John, nor compared the two. Instead he asked him to try segments of the scene several different ways and then choose among them. And this worked. John's inhabiting of Stephen deepened as he grew more comfortable. Occasionally David suggested alternate bits of business to John, in dealing with his laundry or helping her with hers, but for much of the time David listened, encouraged, and largely allowed the actors to find their own ways.

At first Pat remained aloof from John, in contrast to her interactions with David, until slowly, at mid-morning, when they had advanced into the scene, John began to improve. At which point, she watched him with more attention and finally permitted some expression of Teresa's interest.

Furtively glancing, I found David observing motionlessly, his eyes locked upon them. When his glasses slipped down his nose, he did not adjust them, but lifted his head, sitting bent forward, occasionally scribbling notes in the margins of his script.

Just before noon, however, as the actors were discussing a question of timing, he suddenly looked down, blinking, hand to forehead, then rubbed his eyes. I felt faint apprehension rising, a distant trembling. I looked away, closed my eyes. Shook myself, then looked again . . . and found him recovered, and asking them to move about the room freely.

The effect of his request was unexpected. John, freed to use his body, became more expressive and fresh, uncovering an innocence I'd never seen. At one point, the two drew so close I felt he would kiss her, but in the next instant he moved off, taken by Stephen's thoughts.

For lunch, the manager brought sandwiches, coffee, tea, sodas, pie and fruit, which I found myself bolting down, wondering at my appetite. Yet Pat, sitting next to me, kept pace.

Sensing my gaze, she murmured, "No breakfast," and asked if I wanted my pie, which I gladly handed her, declaring my admiration of her trim, nearly-perfect figure.

"High metabolism," she garbled between swallows. "That and the daily work out, which I hate. But there's no choice." She underlined this with a sardonic grimace.

Though undeniably attractive, her slightly triangular face reminded me of a praying mantis, so that I again imagined it must be a little daunting for John, even with this morning's strides.

After eating, watching the others, my mind slipped back to Father, wishing that he'd extended even half of the attention David does here, wishing he'd valued communication, or had been able to understand my halting starts. Not that he didn't care when I was growing up. On his good days, he read to me, took me to museums, hit tennis balls, swam, even took me fishing in Maine, into his silent (sometimes sullen) world, disturbed only by the essential exchanges. But none of life's difficulties, or ambiguities, was ever raised or shared—an immense hole, and waste.

In contrast, David and Pat pass volumes of shared feeling, and possibly history, back and forth in a single glance. Indeed it was so intense, I felt my brow grow hot, my cheeks burn.

In the afternoon, David confined his directing to physical suggestions and to descriptions of the various sets. In passages where there was no dialogue, he narrated, carrying the story and maintaining the mood, and increasingly took every opportunity to praise and encourage John, even to the point of, from my view, transparency. Yet it worked. John began to flesh Stephen out. When, from time to time there was a pause, my mind escaped the room, spinning ahead to the completed profile, to its appearance in *Avenue*, and to the critical acclaim, the hoped-for industry-wide buzz. But in truth I fear I'll not do the subject justice. Somehow over this last year, I find I've grown superstitious, looking for the threads which tie all things.

Abruptly, unexpectedly, the afternoon was over. All went to gather their belongings, leaving me alone, replaying David's careful midwifing these characters into round existence.

Reappearing, David asked how I found the session.

"Well . . . increasingly engaging. The two started so far apart, and yet, by the end, seemed potentially a couple. A little chemistry surfaced, I thought. And David, I was impressed by how much stroking you gave John."

He smiled a masking smile, then asked me if I would like to reconvene this chat elsewhere, where we might eat. I explained I had loosely arranged to see John this evening, but perhaps I could beg out of it, or see John later.

Clearly uncomfortable, David suggested another time, but I told him I'd go buttonhole John and finagle something. And wending my way into the back rooms, I found John alone in his cubicle, penning tiny notes between the lines of the scene.

A mile high after his good work and the copious praise, he uncharacteristically gracefully accepted my suggestion to meet later. "Fine, fine. Come when you can, Christine. Come to the hotel. You know I've moved, to the Plaza. But nine-thirty, ten, whenever. Hey, what a day, was it not? I could kiss that man's feet." And his smile lured out mine.

Pleased, I walked back to find David, but Pat had found him first, by the front door—talking intimately, his hands on her shoulders, hers upon his chest, faces grave. As I hesitated, David called, "Be right with you."

Unsteadily, I reversed once more and wandered back, discovering in the last room, the young manager sitting, legs upon a desk, apparently talking to his girlfriend on the phone, mentioning David's name and Pat's, then turning to a discussion of who was coming to whose digs this evening.

Settling into my own cubicle, began reviewing, indeed untangling my notes, in the midst of which, I heard John stride out, calling, "Goodnight all," its echo boyish in its buoyancy.

Refocused on my work and lost myself within the images of the rehearsal and the director watching, rubbing his eyes.

Eventually a voice intruded, David's at my door, asking if I could wait another few minutes while he made several calls. A glance up revealed his fatigue and revived a fear. Back down at my pages: my notes, black lines, curlicues, under a florescent brightness, incubating in a cubicle. I might've been in a convent or space ship, insulated, separated, from the roar. I closed my eyes.

When at last his voice returned apologizing, I stood feeling faintly bruised, gathered my things, avoiding his gaze. He took my hand. Though I did not pull away, I felt myself stiffen. And then we were on the street.

Evening

Bouncing along Sixth in a cab, slightly apart, I noticed him glance over, before he asked if I was okay.

"Okay? Okay. Yes, I'm okay," I said, but we both heard the catch in my voice, which neither wanted to probe. He, I saw, now leaned back and turned his head away.

Outside my jouncing, dusty window, the desultory buildings of the 20's and 30's slunk by. No Stephen Boylans here, extracting inspiration. No energized stream. What pedestrians I saw were shabby, beaten down, hardly movers-and-shakers. Most, I noticed, were Third World immigrants, here presumably to hitch onto the American dream, while ironically many of the jobs they hoped to find were going over there. How will they find fulfillment?

George Eliot, whose heroines' moral strength I wish I had, wrote that one's inward being is seldom so strong as not to be greatly shaped by what lies outside it. Now we know that genes further, and perhaps minutely, direct our choices. Yet the question remains: what designs and directs our wills? What gives us backbone or determination? Is it adversity or encouragement? Or those tiny blueprints?

My family, despite its fortunate circumstances, has dissolved, leaving as they say, poor issue, Luke and me. And from that one nest, two disparate fates. The roll of genetic dice? Chemistry between parent and child? Prior generations' transgressions erupting like boils through tender skin? Or simply Mother's poor choice, or Father's dour intransigence, his sometimes bullying her and me? . . . Can anyone untangle these things?

I turned back to David, partly in need, partly to reach out. Still staring out his side, his head bobbed gently. I wanted to hold his hand, as he had taken mine, but managed only to place mine on his.

In response, he smiled and closed his eyes. I could not help but fear that his condition may be worsening by the day, and I might see this thing, too, come apart.

Nearing our neighborhood, he proposed that we meet at a local restaurant in thirty minutes, but sensing he would do better at home, I suggested we cook there, and, somewhat unexpectedly, he offered no protest.

Our cab delivered us to his building, one of those white-brick, balconied, sixties designs, which must've looked fresh when first erected but which are rapidly becoming dated, dirty, and a little sad. But the apartment itself was a comfortable, if dark, one-bedroom, with an ample living room, decent bedroom, and modest kitchen. His furniture was even more spare than mine, and he had put away none of his books or music, nor put any pictures on the walls, testimony, I supposed, to his recently reinstated bachelor status.

His blinking answering machine drew him to it where he tapped its replay button and sank into an armchair, one hand around his bundle of mail.

I wandered into the kitchen, finding it odd that I did, but

recognizing that it was hunger that propelled me. Opening the fridge, I discovered a six-pack and little else. "Beers here, David, beers."

"Here, here," he called out just before Martina's recorded voice began listing his office calls.

Returning, I handed him a cold bottle as he scribbled his messages and mumbled to himself. Then drifting back to the kitchen, gazing around, I wondered if I was a bit of a fool for having proposed this. Considered ordering Chinese, but was not in the mood. Peered back into the fridge—just the fridge and me—and discovered a few items in the trays which might be easily prepared. What choice did I have but to cook or crumble?

At some point, he remembered and called out that he'd be right in, explaining, "My dear daughters normally help me stock the place, but both were busy last weekend. Come out here until the chef's ready."

But I was too hungry to obey, until I had things boiling and broiling, whereupon I wandered out to find him reading his mail, a crumpled pile around his feet. Looking up from a personal letter which still held him, he explained in low voice, "An old friend just announced he's moving to Idaho, to start a new life . . . at his age." His eyes reflected his inability to quite understand his friend's desertion. Staring at his knees, he appeared to be recalling something, and then in a deliberate tone, recited,

> I will not well the tears tonight
> nor pull out old passions,
> for though the music sings just right,
> and I lie alone and vacant,
> I'll leave the body slow
> and quiet and hope the night—no moon, no stars
> or wind through the trees—
> will not pry or speak,
> but leave all unmoved,
> and see I seek a barren sleep.

He stopped and searched my face. I was both held by it, and uneasy. I asked about the lines.

"Oh . . . from long ago." He reflected for a moment, brow faintly furrowing, before our eyes met. "While I'm happy for him, I'll miss him . . . Things change in little, unexpected leaps."

"You'll see him, won't you, out there? Or he'll come back to visit you and the city."

He nodded, but his expression registered no solace. Again he found me and said, "Thank you for the beer. I apologize for being no host at all." But it seemed that our minds were carried off by thoughts of new beginnings—until the smell of something burning called me back to the kitchen, where I turned chops and dumped cauliflower from its steaming pot.

"Everything okay?" he called.

"Yes, yes, my nose has saved the day." And soon I was calling, "Da-vid, din-ner." Childhood spondee, nostalgic tones.

"Oh my bones," he groaned but was almost instantly at the kitchen door. "I didn't mean for you to do all of this. I'm supposed to be the cook here."

"What did you think I was doing in here? Composing verse?"

His eyes shone, then fell. "Sorry. Evidently thinking wasn't the operative function. Brain weary, eyes bleary. I apologize."

"All we need are plates and utensils. If you could point me in the right direction."

The simplest of requests, you would think—but apparently not, as he glanced about almost unfamiliarly, bringing fist to his mouth. "Well, either just behind you or in the dishwasher."

Discovering my smile, he explained, not without some mirrored amusement, "Trouble is that each of us, Mandy, Marnie, and I, has a different idea where these things should go."

Nonetheless, after ferreting around, we were seated across from each other, chewing eagerly. And not bad either, I was thinking, as he, too, was nodding, drinking.

"David, did you notice your praise of John left him slightly off the floor at the end?"

"Yes, excellent, excellent," he replied, slicing his chop, eager for a bite.

"Talking John, not chops."

"Yes yes, I know," he hurried.

"You got him thinking and working today."

Pause. Eyes under bristling eyebrows rose to mine. "Indeed . . . This is excellent, Christine, excellent. Rosemary, thyme . . . what else?"

"Soy sauce, a little red wine. And a little too much time."

"No, I like them like this, outside charred, tasty. Caveman's delight."

"Did you hear John warbling out of the studio? It was a side I hadn't known before."

"I did, I did. And Patty did, and Katydid. All pleased." He swallowed. "Pleased as punch, all around."

"You're a magician."

"And you an alchemist. Excellent sauce from the sorceress. Superb choices."

Smiles.

"How did you, David, from amongst all the merry men, find him?"

Chewing his chop, David looked at me considering. "Someone, a friend, a director out there, suggested him. He'd directed John in a play there, said he was directable, was serious about wanting to grow. And so I met him, and tried to get some idea of his range, and whether or not he'd respond to me. And he did. And it was good, and there was light. Indeed he was happy to go over and over some little scenes, trying things. I was surprised, actually."

"Me too."

Pausing, David allowed a surprised look.

It prodded me to clarify what I suspected he knew. "I gather you knew we were an item out there, for a brief time."

He nodded, he knew.

"How do these things get around? . . . I hope that doesn't make you uncomfortable, about the profile."

"Not at all. I have him to thank."

For a short time, our eyes attended to our own plates, but then I heard him clear his throat and say, "Concerning the young man in question, do you mind if I mention something?"

I looked up.

"He's, uh, an attractive fellow, I understand. Particularly, as you know, with the younger set, after "Blackout." Problem is that Amanda apparently has joined the ranks."

"Oh dear . . ."

"Yes. Her imagination, working overtime, has drawn her down to rehearsals, to watch and catch a word—amazing me with her eagerness and forwardness."

My breathing paused as our eyes met and held.

"Unfortunately John seems flattered by it, or maybe he's simply trying to be nice to her—I mean she's half a child—he listens, chats quite earnestly, which of course sends her into the clouds. I've attempted to tell her something of the situation and his reputation, but of course she hears none of it. What do I know of this brave new world? Annoying old Dad . . . I've thought I should say something to *him*, but I didn't want to yet, for . . . well for several reasons. But now I think I'd better."

"David, I don't know whether you want my comments, or might suspect they're self-serving."

"Are you two still . . . ?"

" . . . Sort of."

His eyes shifted away.

"But I would tell her, David, in unmistakable terms, that as he sees it, he's sitting on top of the world, gathering all that he may."

Another nod and setting of jaw.

"I might say something to her, if you wish. Though she may also see it as self-serving. But I remember, David, that I always wished my father, despite the deep divide, had told me what he knew, told me what, and what not, to do. Not that I was frequently ready to follow it."

A faint smile spread up from his mouth. "Pat's noticed it too, and volunteered to say something, although she can be a little blunt."

"Does she think it unwise?"

"You may have noticed that she's not convinced of John's maturity, though I've urged her to keep an open mind. But if it's going to distract her, then I'll have to deal with that too."

"Could you ask Amanda to stay away from rehearsals?"

"I may. But I've promised she could work on the production, part-time out at the studio in Queens, and then upstate when exams are finished."

"Well then, maybe asking John to be more circumspect is the solution."

A flickering glance was sent my way, but then his head bent down near the table, and he brushed his hand across his left eye, then pressed it firmly.

"David?"

"Just a minute . . ."

"Your eyes?"

"Mm . . ."

I waited as he moved both hands to his forehead, holding and kneading his temples with his fingers. "Can I do anything?"

He shook his head gingerly. I attempted thick-headedly to think what to do, but then his constricted voice whispered,

"I'll be all right . . . in a minute. Sorry."

I was wondering if I'd brought this on, and whether I should call his doctor. I tried to imagine his ache, but became aware instead of turmoil roiling inside. Undoubtedly, when he recovered, I should leave and let him rest. The prospect, however, of finding time to talk with him for the profile appeared increasingly problematic.

When he finally straightened up, trying to shake off the effects, I saw that his left eye had grown dark and unfocused.

"David, you okay?"

"Yes . . ."

"Should I call your doctor?"

"No no. I see him regularly. He warned me of these episodes. I've had several. I'll be fine."

" . . . Well . . . I should let you rest." And I stood to clear the table.

"Really Christine, I'm fine. And don't embarrass me further by doing that."

"You've had a long day . . . Can we continue another time?"

Staring down at the table, he frowned. "Of course. I don't want to string this out for you. I apologize for not making time available. I know we've got to work in a few better chats."

"We'll find time," I told him overriding palpable doubt.

Feeling clear-eyed enough to stand, he joined me in clearing and loading the dishwasher. As we did, he said, "I wanted to play you something, a CD of Beethoven's Ninth, the adagio. Do you have a player at home?"

"I do."

"Well take it home and listen. It speaks, at least to me, of the shifting moods, of optimism and sadness, in "The democrat.""

Shifting moods? I'd only just begun Becker's book, but already saw both Stephen and Teresa are subject to such currents. "Well thank you." Alas the Ninth was one of my ex-husband's favorites.

When finished, I collected my coat and notebook, while David squatted searching through a pile of CDs. Then he rose to get his coat.

"David, it's not necessary."

But pulling on his coat, he handed me the Beethoven. Part of me did not want to leave, neither his company, nor his condition. Yet he motioned me toward the door.

Silently we walked the few blocks. The sight of two hooded young men sauntering by in sneakers as large as boots made me glad I was not alone. One reads there are no completely safe neighborhoods anymore. Things have changed, and the root causes are not likely to be soon solved. In Trappers Lake the alternative has been to leave, but here in the city that's not an option for many of the troubled and troubling. I wondered what David's views on solutions were, wondered if his optimism for Trappers Lake was transferable.

Outside my building, facing each other to say goodnight, I leaned to kiss his cheek, cooled by the wind. He took my shoulders lightly and softly brushed his lips across my brow and eyes. The look he wore was sweet, yet detached, as though watching a scene. I wondered at his moods. He began backing away, then waved and turned toward home.

My balance was unsteady as I slipped through the front door and into the lobby, nodding to Frank. Upstairs, tired, I wanted only to listen to the Beethoven. But I had to change for the next stop.

Late Evening

When I emerged again, it was into a cold night and vivid doubts. Did I really need to see John? Waiting for a cab at the corner, so as not to have to tip Frank, I felt the city was deserted, the cabs and I were out alone. And my discomfort only increased as I was sped down Fifth. What did John and I share? Nothing more substantive than the air, most deeply prized when no longer there.

But the Plaza was swinging. People swept here and there, music filtered down from a ballroom, and John was abuzz on the hotel phone. "Jesus, where you been? Come up, come up, my . . ."

"Buttercup?"

"My genius writer."

I cleared my throat and clamped my lips until his cabernet kiss, upstairs at his door, somewhat softened my mood. He then spun off to phone room service for more wine. Still sky-high from rehearsal, he seemed to have been guzzling all night. The silly fool will someday celebrate himself to death.

And on what subject did he press me? Had David heaped yet more praise upon his head? I repeated David's grateful lines about his progress and hard work, after which I quickly inserted my own request for thoughts on David's directing. Yet John could barely attend, throwing out stock encomiums, principally as to how wise David was to let Pat and him have their reigns, tossing his head in equine assertion. Holding mine, I turned away.

Room service arrived, and, while John occupied himself with that, I stepped off to tour his suite. Presumably there was a bed and bath somewhere down the adjoining hall. Et voilà. Plush, rich crimson and beige, Louis the Umpteenth. Florid fantasies swam above the décor of the ersatz boudoir.

As I circled, running my hand over the period reproductions, my eyes landed upon a pile of books on the dressing table, and curious to see what John was reading, I stepped over to leaf through. College textbooks: Modern Theatre, Beginning Italian, and English lit, and for a split second, my spirits rose—John's educating himself—until I discovered several xeroxed Columbia syllabi, and the penned name, A. Loomis. I shut them and moved away, carried by a sudden, frigid draft. Sightlessly I looked around. What to do, where to go?

Feeling unsteady, aware of clamoring voices, I swung in circles, gazing reluctantly at the bed, where now I saw, under its hastily pulled-up spread, signs of sheets sprawled in disarray. I fled into the short hall and there hesitated, trying to decide if I should confront John. But did I want a torrent of lies and self-justifications? Was innocence remotely possible? With John? Yet didn't want to cast myself in the role of the injured, betrayed female. I had known what I was getting into, knew its likely outcome. Was I not passing time myself? . . . As for concerns about Amanda, and David: they are not my charges; indeed I barely know them.

Yet feeling intimations of regurgitation (I could imagine vomiting onto the beige and red carpet, adding my own complementary colors) I saw I must leave. Bracing myself, I strode back into the living room again, where John was opening the wine, whose aroma encouraged my stomach's revolt. Hoped I'd make it home. "John, 'fraid something I ate, or drank, is not agreeing with me."

He turned, bottle in hand, eyebrows rising.

"I cooked dinner at David's," I explained. "May be choking on my own desserts."

"Cooked dinner?" How puzzled he looked.

"Sorry, but I've got to go home. I really don't want to be sick here."

"Well, but what were you . . . Are you all right?"

"I think I can make it. Sorry about the whole evening." I guessed the sharpness in my voice and my rather sour look gave credence to my story.

John glanced back at the bedroom as if now he suddenly remembered. Stepping by, I saw his features unhappily contort, and taking my coat, I fled toward the door, calling, "Good night."

Placing the bottle down, he came after me, suspicion narrowing his eyes—which made it even easier to quickly step to the door. Could it be that with his growing celebrity, one woman per evening was no longer enough? Foolishly I pictured him in bed with her, a comical, mismatched coupling. Unwilling to meet his eyes, I coughed deeply and garbled another apology.

This held him at bay, from where he offered to take me home, but I told him it was only a short cab ride and the hotel doormen would hail me one. "Too much wine probably, John. Too much to stomach," I said, backing into the hall.

He stood at the door, confusion and annoyance wrangling in his cheeks and eyes. Thankfully the elevator came, and I stepped in.

Cab again—so much circling. At least my nausea subsided. My body is so often the better barometer of my emotions than my head, yet remembering his glance back into his bedroom, my indignation once again swelled.

At home, running a bath, I remembered Beethoven and put him on. By the time the adagio began, the bath's enveloping heat had calmed me. The music was more moving than I'd remembered, and the more I listened to the movement's hopeful climbs and wringing descents, the more it and David's life joined to pull at something in me. I could not help but think that these sounds expressed so finely and deeply the best of what men and women are capable. Its intertwining joy and sorrow, its lilting tempos, its chromatic climbs and sudden descents, its reaching and resignation—all speak more eloquently than I could ever, despite some years at this endeavor. Da da daah, da da daah . . . The deep strings sound and fall away, as high hopes are played, then fade.

Mankind, to quote Becker quoting, is but an infinite chance . . . What is mine . . . and to how enhance? One step forward, toward that chance, the next step back, the age-old dance.

April 21st

Early morning, a lozenge, pale yellow, floating indistinctly far out over hazy Long Island, slowly supplanted the sleepless darkness, embedded with images of his rumpled, bullying face glowering over my retreat to the elevator, anger and wine sloshing in his eyes.

Do you suppose he called her immediately after I left? Had she left her books there on purpose, or had he sent her out unceremoniously and forthwith as my hour approached? Who cares. She's old enough to take care of herself. Suspect she's less of a childe than David thinks. But Johnny can get a little pushy when Johnny gets angry. Johnny doesn't like to hear 'no.' Shrank from the thought of watching him again, struggling to instill Stephen with selflessness that's only an act. Tried to weigh whether I should call David to beg off today, though there are not many rehearsals left.

Just before eight, the phone rang as I dimly watched the coffee drip. Who, at this hour?

"You're up?" smirked Kirsten's voice.

"Yes, and evidently so are you."

"I'm usually up at six," she chided, before announcing that she wanted me to interview the latest fashion phenom from Soho, Daemon, assuming I knew the name. When I didn't, she cried out, "My God, Christine, it's good to know there are still a few innocents left out there, who read neither the papers nor the magazines they write for. It's refreshing." She almost sounded sincere.

Yet having vented, she was left to fill the ensuing silence with Daemon's essentials, and what he means to Fashion. But today I had neither energy nor interest. Somehow it seemed better to complete this other thing. I told Kirsten I'd scheduled a session with David.

"Oh? Well, yes, the priority. I'll have William reschedule Daemon. Will you be in at all today?"

"No," I snapped, borrowing last night's anger.

" . . . Well okay. Gotta run. Check with William tomorrow."

How odd our relationship. Can never quite predict whether we'll lock hands or horns, as some competition stirs up love and hate. Perhaps part of it is that we share the bond of having married early and mistakenly, though she, evidently, has sworn never to repeat it, ("Once fooled, twice foolish," she quips not infrequently and without embarrassment.) Indeed it appears that her professional life keeps her adequately stocked, so that at times I want to follow suit—though not just any suit. At other times I sense it rings a little hollow. She treats me like the younger sister she never had, but given my progress to date, I need 'younger.' Need the time.

Thus unexpectedly freed, and eventually injected with sufficient caffeine, I wrote all morning, trying to find the right tone.

> . . . Said Fiona, "Marvin and I have been talking, Eiley."
>
> "This is good Fiona, good," allowed Eiley wondering, then toying.
>
> Fiona paused. Her eyes ran over her own fingers and nails, palm up, palm down. Need work. Sigh. "Your, uh, good work has not gone unnoticed. Marvin is promoting you, to associate editor. You will have some writers."
>
> Eiley felt her breath leave, drawn off. "Ohh Fi-o-na . . . that's . . . that's too kind."
>
> Fiona's hooded eyes watched, considered, did not disagree . . .

At noon I emerged into the mid-day brilliance winking above the crowds. Pushing through the bus's reluctant door at 23rd, I stepped down into sun-baked aromas and lunchtime clusters of brightly-colored outfits, and all manner of faces and hair—bound in ear-ringing noise.

Up in the studio, sunlight and shadow changed dimensions,

erecting walls where there were none, leaving sunpatches shimmering and benches sliced in half.

Like a statue in a corner, Trudi, the actress playing Teresa's slightly older, wiser friend Elaine, studied her lines. Unlike John, she carries her working-class heritage with her, and confided that it's important that Pat and John accurately portray that world. "Hey, it's too easy and tempting to go with all the clichés about the working class."

Liking her straight talk, I asked her how she saw Elaine's prospects, prospects for a woman who'd been married and divorced as a teen, and had a brief fling with Stephen sometime afterward.

She shook her head. "In Trappers Lake? Sweet Jesus, not a place *I'd* ever want to live. Nothin' romantic about it, despite David's notions. What's there? Not a thing, no careers, no 'culchah,' your basic subsistence existence, where people either marry by senior year and scratch out a living, or leave. Hardly a man between 18 and 60 you'd want to have a drink with."

I asked her why Elaine stays.

"Simple. Money. Where's she gonna go? No money, no skills . . . Maybe if she was younger, like you . . ."

"And how does she see Stephen?"

"She's wary; she knows him; she's no innocent. But hey, she knows it's tough on him too. She's a little older than he is, doesn't hold things against him, but warns him not to screw around with Teresa, or she'll have his ass, spread the story, chase him outta town, sink the club. And he knows it, too."

Before I could pursue this, the others emerged from the back rooms: David, John, Pat. Hello, hello, hello. John, with a slightly averted gaze, asked how I was feeling and whether I got home all right. Not answering immediately, I studied him coolly, discovering his cheeks unshaven, his eyes heavy. "I'm better, John, but *you* don't look too good. D'you drink all that wine, all by yourself?"

Frowning, he seemed to grope for the subtext—something new for him.

"Really John, you don't look like you got much sleep."

From his watery eyess leaked unhappiness and fluster. His jaw slid one way then the other, before he turned away.

David glided up, glancing at John. "Did you listen to Ludwig last night?"

"I did. Indeed he stayed with me for much of the night. How about you? Are your . . . are you all right?"

He nodded, pleased with my discretion. "I'm going to read you all a story in a couple of minutes. But there's coffee in the back, and sandwiches, if you want." And our smiles reached into one another quite candidly, as if each sought to know fully the other's thoughts.

But then he excused himself, and moved over to speak with Pat. Watching him, I marveled at his recovery from last night, even as I wondered how he will survive the long pull. At the moment there is an unmistakable sharpness to him, a quiet crispness, a seriousness, but at the same time, in his white shirt which stands out whiter than the cream walls, he seems something of a spirit.

When he moved again, to Trudi in the corner, he was reflected in both mirrors, so that two heads bore down upon her, and all three tipped and rolled, as their faint murmurs drifted across the room. David, I now noticed, was wearing red, high-top sneakers, a sight which warmed my cheeks.

In another corner sat Pat, like Trudi, studying her script. Today she looked dramatic, in shiny, black body suit, matching her shiny dark hair, cut just above her shoulders. I'd originally thought that she might seem too urbane, too confident, a choice to play down-on-her-luck, rural Teresa, but with her fluid face, she can transform herself—here into a hard-bitten, rural girl, worn down by bad choices and bad luck. She'd done it by becoming expressionless and still, and by holding her face flat, her chin down, and using only her eyes. Yesterday, after talking with David, she tried changing her voice, flattening its tone and clipping her words. Sitting there now, she seemed to have withdrawn into herself, much as I imagined Teresa doing, living in her trailer, with two young kids and no adult companionship.

When David left Trudi, he moved out into the middle of the floor and announced that he had a passage from the book he wanted to read. John, I noticed, settled not quite comfortably, off a bit, twisting and tugging at his shirt. The women leaned calmly back to listen. David found his page, adjusted his glasses, and began:

> Somewhere at a crossroads, in a remote corner of the Adirondack wilderness squats the old town, like a transient, unkempt and uncertain. Perched precariously on a slanting plateau by the lake, it's reached by driving through miles of desolate, farm-abandoned meadows and sporadic, under-nourished woodland. One final swoop and swerve carries you over a slate-gray stream to the cratered main street which crawls up among the huddled buildings, tilting this way and that.
>
> More than once, Stephen had wondered, 'What am I doing? Why am I still here? Why have I not found something to do with my life?' And if one were to thoroughly explore the town, one might arrive at the same question.
>
> Yet the town is not without life. At various times, in and out of the country store, sagging like an old hat, come the gnarled, local folk: the craftsmen and woodsmen, the road crew and deputies, the few merchants, the town clerk and sole teacher, and a few mothers with children trailing. Some peer into the windows of the adjacent real-estate office, seldom open, now that the city folk no longer motor up to find their second homes. Across the street slopes the restaurant-and-bar, community watering hole and lone pool table—all in one, one for all. And shoulder to that, the laundry, the sometimes social center, followed by two pale residences, exhibiting the detritus of habitation: clothes drying, toys lying, cat crying, if seldom the inhabitants themselves.

David looked around.

Trudi shook her head disapprovingly. "Not for me. Too many words, gettin' in the way." She shivered and looked down.

Pat had watched Trudi without expression, and now her eyes climbed slowly to the windows. "I found it brought me in. I've read the book and screenplay . . . but here I could feel it, see it, the faded colors, the rotting wood, the sagging frames, the pock-marked street . . . the slow-moving people, young and old, turned in upon themselves."

Looking now to John, I saw him struggling with the two reactions. Glancing at David, picking at a callous on his palm, John muttered, "Well you know, as I think about it . . . a place like that's gonna need a helluva lot more than a club. I mean there's lotsa little towns like that back home, where I come from, and the only change they're gonna see is more farms goin' bust."

"But here John," answered Pat, "here, it's a step, a reasonable step."

John paused, weighing this, then faintly shook his head, evidently unconvinced. Blindly he began searching through his script for a passage supporting his view.

But David did not mind this mixed response. What he wanted was for them to run the next scene while the flavor of the reading lingered. And I was surprised to hear from the outset a noticeable new hardness in their voices, an edginess, interspersed with moments of resignation.

Later David began working John progressively harder, insisting that he try lines again and again, each time with a slightly different objective or emphasis. Indeed I wondered if there was something else at work here. And though John went along, he did so with increasing frustration. Yet David persisted. I felt my own face growing hot, until finally John spun away, spitting, "No, god-damn it! That's it on that one. That's all I'm fucking doing! I've done it every-which-way, so you fucking decide what you want!"

"Okay, John, but that's the level of frustration Stephen wrestles with, isn't it? As he encounters one roadblock after another. He has indeed tried it every which way." With this, David coolly turned to say something to Pat, leaving ruddy-faced John grumbling to himself, and uneasily wiping his palms through his hair.

Before they moved on, however, someone appeared in the

doorway, a young woman, with long, dirty-blonde hair, in whose handsome, if not pretty, features I detected familiar lines. Amanda, I was all but certain. I turned to watch the others, as one by one, each looked up.

Amanda went first to her father, who wrapped her in a warm embrace, her face tilting to him, eyes closing in the bright window light over his shoulder. How tired and tense she looked.

Detaching from him, she apologized, eyes averted, for the interruption, before turning to greet Pat with a resigned, weary half-smile, and then John more happily, under whose gaze and residual anger she seemed to blush, and finally Trudi, before David introduced her to me. As we shook hands, she studied me with unabashed interest, suggesting that my name was not new to her. And then she turned away, mouth pinched, to find a chair.

As the actors launched into the next scene, I peered over at Amanda, sitting off to my left. She'd taken out a notebook and was scribbling away. Attempting to justify her presence here away from academe? Notes for Modern Drama? I wondered if her books had found their way back into her bag. Not surprisingly, I saw that while she attended to all three actors, primary attention was devoted to John. Touchingly.

But what was John doing with this child? What could she possibly offer him? She seemed not nearly as special as he had proclaimed.

Time crawled, as David now did little more than listen.

And then, Amanda and I were alone in the studio as the actors went off to retrieve belongings. I found myself looking blindly in her direction, awaking only when she spoke.

"Excuse me . . . Excuse me, Christine? Do you have the time?"

Feeling as if our ages were reversed, and as if she had information to reveal to me, I did not respond at first, until, with almost dreamlike deliberation, I remembered to look at my watch, indeed study it. "Five-fifteen."

"Thank you." She reached for her book bag, opened it, and slipped her notebook into it, along with familiar bindings, familiar titles. My eyes shied away, and yet I realized that I was curious about how she saw all of this—these connections. "Amanda, how do you think the project's going?"

Seconds passed before she emerged from wherever her mind had run. Warily she eyed me, " . . . Fine . . ."

"And John? How do you think he's doing?"

Impatience, maybe annoyance, played in her cheeks and brow. She shifted her weight and breathed, as if accepting some unpleasant task. "Good. I mean his character's interesting. Maybe it's his best."

"And what about the club? Is that a worthy thing to fight for?"

Frowning, she looked down, before her eyes slid over to me. "What do you mean? . . . Are you interviewing me?"

"No, just curious."

We gazed at one another, but I suspected her mind was also churning.

Maybe out of duty to her dad, she eventually allowed, "I think it's worthy, for their little town. I mean, like, what else? . . . Naturally, I'm sympathetic. To grow up in a place like that, with some of those people . . . must be totally hard."

"But what about Stephen's dream? In some ways it's a very romantic notion."

Moistening her lips, she avoided my gaze, as her emotions seemed to ripple just under her brow. "I don't know . . . It's not easy for people like John, I mean Stephen, anywhere. They have to be willing to stand up to all sorts of crap . . . Everyone has expectations of them."

Of whom was she thinking?

In the next moment I heard her change her tone. "You said you're not going to quote me on any of this, right?"

"No," I reassured her, but I couldn't help prodding a little, "I was wondering, is John popular, at college, say? . . . I did a profile of him last summer when he was shooting "Blackout.""

Head askance, she nonetheless looked closely at me.

"I haven't taken a poll . . . but which profile?"

"For *Avenue Magazine*, came out last Fall."

Conflicting emotions played over her features. "Really?"

I held my gaze.

"You were out there when he was doing it?"

I nodded. "Did you read it?"

Looking away, eyes shifting, she hesitated, "Yes, a friend at school lent it to me."

"And?"

"It was interesting. It explained some things. And I liked the pictures . . . Not that I think the movie was great or anything, but like he was . . ." she glanced uncertainly at me, "he was right, I mean, completely excellent, in the role."

So, her teen fantasy, laminated to a veneer of urban sophistication. "So what are you going to say about my dad?"

Surprised at her probing tone, I replied rather simply, "I want to describe how he works and what makes his films so good, so moving, and so beautiful."

" . . . You know, not everyone thinks so," she informed me, annoyed that I didn't seem to be aware.

I nodded. "And what about you? Do you want to get into the business eventually?"

Apparently a not infrequent question, she replied automatically, "I'm thinking about it. But there're other things I want to do first . . . like travel, study . . . What about you? Do you like what you're doing?"

Nearly laughed. Such a pert turn-about. Could not contain a smile. "Well yes, I meet interesting people, travel a bit, get to write about interesting things . . . I'm writing a story too, about a young woman who escapes to New York."

"Neat . . . But where have they sent you?" she wondered, eyes widening in a familiar manner.

"Last summer to California, to interview John. Other articles have taken me to London, Montreal, Miami."

Her eyebrows rose as she considered this, then asked, "But who . . . who reads that magazine?"

I swallowed a laugh. "I've wondered the same . . . but your friend did. You too . . . You're right, however, most readers are older than you, and I suspect want just a little casual entertainment, a taste. Nothing too heavy."

"Like at a dentist's office," she offered helpfully.

I smiled, appreciatively.

Her expression now softened into that of a girl. Her cheeks and lips suddenly seemed fuller, their paleness turning to cream, as we heard the others returning.

When all had reassembled, David thanked the actors and me before announcing that Mandy and he were off for an evening together—something I assumed was addressed primarily to John.

Shortly he and I were alone on the sidewalk outside, where rather quickly my distaste returned. Watching him watch David and Amanda receding toward Sixth, I tried to control my feelings. But he, oblivious, turned with affected good cheer and asked, "So, you up for a drink?"

As I studied his face, he sensed that something other than acquiescence might be in the offing. Trying to head things off, he hurried, "You're looking stunning tonight, Christine. Your outfit, your coloring, everything, is striking."

"John, I don't quite know where to start."

"Let's start with a drink. It's been a long day, living in Stephen's shoes. You saw how David was riding me."

"Let me just say something, John. I know there's no commitment between us; I know you're just here for a while, but I have not even the slightest desire to be part of your traveling road show, your collection of groupies."

"What are you talking about?"

"I know Amanda was at your hotel. I saw her books."

" . . . Oh, well . . . she was just there to understudy." But the ensuing guffaw came too quickly, after which his face went blank, as if he'd slipped into uncharted seas.

"I'd thought we might establish a friendship this time, but I see nothing's changed."

His face winced. "In fact, Christine, that's not the case."

"It never is, John. Good night."

"But you're wrong, way off."

"Sure." And turning away, I felt mildly triumphant, particularly as chance delivered a bus to board and carry me up Sixth.

Yet, in the herkyjerky bus, doubts swayed with my fellow riders. Was I too impatient? Should I have listened? No, better clean, cleaner, cleansed.

At home, spoke to Kate for a long time, describing the pros and cons of holding a job. On balance, better now than footloose and fancy free. Must be age. And not a word about John. Must be maturity.

"Pregnancy too," she said, "changes perspective. It takes one out of oneself. It's something to live for, Chrissy. Reminds you what's important."

Startled. "You mean it?"

"Oh yes. I needed something . . . And so do you."

"Well, yes . . . but probably not quite the same thing." Yet she alone had seen it—the only other person. And I wondered if writing yet another woman's coming-of-age story would bring me, or anyone else, anything. Tired, I was fearful of the answer.

April 22th

Office days. The ambivalence of routine. Tapping out, deleting, tapping again, white ribbons across a blue screen. This time: reflections on local television and radio news, their sensationalizing and pandering, their lurid stories and blurring of news into entertainment, their buying ratings. Ben and I have been trying to find something fresh: Is this an industry's degeneration, or a society's? Yet we've both been uncomfortable, reporting from our own commercially driven pulpit.

Midday we escaped, fled to the park, away from judgement, commerce, traffic, into the quiet, to clear our heads. And once in the park, as the clamor fell behind, around us unfolded a silent movie: mothers and nannies pushing strollers, older people lining sunny benches, faces tilted sun-ward; our contemporaries jogging, peddling, rolling on their blades, wrapped in inter-galactic spandex.

Pita sandwiches in hand, we meandered up by the museum, groping for the words to express our discomfort. But the soft landscapes—pointillist and pastel—of magnolia and cherry blossoms, tight-fisted azalea buds, limp daffodils drooping over their wilting sheaths, the last forsythia, yellowing into brown combined to distract us, lifting our doubts away, even as I did remember to keep an eye out for Eleanor . . . Eleanor.

Ben's a good soul, seraphic in his clear skin under his wreath of red hair. He listens, notices things, seems to care, and though he's a bit younger, we share feelings and attitudes. I sense he's attracted to me but is careful not to let it intrude.

He explained that Melissa takes time to warm, as she holds much inside. When he told me he, too, wants to write a novel, I wondered aloud if there are not more writers these days than readers.

April 26

Met Lynn, one of the staff photographers, at the office and headed south in her car, to Soho to interview Kirsten's Prince of Rags, Daemon, in his loft.

His androgynous face is as much a garment as his clothing, stitched together quilt-like, through which eyes peer out as from a mask. The piped-in voice seems artificial, too, being neither gentle nor firm. Poor soul. Where will he/she be in a year?

As for his designs, I could only avert my eyes. In this humble observer's opinion, the sole pattern was the utter lack of pattern, or scheme, or beauty. The intention seemed to be the appearance of remnants, or found objects, stitched together, which might have worked had the selection and assembly been more artful. As it was, only sad.

Lynn had trouble finding ways of rendering Daemon's line photogenically, or making it look presentable, or interesting. I turned away. Unaware of our dismay, or possibly in reaction to it, Daemon kept up an indecipherable scat-chatter. Tried to attend, plastering on a permanent-press smile; tried to think of questions to ask, despite the sentiment that the only redeeming aspect of the enterprise was that it provided a living for him and his minions, for now.

Back in the office, pondered what spin to give it. No point in presenting only my own dismay, though state it I would. But the fact is, someone's buying the stuff. Must try to articulate what the public sees in it, even if it will soon pass from the scene. But cannot imagine that Lynn's photos will not reveal the emptiness. And yet both industries, theirs and ours, want the hype, the glitz, the supposed glamour. I can imagine the hew and cry if the emperor is proclaimed to be marching without a stylish stitch.

April 28

Where the hell is this café he suggested? Seven a.m. as I'd wobbled out onto the sidewalk, after too little sleep. Why had I agreed to this hour? Carefully placing one foot in front of the other, hoping my makeup was where it was supposed to be, I clicked along with the hurrying, muttering, suited-set zig-zagging south on Second.

Arrived on time. He was late. My fate, waiting for men. Is this emblematic of their egocentrism? And yet, most likely a phone call had delayed him. So I forced open my eyes to peer around at the mocha walls, the 19th century prints, and the mostly Asian staff—the incongruities—until finally coffee was brought . . . rich and good. Alleluia!

Thus ensconced, I sat wondering if David were not of this city, but rather of a bright mountain village somewhere. But as I closed my eyes, relaxing, a hand trailed across my shoulders. I inhaled sharply, and sat up straight.

"Good morning, Christine," came a voice. "Nodding out, are we?"

I turned loudly in my chair, blinking. His face, close up and smiling, seemed to have sprung from my thoughts. I saw him spinning into the chair opposite, his yellow-green eyes dancing into mine; his glasses splitting the light into fleeting planes of color.

"David."

He tugged his chair to more securely seat himself and make room for the gent behind. "Sorry, I'm late," he exhaled. "Never take a call from your producer first thing. He bears nothing but bad tidings, which is precisely what he's hired to handle. I hope you've ordered. I apologize."

Dismissing the need, I wondered, "Do you want me to ask what the tidings were? Or let them lie?"

He smiled, then dropped his voice. "Oh, the bank's begun balking, once producer Marty Berg began talking to them. Little does it matter, it seems, that all was signed."

Groaning now, he reached for a menu which he unsuccessfully attempted to read. "Marty, thinking he could get a better rate, tried to re-negotiate. But of course the bank's not interested in the least, and now contends we've broken the agreement. So, call in the lawyers; spend more money. Not the way to start the day." His eyes looked up from the menu which he had not seen. Unhappy eyes. He tried to blink them clear, then rubbed them under his glasses. Involuntarily I cringed. He craned his neck around and wondered loudly, "So where is he? Where's my man?"

His voice winged out over the café, suppressing conversation, turning heads, and bringing a waiter, a young Southeast Asian man, trotting our way. "So solly, Mr. Roomis. I not see you come in."

"Good morning, Mr. Tan. Allow me to introduce a talented young writer, Ms. Howth, who's doing a piece for a very important magazine, on cafés—which are the good ones, the ones that offer prompt service and fine food, and which do not. That sort of thing."

"Ohh . . . velly nice, velly nice. Mo coffee, Miss?"

Smiling, I tried to put him at ease. David, how could you?

"But I'll have some coffee, Mr. Tan," David requested, "and muffins for two, bacon, and juice as well, thank you."

Tan's brief bow drew one from David. And Tan again, and David, before Tan backed out of sight. I was not the only patron watching open-eyed.

"Remind me, Christine, to give you the address of the studio in Queens."

"Well give it to me now," I said, taking out my notebook and penning away. Tan hurried back with coffee, muffins, juice, and bacon, peering mindfully at me, his lidded eyes tilting down to my notes. "Thank you, Mr. Tan," I bowed slightly. "Perfectly happy, thank you." Relieved, he bobbed away.

As David sipped coffee and bit into a muffin, I peered closely. So clean this morning, smooth, defined. Soft silver hair, glasses sitting lightly upon his nose—he seemed to change from patriarch to prince, to sui generis, whoever that may be.

Perhaps sensing my gaze, he asked, "So, where shall we begin this morning?"

"I was thinking, David, that what you do is tell stories, dramas, about life, realistic and unsparing . . . What you don't do is comedy, musicals, thrillers, whodunits . . . How did you choose?"

With another sip of coffee, he sat very still, thinking.

"If I had the comedic touch, or musical talent—" a brief, wistful smile spilled out from his eyes—"but I'm confined to poking through the ordinary dark matter which surrounds me." An ambiguous, pensive look replaced his smile. "Who can tell why we do what we do? In some cases, I suppose it seems clear: to fill a need, an expectation . . . Talent, if strong enough, pushes through—something I've witnessed—but for us ordinary folk, we can only wonder what might've come with greater determination, greater single-mindedness." His eyes fell slightly as his thoughts collapsed inward.

"But certainly, David, your doubt has held you back less than most."

His tilting head acknowledged this was true, and untrue.

Leaning closer, he confided lightly, "Emerson, who can jog me alive with his riddles, rhapsodies, and reflections, wrote that we should not forget that we are part of nature and her forces—composed of, created by, embodying . . . and if there are daunting obstacles, yet how often do we find, or achieve, what we've sought. Nature plants the rose of beauty on the brow of chaos."

He watched me as I turned over this metaphor. For whom, I wondered, might this apply? For the exceptional, the optimistic? But unable to quickly reason it through, I asked if his characters' truths came from the brow of chaos.

Straightening up, shifting his legs, he found my eyes.

"Aren't these things all around us? . . . Life sings out its variations. Marnie fears, hesitates, withdraws, while Mandy strikes out recklessly and defiantly. My dear wife Kath, a basically good, honest woman, has refused to join me in searching for a way back— probably understandably—retreating instead into a convent of narrow purity. I have tried to call her out, even as I helped drive her in . . . The question to be confronted is: How are we each picking our way through the world?"

Uneasily I met his eyes, thinking that while it's one thing to see a friend clearly, it's quite another to perceive one's own truths.

"Christine," I heard him whispering, "please remember that this business about my family is confidential."

I indicated I hadn't forgotten, and his face lightened slightly. His eyes now seemed lifted by whimsy. "If we are gossamer beings, there are eddies to ride, cycles to carry us."

Closing my eyes, I tried to board one, but another, practical, question pushed in: "Why then, David, did your lead characters, Horton and Daniel, not find eddies to ride? Why instead did they fall?"

His hands opened, flexed, then relaxed upon the table. He studied them, leaning closer. "Because they chose to fight those forces, rather than ride them, and because when they erred, they fought on, rushed out too far where no hands could reach." David's eyes stared past my shoulder. When he found me again, he leaned back. "On the other hand, if you'll allow more Emersonian nuggets: love's loss lures out re-examination; grief strips bare; death makes room, as the forest fire cleans the forest floor . . . It's dialectical nature, her processes, enchanting me, as I wiggle in her grasp."

My eyes moved down from him to my coffee, feeling these processes prying into me. Holding my breath, I tried to withstand their sharp nails, before spinning my thoughts away, back to him.

"Do you feel that your films have changed you? In straining to get them done?"

His eyes moved uncomfortably over the table before him.

"Work . . . has been the most consistent, deepest connection . . . sadly."

I felt myself start, once more. Felt doubt flow from my frown. More than wife? Daughters? I searched his face. He stared evenly, pensively, before him.

Unexpectedly, inexplicably, I feared for Teresa. "But, well, what about Stephen? Does he reach the same conclusion?"

Blinking, he looked up. "The city revealed to him the possibilities . . . He wants to find, wants to engage, something that stirs and connects him . . ."

" . . . Can that be with Teresa?"

"It can be . . . but for how long, who can say?"

"What about 'sacrifice'?"

"That, too, will be part of it, the ever-changing mix."

I felt my fingers fumbling for my bacon. I became aware of molars crushing, spurting burnt hickory into the corners of my mouth, stimulating glands . . . glands and mind, nourishment for the cells . . . a single bite. Shaking myself, I remembered, "Yet, it is Teresa . . . and Sam and Elaine, who save Stephen."

"In part, yes. They pull him back."

"Is that not a brief against solitary individualism?"

"A case for balance."

"Which Horton and Daniel fail to find?"

He faintly nodded. "Alone in their work, they turn inward. They're not bad people, any more than Stephen is angelic."

" . . . Do not most artists work alone?"

He looked carefully at me. "You work in an office."

"My best work is done at home."

He nodded, reflecting. "Lasting balance doesn't seem to be part of life. Seems indeed an impossibility."

Neither of us moved.

"We are all vulnerable then," I concluded, for myself.

He breathed and looked away, appearing to nod. "Just as there's no complete explanation for why our particular constellation of thoughts and feelings, our particular consciousness, our soul, is manifested in its particular form, so there's no charting where all the nicks and knocks will send us. We can choose our work, but it seems much more difficult to become the person we might wish to be."

"But David, with awareness, do we not gain choice?"

"To a degree. But when my daughters arrived, they arrived clad in their own distinct personalities, one positive, one wary, their choices already narrowed. And, of course, as we all moved on together, it became impossible to sort out what impinged upon what."

Yes, I thought, flashing back through my own past, just when I believed I had reached clarity, something shifted and sent all tumbling once more.

Possibly seeing my dismay, he observed, "Though we construct incredible civilizations, how sketchily do most of us know their underpinnings—not to mention our neighbor, our spouse, our child, our self . . . Perhaps there is too much to know, or perhaps we carelessly, solipsistically, let the surrounding essentials slip away."

As we studied each other through the prism of these thoughts, there erupted behind him a jarring scrape. The gent at his back awkwardly rose, banging into him. David half-turned to pull his chair and make room, glancing up. The fellow apologized. David smiled to dismiss his concern, before turning slowly back.

"You know, Christine, I was thinking that in any objective sense, there is only the slimmest rationale for why I should care about this body, its welfare or survival, beyond the instinct to survive, wherein the beetle crawls on for as long as it is able, once chance has brought this beetle into being."

"It is the vessel of your consciousness."

"Yes, but sometimes I think how easy to let go, to simply open my hand and let the wind take it."

"No David . . ." Yet immediately I felt myself flush. Embarrassed, I looked away. When I turned back, it was as if to discover his gauzy vessel, before the wind took it.

"In the park," he resumed, "I see squirrels playing tag, or watch the birds soar and sing. Nature spews out these variations for no observable reason, other than that a particular agglomeration of cells seems to survive in a particular niche. And we, among them, have this serendipitous opportunity to fill out our time. That's our challenge, in this infinity, this pointless winking. What can we do with our opportunity, our time here? What can we make of ourselves, and the physical world?

"Of course, I would prefer to do comedy, or be able to sing or make music, but I am a bird with no voice, and so have turned to pictures." He flashed a rather self-deprecating smile, before abruptly carrying a kiss on two fingers from his lips to my cheek.

"Thank you," I mumbled heavy-headed.

"A delight," he trilled, "to share a moment in the sun."

Under that brightness I felt a measurable warmth.

"Chris, I appreciate your allowing me to ramble on."

Weakly I smiled, pleased yet feeling he'd opened up many holes.

"Would you allow me one final theory, about the nature of living things?"

Thinking he needn't ask, I nodded minimally.

"It arises, I believe, from nature's basic functions: food-gathering and reproduction. Observation reveals that these functions are exclusionary and often lethal processes, where one creature's gain is at another's expense. Science has found that this system predates the animals and insects, going back to the crack of time, to the basic elements, where collision of two simple elements produced, in their consequent fusing, a new, more complex one. This dialectical process has existed from the very beginning and is in the atomic fabric of things.

"It is a prescription for change, conflict, evolution, variety, but not the immutable status quo. In life, we borrow energy and matter, and, in the end, must give them up. Our physical elements don't disappear but rejoin the dust and air, and yet in many cases we've transformed other matter into something new. A god-like ability . . . yet as Prometheus discovered, there are costs."

Watching, I saw that his attention seemed both consumed and released, and my eyes fell as I attempted to digest all of this. But I heard him breathe and stir. "Christine, how does all of this strike you? . . . I find few who are interested in this sort of thing."

More pleased that he would ask than I dared convey, I noted, "Mothers and fathers achieve it every day, of course, but the transformation you speak of is something I've been trying to implant in Eiley's story. Your questions underlie those she is juggling: What has formed her, and what should she do with this person she is slowly uncovering?"

He looked closer, to see if this was true. I knew inside somewhere I was trembling, but whether from happiness or fear I couldn't tell.

He murmured, "I'd like to read it sometime."

"It's rough; it's early," I warned.

"Well, I'd love to read, or listen to, a draft."

I bowed a little, in appreciation. But his glance at his watch signaled it was time for him to leave for the studio.

"David, I had so many other, nice little, academic questions . . ."

"I was thinking we should meet to look for Eleanor."

"Oh? . . . When?"

"That's the problem."

"I should try again myself. I have time."

His eyes seemed to doubt this. "Well, let me call you. Of course if we find her, what then? What can we offer?"

" . . . To find her a home . . ."

He acknowledged this, then looked up searching for Tan, and raised his hand for the check. Watching his almost Victorian gesture, I somehow felt cast back in time, suspended in amber.

Outside, in the brightness, he promised to call tomorrow or the day after. With a wave and glint, we parted. I drifted down toward the office, feeling a sudden squirming to crack the amber and wriggle out.

May 1st

May Day, on the calendar anyway, but outside there's little vernal about it. Great clouds flow east, over my aerie and the oblivious city and out over the fish-filled sea. Shrubs 'n' flowers shiver in the cool wind and showers. Despite this, I remind myself that today is the first day of the best month, when all Edenic summer stretches ahead. I yearn for its warmth and change, hoping the readiness is all.

In the office, Ben and I kicked another column idea back and forth, this one on The New World Order, from an outline Kirsten had given us, itself a testament to disorder. We joked that our proud leader envisions herself as Secretary General, decreeing, along with peace: chic dress codes, free love, feminism, and global bacchanalia. Much would the world be improved.

We called professors, think-tanks, and diplomats, encountering absolute certainty of opinion about past and present, unmatched, however, by any willingness to predict the future. Thus for all their learning, the good ship Earth is left to sail inexorably on in the dark.

Asked Ben again if he wanted to try another sweep. Hoped it wasn't taking advantage. He smiled a willing smile, and we headed up to 57th and over, past the Plaza, averting my eyes, and under the covering of green. We crisscrossed the east park, past playgrounds, under bridges, squinting toward remote benches, our bodies bent to the gusting west wind. Yet not a single homeless person. Had the city rounded them up? Someone tip them we were coming? Imagined the disappointment in David's voice, his eyelids dropping down.

Returning along Madison, however, we happened upon several, as if the wind had blown them there. And crossing 71st Street, glancing east past the church, I saw the huddled form of an older woman, motionless against a black guardrail. We swerved toward her. With Ben hanging back, I edged closer and, cautiously peering around her shoulder, saw, from David's description, that this might well be her. "Eleanor?"

Her head didn't move, but her eyes did, shifting up to some intermediate point, and then, almost in spite of herself, throwing a fearful glance my way, which she pretended she hadn't. I leaned closer, and she leaned away, reaching for the rail with her left hand, attempting to block me from her field of vision.

"Eleanor, David sent me, to see how you are. You remember David, don't you? He helped you to the shelter."

Her right eye blinked and looked up into the distance, before sliding back to me. For a moment she studied me, then opened her mouth. A hoarse little voice uttered, " . . . Missy?"

"Yes?" I waited.

But disappointed, it seemed, she allowed her eyes to fall back to the church's stone wall.

"Is there anything you need?" I tried again. "David was wondering? Is there anything we can do for you? We'd like to help." But her head turned completely away. No response, no further movement. Poor soul. What does she feel? What does she know? "Eleanor?"

She pushed off from the rail and began rocking slowly toward Park Avenue. Ben stepped up behind me. "What did she say?"

"'Missy,' but I don't know who or what that is."

We watched as she dragged herself away like a wounded animal, before I stepped after her, telling her, "Eleanor, we'll see you later. David and I will come by again, all right?"

"But God knows where she'll be," Ben cautioned behind me.

"We'll find her again. How far can she go?"

How strange, I thought, as we glided through the crowds along Third to the office, that so many of us turn out like this. I thought of Luke, his disease consigning him to live closed in upon himself.

At the office, I left a message on David's machine, telling him of the news and that I would go back to her after work. And I did. But she was no longer there, not surprisingly. Undeterred, I crisscrossed north, and eventually found her at Lexington and 74th, in a doorway. Heart surged. Have her! But to do what with?—even as I was glad the decision was mine, mine alone.

This time when I approached, she did not shy away, though neither did she meet my eyes. "Eleanor, remember me?"

No flicker of recognition, or anything. But I was prepared.

"I have a place for you . . . to wash your clothes and take a bath. And then you can go free . . . Do you understand?"

A shadow passed across her face.

"Wouldn't a bath be good? And clean clothes?"

Faintly her eyes narrowed.

Slowly, more slowly than I had done once before, with the other woman, I reached for her elbow. "Come, Eleanor, come wash up. And then you can go." I tried to coax her gently, but she did not budge, her face tightening in resistance. Uncertain at first, I pressed more firmly, but she held. Girding myself, I increased my force, until, like a boat pulled free from the shore, she floated almost weightlessly, along side.

Carefully, patiently, my hand behind her arm, we made our way down the block. Time lost its way. I held my breath, turning to inhale. Eventually I spotted my building ahead, ever so slowly growing in size.

In the lobby Frank gave me a mystified, then disapproving look, stepping back, squinching up his nose, then covering it, but neither of us said a thing.

Upstairs, I lead Eleanor to my laundry closet and opened the door. "Here, we will wash your clothes, you and I."

I lead her to my second bathroom, which lately only Luke has stepped into. In its white and gray tiles, its empty echo, I imagined we were lost, cut off, in this obscure chamber twenty stories above the frantic streets.

I stepped past her and bent to turn on the water, then straightened to reach into the cabinet for a towel and soap. An extra robe hung behind the door, which I gave her, telling her to undress and climb carefully into the bath, after which I left, hurrying back to the kitchen to open my refrigerator and cupboards, trying to imagine what she might eat.

When I returned, she had managed to get into the robe, a small triumph, I realized. I took her clothes at arm's length to my machine and pitched them in, shaking in extra detergent. Returning to help her wash, I found her using the john.

A short time later, again at the door, I heard water sloshing languidly, and I went in. She was ineffectually paddling, and ignored me. I reached for soap and a washcloth and squatted down by her. She stopped stroking, stilled by apprehension it seemed. Carefully I took her arm and hand and began to wash. The aroma of soap mingling with her sour smells made me gag. Coughing, I faced away, and then turning back I sealed off my sense of smell and slowly scrubbed all I could. She trembled but did not pull away. Her expression remained largely unreadable. Yet as I scoured her back, up and down, side to side, a dim shine emerged in her cheeks and eyes, and her mouth opened slightly. The shine did not immediately dissolve when I stood her up to dry her.

In the kitchen, I found I had to spoon in the soup and rice I'd warmed. Her eyes focused intently, and several times her tongue reached out for an errant drop or grain. But then, with her eyelids drooping, I guided her to Luke's room and its single bed prepared for her. Pushing a few hairs from her forehead, I said goodnight. Her eyes closed. I studied her face, once attractive I gauged, but now lips and nose have thinned, cheeks grown gaunt, eyes sunken. I felt a distant heaviness.

On my couch, tried to read, but she had stirred more than I could identify, and so I pushed myself up to call David, but again reached only his machine. "Call when you can. She's here, in my apartment, bathed and laundered. Did she never so much as murmur her name?"

But he didn't call, though I waited up reading on the couch until midnight. Couldn't help wondering if he was with Pat, or his wife. But eventually I, too, needed sleep, and pulled myself to bed. Checking in on Eleanor, I peered into the dark room from the doorway, and found her eyes open, staring at me. They blinked once, but otherwise did not acknowledge me. For some minutes we watched motionlessly, before I slowly closed the door.

Lying on my side, I tried to imagine her life, but realized there was no way I could give form to her expectations or understand how she sees it all.

May 2nd

What to do with you? Find a home, or someone to take you?
Dawn crawls in, mind drifts, arriving repeatedly back at her.

At seven, propelled by a great sigh, rose to make coffee, and dimly peruse the news, none of which was new. Seven-thirty, David phoned, "Sorry Christine, we were meeting till after midnight. But what a miracle you've accomplished! Congratulations. How is she?"

"I haven't peeked in this morning, but she seemed at peace, as best I could tell."

"Well, you're a saint. If you thought it useful, I could drop by to say hello, before I run out to the studio."

"Do you want some coffee?"

"If you have it."

In a few minutes, he was stepping in, eyes radiating, alert, dancing about the apartment. A smile widened into a gentle hug, which slipped into embrace. I had much to release, pressing against him. In the blur of close-up, pilgrim lips sank into softness, until caution pulled them back. My forehead sought companionship upon his shoulder—until I revived and led him to the kitchen, for coffee, and then to her door.

Knocking, I pushed carefully in, to find her lying on her back staring up at the ceiling. She did not look until she sensed a second presence, then lowered her eyes to us, and, slowly in apprehension, pulled the sheet and blanket entirely over her face.

"It's all right, Eleanor," I soothed. "We just wanted to say good morning. But you can stay right there, if you want to, in bed."

From behind my shoulder, he called, "Hi, Eleanor. How are you doing? Did you get some rest?"

After a short interval, the sheet was lowered, to just below her eyes—a picture so innocent and comical that it pulled smiles from our cheeks, sent our hands feeling for each other's.

"El-ean-or? El-ean-or," I sang. "We both must go to work, to our offices. Will you be all right here? I've left some food for you: soup, bread, rice and vegetables. A little turkey—all in the kitchen, on the top shelf in the refrigerator. If you want, I can make some coffee. Do you want coffee?"

Her eyes shifted slowly from David to me, but nothing more. We stood mutely waiting, until it was clear nothing more would come.

In the kitchen, I refilled his coffee and pressed a piece of cinnamon toast upon him, but, so thrilled was he, he hardly noticed. Within his glasses, his eyes gracefully skated. "My God, Christine, how did you do it? It's marvelous. How'd you get her to come up with you?"

"Just as you did, Herr director. Calmly, but with a steady hand. It wasn't difficult. She's so docile, poor soul."

Smiling at the cabinets, windows, me, he exclaimed, "I don't know whether to be more impressed or relieved . . . Of course the next question is what to do? Martina said she'd make some calls, to find some facility, or home. Maybe a private home. Apparently the state will pay individuals to board people. But it would have to be chosen carefully. What do you think?"

Yet we both recognized that her state, and her perceptions were unknowable to us. Tilting his head back to swallow the last of his coffee, he peeked at his watch. "Unfortunately I have to run, but may I call you later? And possibly come by again?"

"When?"

Another frowning glance at his watch. "Nine? Ten? We've got rehearsal, after shooting, followed by a production meeting. Is that too late?"

No, no . . .

He leaned forward; our cheeks brushed lightly, a glancing kiss, as hands held hands, and arms. I heard some interior cry.

"Christine, I can't tell you what a weight you've lifted . . . one that's begged for months . . . Thank you . . . I'll call you later." And with a final blur the door was closed. The air, stirred, soon settled.

In her room, I found she had neither moved nor changed her expression, turtle-like. Decided to leave her here until Martina or I find some solution.

Outside, bright sun drew me quickly along, down to the office, eager to relate this to Ben. Melissa was with him, and she, for the first time in my experience, put aside her reserve and expressed interest, indeed enthusiasm, suggesting adapting Eleanor's story for the magazine. But somehow this seemed wrong, even tired, particularly as Eleanor is a blank, and our ability to help her is uncertain. Where will the substantial care, time, and money come from? With, in all probability, her wires hopelessly crossed, what could be done?

Evening, May 2nd

Walking into my lobby after working until eight, I was called aside by Tony. "Christine, uh, one of the maintenance men found a woman outside your apartment, by the service elevator. Frank said she came in with you last night. They, uh, I mean they tried to talk to her, but uh . . . Well, you know. Your door must have locked behind her."

"When was this?"

"'Round two o'clock, I think."

"Is she upstairs?"

Distress pressed vertical lines into his brow. "Uh . . . you see no one knew what t' do; we didn't know where t' reach you, so they called d' hospital, and they of course, referred us, that is Mike, our chief, to a shelter, which in turn, uh, sent a van."

"Oh no. Which shelter?"

"I have the number."

I thanked Tony and rushed upstairs to call, and, after the usual holding and ear-offending extension-switching, was told by a thoroughly disinterested woman that she'd been let go.

"Let go? Where?"

"Right here, Ma'am. The report was: she was clean and didn't have no immediate problems."

"But she has no home!"

"She was bathed; her clothes were clean. We don't have no extra room for d' ones like that."

"So you put her back out on the street?"

"Didn't have no room, Ma'am."

"Then why did you bother to pick her up? And why didn't you bring her back where you got her?"

"Didn't have no authorization."

Anger and frustration clogged my head. "Where did you release her?"

"Like I said, right outside, Ma'am."

I swore to myself that some of the people running these institutions should be institutionalized themselves. "When?"

"Six, Ma'am." Click, gone.

I sank onto my kitchen stool. Should I rush off to look for her? Of course. Could not simply let her go. And so cabbed west, to search the West side streets, from 86th up to 96th, between the parks, but by then it'd grown dark and shadowy, eventually sending me back empty-handed. Where could she have gone? Some doorway? Some bridge? The entire experience will have confused and frightened her.

Starved, let down, wanting to cry out, I peered into my fridge. She'd touched nothing, ate nothing.

Waiting for the microwave to count off the seconds, I heard the lobby intercom buzz. David, I exulted. "Uh, Miss Howth, a Mr. Trevelyan."

"Wha?" What the hell does he want?

"Miss Howth?"

"Listen, Tony, could you put him on for a second?"

Fumbling and muffled grunts preceded him. "Christine, it's John. I just need to talk to you for a few minutes."

"So go ahead, talk."

"Not here. It's personal. Just a few minutes."

"I'm in the middle of something."

"Christine, come on. I'll make it quick."

" . . . Oh for Pete's sake!"

I met him at the door.

"Christine, I need to explain what's going on with Mandy and me."

"Why do you think I care?"

" . . . I realize it's my fault, but I want to come clean with you, so you don't think I'm the kind of person . . ."

"You are." I felt my mouth curl with distaste.

His face clouded. "Just hear me out."

Again? And yet there was something different about him.

I stepped back to lead him into the living room where he sat across from me on the couch.

"First, another apology is in order. I realize that, and I do apologize. You mean a lot to me, but I uh . . . what's happened is that, well, I've fallen in love with Mandy . . . I know you'll laugh and think I'm pulling your leg, but I'm not. It's true."

Just able to restrain a snort, I reminded myself it's Eleanor I should be attending to.

"Christine, I appreciate you and what you did for me. Really. That profile was a big step forward for me. You took me more seriously than I had myself. You saw more potential than I did, so I wanta thank you, which I never properly did—though in our lovemaking, I wasn't just going through the motions."

None of this felt quite real. I heard him continuing, telling me that it started off as an effort just to be nice to the director's daughter, but then he found they talked well together.

"Talked well? John, she's nineteen."

"I know. But we get along. Maybe I'm nineteen . . . You know, Christine—I mean I respect you, but you've always made it clear how much more . . . well, educated you are, than me."

"Nonsense John, you were thinking of only one thing last summer. And in any case, that was never my intention."

"Yeah well, I know I never went to college; I know your husband was some sort of intellectual, but there are different ways of living, you know."

"Yes, I know, John."

"Even now, you come across as superior."

"Well I'm sorry, but I can swallow only so much BS. I thought honesty was the one thing we owed each other."

"Last summer, I knew you were getting over your divorce and saw we weren't, well, like I said, a match . . ."

I looked at John, wondering if he thought this was true. There was little evidence then of even modest reflection. "And this time, John? What were you thinking?"

"I don't know. I was open."

I looked away feeling weak with hunger and disgust.

"But I wanted to explain about Mandy and me."

"A subject in which I have no particular interest, although I hope you'll realize who you're dealing with, and what your effect on her might be—not to mention on David."

"She's not helpless. She's not a child. Growing up in the city, and with a father like hers, who's no angel, woke her up early."

"That doesn't mean she's ready for the boundless concupiscence and self-regard of a Hollywood star."

He shook his head. "Whatever that means . . . I thought you tried to see beyond the clichés."

"I keep trying to."

"Last summer it didn't seem to be a problem for you."

"I was slow, out of practice. Dreaming, I guess."

"Maybe what you don't understand is that I care for her."

"Fine, this week and maybe next, but then what?"

"You're hard, Christine. I'm telling you I'm serious. If you can't handle that, there's not much I can do."

"Listen, none of this is really to the point."

"And she's probably coming back to California with me, after the picture."

Groaning and standing up, I exclaimed, "Fine, John, I'm glad you kept me in the loop, but I'm starved and I've got to eat something. Is there anything else?"

Standing also, he said, "No, that was it . . . but I was hoping we could stay friends." For emphasis, he stared unhappily from under his dark eyebrows, much as he did with the young things in "Blackout."

"Friends?"

For once he was silent.

"John, I hope you'll think of the poor girl from time to time, and not just . . . you know. She's probably endowed you with all sorts of inalienable virtues."

His mouth twisted with disenchantment, and I turned to lead him back to the door, where he paused. "I hope you'll give me the benefit . . . of some understanding."

"I'll do my best."

" . . . Christine, can I give you a hug? Just to . . ."

Wishing he'd just go, I opened the door.

"It'd mean something to me."

"Look, John . . ." I forced myself to meet his eyes, "in time all of this will be forgotten. It's served its purpose, and you don't really need my seal of approval for this other thing." Yet I saw that he was bending toward me, and felt his lips pressing against mine. I closed my eyes and mouth, trying to push away, but couldn't overpower his hold around my shoulders. I tried going limp, as his body pushed me back. There is a part of me . . . No, no longer. Finished, away! His force, his presence, were repellent, and that enabled me to twist away enough to hiss, "No John. Stop, for God's sake! Are you out of your fucking mind?"

With that, he released me, leaning back, his face lost in the overhead lights, before he stepped through the doorway and disappeared.

With a shiver of revulsion, I closed the door and locked it.

My mind whirled through sky, bleak and blank, reaching for something, sure of neither form nor purpose.

May 4th

A swarthy Russian cab driver was driving me across the upper roadway of the 59th Street Bridge. Twisting back in my seat, I surveyed the Flash Gordon metropolis, impossibly plastic, clear and close.

Once over the bridge, however, all flattened into the functional and ugly, as if the East River separates worlds, as indeed it does. Through blocks, then miles of low, unpopulated, indistinguishable structures we drove, where neither design nor taste was evident. One might argue it's money that's missing, but I contend it's thought and even a minimal visual sense, as if people here have refused to use the brains and eyes God gave them.

Eventually, rising like a hill town from this drab plain, appeared the great studio. As we approached, the main building sat poised like an art deco aeroplane, which having landed, found itself hemmed in by shacks springing up weed-like overnight.

Gazing out as we swooped in for a landing, I was delighted by the faces of those converging on this magic-making factory, an array of ages and styles stretching across the decades.

Following them through revolving doors, I entered a high-ceilinged, semicircular lobby, behind which ascended a marble stairway to a semicircular mezzanine and balconies beyond. As in Grand Central's concourse, voices and sounds quietly reverberated—a din rising from the years. Collecting in clumps, people sat or stood gazing, chatting, sipping coffee, waiting for the hour, while behind them, supporting the mezzanine, jade green columns curved away to left and right, standing out from pale French blue walls and marble meer. Oh yes, my dear, it was so.

I asked a security type, sleepy-eyed in his raspberry-colored uniform, where I might find D. Loomis. Awakening, eyes blinking, he turned and pointed to the stairway. "Me-me-mez-zanine, Miss. Right up there." His eyes ascended as if he yearned to go.

Muscles burning, I pushed up the curving stair, until at the top I was confronted by two corridors, bounded by mirroring glass doors, receding into darkness. Asking again, I was sent along, bending and squinting to read the titles by each door, until finally: Mandible Productions. D. Loomis, M. Berg. Pushed into a glassed-in anteroom occupied by a solitary woman reading beneath two vine-shaped deco lamps and seated in a dark green leather chair. Entirely in black, head tilted into a magazine, she was striking. As if she sensed my scrutiny, she glanced up. It was Pat, her hair set quite differently. Her eyes squinted, her mouth fluttered in silent hello, her smile appeared and disappeared. I wondered if she resented my friendship with David.

"A production meeting's in progress," she murmured, "organizing the day's shoot. David, Graham, Rudi, Peter of Sound, Debbie of Continuity, the gaffer and the grip, Hillary of Wardrobe, and Georgina, the set designer—all people you should meet." A final perfunctory smile and back to her magazine. *Avenue*, I noticed. My, my.

Barely had begun jotting in my notebook a few impressions of the place, when the inner door opened, disgorging the aforementioned lieutenants. Rising with determined swiftness, Pat slipped through the stream, closely observed by the men's panning heads.

About to return to my notes, I noticed shoes and chino pantlegs arrive before me. Graham, the line producer, introduced himself and welcomed me to the production. He was tall, trim, and blond, with a surprisingly deep, commanding voice, and though he uttered only the prescribed sentiments, his eyes, taking in more, were intelligent, aware, and apparently sincere—for all of which I was pleased on David's behalf.

Almost immediately upon his departure, Pat glided out again, a cool smile frozen across her face, never a glance my way. I picked up my things and stepped into the sanctum, to find David studying a schedule spread out upon his desk.

To my good morning, he looked up, smiled, and came quickly around the desk, sliding into our now customary embrace, warmly, truly, briefly.

He gave me the number of the sound stage in which the shooting would begin in about forty-five minutes, and then suggested that, as I had not been here before, I might enjoy exploring, while he attended to a series of people and details.

"Get lost, you're saying?"

"Enjoy yourself," he preferred. A pause, another gentle hug, a tap of a kiss, and I was off.

Back across the marble floor and down the polished stairs, to meander through the heart of the studio: three corridors leading to the sound stages. Twisting and turning past and through collections of people, I dodged dollies and carts carrying all manner of things, past runners and sitters outside various productions: commercials, TV shows, other movies, I gathered from glimpses and signs. I watched casts and crews mill and palaver, and, seeing one open door, peeked in. A television production crew was changing walls: one pink corner was roughly pried up and marched away, as its light-blue replacement was dollied in, and maneuvered by a legion of arms into position—after which, all stood back to admire their work. Windows followed, then blinds, curtains, carpets, all bobbing on backs, while up in the rafters, spot and flood-lights were flicked on and off, focused here and there, until the lighting director signaled 'a lock.' Now furniture bumped in, cartoon figures astride human legs, and when all was in place, the actors materialized magically. And lastly, in the middle, the director—a woman, I was pleased to discover.

Behind me, in the corridor, erupted squeals and peals of tiny laughter, as a gaggle of school children straggled by, chained hand to hand, herded by impossibly young-looking teachers. Some of the little ones stared up at me as they tottered by, wide-eyed, smiling.

Farther on, an angular, heavily made-up model, a pharaoh queen, waited for her commercial, surrounded by a retinue of attendants who paid scant attention.

Now aromas and people carrying food hinted that the cafeteria was not far. I bought a coffee and bagel and sat at a table to gaze upon the scene.

Last year's "Blackout" was shot on-location so that I never entered any of Hollywood's studios. But here it seemed a mixture of subway and circus, with something joyful about its communal throng, and its seeming to exist out of time. Yet looking more closely, I saw not all were exuberant. Some waited bored, dispirited, heads and shoulders, and even eyelids, sagging.

Today's set was the interior of Teresa's trailer home. The scene was of her putting her two children to bed, after which her friend, Elaine, arrives, and they sit together in the tiny kitchen and discuss (what else?) Stephen and his dream, interspersing reports on their fellow citizens, caustic comments and funny ones, mostly by Elaine. There is some discussion of what Stephen is up against: fear of change and concern about incidents of drunkenness, noise, and vandalism—notwithstanding that the club, or cabaret, is a mile out of town along the highway.

Taking a seat in one of several unspoken-for chairs near the door, I reflected on the effort and energy assembled simply to tell a story. David's quoted analogy seemed indeed apt: "the modern equivalent of medieval craftsmen assembling to build a cathedral to God, called by devotion, sustained by their daily bread."

David appeared across the set, moving visibly charged among the crew preparing for the first scene. Off to the side he saw the two tiny children cast as Teresa's kids and went to them and their mother dressed to the nines. Squatting, hands on knees, he spoke with the kids and shook the mother's hand. All beamed back, before he, sleek and gray today, moved on to the camera, waving to me as he went, glasses glinting under the lights.

Before he could bend to the camera, however, Debbie discreetly called that Kath was on the phone. He straightened, glanced at his watch, took a step, then stopped. In a low voice, he asked Debbie to inquire if he could, barring an emergency, call her at lunchtime. Debbie hurried back to the phone. David didn't move, head tilted forward, until finally he sank down onto the dolly seat and leaned to the eyepiece.

Now pirouetting onto the set came the two actresses, and David sprung up to greet them. How different the atmosphere here compared to that on the frantic, outdoor "Blackout" sets, which reflected that director's demeanor and lack of organization. Here in contrast, all was calm, providing the nuances their space.

As the moment for shooting neared, more people arrived, some attending to details, others waiting, arms folded. Rudi, the Director of Photography, who does most of his own shooting, conferred with David and the gaffer. Peter tested the various mics. Props, make-up, and costumes were checked by their respective overseers, and Debbie, who earlier introduced herself, took notes between snapping and labeling Polaroids of the set.

The first shot dollied with Teresa as she, tired from a day's work, moved heavily through her confined trailer, getting her girls to bed. But the shots of the girls read too cheery and bright-eyed, so that David went to them and, I managed to hear, explained, "Young Ladies, in this scene, we're pretending it's early, too early for you to want to go to bed, okay?"

The girls hesitated, unsure how they were expected to respond.

"So, you're not happy, right? But also, we're pretending your mom is real tired after a long day. So even though you'd rather hang around and play, or have her read to you, maybe this time you can help her out."

The two, watching David, began to catch on.

"You can show her you're not happy, but, at the same time, I want you to see she's pooped, worn out, and so, tonight you go along. You know? You go to bed, without any fussing."

One got it, and the other followed. I glanced at the mother to see how this sat with her, but her eyes swam dreamily between her girls and David.

In the next take, the two little girls were noticeably different, dragging their feet, wearing long faces, yet complying, aware of their mother's state of mind.

Pleased, David turned to the next scene, asking Pat and Trudi if they had any questions. Whey they indicated they were ready, he returned to his director's chair. After the first two takes, he asked for a few small changes, doing so by posing questions and allowing them to arrive at the answers. They picked up his cues almost immediately, and, by the fourth take, everyone was pleased with the emphasis and naturalness.

Debbie now stepped forward to announce the coffee break. In an instant, it seemed, the set was emptied.

She came over asking, "Do you want to join me, Christine?"

"Thanks, but it all flew by so fast, I need to sit here and try to write down what I think I saw . . . Maybe lunch instead?"

A nod and a smile before she turned and strode off.

Rather than into my notebook, however, I stared at the magical gray camera perched alone atop its dolly. I was tempted to get up, turn it on, and play the scene myself in this almost doll-like setting. As I scribbled thoughts and impressions, it occurred to me that I hadn't seen John, or his young protégé. Sitting there, I wondered if I had not imagined the whole thing with Amanda.

After a while, as I saw no sign of the coffee break ending, I decided to stretch my legs, and possibly stir myself with more caffeine. But in my preoccupation, I soon found myself in an unfamiliar and increasingly less-trafficked corridor, until eventually alone. About to reverse direction, I noticed ahead a door open and a man step out, his back to me. Yet instantly I knew from the way he moved, it was John. About to call out, I hesitated, and, in that moment, saw a young woman glide out, slip under his arm, and together walk languorously off, in post-coital ease. Turning and retracing my way, I scolded myself that this little scene was nothing to me, was old news, and that he was history. And yet I felt kicked.

Back in the cafeteria, coffee steadied in two hands, I slumped into a chair. Once again Debbie appeared before me, and despite my irritation, I asked her to join me. She pulled up a chair, bubbling over about the first scenes. "I so enjoy watching those two women. They're so good, responding, feeding off each other."

I agreed, but I wanted to hear her thoughts on David, for although she didn't say so directly, she was, I could see, enamored—doubly, as an aspiring director herself, feasting on the opportunity to work with him. I asked what she thought of David's theme running through his last three films.

"What? Pursuing one's vision?" she asked.

"Yes, the compulsion, and the costs."

She paused, reflecting. "I've wondered about it, of course. I'm not sure any art is worth those costs."

I told her that for years I'd had much the same reaction, yet biographies and life itself have revealed that great art, that which enriches us, frequently comes out of unnatural focus and imbalance, often harming the artist and those close.

Apparently uncomfortable with this, or at least with any implications concerning David, she avoided my gaze. Or maybe she thought I was attempting to elicit a little dirt for my profile. Our conversation faltered. Fortunately it was time to get back.

Returning to the set, I took up residency in my chair and opened my notes. Rudi stepped over, smiling down from his large, grayish head—chiseled Elsinor granite. "Are vee taking da proper quantity uff notes?"

I smiled, standing to introduce myself, and though he kissed my hand urbanely and was disposed to chat, he exhibited some preoccupation or unhappiness he seemed to want me to notice.

When I didn't pick up his cue, he tried another tack, "Why are you sitting off here by yourself? Come sit by d' camera, vhere you can see better. I give you a little inside insight."

"That's very kind. I'd like that."

He permitted his mouth to slide into a kind of half-smile.

I asked where he was from.

"Budapest . . . You know?"

"And of royal blood?"

"We are all royal dis or royal dat, each in our own little way, in our own little rat hole. Princes of darkness, princesses of light." Motioning with his head, he urged me to follow him to the camera, where he had me sit on the dolly's seat and peer through the eyepiece. There I discovered the trailer's interior, its cramped kitchenette, with Pat sitting at a tiny table studying lines. I felt as if I were by her cheek, running the scene along with her. The world fell away. I could see her lips moving slightly, and was enchanted when she craned her head back, making a mental note, stroking the dark hair over her ear. Rudi called to her, and she started, glancing around before staring straight into the camera, smiling at first, then dissolving into thought.

Rudi whispered, "I pan da camera left now, den pull back a bit and den move in again."

I flew around the room, a witch, able to dive and arrive at will. Is this what entrances David? Worlds to shape? Intense, ideal, malleable. Go anywhere, create anything. Pulling back from the eyepiece, I exclaimed, "Why, that's magic!"

"Yes," he exhaled with faint ennui.

"Rudi, how do you two choose shots? On this your fourth picture together, do you work it out ahead, storyboard it, or on the set, or a combination?"

He looked at me, then away thoughtfully. "Yes, all dose tings. We are lucky, you see, dat we see tings in similar vays. Of course we talk and talk, but we begin very close."

"So it's give-and-take all the way through?"

"Dat's what it's about. Though we know each other, da possibilities are infinite. But he selects d' best."

"Must be fun . . . and satisfying."

"It's da only vay. One is always seeking something new. One doesn't want to repeat and repeat. Working by rote, is *tot*—dead."

"You work for other directors?"

"Of course. And next year I direct my own picture. You know in Hungary, I was a director."

"No, I didn't know," I said, suspecting I was about to hear.

"I was young, of course. And d' budgets were very small, not da best. We have a drink sometime, 'n' talk. I give you a little history of movies. Mine vere never picked up over here—too subtle, you know. But here comes Graham. I must get ready."

And Graham came striding out into the set, exhorting, "Come on, people. Let's not find other ways to delay this further. Rudi, your lighting all set?"

I retreated as Rudi began calling to his assistants while checking through the camera. David entered talking closely with John. I faced away involuntarily, to scribble notes on Rudi, and indeed, did not really look up until the first take was rolling.

But I was not alone in feeling that something was off. Almost immediately David stopped John, who had not quite found Stephen. There was no presence, no interior life, no concentration, as Pat's sharp-eyed displeasure confirmed. Even Peter's brow was lined with doubt as he replayed the segment. David now lead John to the edge of the set. They conferred and returned to try it again, but John-boy didn't have it. Shot his wad was my guess.

Growling, David again escorted him away, presumably to some place where they could run lines and find concentration. I wished I could follow and listen. Made a note to ask David later.

I looked to see if Amanda had made her appearance, but she was not to be seen. People puttered with their equipment; Pat paged through her script—all sought ways to deflect this shared embarrassment.

Eventually David and John returned. John's expression had darkened. He seemed unaware of the set and crew around him.

In the ensuing conversation with Teresa, bitterness cut into Stephen's brow and laced his words. "Some of 'em were ready to spit on me! Turn their backs. People I've known all my life, who knew my parents . . . What do they want? For us to pack it up and leave, one by one, till nothin's left? As though they've done a damned thing here, all these years!"

At the end David went to and quietly congratulated John.

Now, as they prepared for close-ups, Rudi turned and motioned me to run up and look. In the dramatic, light and dark lighting, the actors' faces were etched with concern. Somehow David had found a means for John to reach in more deeply than anyone thought possible. The entire set sensed it, and a silence descended unbroken for minutes on end, while David stayed close to John, serving as his sole connection, glancing at Rudi and Peter for their hushed reports.

But as David remained exacting, the takes came slowly, sometimes four or five per shot, sometimes more. I overheard whispers of overtime spread discreetly among the crew.

At one point, sharp cries drew all faces back to the actors, where Pat and John were cajoling David to allow her or his character an emphatic gesture to cap the scene. Although David gave both their say, he favored John, citing the dramatic thrust. Pat spun around, throwing up her arms, crying out, "That's shit!" and stamping away toward the exit. David hurried after her. In the shadows, their arguing flared back and forth. Surprisingly David pulled out a cigarette, lit up, and drew in rapidly and deeply before finally insisting on a compromise.

As the last shot was readied, I gazed around in delight at the contrasts between the richly detailed trailer and the stark, functional studio, between the made-up actors and the pale, T-shirted crew. Two parallel worlds: the crew, raw, unadorned, touching in their simplicity; the actors, eyes-flashing, expressions heightened, gorged with life—Gods. A chill raced up my spine.

In the afternoon, there followed an animated scene between Stephen and Elaine in her apartment where they discussed first the cabaret's local politics and then Teresa, whom Elaine was determined to protect. "Listen . . . I don't have to say anything more, do I?"

Stephen, eyes to the floor, turned in place, hands in his back pockets. "No . . . no . . . ."

"'Cause you know what I'll do if you fuck up, don't you?"

How different the chemistry between John and Trudi. Pat, it seems, comes with definite expectations, which, if aren't met, affect her demeanor, whereas Trudi is loose and open, but, when necessary, is also direct and no-nonsense. As Johnny is at ease with Trudi, the give-and-take warmed and relaxed them, and everyone, and the scene proceeded quickly.

Just before seven, David stepped out into the set next to Elaine's sofa. "I'd like to thank everyone for a long day, and for keeping your energy up, for sticking with it through that difficult patch. I particularly want to thank John for making the effort to get it right, and for having patience with himself and with me. It's no easy task to match concentration and intensity, day in day out, week after week. And the actors have been at it for some weeks now. and I want to thank them, and the crew. It's a long haul, as you know for everyone, and we've got to help each other . . . maintain our levels, even when we're tired and frustrated. So thank you all, and see you tomorrow."

Evening

Rattling up over the bridge, as the two men rattled on about today's shoot, and tomorrow's, I, from our cab window, gazed ahead and downtown into the low sun silhouetting the buildings. I was tired and closed my eyes, listening to the rhythm and whine of the tires. In this monochromatic world, in the flickering light, wedged between David and the door, with Mandy on his other side and Rudi in front with the driver, I felt abducted, bound back into the last century, in a carriage, or one of the early 'Els,'—perhaps to avoid the uncertain future, or perhaps to reconnect with the indistinct past from which my parent's deaths have cut me off.

As we approached our neighborhood, Rudi turned back toward us, glancing at David, then me. He proposed that he and I have a drink or dinner. I accepted, surprising myself, for I didn't much feel like it. Maybe it was for David, or the profile, or because I didn't want to be alone this evening.

When we stopped outside my building, I extended a hand to David in goodnight, called to Mandy, still hidden down beside her father, and pried myself out of the cab.

Rudi and I were left somewhat unsteadily facing one another in the gentle breeze of twilight. He asked if I wanted to freshen up upstairs, but I decided to hold that option in reserve, if escape was needed.

Off we went, gliding west along the quiet side streets to Madison. In the yellow light, Rudi's distinctly European features and surface savoir faire added to my sense of displacement. The avenue seemed to have regained a bit of its old glamour, with couples beautifully dressed, flowing north toward home. I gazed into my favorite windows as Rudi pointed out locations where he'd filmed.

As we walked, I noticed that Rudi appeared to wrestle with some thought. I guessed that if he were not David's friend, he might have felt less hesitancy to express it.

At sixty-ninth, we swerved east off Madison and into a tiny bistro—six tables, a bar, and barmaid whose dark hair and pale French face might have lurked in a Manet. The seated patrons studied us carefully as we worked our way to the last free table near the bar. Several of these chic, if casually dressed boulevardiers seemed to know Rudi and sized me up as his latest consort. Certainly that was the expression on the barmaid's face as she swung out from behind the bar with a bottle of Côte du Rhône and menus.

Rudi introduced us. She was Françoise. Her shoulder-length, brunette hair, hanging in half-moon curve, and her perfect make-up, made her the quintessential Parisienne, at once aware and self-possessedly remote. She was also several years older than I'd first thought, and, I couldn't help but notice, seemed to share with Rudi the easy intimacy of ex-patriots, or lovers, relieving my worry that I might be too much Rudi's focus this evening.

As we relaxed over our first sips of wine, I steered the conversation back to the city: the feeling of New York's former elegance and grace, which the taxi ride and our walk had evoked. But Rudi maintained that the images and memories were illusions, grand illusions, properly forgotten.

I disagreed, allowing that while the elegant buildings and streets were not representative of all, they constituted a center and contributed beauty and style which all could share.

He dismissed this. And though we went back and forth, he remained adamantly against assigning any lasting value to that former, limited elegance. I found myself wondering where his view might have come from. Was it intellectual or political? Did it rise from his Communist-era schooling, or something in his psychological makeup? It was surprisingly sharp and unyielding.

Several times, Françoise returned and spoke with us, and she, like Rudi, carried some faint sadness or melancholy in her dark eyes. I asked her if she liked living here.

"Oh yes," she smiled, and explained that she felt there were many more options here for her than in Paris and hoped to eventually open a boutique downtown.

When she noticed my eye fell to her hand and its wedding ring, she smiled a strange, mixed smile and said that it was something she shared with Rudi, that they were both married to people who could not live here in New York.

Rudi appeared mildly put off by this revelation, but then perhaps accepting the fait accompli, explained that his wife, who lived in Budapest, had tried it here, but had fled back. He visited her as often as his schedule permitted, but . . .

Possibly this was what he wanted to tell me all along.

Françoise asked if I was of Irish or German descent. "Your face holds a bit of both—two distinct feelings." Her almond-shaped eyes within her long, dark lashes waited and watched.

Surprised, faintly uneasy, I congratulated her. She was exactly right. Mother Irish, Father Irish and German—a volatile mix, I believe, which has left me the lone witness and caretaker.

Françoise smiled gently, while Rudi studied my face, perhaps more closely than before.

When Françoise returned to the bar, with a swaying gait that enthralls many men and which seems displayed without self-consciousness, I managed to turn the conversation back to David. "Rudi, what are his strengths as a director?"

He looked down, not entirely happily, working his jaw.

Then he looked sharply up at me again. "Well, what I can tell you first is . . . he has a very good eye, and a clear vision of da way he vants tings to look, and he is good wid d' actors. He cares for them, particularly da women." He glanced at me meaningfully, eyebrows arching. "And he gets good tings from dem, all of dem, gets deir best . . . and, above all, I like him as a man."

"That sounds pretty good."

"Da best, da best I know uf."

Focusing in, drawn by his candor, I nodded appreciatively, after which we ate silently for a time.

But at some point he cleared his throat and spoke, "Dere is one other ting I might say about David." He waited until he had my attention. "Doing dese films is a considerable burden. Although he has Marty and Graham to handle many of the details, d' essential responsibility for everyting falls on his shoulders. . . . And I don't think he is fully recovered from d' last one, d' "Kestrel" . . . Also, as I gadder you've heard from one source or anodder, his marriage is in serious trouble. So, I guess my point is, if you'll excuse me, he needs rest . . . he needs to simplify, not complicate."

I stared at him, aware of some checked indignation. What did he believe he's protecting David from? He held my gaze for some short time, before he resumed eating. Several sharp rejoinders resounded in my head, but I restrained myself.

For a while, we were again silent, and although our conversation did, in time, find other subjects, clearly our differing perspectives dampened things.

When we were finished, we said goodnight to Françoise, who urged me to come by for a drink sometime, before she smiled at Rudi with a certain familiar acceptance, and they kissed in the French manner.

He walked me home through the now empty streets glistening from a shower which passed during dinner. I sensed continuing agitation in him, but did not want to ask him about its source. Certainly I did not want any return to his warning. We kissed formally, cheek and cheek, and said goodnight. But I saw that the lingering frustration was thick in his eyes as I turned away.

May 10th

Images from the studio will not leave my head: its labyrinthine corridors leading to bowers of light, clumps of people, the swimming sets, the spasms of intensity encased in blocks of stillness. David presiding, gliding, darting here and there, whispering, raising his wand . . . revealing what can be done.

But how to take Rudi's warning? . . . Annoyed . . . Did he really think I could divert David from this process, even if either of us were open to diversion? More likely it was his own problems. No doubt he wanted stroking.

In the office all day, editing a piece with Ben. And now, in the evening have returned to chase after Eiley.

> . . . On the following Sunday, Eiley took another step,
> shearing her hair short, neither a sacrifice or a mutilation,

126

but a signal—which left her looking both doll-like and dangerous. Or so the looks she received suggested.

Then she went further, dying it black, jet, and began wearing black lipstick and wildly different outfits, began using the effect to give expression to the anger, from home and from the frustration around her at work. She was acquiring a reputation for Down East flintiness, for not suffering fools gladly. This both pleased and worried her. She wondered where this vehemence came from. She feared the answer lay in her father's glowering face, whose image swept down from Deer Isle in the night winds . . .

May 12th

Today, dragging myself home, found a letter in my box.

My Dear Christine,

Two a.m., too late to call. So this in apology, for not getting back to you. I assume Martina reached you, about my schedule, gone off the edge. Long days, little sleep, cut off from life outside, while the project tears along.

Yet have been thinking that, though you and I hardly know one another, some glimmer has passed between us, and though reason cannot account for it, and though my schedule, my situation, and my record would all seem to belie it, I feel something shared with you, beyond our respective needs to talk.

And so I want to formally invite you to come up to the Adirondacks for a few days, to watch the process. There's a different dynamic on location, than what you saw in the studio.

For the next few days however, I must beg off any rendezvous. Too many meetings, rehearsals, days shooting, in too few hours. But next Friday, please come to the apartment at eight, where after the shoot, Graham, Rudi, and a few others will gather for an end-of-week beer. But once they've had their say (the purpose of the gathering) they'll be eager to leave.

Marnie will also be here for the weekend, but she retires early, and we may finally talk. So please come. With the trek up to Trappers Lake looming, time is ever more precious.

You see that despite some experience, I live a careening life. Only when this film is done, may I, with luck, find balance again.

Regards to Eiley, and with more warmth than I dare express,

David.

Read it once. Read it again. Have feelings rushed too far ahead? Or is it other things?

May 14th

Kirsten called me in this morning. Scribbling and not looking up, she asked, "Do you have a current passport?"
"Yes."
"And how's your French?"
"Passable."
"Then you're going with me to Paris, in mid-July."
A slow-motion jolt, a distant, warm current ran through my head. "Paris?"
Looking slowly up, she allowed a thin smile.
"Oh, well . . . what a treat! Thank you, how wonderful!"
"You'll be working, so no thanks is necessary. But there'll be some interesting people you'll meet, and I mentioned it to Laurent on the phone the other day. He's eager to see you."

" . . . That was foolish of me." At the moment, could hardly picture him.

"Foolish? Why? Why say that?"

"Married men are not what I need."

"But his is a special circumstance, I believe. And from what I hear, that hasn't held you back with your director."

My face grew hot. Felt drops on my brow forming.

"Christine, you needn't blush. You and I know something of first marriages, and other unwise choices . . . Anyway, you'll need some clothes, as I'll want you at several meetings with me. What's your schedule look like?"

"Loomis thinks I should go up to the Adirondacks, to watch the shoot, sometime in June, I believe."

Her heavy eyes considered this. I knew generally what she was wondering, but I also knew I owed her no explanation. I maintained my business face. Eiley would be proud.

"Okay . . . well, let's see." She pulled her calendar out.

"I'm travelling later this month and much of June, so maybe this weekend we could pick up a few outfits. How about Saturday?"

"Fine."

"I'll pick you up, ten o'clock, downstairs." Penciling it in, she glanced up, then picked up the ringing phone—as always, my exit cue.

Dizzied by the prospect, even as I was amused by her assumptions, I returned to my own office and to work.

After five, I walked up into the park, needing to unwind. I walked rapidly, aware of little. Although in time I remembered, I saw no one who might have been Eleanor. This heaviness dulled the other prospects. For months I'd had my solitude and grief, until suddenly it sloughed off, like snakeskin . . . Yet what I have now feels not quite earned or connected. Not quite mine.

> How slim the membrane
> 'tween joy and sorrow
> 'tween love and loneliness
> past and 'morrow.

May 20th

Long weeks, too-short days. Time accordions a wobbly tune. Have not seen David—a feeling which inflates into an ache. But why? . . . He intrigues me, with his whimsy and his magic.
This, despite his dark clouds, which I hide from myself.

> . . . After work, some of the assistants would gather around Eiley's desk, mostly for casual chitchat, but sometimes manuscripts were discussed. They were eager for her insights, but what lured them most powerfully was her comments on how they, the assistants, might make it up to associate and beyond, as she had so rapidly.
>
> "It may mean," she whispered low, with her new authority, "going out, finding new authors, new voices, new ideas . . . It may mean incubating them . . . even masturbating them, milking them for their eggs, juices, seed . . ."
>
> All watched her, none moving, none speaking. She could not tell which, if any, had the fiber for this . . .

May 22nd

All were gone, fled from the office, to their weekends, their spouses or lovers. I wandered through empty corridors, past darkened desks, shadowed cabinets. Part of me wanted to stay, in the stillness, in the lightless quiet, allowing thoughts to come, hoping to encounter some essential kernel of myself.

But eight-thirty delivered me to David's somber door, 18D, where the rise and fall of voices within, the clink of glassware, set me outside some Elizabethan pub.

Knock, knock. The volume dropped, the door swung open, Rudi's full gray face once again filled the frame, a gargoyle, slightly flushed.

"Ah. The Czarina. Welcome." Stepping back, he bowed, obscuring his ambivalence, unveiling Debbie waving, Graham and

Peter straining to see, and the younger, rounder, shorter daughter, Marnie, blank-faced. From the kitchen, came David striding, drying hands, stretching wings, greeting me with a proper kiss, announcing they were wrapping up.

Behind, Rudi tapped my shoulder, holding a drink between thumb and forefinger, and a camera in the other hand. "My dear, some schnapps," handing me the drink. "And then, please, a few snaps," handing me the camera.

I slipped a sip, hoping it wouldn't undo my balance.

David called his reluctant daughter, one arm reaching, embracing, consoling, as she leaned the other way. But he managed to sit with his dimpled girl at the center of the couch, and the others edged in on either side. Squinting through the camera, I asked them to smile, but saw they were already—laughing at my attempt to hold my liquor and my framing. I put the drink down and clicked off a few.

Then up popped cork-like Marnie, from the sea of voices. The rest called for me to join them. I stepped with care, my head now swimming, to the couch and sank through heat and odor, down to David's side.

One click, then another, released all to gather bags and jackets and flee for home, to reclaim their personal lives. With hugs and byes they were quickly gone, leaving David, Marnie, and me rooted to the floor.

I sought David's eye for some hint of what might follow, but he was moving back to his desk, "Excuse me, just a minute. I need to do a little jotting."

Marnie and I stood stranded over Persian whorls, until I tried, "Well, they were a lively group, don't you think, Marnie? Too bad the actresses weren't here as well. Do you know them?"

Whether from irritation or awkwardness, a forced smile slanted across her face, before she turned to collect and take glasses to the kitchen.

From behind me David called, "Marne, is our supper ready? Could you take a look, hon?"

Now I heard his footsteps, and felt his warm hand sliding up my back. For an instant, an embrace wed us—part payment for those canceled trips—before we parted to spare his daughter another start.

Soon we were settled around the tiny table. But before our first bite, the phone pulled Marnie up and into the bedroom.

David tried to eat a little before the expected summons. "David, I received your letter. Thank you . . ."

We looked at one another for signs of feeling.

He whispered, "I hope it didn't give you fright."

"Quite the contrary."

He reached for and squeezed my hand, before Marnie peeked out. "Dad, it's Mom."

A guarded glance, a sobering pause, and he was up and striding, past Marnie drifting back, her ears alert for angry tones. The bedroom door was closed; she sat, her eyes dropping.

I tried a little eating, a little wine, then asked her how she found this filmmaking.

Glancing up from under her thick eyebrows, her mother's contribution, I gathered, she answered without the slightest hesitation, "I hate it."

Oh dear . . . not a lot of openings there. And hates all those associated with it, I feared. I explained that I was writing about her father's work, but this elicited not the slightest spark. But then, neither did her dinner, which she forked listlessly, leaving me to observe that she still carried her childhood roundness, in place of Mandy's female curvings, and not yet any of that mental sharpness. Thus do run our different schedules.

I asked her what she likes doing in the city.

Shaking once her unhappy head, she replied as if nearly dead, "Oh, I go to school. That's enough for now. I'm not one of the precocious ones."

Remembering my own adolescence, I felt some sympathy for her, for I was not free of teenage reluctance and self-consciousness. On the other hand, when someone showed genuine interest, I did respond. But her attention may well have been on the phone conversation in the bedroom.

When David returned, his pale coloring suggested the conversation had not been easy—something I assumed Marnie read more readily than me. Yet he made no mention of it, and shortly our talk circled back to the assemblage just left.

"They're as harmonious a group as we've had," he told me, "and yet each is interesting in his or her own way. Debbie, for instance, who's new this time, has already done some lovely student films, and may someday be a fine director. She's got an eye and feel, and she works wholeheartedly for us."

"You do the hiring?"

"No, it's Graham who finds them." David looked at Marnie. "Sorry, Marne, for talking shop. Christine, Marnie's become quite a soccer player. She's made the varsity this year."

"Dad . . ." she squeaked, "could I be excused? I have some homework to do."

I felt myself recoil, and saw David stiffen.

"But Marne, it's Friday night. Won't you sit and talk with us a while?"

"I really need to work." Her face and body twisted, all but pleading her agony. With little choice, it seemed, David freed her with a disappointed nod, and this sent her fleeing from the room, back behind the bedroom door.

Awkward moments followed, as we pushed at and ate our supper. "David, I feel bad, taking her dad away, her busy dad."

Slowly, he met my gaze. "Christine, it's not you but I who should apologize. I've always hoped these gatherings would lift her out of herself, provide a little life and lightening, but she's not ready. And I never learn, it seems." He looked away and brought his hands over his eyes, slowly rubbing. Then glancing at her door, he lowered his voice, "I've tried to talk to her countless times, but the hurt is too deeply rooted. Time, I'm afraid, is what she needs—as do we all. And is what we lack."

"But . . . well, how about friends and school? Does she find enjoyment there?"

A sadness dulled his face. "Yes, I think. I've met two or three of her friends on weekend afternoons. She's not alone in having troubled parents. I've heard them talking, comparing stories. It's sad to hear . . . But school she likes, and does pretty well. Kath read to both girls for years, and I did when I could, with the result that both are interested and read on their own. A source of solace, I hope." Now dropping his voice still more, he asked, "Would you mind if I relate one incident which, alas, captures our respective frustrations?"

My eyes moved across the troubled regions of his face.

"Marnie and I were in the Frick Museum not so long ago. I'd suggested it because it confers a feeling of peace and elegiac retreat from the city's hard exterior, at least to me. But I realized too late she would see it differently—dead and dowdy, no doubt—deepening her perception that I neither attend to her needs nor understand her—which to some degree is true."

"I remember standing before a Whistler, one of his long pale women who, if elegant, does not smile, and who seems to be waiting for something which may never come, and I wondered if this is how Marnie sees her life, dependent on parents who never quite arrive for her. When I asked her if she liked this Whistler, ""Nooo, no way,"" came her girlish whine.

"You do that well, David."

"Years of practice . . . When I asked her what didn't she like, she only squeaked, ""Oh I don't know . . ."" And moved on.

"Following her, I said, 'I like it, its unspoken emotion.'

""I know Dad. You like sad things."" It seemed a voice penetrating in as from the edge of sleep. I felt her hurt, her bitterness, her pessimism . . .

I tried again, 'But Marne, there is both sadness and happiness to life, which we all experience. It's part of living.'

""No kidding, Dad.""

I could not help but smile at David's rendition, so apt was the pitch, and he, noticing, let free a fleeting brightness.

"It was not the first time I've found she's several steps ahead of me. And yet when I catch up and speak with candor, she reacts as if it's harsh, and withdraws in stony silence. I throw up my hands, often, when she's not looking. But this time, tried once more, "I didn't realize that you felt such sadness. Do you want to . . . ?"

""You're so oblivious,"" she sighed.

David shook his sagging head. "I fear that as long as she will not discuss her sadness, she'll remain trapped in it."

Reflecting, I wondered where their solution lay. "She expects you to know her, as perhaps ideally we all should know each other . . . but it takes time . . . I could only begin to understand my own Father's difficult mix at the end, in his last few months."

David's eyes grew softer now and quiet. Hesitantly he continued, "As we were about to leave the museum, she said, ""Dad, I know you'd like me to want to stay.""

'No, not at all,' I replied quite honestly.

""But I'm just not the artist that everyone else is in the family."" she said.

Looking down, he murmured, "She feels she's out there by herself. Kath has her crafts business. Mandy seems to want to follow me . . ."

"How do things go with her mom?" I wondered.

"From what I understand, they continue to have their good days and bad, good weeks, months, and bad. Unfortunately neither Kath nor I have large families to offer support or a sense of belonging. Our parents have died, our cousins wandered off.

"Anyway, about to leave the museum, she blurted out to me, ""You know sometimes I think I was adopted.""

"When I recovered from this cry, I remembered I'd read it's not such an uncommon feeling, or fear, among kids, but when I then tried to put an arm around her, she squealed and pulled away. Unfortunately a passing family of four, including a daughter slightly younger-looking than Marnie, apparently witnessed this, smiling uncomfortably. And this, for Marnie, intensified the moment, while for me made it all too clear that despite my intentions, I'd pushed her further away."

Caught by his quandary, we looked helplessly at each other.

"I'm sorry," he apologized, "to go on about all this."

"It's difficult . . . I wish I had something to suggest."

Our eyes held sadly on the other.

"You've already brought me a little infusion of Spring," he said.

I looked down, but then reached for his hand, which I held and studied. Long fingers, creased knuckles, veins branching, pale colors, neither young nor old. I carefully gave it back.

He breathed. "Though you and I hear, and dance to, similar music . . . still I must remind you how unsettled things are. I can only suggest that we go slowly, even as I so enjoy looking at, and talking with, you. I need you much more than you could need my friendship." His warm smile moved over my face.

"No, David. That's not true. There's no one else to share what we do."

His cheek tried to smile again, "I must tell you that Kath and I are attempting to make some decisions . . . something we've avoided. It's gone on too long. And the girls suffer more than we."

I felt this burden bowing my own head. "I know it's so difficult for families to break old patterns."

Inhaling, he looked vaguely around. "I've long seen that I don't bring Kath happiness. I did at first, but no longer . . . I've kept thinking that if we could just find some common ground, but we never quite do. We've perfected evasion. Probably I should accept that we've changed, or that maybe it was never quite what we thought."

"You've been together a long time."

He twisted his mouth. "In the beginning, it was good. We each had a life, work, and each other . . . But the kids, the movies, stretched our energy and our patience. I probably shouldn't have become a father. But now . . . I won't live like this, any longer. I don't have the time." With quiet petulance, he spit this out.

Studying the table, he explained further, "Much, most, was probably my fault, but I couldn't get any discussion going. Kath withdraws, like Marnie . . . And while I can understand, nothing's gained. Over these months we might've talked, but she's refused . . . Now, after months of solitude, I will no longer sit home alone, night after night . . . But I go on again. Sorry."

Watching him, I shared his dismay, and began to tell him a little about the frustrations of dealing with my brother, whose life could measurably improve, if only . . .

But this only deepened his despondency. "I suppose that as the elements which made us are mixed, so it shouldn't surprise us that our behavior is also mixed."

For some moments, we sat pondering, before he asked me if I wanted coffee. We took our dishes into the kitchen. There we began talking about the Adirondacks, to which he would soon be going. I pictured the hemlocks, pine, and spruce sprouting out of rocky hillsides, still pocketed with snow—though Spring has come, on the calendar. I imagined the warmer winds rushing up the mountainsides, heard the boughs clicking, creaking.

Blackout. Eyes closed. Seated together again on his couch, a short time later, with our coffee, he began speaking of Stephen, "I worry that the message of his story may be misleading, because the forces opposing change are probably more powerful and more intransigent than we portray. Inertia is hard to overcome. The cases of real success may be few, I fear."

"And yet David, what choice does Stephen have? To give up would be a kind of death."

He looked down, nodding once. "If he is to stay there, he has no real choice."

We glanced at each other, as we considered this. I became aware of a darkness suffusing his eyes. His features grew pained. He turned away, bending, whispering, "Damn . . ."

"What?"

"Eyes again."

"Oh dear." I slid closer. "Anything I can do?"

" . . . Just have to wait . . ."

"Is it painful?"

"No . . . not really."

"Can you see?"

"With one."

" . . . Does it happen more frequently now?"

But he did not answer. I wanted to do something. "Can I get your medicine, or . . . ?"

"Sorry," he mumbled. "Fraid it's hard to talk, to concentrate, right now. Feel a little dizzy."

"Want to lie down?"

"Maybe . . ."

At this moment, I sensed another presence, and looking up, found Marnie peering out from the bedroom door.

"Dad?" She studied him, then me, unhappily.

"Hi, Marne. Have a little headache," he told her.

She didn't move.

"Did you get some work done, Marne?" he asked, making every effort to speak normally.

"Dad, is it something you ate or drank?"

" . . . Don't think so, though maybe. Do you want me to take a look at anything you did?"

"How 're you going to do that, Dad?"

"This'll go away in a bit."

She pondered, pinching her lips. "It's late, Dad. I think I'm going to go to bed."

"Well, I'll come in, in a minute."

She paused and involuntarily glanced at me, then blurted out, "You don't have to."

"Give me a couple of minutes, Marne, till this thing goes away."

She waited for several seconds, then murmured, "Okay," before leaning back out of sight, into her room and closing the door.

I looked down at David. Slowly, eyes closed, he leaned against the sofa back. "Chris, could you turn the overhead lights off? The switch is there." He pointed to the wall behind.

As I stood and stepped to flick it off, I decided, "If you're okay, David, I think I'd better go."

" . . . Do you think this God we doubt is teasing us, Christine?"

"Yes, verging on the malevolent . . . I'd like to ask him why . . . and I wish I could do something for you."

"You have . . . Perhaps he wants us to notice the perfect irony."

"I refuse."

"In any case, it's temporary, and I can sleep tomorrow morning; no meetings right away . . . I'll call you."

"David . . ."

"What?"

"Rest is what you need."

He pushed himself forward now, elbows upon knees, head down. "Sunday maybe . . ." But making an effort to open his eyes, he winced in pain. I moved over to him and took his hand. He covered mine with his and brought my fingers to his lips. I bent and kissed his brow, and he in response, eyes closed, kissed the air.

May 24th

Below, the city gently murmured. People were stepping out to church, buying the Sunday paper, walking the dog. And we might meet, he and I.

The sun was slowly drawing out memories from Friday night. For Marnie's sake, I should not have gone, while for us, it was too short.

His affliction has haunted me. Should he not attend to it more than he does? And attend to Marnie? Yet the film's momentum, its money-driven schedule, its mass, pulls all after it.

Hearing the phone calling out, I moved back inside. He was there, suggesting we meet in late afternoon when Marnie goes off to a movie with a friend. "We might walk in the park, if you like, around four or five. Maybe we'll stumble upon Eleanor."

"David, I feel bad for Marnie, about my intrusion Friday."

"That's for Marnie and me to work out."

"If I hadn't come, you two would've had time."

"Chris . . . I've made time for her recently. Unfortunately, we have not yet found ways to talk."

"She's young."

"She's too much like her mom. I'll keep trying, but I can't do it by myself. I thank you for coming. Sorry that once again it was cut short."

"Do you think the tension made this other thing worse?"

"My eyes? . . . God no!"

"Maybe you're trying to do too much."

"If anything, it's that I'm not doing enough."

"But David . . ."

"Could we talk later, when we meet? She's waiting."

Hanging up, and about to return to the terrace, I heard the intercom buzz, the lobby calling up, "Uh, Miss Howth, ya brotha's down here again."

"Okay, send him up, Frank."

When I opened the door and greeted him, he neither replied nor met my eyes, but stood head down, waiting for me to step aside and let him in.

"Coffee, Luke?"

"Uh, no thanks."

"Well then, what's up?"

"Oh, uh . . ." An unhappy, accusing glance was slung my way "Uh, someone broke into my place . . . trashed 'n' stole all my stuff."

"My God! . . . I'm sorry. That's infuriating!"

Under his eyebrows, his forlorn expression spiked up in anger. "Yeah, they got my television, my Walkman, and my papers."

"Papers?"

His face sneered in mocking disbelief. "That's right, my papers, my personal papers. I can't go back. They'll have all my information. My bank account, everything."

"I'm sorry. Really . . . Tomorrow maybe you'd better call the bank."

Resentfully he stared at me, then down at the floor. "No kidding. Well, uh, listen, could I, uh, stay here?"

"Of course. For a night or . . . ?"

"Uh, maybe two, or three. Until I get a new place. I mean if it's not too much trouble. I mean I wouldn't want to put you out or anything, up here in this palace your husband got for you."

"Luke, I was just trying to understand what you need. Of course you're welcome. I'm glad to have you."

"I hope they don't try to call me here."

"Who?"

Vexation tightened his mouth, before his head fell under the weight of adversity. I reached out and touched his shoulder, but he shivered and pulled away.

"Luke, do you have money for a new place?"

"Why? 'Fraid I'm going to ask for money? Some of Dad's money he left you?"

"Luke, whatever money he had, he left to both of us, and when the estate 's settled, we'll split what's left. But if you need some, I can probably get some."

"Listen, uh, don't hassle me about money. If I need some, I won't come to you."

"But what about a place? Do you want me to make some calls, talk to an agent?"

" . . . Uh, I'll let you know . . ."

Not one of his good days, I told myself, turning toward the kitchen, asking again if he'd like anything to eat. Instead of a reply, however, I heard footsteps scuffing off, and looking back, I saw him disappear into the spare bedroom, the carom of the closing door echoing sharply off the bare surfaces. Hoped he'd find no sign of Eleanor.

Made myself another coffee. How long can he go on like this? I'm the only one who knows he exists, or cares. Can I allow myself that thought?

At four, with the May sun still high, David called to suggest meeting at 72nd and Fifth, and a short time later, picking him out among the crowd, I felt my spirits lift.

Taking my hand, he led the way between wobbling rollerbladers, downhill to the boat pond, where his eyes bounced with sparrows bouncing around the bushes, with starlings milling stifflegged on the grass, and chickadees dee dee deeing in the branches. "How well these feathered bundles have adapted to city life," he mused, "even as they seem more wary and wild than the pigeons and squirrels. I wonder what they might say to us about the city."

"The pigeons might ask us why the hell we've installed kestrels up in the towers, to dive on them."

His eyes caught the sun, which closed them. "To rebalance the balance we've undone."

Ahead I noticed many of the azaleas were fully blooming, preceding those on my alpine terrace, where Spring lands late.

Another flash, this time just above our heads, sent us ducking together, throwing up our elbows, even as we saw it was only a seagull gliding down to the pond, its body tilting effortlessly, adjusting its descent.

"David, do we do anything that sublimely?"

David re-gripped my hand as we leaned into the uphill path. "Occasionally."

"Such as?"

He turned and pulled me urgently to him and kissed me fully. My eyes closed and for some moments the day disappeared—its sounds and light and trees.

Releasing each other, we regained balance and composure, and resumed our walk, slowly, unsteadily at first, dreamily uphill, under the trees.

"David," I asked, after an interval, "where among the possibilities was that? . . . Mere impulse?"

As we walked, he seemed to gaze to the horizon for the answer. "It was life crying out . . . reaching out."

"Forgetting . . . its own warning?"

He weighed this. "Maybe . . . I'm sorry . . . But I should tell you that Kath and I have reached a decision, having spoken over the last day or two. Friday night's phone call marked the final stage . . . We've concluded that we cannot repair, cannot resume, cannot regain . . . what was good. And so, will divorce."

I closed my eyes. "I'm sorry . . ."

"I have not yet told either Marnie or Mandy, nor has she, I believe."

We walked silently, for some time, passing the museum and turning west to the playing fields. Baseballs and softballs arced through the pale blue sky. Shouts drifted up above them, dissolving in the breeze.

"I told Kath that I felt we'd lost hope, lost any way back. And time is not infinite. She did not dispute it. We'd tried a therapist, but it hadn't helped."

My legs felt heavy as we now crossed the Great Lawn. Our feet seemed to sink into the grass as we tried to wind between teams or lone individuals standing silently in the field—individuals who never glanced or seemed to notice us. This heaviness squeezed out a suggestion, "David, maybe we should suspend our talks . . . give you some time."

Head tilted forward, he looked at me, then looked away. "I'll be going north soon."

I could not look to read his face.

I heard him breathe out, "Maybe a short time." A sardonic half-laugh followed. "As though we've had much time."

"I feel bad for you, for both of you." Now, able to turn, I saw his expression: sad, fallen, motionless.

We walked downhill and onto the west drive, joining the stream of whirring tires and padding feet.

"Christine, this stretched back for us a long way. It became a terrible weight."

Well did I know.

He now steered us over to one of the side paths, and stopped. He turned me to him. "Maybe you're right, about time-off . . . There're too many things up in the air. I find myself enjoying our talks too much . . . I fear it's an escape, a needed but too-easy distraction."

Even more than his words, I found his darkened eyes and pursed lips expressed his distress.

"Listen," he began again, "would it be unfair, would it wreak havoc with your schedule, to delay our talks until you come upstate?"

I felt something drop through me. On one hand, I could understand, on the other, fear edged in.

"Maybe, if you could, that would allow us a fresh beginning, a clearer perspective, without everything crowding in."

"David, that's fine . . . but the movie will still be there, needing you."

"Yes, but things will be simpler."

I hadn't expected any of this when I agreed to come out to walk. Now the prospect of delay, however understandable, stabbed inside, making me withdraw a little. I wondered if the profile would ever get done.

We turned again and soon reached the transverse across 72nd where we made our way to the plaza above the fountain. In our silence, his substantial burdens buffeted my mind, spinning through it, disorienting me. I noticed him stop to study something ahead. Following his frowning gaze, I discovered on a shadowed bench an older woman sitting, rocking slightly.

"Eleanor?" I wondered.

We studied her before edging closer. Softly he called her name. She stopped rocking but did not look our way. She seemed thinner, I noticed, and more pale. We took another step before I tried, "Eleanor? . . . Eleanor, hello."

Now fearfully, she looked over at us, but with no bump of recognition—instead a perceptible shrinking into her coat, as her eyes slid away, seeking escape.

"Do you remember David or me?"

She pulled herself forward in her seat, eyes moving over the ground ahead.

"We were taking a walk," he told her, "on this Spring afternoon."

"Do you need anything?" I asked. "A bath? Are you hungry, Eleanor?" . . . 'El-ean-or!' my brain cried, 'It's Missy.'

Dimly, as if she'd heard me, she peered carefully up, silently. What did she see, what did she remember? There must be some recollection, of the apartment, the bath, before she wandered out and was taken off. Did she think I sent them, the men in the ambulance?

She looked away. A sparrow hopped near her shoes, cocking its head for crumbs. Eleanor cocked hers toward us.

"Are you hungry, Eleanor? Can we bring you some food?" David softly offered.

She seemed to relax slightly and give up thought of flight. The sparrow bounced away on toothpick legs.

"Christine, why don't you sit with her, and I'll run over to one of those carts and buy her something."

"Do you suppose they have anything she might eat?"

"I'll see."

And so I turned and slowly lowered myself onto the bench with her, not too close. After first saying nothing, I decided to talk, tell her something—about my brother—if only to extend the sound of human speech. "Eleanor, my brother Luke is staying for a short time in my apartment, where you stayed. Do you remember? He's looking for an apartment, which is not easy to find these days, as you must know."

But she did no more than stare at her knees. Possibly the attentive stillness in her eyes suggested she was listening, and, hoping that was so, I went on, expanding the story to include Father and eventually Mother, who has become as much a shadow to me now as this woman by my side.

David returned with a pita sandwich, lemonade, and a pretzel. He held them out for her to take, but she didn't move. I motioned to the bench next to her, and he placed them there, then stepped back around me and sat, taking out a list of organizations which could possibly help her. We discussed them in conspiratorial hush. I was fearful that anything but the gentlest of approaches would drive her further into herself, and away from help. We concluded that he should again run off to phone the agencies, to see if we could bring her in. And once more he did, and again I talked to her, this time about his film and the studio. But I soon concluded that, to her, it was only a drone, babble, and I fell silent.

Around me the park noise grew distant. An unhappy premonition preceded David's reappearance, and was borne out, first in the irritation lining his face, and second in the news that the eastside agency had no room, while the only one which did, in

Roslyn, Long Island, didn't admit on Sundays. He sat heavily with groaning exasperation.

"I could take her there tomorrow. I have a car."

"Could you?" His face tentatively brightened. "Do you have time?" Our hands, like squirrels nosing under leaves, felt for each other's.

"Yes."

"And what about tonight, do you think?"

"I don't know . . . Luke would probably go nuts, bolt, if I brought her back."

"And I have to work, which would mean I'd be dumping her on Marnie. We have no extra room or bed."

"Returning to the shelter might dismay her."

He agreed.

"Perhaps she'll be okay this evening," I offered, despite remembering my earlier experience with her.

Glancing over, I saw she had not touched the food. I slid closer. She straightened rigidly. I placed the food on her lap and moved the lemonade next to her. "This is for you."

No response—leaving the three of us uncertain and still. I glanced at David, and found him checking his watch.

I turned to her, "Eleanor. We'll see you tomorrow. Will you be here?"

Her eyes blinked—dark glass, as unreadable as the sparrow's eye. She stared down at the earth.

Reluctantly we stood to say goodbye. She didn't appear to notice. "See you tomorrow, Eleanor."

Nothing. We backed away uneasily.

Passing a policeman, we told him about her and asked if it was safe for her in the park. He did a kind of double-take, and then, largely to placate us, it seemed, assured us in stiff, rote rhetoric, "Oh yes, ma'am, no problem. Her person's perfectly safe here. I mean we run regular patrols throughout d' premises. In fact it's safer in here than on da streets." Something in his glazed eyes wondered why we cared. Wandering back toward Fifth, David confessed, "Christine, it was never my intention to dump all this on you. I'm afraid I thought things were solved when I got her into the shelter. If I'd thought about it a little more, I might have realized."

"Maybe tomorrow, David. My brother's condition has taught me patience."

Under a frown, his thoughts ran through these situations, it seemed. He took my hand but did not look my way as we walked back to my apartment building. We agreed to talk on the phone about Eleanor, or, if I needed to, about the profile, but otherwise would begin again up in the mountains. Our embrace, which started as a mere goodbye, lingered. I found I couldn't let go. Our cheeks brushed, then pressed together. I don't know for how long.

May 25th

A cry feels caught in my chest. But for whom? Who does it mourn? . . . No lack of candidates. Why, I wondered, are the links in some lives so fragile?

Luke, who was in last night when David dropped me off, was not when I got up. And as he'd brought next to nothing when he arrived, there were no signs as to whether he'd be back. If not, there's someone else who could use the bed.

I called Martina, who informed me the Roslyn home will accept Eleanor, if we deliver her. And so, after calling my office to explain, out I strode, eyes forward and dry. Out to the park to collect her, gliding west into a warm, gentle light. Back to her bench, but perhaps not surprisingly, she'd moved. I swept north past the theater and around the Great Lawn, through the playgrounds, by the tennis courts and reservoir, past any bench I saw. Then down through the west park. I asked a policeman, then a parks worker, but neither remembered a homeless woman. Following the lower loop, rounded the bend and back up again, up past the zoo. She was making me earn my triumph. Up through the Eastside, along Fifth and back in, telling myself that as she was such a small bent object amid the bushes, benches and trees, I might easily miss her.

Alas, began to tire, could not march forever, with anxiety bleeding off energy. Retraced to the boat pond, then left the park and wandered heavy-legged to 71st Street again, and 74th, and to several churches. Where are you, Eleanor? Why do you hide? Wouldn't it be better to find a home?

Hours passed, then the entire day. I kept thinking, one more corner, one more bench. But felt my heart beginning to labor, my head growing heavy. How can she have disappeared? I looked everywhere. At last, my legs, and lungs, and body succumbed.

Upstairs, sank into a bath, defeated, guilty . . . What would I tell him? That she was nowhere? In some doorway I missed? . . .

Had she done this purposely? Why did we not take her yesterday? What were we thinking?

Called Kate. Out, and David too, of course. Left an account of my failure on his machine. Felt achy, as if the flu had infiltrated. You would think he could find a minute to call.

At eleven, it was Luke who appeared—in place of the hoped-for call from David or Kate—with no explanation as to where he'd been. He went straight to his room following our typical non-exchange at the door. Mercifully, sleep beckoned. Back, legs, head, all pounded into putty.

May 26th

Tried again of course, without much hope. Called police, Parks Department, several hospitals and shelters. Found nothing but futility.

Kept my door closed at the office. Though Ben didn't make his usual visit, Melissa did, asking about Eleanor. After she'd heard the latest, she concluded that probably what we ought to do is tutoring. "Tutor students in reading and writing. It's where our so-called talents lie," she breathed. I suggested she mention it to Kirsten. She said she would.

Yet I felt thick and heavy-headed. In place of seeing David, tried openings for his profile,

David Loomis, an onomatopoetic name for a man of fine lines, soft silver, and round-eyed wonder. Indeed the name may once have been 'Luminous,' for such is the aura encountered in his presence. But while his face is not noticeably lined or sad, it is not without the imprint of difficulties, not without a pale tightness . . .

May 28th

At home after work, found a note from Luke lying on the kitchen counter, saying that he had a new place to live and wouldn't be bothering me anymore. But he included no address or phone, nor any personal word. As I expelled my exasperation, I reminded myself of the stresses and limitations he labors under. Still it's hard to know how much to emotionally invest, when little appears to benefit him, and there's nothing coming back. Does one simply accept the hand that's been dealt him?

As for Eleanor, did try yet again, but failed to see anyone remotely like her. I imagined her outline hunched on some bench, her face grown ever more thin. I wondered if somehow she was waiting for the indistinct shape, that to her, I must have been.

June 6th

People flee the city now on weekends, leaving it quiet and subdued. Above my terrace an entire cotton continent flows silently by as I lie down, stretch out, then rise again, unable to focus on anything but Eiley.

> . . ."I see what you're attempting, Eiley," came his throaty warning, "but it won't fly."
>
> "But flying, Marv, is precisely what we need, to lift the expectations of our readers."
>
> "Eileen . . . please . . ."
>
> She turned away to hide her frown, her disappointment that he would reject this experiment . . .

149

Threw myself upon my bed, rolling stomach to back, and back to front. Not even sleep would come. Pulled myself up, drifted on the terrace, under the seamless overcast. Attempted to inhale a needed, deep, fresh breath, attempting it over and over again.

SUMMER

June 22nd

Alarm snatches me from a dream, and I stretch into the prospect of a different world: outdoor days, walking the earth, wrapped in a single layer, and the Adirondacks rising cool and green—Himalayas, to my mind.

Packed and ready. No last minute panic, everything pried into three bags. Need only the traditional coffee and toast, on this first day of a new week, a new world, a-twitter. To the Uplands!

Dragging bags to the elevator, their weight protested I'd brought too much. Too late. Pushed, kicked them in, and descended to the dungeon, two levels below the street, two above Hades, shadowed, still-life caverns of soot and grime, where autos dolefully sleep, motionless hulks with grills of crocodile smiles, waiting to snatch any straying resident. Arms and shoulders aching, yet I dared not put down my bags, onto the inevitable grease smear. Skirted sheets of newspaper, beer cans and oil cans, dark shadows, rodents hiding, until finally under a film of grime, my hamster, my kneeling red roadster, the toadster, my sometimes escape machine, my neglected, tiny Plymouth, tearfully in need of a bath. Threw the bags into the back seat, shaking her carcass. Pumped its flimsy gas peddle, attached it felt, by a paperclip. She coughed, convulsed, hiccuped. Tried again. Remembered. Pulled herself out of bed, snuffling, 'I think I can, I think I can . . .' A glance back at her stall, the unswept corner, before we crawled, in first, to the ramp and up, with much revving and recalling, until by the time we'd reached the sidewalk, I could barely hold her back.

Crossing on the sidewalk, an older woman froze in the head-lights, as it were, then raised her cane to strike a blow. The hamster's continued rusty revving, rocking on the incline, widened her eyes in defiant fear, before I waved her on.

And then we reached the street, a slash of morning sun ahead, and squealed onto Madison, to begin shussing north between the careening cabs and buses, none of which could match our nifty nimbleness. Hunched low we streaked through shadowed Harlem neighborhoods and crossed the cratered bridge to the Deegan. Pressed her to speed faster, round the moon-size potholes, past the blurred graffiti and bleaching garbage, accelerating through the Bronx, praying, holding my breath. Hallelujah! The little thing hummed and shook, its tiny engine straining to hold the pace I asked. Dominatrix. Christineabad. Past Stella D'Oro and Van Cortland, Yonkers raceway, the old Wanamakers, into the great beyond.

Held my breath crossing zee Tappan Zee, where to my left a last glimpse of Mordor, and to my right, Hudson country, palisades opening to a more gentle prospect, rising faintly into pale empyrean.

I pictured the working host ahead, David, Pat and Rudi, and Johnny boy, while the real denizens squinted from afar. "Oh, do not forsake me, oh my darling . . ."

With little traffic on the Thruway, flew along accompanied by the sun, and through passing trees glimpsed strands of David's silver hair, his flashing eyes. Cracking the window for air, the roar drowned all other sounds. Closed it, and in the humming we flowed by lush glades, green ponds, fields sparsely-treed savanna-like, story-lands adorned in Spring's gentle hues—one Earth of overwhelming richness through which I traveled back in time.

Turned on the radio, a seamless ribbon of pop, crackle, and rock, all bleeding together—never a second's silence. Day-dreams rode this carpet of percussion in pulsing images: father driving us in the big, old station wagon; the radio crooning Sinatra and Patti Page half-heard; an early boyfriend, Mark, walking me to the movies; summer canoeing along a placid stream, peering up through the layered foliage; an endless trip through endless days, the sequestered world which formed me, and which has led to my questions: Why have I not reached out beyond that world? Does some fear hem me in? Some weakness hold me back from the steps I need?

In time, other landmarks: the Northway, signs for Lake George, the Fort Anne strip of gas stations, where I stopped to buy two bags of chips and a diet Coke. Then at last, off the highway, climbing, curling up toward Lake Placid and the deep Adirondack. The rhythm of the wheel, right, left, right left, left right. Climb, twist, climb, dive, then climb again. The highwayman comes rising, rising, north by northwest, past rock-strewn streams and strangled ponds. "Oh do not forsake me . . ."

Growing tired, squinting eyes begin aching, bottom numbing, shifting in my seat. Counting the miles, wondered how I would be received. Will they think I'm pursuing David, to distraction?

Turning my mind away, I wondered if I could have survived such a trek in the 18th century or earlier, when travel was measured in weeks, when Cora and Hawkeye dodged and fled over these peaks and valleys. Were not people tougher then?

And finally, just after two-thirty: the outskirts, the familiar stream, and gas station, and last rise. Yet the town itself was larger than Becker portrayed, and more varied. I saw ahead the video store, the dark real estate office, the white church above the town, but other streets too. Becker shrunk it down.

A clump of vans, trucks, light stands, dolly tracks, and crew members, hands in pockets, a scattering of extras waiting for cues. Driving up, I recognized Peter, the sound engineer, looking through a case. I pulled over to ask him how things were going and where I might find David. At first he didn't recognize me, thought I was a tourist or was coming on to him. Turned taut and cool, until remembering, blushed and blurted, "Oh . . . sorry, Christine. In there, in the diner," before he hurried away.

A P.A. tip-toed up warning me away from the front door which was in the shot. He led me around back, in through the kitchen, careful not to make a sound, to where I could see a shot just beginning. A town councilman entered, searched for, then approached the booth where Stephen, eating, read the local paper. The councilman, a big man of perhaps sixty, cleared his throat before announcing to Stephen that the zoning board had denied his request for a club permit. Having uttered this with some apprehension, he began to back away, then turned to stride for the door, but Stephen, recovering, scrambled out of the booth and ran after him, tracked by the dollying camera, tight on his anger-darkened face, now almost unrecognizable. Several days' growth sculpted and sharpened his now ruddy features above his rough country clothes. His eyes stared out, intense, determined. I was startled, thrilled. Somehow together they'd combined to turn John into Stephen Boylan.

Drawing even with the councilman, trembling with indignation, he asked the other about the reasons for denial. The older man told him it would be a disruption to the town.

"Disruption? It's a mile *out* of town!"

"And we don't want all the kids goin' there."

"Kids? No one under eighteen will be admitted. State law," Stephen proclaimed, voice ringing, close to raging.

"Nor do we want the noise 'n' drinkin' and the ugliness."

Stephen's eyes closed down in fury, nearly disappearing. Yet he managed to restrain himself, jaw working, realizing that he'd get nowhere with this fellow. Sucking it in, he growled "I was told we'd get a hearing, with the board, and I intend to."

The other man shrugged and began to turn away again.

"Sam promised it, and I'm gonna hold him to it."

"The board's made its finding," the man snapped with finality.

"Not without a hearing it hasn't! It's improper, and Sam's bound to see that things are done proper. You people think you can forget the rules and run things to suit yourselves."

"We live here, young man, and we've been here a lot longer than you have," the other hissed, now quaking. "Who d' you think you are, comin' in an' tryin' to tell us how t' live?"

"Yeah well you're not the only ones livin' here. We've asked the people, and most of 'em want it, most of 'em support us, includin' Sam! You had your chance, while the town was dryin' up, and what'd you do? Nothin'! Not a damn thing. So now it's our turn. We've got the signatures, and we're not lettin' this place go t' hell any further. You hear?"

The other man shook his head and began to leave. Stephen grabbed his shoulder as if to yank him around, but then on second thought let go. The other man, slightly larger than Stephen, if older, turned back and raised his eyebrows as if daring Stephen to do something. But Stephen spun away, wiping a hand across his eyes and brow, across his face gray with fury, and hunched back to his booth, passing the few surprised patrons. The camera tracked with him like a shadow, until he threw himself down into his seat.

David's voice called out "Cut," releasing a cloud of voices and tension from among the watching. But unable to see David in the throng, my gaze fell back on John still rigid in his booth. After a moment, as his body relaxed, as the anger drained away, his head rose, and our eyes happened to meet across the room. At first he reacted not at all—a blank stare—until something clicked. He blinked and allowed a slow softening to replace Stephen's hold. A hand was raised in hello—the most mature expression I'd ever seen him make, and I returned the acknowledgement. But our attention was diverted by Graham calling out for another take.

Opening my briefcase, extracting pad and pen, I groped for words to describe the scene, while around me in the narrow spaces near the counter, maybe fifty people stood working or watching. Feeling I was in the way, though no one said so, I squeezed back to a wall behind the counter, not far from where bacon and burgers sizzled on the grill. I asked one of the cooks if I could order something. His narrow dark face, French to my mind, glowered with impatience as he flipped the burgers. "Is it possible to get a BLT?" I repeated, trying to catch his eye. And though he nodded, he did not want friendliness, I saw, and I wondered if he resented our presence, despite the prospect of a little extra cash and novelty. Perhaps the contrast in prospects was painful or irritating, or maybe he preferred the peace and quiet here. Whichever, I realized that his feelings, his views, his life were completely opaque to me, though he stood but three feet away.

Turning to note the costumes and gnarled faces of the extras, many of whom were local, I felt I'd stepped into an all-male lodge, a world of hunters, where even the women dressed like woodsmen. The only two who didn't fit were Debbie and the actress playing the waitress, a young pony-tailed blond who might have stepped out of the '50s and who couldn't keep her eyes off John.

Among the crew members, I detected an intensity not visible in the dispassionate efficiency of the studio. Indeed everyone here seemed to have absorbed the stark, local reality. And like gusts rustling through trees, energy swept the room, in cries and debates and directions, rising, subsiding, then rising again.

Someone slipping deftly through the crowd brought John a fresh coffee for the next take—Amanda—and despite my avowed disinterest, I felt myself flush and look away, only to see the blond waitress watching eagle-eyed Amanda's every move.

Now the unhappy chef slid my sandwich onto the counter in front of me. I fumbled for my wallet. Can Amanda's exams be already done? Eager for my sandwich, I found I could barely breathe, and with the next take about to start, a small panic came. I lurched forward toward the counter, dumping my notebook and pen—a clatter which brought fierce cries of "Quiet!" and "Shhh!"

The chef silently pushed a cup of coffee my way, this time with a sympathetic smile. I felt he'd been watching me and perhaps saw I was, like him, not integral. I whispered thanks to him, as I tried to eat and scribble. But the taste of food only increased my hunger, awakening my stomach's groans as I attempted to peer over heads at the scene.

Close-ups followed. Between them, I was able to gain glimpses of David, standing talking confidentially with John, his hand on John's shoulder. When I couldn't see David, I looked around. The chef, now friend, asked me what I did, and I explained. Then asked him if he was French-Canadian.

"Mais oui. But tell me, how did you guess?" Yet his sarcasm was gentle, and I told him, in French, that my sandwich was the best thing I've eaten in a week. He smiled thinly, saying that the closest real food was in Montreal or Quèbec—where, however, there was no work for him. He wanted to go to New Orleans, and asked me if I wanted to drive him there. I laughed, "Mais Monsieur, I've just arrived."

Gazing around, between bites of my sandwich, moist with mayo and bacon, I was entranced by the faces in the crowd: mountain men, delivery men, blue-haired housewives in down vests, waiting for their shots. At the far end of the room, four lumbermen played pool, with seldom a glance toward the filmmaking.

At length Graham's voice reached out across the diner a final time, "Okay people, that's it for today, that's a wrap. Thank you all."

Checking my watch, I was surprised to find it was nearly five. I heard Rudi explain to someone that, though still light, the sun had just disappeared behind clouds.

People began to work their way out. I thanked my French friend, who invited me back, as Françoise had. As I told him I had no idea what the shooting schedule would be, I reflected that there is something steadfastly solitary about these French seeking a new start here. They seem un-phased that they are outsiders. They seem to wear their own ambience around them like a cape.

Pushing through to David, I found him sitting in the end booth, going over notes with Debbie. I looked around for John, but he had disappeared, with his coffee girl.

Looking up, David brightened, "Christine! Good, you made it."

Debbie too looked up and smiled with somewhat less luster.

I told David that I'd arrived in time to see the master tracking shot, and was impressed with John's performance.

He looked at me thoughtfully. "I hope it was so . . . It was the last two we wanted to print, wasn't it, Deb?"

Checking her notes, she confirmed this, before David asked, "Deb, there's a room at the inn for our friend, is there not?"

"Room 121," she replied, glancing down at her notebook.

They'd developed, I saw, an implicit understanding.

David now told me he was scheduled to rehearse Pat and Trudi and invited me to watch. But seeing that he was tired, I found this prospect uncomfortable, and so declined. Besides I wanted to stretch my legs and get some air and see the town. Dinner, he said, would be at 7:30, down the street at the Elks Lodge.

And so I departed, leaving him to Debbie. Outside the crowd had largely dispersed. In the lower afternoon light, the town appeared more picturesque, in its shadows and odd lumps and muted colors. Two boys, maybe thirteen or fourteen, circled up to me on their stripped-down mountain bikes, thinking, perhaps, I was an actress. "Hey," barked one, "you on 'E.R.'?"

"Nah," overrode the other, "you were in "Volcano" weren't you." When I told them I was only a journalist, their faces fell blank, annoyed. Rearing up haughtily on their back wheels, their tires spitting pebbles, they peddled vigorously away. Watching, I nearly collided with a mother, close to my age, but heavy and languidly cow-eyed, trailed by her pudgy 10-year-old daughter, waddling by, gazing up with wonder. I tried to smile back, even as I felt some vague sadness.

Meandering uphill past small houses set haphazardly on the slope, I reached an old barn which had for some time been a garage, and inside I dimly made out two young men working on two cars side by side. Their voices, in clipped cadences, drifted out to me, one high-pitched, the other deep and almost swallowed. I paused to listen unobserved.

Low voice: ". . . and so she says, 'Yeah I'd sell it to ya. Wha d' ya think it's worth?' and I told her."

High voice: "Whaja offer?"

Low: "Five hundred." Both cackle. High voice whistles.

Low: "Well why not? Wha's she know?"

High: "Her pa 'll skin you."

Low: "I told her not to mention it, to him or anyone."

High: " . . . You like her?"

Low: "She's alright."

High: "You dump her, and it'll all come out, and then her Pa 'll be comin' round here."

Low: "I'll be long gone."
High: "Oh thanks. Where you goin'?"
Low: "Haven't decided yet."
High: "You ain't goin' nowhere."

At this point, they must have noticed me, for I heard a hissed, "Shi-it . . . Who's that?"

I moved on, amused in part, in part disgusted.

On another street, stumbled upon Rudi and his camera assistant, Michael, wandering, scouting the town for end-of-day shots, when the low light offers dramatic contrasts with the shadows and shadings. They invited me to tag along.

Watching, as they stopped to study the various streets and buildings, I saw that Michael's face was handsome and warmed by a self-effacing smile which he threw my way when Rudi peered through his viewing lens or studied the light meter, calling out readings and lenses for Michael to record. I rather liked taking the time to look and consider, and liked the idea that the enterprise went forward without David's presence.

As we wandered, I began to notice individual flourishes on many of the older buildings built early in our nearly depleted century: the lattice work around porches, the fasciae lining arched windows, the columns and cupolas. They carried me back to the period of my childhood when the restlessness of change wasn't omnipresent. And yet I recognize that we need both, at different times, change and stability, the familiar and vehicles for change. The few passing cars seemed to embody this, rolling by, engines gently throbbing, beneath their drivers' motionless gazes.

A sudden breeze carried the damp pine breath of the forest, and prompted Rudi to pull his jacket around him, buttoning it with a shiver. I caught Michael studying me.

By seven-thirty, we'd arrived back at the Elks Lodge for dinner and found that our number, local and city, cast and crew, had swelled to over sixty. Rudi led us to the center of six round tables and seated me between Michael and him, just as David emerged from the back room trailed by Pat and Trudi. David sat next to

Rudi and Pat next to him, while Trudi, Debbie, Graham, Peter, Hillary and a fellow I didn't know settled into the remaining seats. No one asked about John and Amanda.

Above the constant buzz of conversation, highlights from the day's events—frequently humorous—burst brightly over the table. Michael, on my right, asked about my work and life, having recently moved down to the city from Boston. And though he was young, I fantasized showing him the Village, Soho, and out-of-the-way streets and alleys. But Rudi interrupted with thoughts about how to shoot Trappers Lake, and Michael and I never quite got back to city life. At some point, I asked Michael quietly what's the best thing about working with David, and he whispered, "the people," including, it seemed from his gaze, me. I nearly laughed, but must confess it made me feel ten years younger, for a moment or so.

Separated by Rudi, David and I exchanged hardly a word, though our eyes met. But he seemed to have regained energy in the rehearsal and now with dinner. And after dinner we took our chairs over to the other side of the hall to watch the dailies, some of which were silent and some were synced up to their soundtracks. In their somber beauty, made poignant by the stark rural faces, a number of which are French-looking like my chef, the compositions created a medieval aura, a rich heaviness, against which Stephen, and Teresa, and Sam the mayor must struggle. Indeed, set in this almost primal place, there was something archetypal about it, which pleased and moved me and lifted my hopes for the film.

Following the dailies, which drew applause and bravos, David stood, as was apparently the custom, to thank everyone for a good day's shooting, and to announce that a jugband had been hired to concertize at the club on the weekend—eliciting more applause and whistles. Graham then took over to announce tomorrow's schedule.

Afterward I followed David's car back to the motel, accompanied by both Rudi and Michael who weighed the poor hamster down to her limit. At the motel, Debbie brought me my key and showed me my room, and my two shadows brought in my bags, then stood around wanting to talk. But exhausted, I apologized and sent them out.

Running a bath, I looked forward to crawling under the covers, but, as I was about to step into its inviting heat, a knock caught me in mid-step. I suspected it was him and threw on a robe to open the door.

Both tired, we managed wan smiles under the motel's inadequate lighting. The lines in his face were deeper and more marked, I saw as he stepped in past me. Closing the door, I wondered where and how to begin, even as I knew it was an embrace I wanted. Perhaps he felt that too, for he came forward and we held each other, cheeks gently touching, riding the full pulses of our breathing. And yet I could not help but notice he felt almost fragile, and this revived my concern, as we clung to one another.

When we pulled back a little, we studied each other, wondering perhaps, who this other person was. A sideways glance toward the bed conveyed his need to get off his feet, and so we climbed onto it, propping ourselves up against the headboard. We talked in fits and starts, filling the other in about our time apart. Seeing that he was cold, I rose and threw the extra blanket over him.

We did not need more really. He had no energy for exhaustive chat, and so we held each other and exchanged a few details of work, the wilderness, Eleanor, and the city. When he felt himself dozing off, he said it was time to leave for the undisturbed rest he desperately needed. The daily pattern would bring Graham and Rudi to his room at six for the production meeting that charted each day. A long hug by the door—both sad and happy. And then I was alone in my bed—too late for my bath—shivering and pulling the blankets urgently over me, attempting to hold still in the surprising quiet.

June 23rd

Following breakfast at the motel, we were collected in an old yellow school bus that groaned along behind several equipment trucks into the back country. Off the main roads, we zigged and zagged upward for half an hour past brown fields and green-gray woods, finally entering a forest of deep stillness and shadow. Another stretch of creaking through damp woods and slants of sunlight brought us to a clearing along a stream, at the far end of which tumbled a falls pitching down between granite boulders crowned by a stand of hemlock.

Lulled by the long ride, I floated aimlessly trying to wake myself, as the crew marched back and forth unloading equipment. Out of a dream, a new, yellow Mustang convertible glided up beyond the trucks. And who was it but Johnny-boy stepping out from behind the wheel, with Amanda, looking young and pretty in her blue-jeans outfit. Helpfully, this worked like a dose of caffeine. I shook my head and turned to see if anyone else had noticed. But occupied by their well-practiced routines, not one looked up. I moved slowly toward the falls, listening and gazing into its flow.

David was off to the side talking with Paul Ceccini, the actor playing Sam the Mayor, while Rudi and Michael and others prepared the camera, dolly, tracks, and reflectors, while still others set up lights to augment the levels in the shade.

Michael, in passing, smiled good morning, inviting me to gaze into his pleasing symmetrical features. Someone touched my shoulder, and I spun to find John. He smiled slightly through his dark stubble, "Sorry I didn't say hello yesterday, in the restaurant. How are you? You're looking well."

"And you too, John. I thought you did well yesterday."

Pleased, he smiled modestly, handsomely. "Thanks. How long you up for?"

"A week."

"Good. It's terrific up here, even in the rain. It's been an experience, to reconnect with the country."

I looked at him, doubting, somehow, the depth of his reconnection, and wondering what beyond the film we could talk about. Relationships like ours leave little once they pass, and, in light of that, it's difficult to explain the energy they summon. The imagining is all, it seems.

Frowning now, John dropped his voice, "Christine, I, uh, have been a little worried about David. He's seemed tired, and his eyes 've been bothering him; he keeps rubbing them and pressing them. But I, uh, haven't found a way to ask him about it. Guess I've been afraid to, but Rudi's noticed it as well. Rudi thinks he needs rest, but of course the question is how or when."

Indicating I was aware of the problem, I looked away, wondering if he, also, was urging me not to distract David. Possibly unsettled by my silence, John took a step back. "If you have any thoughts or suggestions, Christine . . . otherwise, hope we'll find a moment to talk sometime."

Nodding, I turned back to the stream. Closer to the falls, I saw David walking with his arm around Amanda, talking together heads down. Looking back toward the camera, I discovered Michael studying me again. I waved, trying to imagine how he may have seen my brief encounter with John, supposing that he's heard something of our history.

As I settled upon a large flat rock, another car bounced up, disgorging Pat and Trudi, come to watch, despite it being their day off. They called out and waved to me as they headed over to Candace, the make-up person, who had begun to prepare Paul.

The first shot was of Stephen negotiating a descent down the steep hill above the stream, having earlier climbed up into the woods to ponder alternatives and burn frustration. The camera, set up near me, would follow part of his precipitous hurtling, but the second shot was more involved. They gave Michael a camera and tied him into a boson chair attached to a cable, so that several of Stephen's leaps could be captured with some sense of the drop, speed, and danger. A stunt-double had been brought in for the day to step in for John, flying, free-falling down over the last boulders and drops, one misstep from a bone-cracking crash.

Michael, I could see, was thrilled to be filming this, and barely attended to Rudi's instructions on framing and focus. But finally after much preparation and rehearsal, they filmed the sequence, not once but three times, the last of which neither Pat nor I could watch—in my case, peering instead over at David, who twisted with each vault and pumped his fist with each landing. I was astonished. How different are men.

A less risky scene followed, where Sam the mayor was waiting for Stephen when he bounded up breathing hard, adrenaline pumping, alive from gambling on the rocks. Ceccini, a New York actor, conveyed, nonetheless, a rural sensibility, in his broadly round face. In contrast to Stephen, his demeanor was relaxed and loose, swinging between humor and shrewd strategizing, so that once again, I felt David had chosen well. Watching Paul, I saw that he simply *was* Sam, and his naturalness played intriguingly against Stephen's edginess. Although they are allies, they come at the struggle with the town's factions from quite different angles, and eventually Stephen comes to realize that Sam's approach is the more politic and effective, and to that he bows.

By lunchtime everyone was famished, after the extended, dramatic takes in the fresh mountain air. Most threw themselves down on rocks by the stream to refuel, doing so with such concentration that there was little chat or laughter. But all was abruptly diverted by an echoing splash from the pool at the base of the falls. Heads swiveled around to discover, in mid-air, Dave, one of the grips, arms binding a perfect cannonball, about to land on top of Michael who exploded the first—neither with a stitch on. Another fellow, who I didn't know, followed—a ball of hairy white bacon hanging for an instant above the pool, followed by his ca-plash and crows of delight and howls of discomfort, as the water this time of year could not run much above freezing.

Now Pat and Trudi arose and brazenly stepped over to look, which initially kept the three males stuck in the icy pool, arms around themselves for modesty and warmth, until they saw the women, laughing and staring, were not about to leave. Summoning their own pluck, they climbed, crawled, and scrambled out onto the rocks. And while Michael ran, bent modestly for his jeans, and turned away to pull them on, Dave and the other, less gracefully proportioned, out-brazened the two women by slowly walking up to them, until Pat and Trudi burst out laughing and retired with broad smiles, delighted with their effect.

The afternoon was spent high in the rocks and paths surrounding the clearing, shooting Stephen's prior wanderings. It took time to set up the tracking shots which David wanted, but he felt the movement through light and shade would convey something of the extremes and uncertainty Stephen was experiencing in taking on the town's old guard. And so, although this activity itself was simple, David was even more particular than usual about the light and movement and framing.

And I, high on that steep hill, watching and carefully moving along the ledges and slopes and through the strong sunlight and shade, found myself replaying contrasts: the fortunate circumstances which bore me, the little I have done with them, the too-frequent inadequacy in communication—all the while watching he who incarnates the surefootedness, concentration, and courage required to follow instincts along an ever-changing, unknown path.

Evening

"Christine?"

"Yes?" I was in his motel room, sitting on his bed waiting to take a walk, while he, bent over his desk, scribbled a few notes.

"You know, last night, I dreamed I was making a short film, maybe five minutes, of shots from that hill, of a man, or woman, making her way up through those woods, ever upward, through shafts of light, becoming ever more disoriented and detached . . ."

"Detached from what?"

He looked over, blinked. "The habitual. The usual sense of one's self. One wobbles, one feels one may fall. And yet it can also be freeing . . ." He looked down, eyes unfocused. But now his head tilted, and I saw that his thoughts had moved on. "You know, I've been racking my brain to get John to rise to the story and the situation. And have been sometimes pleased, sometimes not. But a while ago, I happened upon something unexpected. Amanda, who's seen my frustration, my failure to reach him consistently, put aside her infatuation and began speaking to him about Stephen, began coaching him, giving him suggestions as to how he might fill out Stephen. Indeed he's let slip as much. But only when I stepped back, did I see it: that it's she who's picked up my burden, coming up with things that neither John nor I had thought of. So, for all my absorption in this thing, it's my daughter, whom I have not very much helped, who's helping me."

Watching him, I saw this revelation occupied him, until, with slight bemusement, he looked at me again. "And surprisingly, we've both been smart enough to use it."

"Has anyone else noticed it? Has Pat?"

It took a moment for him to find me and study me. "She's noticed the improvements, certainly."

In spite of myself, I asked, "Has Pat's new friend come up?"

He shook his head, "No," and glanced briefly at me.

Something pressed me to add, "She's still cool toward me."

His frowning stare focused past me, across the room. "Give it a little time, Chris . . . As you know, Pat and I have been through some of the same things these last several years, shared the good and bad. I'm lucky to have had her friendship."

Feeling my face grow warm, I avoided his eyes.

For some moments we were quiet, until he stood, ready to walk. "Shall we go?"

I pushed up and off the bed, and moving toward the door, I asked, "Did I tell you that Kirsten's taking me to Paris in July, to work with her, on the merger with a French magazine?"

"No, you didn't. But that's wonderful." And yet his expression appeared puzzled.

"I'll be meeting her colleagues there, have a chance to revive my French, see a new side of the city."

"How lucky, how perfect." He paused behind an uncertain smile, then reached out for my hand. Together we stepped outside.

It was dark in the parking lot. We slipped arm-in-arm and walked toward the road which was distinguishable only by being darker than everything else.

"When we're finished shooting," he said, "I'm going to take a week, before we get into the editing."

Through the dark, I looked over at him, faintly making out his glasses, nose, and one eye.

"Maybe I can lure you away from your boss, and you and I can go somewhere . . . get to know each other." Now as his head tilted farther back, I could make out the line of his cheek. We stopped walking, and turned to each other, two shapes darker than the night around us.

June 24th

Rain returned today. They'd made alternate plans, including letting David sleep. For while they didn't know what was wrong, they saw something was—strain, fatigue, they guessed. When Graham asked me if I'm aware of anything more, I believe I was convincing in my denial, yet it cost me a palpable headache.

Rudi and crew moved around the town, picking up shots he'd discussed with David. The actresses, their attendants, and I went to the diner for cafés au lait, but it turned out it was my French chef's day off, and so we contented ourselves with regular coffee and girl-world chitchat.

After lunch at the Elks Lodge, with the rain now falling intermittently, and David refreshed, everyone gathered for an exterior scene of Stephen walking through the neighborhood, reminding supporters of the club to attend the Sunday town meeting at the church. At mid-point, Teresa joins him, and there's a moment when they stop in the midst of a downpour and embrace and kiss. Watching, I felt it the length of me—their bodies and arms wrapping around, the rain running down their faces. And they did it twice, three times, freshly, impulsively, as directed by David. From just beyond the semicircle of crew and actors, I stared through reluctant eyes, trying to summon a full breath, startled by Pat's ardor. How sensual and carnal and desirous she made it. How uncomfortably riveting. From where did she summon *that*? With her wet hair in strands over her cheek and brow, and her upturned face moist and glistening, she seemed closer to Amanda's age, and to a degree she seduced John, leaving him, after the shot, speechless, looking for her, throwing sharp glances after her, and around to see if anyone else had noticed.

In the evening, David rehearsed the next day's climactic scene, and I watched, once again amazed at the energy he found. It is his work, I am realizing first-hand, that brings him life, that takes his love, that consumes him, each day throwing all he has into it, until the well runs dry.

June 25th

Pale yellow sky hanging above an airless stillness portended a hot summer's day. The day's scene, the climactic town meeting, would be up at the old church.

By ten the sun had nearly burned off the haze around the steeple. Wandering among the gathering extras and townspeople, I felt it was Sunday, as they, dressed in suits and dresses, ambled about, or stood talking and commenting to one another. Soon several were dabbing their brows and pulling off their jackets. As others arrived, the buzz of activity seemed to expand, filling the air. Both the real and fictional residents brought salads and pies and handcrafts to barter and sell from tables in front of the church— all to be included in the opening shots. There they visited with one another, tasting and inspecting the offerings. At the same time along the side of the church, but out of framing, rows of additional tables were set up for the lunches and refreshments catered by the production company. More tables for Candace and her assistants, and for all the costumes, were placed in front of two huge Winnebagos serving as dressing rooms. Still other tables were designated for props, and for the technical departments: sound, lighting, camera, and grip.

Now, through the increasing brightness, groups began to stir as bunches of extras were summoned up the front steps into the church. Winding through them, I heard murmurs about the fictional debate, neighbors taking one side or the other, or finding parallel issues in the real town. Frequently I saw it was age that divided those who were willing or not willing to take a chance to save the town.

The first shots established the town's people. David moved quickly through the local extras, sizing them up in brief conversation, and then asking for some exchange or comment or observation. These responses were shot in a variety of ways: handheld, locked down, or tracked by a dolly—from which, I assume, he will select the best, months from now.

Immediately after lunch, the pace quickened. The remaining actors playing the principals were summoned inside for the master shots. I stuck close to Rudi and Michael, as it would've been impossible to follow David hurrying from actors and extras to Rudi, Peter, and the crew.

More than usual, Graham kept the machinery turning and kept each department and all groups of extras on schedule. And although for much of the time in the church chaos appeared to prevail, regularly all quieted, order was restored, and shots were ticked off.

The debates themselves, in front of the congregation, were unexpectedly engaging: a kind of prickly, swirling discussion between members of the two sides, with additional points thrown in from the pews. And, as I saw in the restaurant, opinions quickly boiled over, heated by the belief that life as they knew it, or hoped it could be, was at stake.

In many ways, Sam the mayor was the most interesting of the characters. In his role as mayor of all the people, he was the most aware of all views, despite his intention to win support for the club. Part Mark Antony, he disarmingly denied any special pleading, in a casual, self-effacing way, while subtly making his case. "Now ladies and gentlemen . . . uh, the reason we're all here is not only . . . not only the specific proposal before us, but, uh, to discuss the fact that our community's been goin' through hard times. For nigh onto five years now, we've been hurtin'. Jobs 'n' people been walkin' off, which is bad enough in itself, but the ripple effect is that our tax revenues have fallen; meanin' less money for our school, and almost none for our roads. It's meant we've had to cut back Chief McEvoy's salary, and Clare Minelli's too, though she's given twenty years of her life to this town, and educated most of us . . . or tried to . . . Why, if this keeps up, your mayor's gonna hafta be cuttin' his own salary down a little, too."

Light, nervous laughter rustled through the pews.

"As a matter of fact, as most of you know, the mayor, for the last three years, has forgone his salary entirely . . . which is good for the belt line," he says patting his stomach, "but tough on the wallet."

Someone cried out from the pews, "Hey Mayor! We pay for what we *get* 'round here!" And an older woman half-rose to call, "*All* you people sittin' on the board should be payin' *us* for the privilege ah sittin' there, 'n' doin' nothin'!"

A great cheer briefly rose, followed by a general stirring, as the lines and laughs were passed around and repeated.

Sam smiled. "I know, I know, ladies and gentlemen . . . I don't disagree, in principle. But believe me, we *do* pay, at moments like this, to hafta stand up here and be held accountable for an empty cupboard . . . It's no fun—a sad state, despite the many bits ah wisdom you all've whispered in my ear over the years. I assume it's the same for the board, eh, Harvey?"

But Harvey Thomas, the opposition leader, sitting at the oval table to Sam's left, didn't react.

"Ladies and gentlemen, I might just say that if I'd taken some of your heartfelt advice, I'd be residin' in a spot far south ah here, an extremely hot place not infrequently referred to in here on Sundays . . . which, as I look around at some of your faces, might be preferable."

A tittering again rippled through the gathering.

"But to get back to my point, ladies and gentlemen . . . we have looked at our situation and watched with deepening frustration its downhill slide for these past five years . . . and so, have finally concluded that somethin' hasta be done. Somethin', somethin' bold, somethin' *new* . . . We kin no longer sit still."

Unequivocal cheers and applause from part of the crowd. And when things quieted down again, Sam went on, dryly and sometimes downright amusingly, making the case for the club, first as a source of revenue for the town, and second as the first of several town sponsored projects to bring back life to Trappers Lake. "What we wanta do, folks, with the extra money the club can give us, is not only pay the chief and Clare but also finance some other new businesses, ones that have a reasonable prospect of workin'. We might try to get a motel built here, on the lake. We have this beautiful lake right here, and we don't use it enough. We don't take advantage. Some have suggested a little more upscale restaurant might be somethin' to go with the motel. Then the summer visitors we do get, won't have to drive twenty minutes away just to eat 'n' sleep. There are a number of small businesses we're thinkin' could be successful here, with a little start-up capital, businesses which can bring in more revenue for the town. We've gotta think of ways to use and beautify this home of ours. Fur instance, we might create a town green so we can all come together in the summer months . . . Frankly, there're alotta things various people have suggested, and we see this club as the first of many."

But the opposition was not without its arguments too, as articulated by old Harvey Thomas, the head of the board, still strong and sharp at sixty-eight. "Now Sam is a good man and has the town's best interests at heart, if not in his head. You see, he may have forgotten that only ten years ago, we went through this same thing, same ideas, for the same reasons: get some new enterprises goin' and the town'll rise again. Just need a little money . . . Problem is: What if the new businesses don't take hold and make money? Then the town's stuck with the debt. Just like ten years ago, when we woke up one day to find the businesses had failed, and we'd spent all our tax money, and still owed Chief McEvoy, and Clare, not to mention other bills and county taxes. And so I ask Sam, just *who* is it that's gonna come and make this club such a success? Where're these people, these patrons with money, gonna come from? . . . Oh, some young people from around will come for a while, but experience tells us they cost as much money to police and clean up after, as the little they spend, and the elements who come are not those who're gonna encourage good families and good people . . . So you see, Sam, it may look nice on paper, but experience gives you a little clearer picture of the prospects."

But Sam, too, was prepared, listing off solutions to Harvey's problems, including an estimate of where patrons might come from: the towns within an hour's drive, including two college towns.

"And finally, Ladies and Gents, the outlay by the town will be minimal, thanks to the hard work of Stephen Boylan and Teresa Aucoin and others."

As the debate swept back and forth, as the different speakers stood and made their points, I watched the local extras straining to follow each word, leaning one way or another to see each speaker, and then turning back to one another to comment or argue. And the unsolicited murmurs, catcalls, and laughter seemed to come equally from both sides, not only because David directed it, but because the locals found merit in both sides. And such was the intensity of interest, that several times David cut away from the debate itself to film reaction shots of those residents who were thoroughly caught up.

At some point, Stephen, seated on Sam's right, rose to make one final argument for the club, "People, one last thing . . . If we don't do this, it's likely someone else will, somewhere in the county. And that's gonna siphon away the last of our young people . . . Fact is, if there's no hope here, what's gonna keep us here . . . those few of us who are left? . . . You see, what we're really decidin' here is the future for all of us, the life or death of our community . . . For you see ours wouldn't be the first one that's died up here . . . but it would be one of the more tragic, with all our natural potential. So, we have that choice now, and I urge you not to sit passively by . . . but vote for a chance, vote for a little imagination, vote for a little guts."

With this, a number of the younger people stood up and whistled and whooped, and even some of the older people applauded, but Harvey Thomas's face just grew tighter and darker.

Eventually a hand count was taken, and the supporters won by about thirty votes, of the approximately three-hundred-fifty cast. In the course of the count, I spotted for the first time today my chef from the restaurant, and we waved to each other, as he sat cast with the younger, hopeful faction, from whence came, after the count, most of the noise and celebration. On the other hand, taking a cue from Harvey's obdurate stance, many of the nay-sayers would not concede gracefully and refused to turn and shake hands.

Now Stephen stood up one last time, raising his hand for order, and when quiet settled over the gathering, he addressed primarily the opposition: "Those of you who have opposed this idea—I hope you won't hold it against us that we wanta try somethin' beyond what's been done . . . But you know, we're still all one town, so let's not let bitterness divide us. We're all still livin' here, so let's not have everyone walkin' around mad at each other . . . The club is supported by the majority at the moment, so those against it should try to give it a shot, and if it causes problems, well, then we'll all deal with 'em. It's not all carved in stone. It was never our intention to open a den of iniquity, but rather to bring new life to the town . . . We see the club honoring different tastes on different evenings. It's not a panacea, but it's a start, if we get behind it and make it ours."

One last time expressions of general support swelled up from the pews. But only a few of the opposition showed any signs of coming around. Harvey and his closest cronies bowed their heads as they slowly stood to gather their jackets and papers, before they stiffly edged out of the pews and trudged back up the aisle.

With this, a quiet spread over the congregation. The victory was understood to be a mixed one. Only gradually, as most pushed up and turned to make their way out, did a general murmuring return. Some were indignant, some confused; many sought support or clarification from their neighbors as they shuffled toward the doors.

Outside on the steps, and on the church grounds, David directed a rapid series of handheld shots, of the varied reactions and of the faces, hot and drained and thoughtful in the late afternoon sun. I kept close, watching how he concentrated on coaxing credible reactions from the extras, many of whom were tired and wrung out by the noise and by the long, hot day. He began by engaging them in conversation, about anything, and then bent it toward the town's issues. When he felt they were ready, he threw them a question or asked for a reaction to something he said—and Rudi filmed it. And while it didn't always produce something useable, more frequently than not, it uncovered something genuine and thoughtful.

Later, as I moved among the locals, I overheard exclamations as to how good the actor playing Harvey Thomas was, how chillingly credible. And I watched as a number of the locals stared at him, expressing their disapproval of his inflexible stance.

Not far away, the professionals gathered around Jonathan Alter, the actor playing Harvey. He stood with his tie loosened, his blue suit jacket hanging from his shoulder, as all chatted and joked, beers in hand. Jonathan, I saw, was popular, affable, and quite unlike Harvey. Yet I could see that a number of the townspeople could not quite accept that Harvey and Jonathan were two different personalities. They watched him, wondering if the man before them, smiling and talking, was not really a troll, ready to steal the town's soul.

Evening

Moving in and out of long deep shadows, carrying, discarding, cleaning, the crew, extras, and townspeople willingly, if wearily, wrapped up. Around the church in the gathering dark, in all directions, shuffled bodies carrying loads of all shapes and sizes, heads and shoulders bowed under the weight and hours.

Michael, in passing, whispered, "Hey, quite a day."

"A swirling circus of a day!" I called back.

Rudi, listening as he wrote up notes on the various reels, raised a skeptical eye, having seen it all before. Above him gleamed the white steeple in the last moments of the sun, while the air beyond was still and clear. Inhaling, Rudi now loudly pronounced, "You know, it was da town's day today." And he paused to watch the townspeople packing.

"The people's day," called David, consulting with Debbie on shots and scenes, "It was their ocean that floated our boat." His eyes laughed above the creases 'round his cheeks.

Now Jonathan Alter called to him, "In reality, David, the club would be an imprudent gamble."

As if yanked, our heads snapped around toward him.

Dave-the-grip called out in passing, "Hey, Harvey baby, life's a gamble." And his chubby smile squeezed his eyes into lines as he lugged a heavy tripod toward the trucks.

Loudly Jonathan replied, "Which is fine, so long as people gamble with their own resources, and not others'." And he protruded his lips ambiguously.

"But our make-believe town vas down and dying," replied Rudi frowning. "Vhat choice did dey have?"

"Until today, when the town sang in its chains like the sea," sang David, moving away.

To which Paul Ceccini called, "Splashing us all in a spray of hope."

"In a chorus of voices," refined Peter coiling cables. "On the sound track, a choir of the mountains."

Thus diverted, the wrapping was soon done, and we rolled downhill on rubber legs to dinner at the Elks Lodge. Entering the hall, Trudi, Pat, Candace, and Debbie formed a chorus line arm-in-arm, kicking up, and singing, "Gonna wash that man right outta my hair . . ." until cat-calls and cries drowned them out, and the steaming food summoned us to the tables. Settling down next to David, I told myself it was indeed the richest of days: a world unto itself, all tripped into motion and rippling debate.

Graham and David decided to postpone the dailies, freeing everyone to eat and collapse, which many did, although others lingered at the tables to unwind, recount, and listen.

When we had eaten and set down our forks, David, I noticed, succumbed to a great yawn, stretching back in his chair. I offered to drive him back to the motel, but he, rising, dropped a heavy hand on my arm and kindly shook his head. Pushing off from our table, he strolled slowly among the others still seated, exchanging compliments and comments: "Good day, David!" "Great job." "Well done, David." "A joy . . ." He smiled, congratulating and thanking them one by one. Eyes followed him even as they continued chatting with their neighbors. Above all, I was coming to see, it was the unique and memorable faces he'd chosen for the various characters that will bring alive the personal and political dramas. Each seemed fresh and authentically engaged.

Not until we were alone and climbing into his rented Ford, did I have the chance to tell him. "David, it was a parade of striking faces, and moments. Paul was great, Jonathan chilling, Johnny convincing . . . A world unto itself, a delight to be in the middle of. I was impressed with your handling of the extras, how you got them to act so naturally. For me, the boundary between story and reality wavered, and disappeared."

He ran a hand across his eyes. "The trick is to size up what the extras bring and what they're comfortable and uncomfortable with. With experience, you begin to see the patterns: the way they can speak in front of a camera, what they can say easily, and you go with that, aware that you must be ready when they are, because they can't reproduce it on demand like a pro."

Now, however, as he drove, I saw him flinch, saw an eyelid close, then flutter, as if a speck had lodged under it. He slowed the car, rubbing the eye, squinting ahead with the other.

"David?"

"Just a minute . . ."

"Shall I drive?"

"Hold on . . . Sorry . . ."

After a moment, he seemed to recover, and my mind swung back to the church. "Another thing I noticed was how good Trudi, Pat, Paul, and Jonathan were in helping the locals with their concentration and bits of business. It made the extras feel part of the production, I think. It inspired them. They looked so pleased."

"Trudi and Paul love that. Although I suggested a few general ideas to the extras, the specifics coming from the actors were more effective."

"Well it worked," I declared, recalling the faces.

But now gazing distractedly ahead, I noticed the road grew particularly dark as it appeared to swerve left under boughs of great evergreens. I glanced at David, but he stared motionlessly ahead, and as we approached the curve, he made no attempt to slow. "David!" I called. But too late.

Going in too fast, he managed to turn the wheel only as we reached the gravel shoulder. The car's tail swung out skidding sideways off the edge. We hit something, then shot ahead again, down a small embankment, into some trees, lurching, bouncing, and grinding over bushes or saplings, before smashing head-on into two larger trees which stopped us dead.

Fortunately my seatbelt held, but his was not on, and I heard his head hit something, the wheel or windshield, before the tilt of the embankment sent the car into a slow-motion roll onto my side, bringing him down heavily onto me, pinning me against my door.

Something, another tree maybe, prevented us from rolling farther, but left us on our side, rocking against this swaying support. David didn't move, his weight pressed my shoulder with increasing force against my window. I called out, cried for him to move, but there was no response. Fear now rose up, building into a silent scream. The car might catch fire; the trees may give way, sending us hurtling; the others returning to the motel would miss us, as we'd rolled too far down the embankment to be seen; rescue would find us too late; we'd burn or freeze, trapped in this metal tomb . . . David was already dead.

But then some twitch or movement chased that fear. "David!" I cried again.

Nothing at first. Then a faint groan.

"David!"

Silence, save for the trees or branches creaking and cracking. As I tried to shift, the car shuddered.

Somehow I swallowed my panic. If I were to move at all, I needed to summon all my strength. Wedged against the door and window, I needed to budge him and squeeze out from under. I felt for my seatbelt, following it down to the buckle, which unfortunately was pinned by his body. In moving my arms to release it, he slipped more completely against my chest, making it difficult to breathe, let alone move. Again I needed to quell my fear, now of suffocation. I wondered if I could twist and work my way forward to where I might edge around him and get up to and out his door. But the more I twisted away and inched forward, the more he slipped toward my door, until most of his weight pressed upon his neck and head. Reaching behind him, I managed to guide his head, then shoulders, so that he slid more onto his back, while I squeezed up and over him.

Gradually I was able to maneuver and stretch toward his door. But just as I reached for the handle to try to push it open, he groaned and gasped for breath.

"David!"

" . . . Ca . . . can't breathe!"

But there was no way to quickly reach down and lift his head. I saw that I had to somehow get out, turn around, then reach back in. And so by gripping the side of the seat and pushing off from first my door and then the dash, I was able to get close enough to turn the door handle. But pushing it open, straight up, seemed beyond my strength, and for some moments I crouched there, aware that David needed to be moved. Then I tried turning onto my back and using both arms to push the door away from me, also finding new and higher footholds from which to inch upward. At last, I was able to shove the door so it stayed open, and then pulled myself up, turning as I did, onto my stomach.

David groaned once more, and I saw him roll and move a bit.

" . . . G, God," he coughed, then pulled himself farther into the footwell so that he lay mostly on his back.

"David, can you hear me?"

"Wha . . . what's happened?"

"David, you breathing okay?"

No response at first. Then, " . . . Christine?"

"I'm here. You okay?"

A groan. "Wha . . . Did we crash? . . . I don't understand . . ."

"Yes, we slid off the road. How are you?"

" . . . Lousy . . . head hurts."

"Wait a sec." Now I pulled myself out onto the side of the car enough so that I could stand on the side of the front seat. David was reaching awkwardly up for a handhold with which to pull himself up.

"Is it . . . night?" he asked gasping.

"Nearly. Can you reach the steering wheel?"

"Where is it?"

"With your left hand, reach higher, over your head." But I saw he couldn't, and so I pulled my legs out and swung them back over the rear door, then lowered myself back in head-first using the wheel and dash for support. Inching down, fearing that if I went too far, I'd tumble in again, I was finally able to just catch David's fingers and direct them to his side of the wheel. "There. Can you pull yourself around?"

Still grunting, breathing with difficulty, he was able to do this until his head was nearly upright, his back against the door. But there he could move no further, and, as I was sure there was no way I could lift him, I pushed myself back out.

"Christine? You there?"

"Yes."

"There's no light down here."

"It's growing dark."

"Can't see a damn thing . . ."

He felt for his wristwatch and held it in front of his eyes, but couldn't make out its luminous dial. "My God," he whispered, "I . . . can't see at all."

"What?" slipped out, as I peered down to see him.

"Chris, it's happened. I can't see . . ."

A pounding now filled my ears; my heart thumped wildly. Yet over this, in the distance, the sound of a car could be heard coming along the road. "David, a car! I'm going to see if I can wave it down."

Though he didn't respond, I pushed myself back out onto the side of the car and turned to peer up the incline. In the pale twilight, I saw the embankment, steep, but not too far away. I didn't know whether to jump and turn onto my stomach and let myself down. But with the car approaching, I knew I must move. I noticed a smooth, leafy spot near the back door and decided to jump, attempting to land on all fours. I managed to land feet first, but my hands thwacked down against the bank, and I was dimly aware of slicing something before I scrambled up. From the direction of Trappers Lake, a car indeed was coming. I stumbled out onto the road, waving frantically.

The car slowed and pulled over, and I ran to the driver's side. A man pushed open the door, stepped out, and stared at me with surprise. "Christine?" It was my friend the chef.

"Bertrand! We've had an accident."

He seemed mystified and looked around. "Un accident?"

Pointing behind me, I explained, "Our car ran off the road. David, the director, is stuck inside, down the bank."

Slowly Bertrand's eyes swung to where I pointed.

"Come, help me get him out."

Bertrand now reached back into his car and turned off the engine, before I led him to the embankment. There, glancing at my hands, he said, "You are bleeding . . ." He attempted to inspect the cut, grasping my wrist, but I pressed both against my sweater. "We've got to hurry."

But he again took my right hand and studied it intensely, then stared at me. Pulling it back, I urged, "Please, Bertrand." His gaze now slid down to the darkness, frowning, but when I began climbing down, he followed. Both of us skidded on heels and hands, then ran side-stepping over to the car.

Gingerly, Bertrand edged behind the big Ford to see what was holding it on its side. When he returned, he said, "Fortunately, there are several trees supporting." He studied me again, then glanced up at the car.

I called "David?" But there was no reply.

Now Bertrand turned and again walked to the rear of the car, then came back, studying the open front door.

"Maybe here," he mumbled, reaching up for the door frame.

"Christine, help me." And he jumped up grabbing hold,

dangling and calling, "Quick, give me . . . let me place a foot on your back. Hurry, turn, face the hill."

Uncertain I nonetheless complied, feeling foolish, yet bending toward the incline. I heard him grunt, then felt a shoe press down near my hip, then waist. He grunted again pulling himself up. A hard, heavy thrust against my lower back felt for an instant as if it would snap it, pinching and digging in at the same time, impossibly heavy. I cried out, but then it was gone, and I looked up to find him up on the side of the car, peering down in, and apparently talking with David.

"Bertrand, how is he?"

Peering back over at me, he muttered, "He's able to stand a little, against the other door. He thinks he banged his head; he remembers nothing."

I wondered if David still could not see.

In time, Bertrand got David out onto the side of the car, and once he had jumped down as I had, we both eased David down feet first to the incline. Feeling dizzy, he bent over for a moment, but shortly afterward we helped him climb back up to the road. There I saw that had we skidded a few yards earlier, we would have shot off a cliff. Ragged, tumbling images turned me cold. For several seconds I could barely breathe.

Bertrand asked David if he wanted to go to the hospital, thirty minutes north, but David recoiled "No!" And turned away. "No thanks . . . Just need to get back to the motel." And so we helped him into the front seat. After closing David's door, Bertrand held mine, but as I moved by him, he grabbed my shoulders and pressed a kiss into my mouth before I could slide in. I twisted out of his grip and fell in onto the seat. Not wanting to delay our return to the motel, I said nothing, wiping my lips, feeling revulsion and a sharp disappointment in him.

At the motel, I climbed out quickly and opened David's door. He swung around, and I helped pull him up. We took a few unsteady steps, then paused to wait for Bertrand, who, when he'd closed the car door, reached for David's other arm and shoulder. Together we brought David to his motel door. Meeting my gaze,

Bertrand smiled, then squinted at David and said, "I think he will be all right."

"Thanks, Bertrand," I replied through mixed feelings.

His tilted head waited for more, but David had found his room key and pushed it into my hand. I nodded to Bertrand, then turned to open the door.

Inside David's room, I led him to the edge of his bed and helped him sit. I brought him water which he eagerly sipped, but the various pains grew more insistent, so that he groaned as he tried to move. I saw he was barely able to hold himself up, and that he kept his eyes tightly closed. "David? How's your head?"

Gingerly he rotated it.

"Can you remember anything from the accident?"

He thought, then shook his head.

"You may have a concussion . . ."

He digested this and frowned. "I suppose . . . Could you see if I have any aspirin in the bathroom?"

I went to the medicine cabinet and returned with a bottle. When he'd taken two, I asked, "Sure you shouldn't go to a hospital?"

"No, that's the last thing . . ."

"Well, is there anything I can do?"

He didn't reply, leaving me to watch in silence. I moved to the end of the bed and sat, now aware of my own fatigue and soreness. For both of us, I imagined, the implications were beginning to pile up. I pushed myself up again and moved to lightly touch his head. His hand felt for mine. I brought my other hand on top of both. We were silent for a short time, until I asked, "So, David, what shall we do?"

" . . . I'm thinking . . . Still can't see a thing." Straightening up, he inhaled with pain.

"Do you want to call your doctor in New York?"

Feeling his head carefully, opening his eyes slightly, he murmured, "Yes, suppose I should. Where's my briefcase?"

Only then did I realize we'd never retrieved it. "I'm afraid it's back in the car."

His mouth opened and closed, brow furrowed. "Where?"

"Back on the road to Trappers Lake. Shall I . . . ?"

"I need to get it back . . . but, could you dial information in the city for me? And then the number."

I made both calls, reaching the doctor's service, where the operator was surprisingly helpful and predicted that the doctor would call back within the hour—the gist of which David heard.

"What about Graham? And Rudi?"

"Mm, what, what to tell them?" For some moments he pondered, then exhaled, "I had a plan, in case this . . . in case something happened. Maybe bring them in, one at a time. Rudi will direct tomorrow anyway. We'll keep it among us, until it passes."

"Is that a possibility? That it could come and go?"

"No one knows. The doctors certainly don't. But I must believe it will."

I went to fetch Graham, saying only that David needed to see him. And when he first stepped into David's room he noticed nothing amiss beyond signs of David's evidently continuing fatigue.

"David, I thought we did well today. I assume you were pleased, got what you wanted?"

"Yes, thanks Graham. Unfortunately, there's a little problem."

Looking closer, Graham began to sense there was.

"Driving back here, I had an accident; the car skidded off the road. Fortunately Christine's okay, but I bumped my head. At the moment, I can't see the fricking hand in front of my face."

Graham blinked, then glanced at me, unhappy to find my corroboration. Slowly he breathed and looked back at David, studying him. "Shouldn't you see a doctor, David?"

"I've put in a call to my doctor in the city. Aside from this little inconvenience, and possibly a mild concussion, I'm all right." One side of his mouth twisted up sardonically. "The car, by the way, is off the road, back toward Trappers Lake. Maybe you could get someone to go back and get my briefcase. And get the car towed. But first, we have to decide what to do . . . I'm praying that with a little rest, I'll regain things . . . Anyway, tomorrow, Rudi will direct. Do we have enough pick-up shots, and simple scenes we can shoot?"

"I'll check . . . but what . . . will you stay here 'n' rest?"

"I'll see how I'm doing in the morning."

". . . Well David, I'm sorry . . ."

David seemed to dismiss the need for sympathy. Graham asked, "Shall I get Rudi? I think he's back."

"Yes, but not a word of this to anyone else. It can't leave this room."

Graham understood, indeed did not seem as shocked as he might. With a sober evaluation of David and a glance at me, he left. I looked at David, bent over a bit on the bed. "Do you want to get comfortable, David? Sit up more against the headboard? Take off your jacket?"

Together we managed this, and he stretched his legs out on the bed just as Rudi stepped in. The phone rang, and I handed it to David. While he spoke to his doctor in swallowed, barely audible clips, I told Rudi the story. He looked at me heavily, accusingly, it seemed. But I had no interest in dealing with his suspicions. Rather, I needed to take care of my cut and bruises, and so excused myself, telling him I'd be back in a while.

In my bathroom, I discovered lumps on my forehead, arms, and legs, and how tired I looked. I ran a bath and washed my sliced-up hand, shaking it and growling at the stinging.

Perhaps the bath's soothing heat released pent-up stress and fears. Tears came slowly, then unrestrainedly. I covered my eyes, as my body shook. What will happen to him? And to this worthy communal effort?

In time, I dressed and headed back to his room. When I knocked, it was Graham again who cautiously opened the door. Entering, I found David lying flat on his back on the bed, forearm over his eyes. Rudi had left. Graham explained that the doctor could only recommend rest and say that there was a fifty-fifty chance that his sight would return, probably somewhat reduced.

Looking at David, I saw his lips pressed tight, fists clenched. Graham asked that I be present at the shooting tomorrow, for the appearance of normalcy. And then he said goodnight.

Moving over to David, I asked if he was feeling any better.

His forearm moved down away from his eyes, and his head turned one way, then rolled back. "Major headache."

"Did the doctor suggest anything?"

"Tylenol." His down-turned mouth expressed irritation.

I saw the aspirin bottle on its side, empty. "What about a hot bath? I just took one. It's very soothing." But he didn't seem to hear. "David?"

"What? . . . Yes, well maybe . . ."

"Shall I run one?"

"Okay."

I did, and when I returned, I sat on the edge of his bed and reached to lightly touch his shoulder.

"Sorry about this," he murmured. "Should've let you drive."

"Shh . . ."

"Not good judgement. Stupid."

I squeezed his shoulder.

"I get in the mindset that it's better to do things myself. Problem is, after time, months, it's too much, things fall off: energy, ability, resilience."

"You're still resilient. You'll recover in a day or so."

" . . . I can't even remember what happened, after walking out after dinner. Can you?"

"I don't know, David, whether you simply didn't see the turn. It was very dark."

"Was I dreaming? Was I just not alert?"

"I think you saw the turn too late, and we skidded off."

" . . . I must have really whammed my head. Thank God nothing happened to you."

I touched the back of his neck, squeezing it carefully.

"That's good . . . Just attach a new head."

For some minutes I massaged, with my good hand, his neck and head and shoulders. At length he said, "Maybe I should see if I can get around."

"That can wait till tomorrow, no?"

He frowned. "I need to see if I can get to the bathroom. You know, I stepped out measurements, in case."

I looked at him, aware of some distant thump of apprehension. "The only question was when," he mumbled to himself.

Although I'd understood, still the blow resounded.

He began feeling for the edge of the bed, then carefully stood and inched along its length and around its foot, before turning and sliding his feet cautiously, arms out, to his desk. "There. Not too bad." But his features furrowed under the difficulties. "Christine, where are you? Come here for a moment."

I moved over to him by the desk and helped him drape an arm over my shoulders. As I supported him, I felt him trembling and looked into his face in the brighter light, finding lines of pain, his forehead puffed and bruised. "Shall we go back?"

"No. Not yet . . . I want to think . . . what's possible."

"Your bath must be ready. Shall I help you get in?"

An ironic snort. "I won't subject you to that."

"But can you manage?"

"I will." With that he began to make his way back to the bed.

"Do you want me to stay?"

"I'm a mess . . . I feel as if I may be sick . . . but I've got to think this through, particularly in case it doesn't clear up."

Following him, I reached for his shoulder, then laid my brow against his cheek. He turned to kiss me. I felt myself breathe deeply, "David . . ."

He tipped his head down a little. "Is this the result of fatigue . . . my eyes, or something else? . . . Has that which brought me this far, now sent me falling?"

He expected no answer now, I knew. I suspected this tumbled out from pushing too hard and too long. I touched his face, finding a strange satisfaction in not being seen. He reached out for his bed again. I leaned and kissed his ear, then let him go. "I don't like leaving you."

His face fell. "Me neither . . . but need to, need to think." Turning, he tried to kiss me, his lips popping in the silence of the room.

I took his hand, holding it, fingers around fingers. But shortly he released his hand; his mouth wavered; his lips formed and reformed some word or words. I touched his arm and moved away to the door.

In my room again, I wondered if I should go back. But he needs quiet, clarity . . . I tried to imagine his darkness, pitch black, airless. I was breathing hard. Why did he insist on driving? Habit? Self-reliance? Control? Will? . . . And what now? What will happen to the film . . . and all that flows from it?

June 26th

On the cusp of sleep, found myself swimming deep down, under ice, then rising through pale blue water, into a room where, through the projector's flickering, came an older woman serving tea, never gazing at me. Several young men seated on stools leaned my way. The steam rising from my cup coated my lip. Enveloped in sweat, I was burning on one side, freezing on the other, crying that I must get up and away.

Waking I found my bed drenched. Arose achy and sore. Showered away the night sweat. Examined bruises, dressed, walked to his door.

Rudi, the speakeasy doorman, cracked it open, searching past me for unwanted observers, barely acknowledging me. Inside, David was sitting up very straight at the desk, fully dressed, eating breakfast, turning his head this way and that toward the curtained window.

"Good morning."

"Chris! Hello! Look, it's come back. I noticed it when I awoke; I could distinguish light from dark." This he showed me by rotating his head, mouth open in astonishment.

Coming forward, I touched his shoulder. "That's good, very good."

"And tomorrow I shall see. I'm absolutely positive! It was your bath that did it, the heat sinking in, the dead man's float, then sleeping flat out, and when I opened my eyes, voilà!"

Rudi watched David with embarrassed uncertainty. His eyes stopped down and ranged over the floor. Glancing at his notes, he asked, "David, is dere anything else you vant me to pay particular attention to?"

"No Rudi, I think we covered it. I want, as we said, the town's idiosyncrasies, its physical presence, to be the stage, sometimes presented square on, other times at odd angles, but seeking out clear, vivid shapes."

"Yes yes," nodded Rudi.

"Use your instincts."

Uncertain, Rudi studied David briefly, then moistened his lips.

"Okay, see you two later," David said, dismissing us, turning away.

Although I'd hoped to talk to him, I saw that Rudi was ready.

Under crisp white clouds and a northern wind, the town seemed to float like a derelict galleon. We roamed with Rudi, like children, as he picked up shots and short scenes, first in the town, and then at the club and in the countryside. And unlike Graham, Rudi did not seem weighed down by the situation. Indeed he seemed more excited and alive than usual, and moved everything along with snappy precision, which pleased the crew. To them, all seemed under control. No whispering of David's whereabouts.

At lunchtime, I drove back alone to the motel, where I found David's door open and him moving around almost confidently, his hands out at his waist. He announced he'd been outside, into the parking lot, navigating by the sun. "And tomorrow, Christine, tomorrow, maybe not all the way but enough."

There was little evidence of the crumpled figure of last night, though his hair needed brushing and his sweater straightening, which I managed despite his ducking and pulling away. "You embarrass me. Tell me how Rudi's doing?"

When I told him things were flowing along, he seemed relieved.

"By the way, Mandy came by, but I pretended to be asleep, didn't answer the door. I felt bad, but I think it was best. What do you think? Was I wrong?"

"I don't know."

We were silent for a moment, until a mild bemusement stole over him. "She and I are going through a period of secrets." The corners of his lips twitched with conflicting inclinations. "Listen, Christine, may I ask you, after dinner, to take a walk with me? I'll be stir-crazy by then. Will need some air, need to stretch. My mind's spinning, racing."

"Of course, David, I have no other dates."

"To the dismay of several here."

" . . . You should take it easy, no?"

"I have. I will. Until tomorrow."

He was alight, I saw, anticipating tomorrow. And drawn by this, I moved forward to hug him, indeed to kiss him hard. Then I left him, his arms out, turning robot-like. "Later. Later. Don't forget."

About to enter my room before driving back to the club, I saw the Mustang convertible drive up, and its driver, Amanda, lean out, "Christine . . ." As I waited, she got out. "Have you seen Dad?"

"Yes."

"What happened? I haven't been able to find him or reach him by phone. Where is he?"

"Have you tried his room?"

She glanced behind me toward it. "Yes, but there was no answer."

"He may have been sleeping."

" . . . Well, what happened? Someone said you were with him."

I told her the story quickly, during which she avoided my eyes, growing visibly agitated, her fingers pulling at three thin silver rings. Did she feel embarrassed for her father? Now as she glanced at me, dark lines of resentment appeared under her eyes. "I was going to call Mom, but what . . . what would I tell her?"

"I think he hopes to return to work tomorrow."

She squinted at me from under her eyebrows. "Oh . . . really? . . . So maybe it's not so serious."

I watched her weighing this—she who had recently crossed over into womanhood. "Has he seen a doctor?" she asked.

"I don't believe so."

" . . . Why not? Didn't you make him see one?"

"Make him?"

Her eyes flashed at me, then threw their indignation at the ground.

"Why don't you try his room again? He may be up and around."

She appeared to ignore this, looking out across the parking lot. "Some people have said he's having trouble with his eyes. Of course he's been tired . . ."

Our eyes met, then darted elsewhere, and back. I felt myself growing annoyed. How could she not have seen?

"He won't level with me," she explained—admitted.

"Well talk to him, ask him. I don't know what else to suggest."

With frustration puffing her face, she turned away. "Well, thank you. Sorry to have bothered you."

"No bother. Go see him."

She paused and peered back at me, shaking her blondish hair into place. "Sorry if I've been a problem. I haven't meant to be. John's said some very nice things about you."

Again our eyes held, but hers did not mirror those sentiments, before she turned away and strode toward his door.

Through the afternoon, I paid attention to Rudi, to discover differences in directing styles. It wasn't hard. He lacks the rapport with the actors, as well as the magical, altering quality that David brings. And perhaps realizing this, he wisely kept the discussions of the actors' choices to a minimum, asking, when there were questions, how David had left it. To me, it seemed that David's presence floated above the company through the afternoon, its guiding vision, in absentia.

After dinner at the Elks Lodge with Debbie and Trudi, I drove the hamster back to the motel, and knocking on David's door, found him dressed, ready to go, wearing a windbreaker and dark glasses.

"Hey, swank," I commented, laughing.

"It's swank or swim. For God's sake get me out of here! Let's skedaddle, let's hit the road, make tracks." And with startling agility he slipped up to me, kissed my cheek, then slid around me and out to the covered walkway, feeling his way, fingers out like feelers. He whispered, "Anyone around? I don't want them to see me like this."

I assured him we were safely alone, as most were at the jug band concert. He took my arm, and we made our way out through the motel drive and along the road.

Suddenly he released my arm and used the lip of asphalt to navigate, only occasionally reaching out to me next to him.

He asked me about the afternoon, and I described the scenes and shots I remembered, and told him that again all went smoothly.

Deeply he breathed, "Thank God for Rudi."

Now his head jerked around, tilting, as if he'd heard something. Then exhaling, he let it go. "You know the cleaning lady at the motel told me that there are wolves, and even bears, roaming these roads."

My hand went to his elbow. I felt myself clearing my throat.

"Trained bears, she said."

I released him and blew in his ear.

"That's precisely how she told me to get rid of them."

We walked on, quite happy to be alone in the dark.

Ahead to our right, a somehow-glowing stand of white birches appeared, a few yards off the road. When I described them, he wanted to touch them, and so re-grasping my arm, we slowly climbed down into and across a ditch, stumbling and clasping each other, and up a slight bank, where he reached out cautiously to one of the flaky white trunks and ran his palm down over the cool, smooth bark with its papery tufts. Where one peeled up, he pulled a little off and smelled it. "Dry, faintly herbal. Its own smell."

He took both hands and ringed the trunk of one, then patted it, as if to gauge its heft. Then using it for support, he tilted his head back and quoted quietly, "When it is dark enough, you can see the stars . . . Must not be dark enough." His pale right hand snaked out, reaching for me. "Onward."

Back on the edge of the road, moving along easily, I heard him inhale, as he does when he wants to tell me something. "Walking like this, in this stillness and fresh air, even in my double darkness, restores calm, perspective. I can breathe again, swallow my fallibility, find the temerity to push on."

I looked over. "That's no surprise to me."

"Maybe something good will come of this," he breathed.

"Your dialectic?"

"Maybe . . . As long as it's not the end."

I reached for his arm, and we walked on silently for some moments, until eventually he said, "Chris, I hope you will continue to push yourself."

"Why? How do you mean?"

"Don't let things distract you, pull you off your focus."

I looked at him through the dark, able to make out the lines of a frown. I saw his lips part. "I think we both expect a lot of Eiley. Don't stint."

Where had this come from? Why had he said it? Peering over again, I found him holding himself tall, chin up, as if daring fate to deal another blow. I told him, "I'm ready to squeeze out my best."

We walked on, ruminating perhaps. Twice when he stumbled, I was able to catch and steady him, gripping him under his arm.

At the edge of light cast by the motel, I stopped and turned him so that we faced each other, then slipped both arms around him, under his jacket. I pressed him tightly against me, laying my head against his shoulder. His heart pounded so insistently that I thought anyone nearby must hear it.

On his door, I discovered a note from Rudi, and read it to him. 'David, Need to meet about tomorrow. Call.'

Leading him in, I saw in the light that he was tired, as he side-stepped his way to the bed and phone.

I left him for a while, but later he called and I returned.

We didn't talk but held each other, first sitting on his bed, then lying down, and when it grew quite cold, sliding beneath the covers. Turning onto my side, I pushed him over onto his stomach so that I could rub his back. He lifted his head. "You are a gift."

"We are, as you said, a chance."

"I want an explanation how you came into my life."

"It was very simple."

"The series of coincidences that led to it. How far back must one look?"

But as our minds wandered after them, we saw they spread and wove like roots. And somewhere, along one of those paths, he was soon gently snoring, breathing particles that must have had their origins long ago.

June 27th

Awakened by a phone, I rolled over to find, in a beam of morning light, a silver-maned man at his desk, leaning, pen in hand, talking into the receiver wedged on his shoulder. "That's the extent of it, Nathan. One's working 'bout seventy percent; the other's balking—resting, I assume . . . Yes I understand . . . Cross that when I come to it . . . Yes I *am* taking it easy, as much as I can . . . And yes, taking your medicine, too, although what good . . . Okay, okay . . . Listen, I'll call you tomorrow . . . I expect to be back to normal . . . I know, I know you warned me. You've done your duty. Bye."

Hanging up, he scribbled something urgent on the pages of his script.

"David?"

Engaged by his work, he twisted to look at the bed, then me.

" . . . You're looking at me," I exclaimed.

"As you are at me, my lady of the birches—of thee I sing."

Arms and legs thrashed to get out from under the covers. Just remembered to pull the top blanket around me as I went.

"Modesty's not required, or even particularly appreciated."

"It's come back . . ."

"As I said it would."

My cheek grazed his forehead and nose. My hands slipped around his flannel shirt so I could kiss him fully. Pulling back, I found one eye squinting hard, the other dimly following, his face a half-dozen hues. My heart leapt.

"Are you all right?" he asked, gazing up.

"Yes, yes." I blinked back the blurring. "Oh David, thank God!"

"Well . . ." One eye bore into mine. "As you can see, one's working, the other isn't. Not yet."

I stared, at one and then the other. "And what did your doctor say? I assume that was him just now."

He swiveled and looked away, then shrugged. "Not much. Take my medicine," he laughed, "As I am." He peered back up at me.

I took his hand, and, in looking into each other, I saw dark pigments in his yellow-green iris. Perhaps we gazed more clearly than ever before, without distraction or patter. I brought his hand to my lips, trying to understand how it was connected to that eye, and wondering what emotions must be throbbing in him: hope, and the relief of having reached the surface again.

But I was not alone in wanting to celebrate his return. On today's first location, I watched Mandy greet him, unabashedly embracing him, her cheeks glistening. And I watched others studying David to see how he was, and whether he was the leader they'd known, sitting, hiding behind sunglasses and a white N.Y. Rangers hat Graham had given him, occasionally puffing on a cigarette, barely moving. People came up, bent down, talked quietly with him—their elder. And Rudi served, with the modest glow of satisfaction, as his eyes, even more than usual, describing shots, rather than having David stand to peer through the viewfinder.

I, on the other hand, became invisible. People ignored me, with the exception of Debbie and Trudi. Perhaps some attached to me whatever blame they required—temptress, parasite, vagabond . . . One can never know the cascading dramas acted out in others' heads.

As for David, leaning on one arm in his chair, one eye alert, the center of his pale face, crowned by a wisp of silver hair and his white hat, he seemed not quite of solid matter, but rather an assemblage of planes and light. His fingers came alive, tenting, pointing, summoning, writing, wiping his brow, pushing away strands of hair, tentatively pulling at his eyelid. Watching, I realized that despite his fragility, he alone had the comprehensive understanding of the ideas that brought and held this assemblage together.

In the afternoon, as they shot Stephen and Teresa at the club, before opening night, I felt my thoughts sliding ahead. I became aware that, by the end of this day, I would have observed pretty much what I needed to write my profile. And maybe for David's sake as well, it was time to leave—the point of diminishing returns rapidly closing in. Whatever might develop between us would be better to explore in the future.

His revival, and his gratification with the performances in the club scenes, made it easier for me to tell him that my work was done, and I would leave tomorrow. I couldn't have told him while he was locked in darkness. Yet now, when I revealed this, he seemed shaken, caught off-guard, standing up to face me, swaying a little, in his room before dinner. "Christine? . . . Really? Tomorrow? . . . But do you have to?"

"I should get back . . . I need to."

"But why not stay, Chris, a few more days?"

Weighing this, I realized my entire body was leaning home.

He canceled rehearsal scheduled after the dailies, and after I'd said goodnight to Debbie, Trudi, and Rudi following dinner, we returned to his room together.

There, I began to feel guilty, that my announcement appeared to cancel the day's several deep satisfactions. His fatigue seemed suddenly more evident, and even his good eye appeared to give him trouble. He sat by his desk and closed its drawer.

"David, I feel like a thief, even as I know I must go."

"Then stay."

"It may be best for you, and the movie, if I leave you for a while."

"Nonsense. Stay. You were planning to."

Under a weight, my head tilted down. "I've got to get back."

He turned away in his chair, pulling my heart.

"I won't see you for weeks," he realized in a low voice.

I went to him and touched his silver hair.

"How about coming up for a few days, maybe over the Fourth?" he suggested.

"Maybe. I don't know . . . I don't want to distract you."

" . . . Chris . . ."

"David, you warned me away."

He reflected, appearing to doubt that this was true. "That was before . . . and I thought we'd have more time . . . I feel, despite everything, we've grown closer."

"Yes, but while I feel that as well, there's another thing. Since the accident, people have grown a little uncomfortable with me around. Whether it's justified or not, I don't want to become a controversy . . . and I need to return to my story."

"Sometimes one has to be steadfast, cast off suspicions."

"David, time apart will not change things, will it?

Painfully, and unhappily, he glanced up at me with his one worn eye, his face lined and suddenly older. I shivered as I tried to get hold of my feelings, but it seemed as if years of sadness had surfaced in his face. And watching that, I could not stand apart. I bent to kiss him, and he reached around and pulled me to him, where I could feel him shaking.

"But must it be now, and so suddenly?"

"Yes." I surprised myself, that I was adamant. "But we have tonight, and future nights. And what we share won't vanish."

His head swung away. "Things do . . ."

"We have much to bind us."

He did not move, until slowly his head fell slightly.

I felt him inhale, and regain some level of strength.

"David, should we talk about the profile, and how to deal with this?"

"Not tonight. We can do it by phone, the later the better. . . . Your leaving feels too abrupt."

"I don't disagree. But the accident has changed the atmosphere. It feels hard to justify our time together, when so many need your attention."

"Maybe . . . One wants to think, despite all the evidence, that things move progressively, from bad to good, good to better, from

Spring to Summer . . . but there are little deflections, collisions. Things are redirected, slightly, or mightily, and one never quite gets back."

"Are not the seasons, and life, circular?"

"Not perfectly." His one eye searched mine.

I wondered how he saw me, and my decision. I wondered how close I was to staying. "Trust me, David. Trust us."

"I would like to."

When we ran out of words, I helped him onto the bed, where we held each other. Later, undressed, I massaged his back, neck, and head, then shoulders, ribs, soft hair. I explored the slim layer of muscle running down along his vertebrae. He groaned a bit as I pressed and squeezed. In little movements, spasms, life seemed to squirm back in. With a great inhaling, he rolled over on his side and pulled me to him. We seemed to take the measure of each other's length, touching at points, then allowing cool air back in between. His touching stole my breath, and I spilled over onto my back. He moved over me, pinning me, then rising slowly up, kneeling, slowly lifted me to him. I feared that I would make too much noise, until it seemed a great gust rushed past, and carried all concern away.

I fell into sleep, then lurched out, thinking that my decision to leave was both mistaken, and best—selfish, cowardly, utterly wrong, and yet, essential.

He hardly stirred. I touched his hair and neck and listened to his breathing, and lay my head gently upon his back. I pictured the townspeople in the church singing . . . a hymn. I imagined I was singing with them, but then realized I was crying, over our separation, and over my control of my emotions, and over the control, at some inscrutable cost, of my life.

June 28th

Walking through my rooms, staring out at their views, and at my two paintings, the familiar black ridges and crosses, their soft matter missing. Paging slowly through Eiley, after which I pick up and carry around, like a newborn, the armful of mail, crumpling and discarding as I go. But underneath this load, another, more heavy: What if he can't finish? What if all that he has talked of has slipped away, into the past? I imagine the weight he must shoulder, the worry—and beyond, the inexpressible loss, of his freedom, to work as he wishes.

June 29th

Walked to the office, to connect and resume. Everyone asked how it was . . . in his room.

Leafing through replies, I saw their expectations had risen up on toe. "Oh . . . well . . . it was beautiful, up there, in the mountains and trees. The movie was wonderful. Its story will please."

Through the morning they came and went, gathering around, waiting for a word. I described what I could, what could be called down from the mountains.

Fortunately, Kate phoned. "Chrissy, you're back! How did it go? It must've been great."

"Hi Katey . . . God, don't know quite where to begin."

"Begin by saying you'll come out to the beach, over the Fourth."

"Really?" I could hardly picture this. I felt I needed to be alone, get back to work. "Larry won't mind?"

"Nooo, you know he's a fan. So you'll come? Give us a yes."

"I have tons of work. Have to write up all my notes, pick up with Eiley."

"You can work out there. I'll leave you alone. But you don't want to stay in the city by yourself."

No? But I do. And maybe I should.

"Come on, Chrissy. I need you . . . And you love the ocean."

"You really don't mind if I work?"

"Nooo, Larry works all the time. I see him at meals or parties, just like here. Come on, it's summer."

" . . . Okay. Thanks." Maybe it would be better, not to hole up and obsess.

"Good! Now tell me everything. I want all the details."

In bits, and whole pieces, I told her the story, except for the accident and its aftermath. But toward the end, Kirsten stuck her head in, and I got off.

"Chris, two friends and I are meeting for dinner at eight. I thought you might join us. To welcome you back."

"Why sure. Sounds like fun. At eight?"

She threw back a nod as she hurried away, calling over her shoulder, "William's got the address."

Worked on a piece, until finally, late in the day, could put it off no more. Pushed my drafts aside, placed a clear sheet in front of me and wrote to him . . . for me.

David Dear David,

I was numb as I got into the car. Barely noticed the miles. Here I feel mostly the heaviness of your absence and your predicament.

Yet the decision seems right. (I repeat this because I need to convince myself, against all feeling.) It is, in reality, your world up there, and you don't need added burdens and responsibilities. You shouldn't try to serve two mistresses at once. (Sorry)

But know, David, that somehow you have invaded, have worked your way into, my core. I feel your presence. I start and look sharply around.

I hope that the distance and distraction will not wear away our connection. It's something unique in my life, something I've never had, and which I know cannot be replaced.

Love,
Christine

Evening

Intimate restaurant, candlelight played over features. Kirsten's two friends, her contemporaries, seemed initially plastic and cool, until with time and some wine, they grew more animated and individual. They shared stories of surprising humor, and I saw why Kirsten liked them. They asked me to describe Loomis and the Adirondacks. Looking into their faces, I saw eagerness in need of joining, spaces in need of filling. I told them of the high hill in the afternoon and the dark walks at night, the shadowy bears and luminescent birches. I mentioned the café and my French chef, the sizzling grill, the soul-stirring coffee, the Bruegel crowd, the stream and boys in the air.

They asked if the motel rooms were comfortable, the lake picturesque, the woods dark and deep.

"Oh, yes . . . yes," I recalled leaning back, parting my lips in the smile of replay. "It was all so fresh and un-spoiled. The cast and crew were so charged, so physical and focused—all like nothing I've known."

Silence. Breaths held. Kirsten averted her eyes. Looking closely at the others required a muffling hand, hiding a smile, but maybe a cry inside.

"Well," interjected Kirsten wearily "be that as it may, it's not for me anymore. I'm afraid I find that pastoral business gets old quickly now, and in any case it's bad for the skin—the wind and sun."

Serious nods from the two—whether from intimidation or concurrence, I couldn't tell. Hid my own ambivalence deep in a draught. One of Kirsten's friends, Jen, is also recently divorced. Her dark eyes I found captivating, her newly liberated mind hungry. She wants, she confessed, to write. Yes, join the club. But she, I saw, tells a good story. An account exec at an agency, where agility is all, she misses nothing, and tonight she ended her tales with real snap. Indeed, with sly observations and unexpected wit, she had us all painlessly laughing.

June 30th

The following morning, Kirsten came in asking for the blood 'neath the nails, seeking to paint the exalted with pigments of commonness. "So tell me, really, how did things go?"

I turned in my chair, catching a glimpse of the city outside. "It was as I said, a circus of light."

"Oh come on . . . What about you two?"

"We get along."

She sniffed at the glossing. "So obviously his marriage is finished."

I hesitated, aware that my forehead was creasing.

"And you are, or were, the reigning princess? At least until you departed."

From under my frown I felt a snort warring with a sneer. Annoyance shuttered her gray eyes. Must she spell it out? "Did you never ask about his reputation?"

"Which reputation?"

" . . . My goodness, Christine. Hook line and sinker? You think he's a monk? You didn't ask him about the various actresses?"

Felt my body tighten. The usual beads began trickling, as my expression, I knew, grew less happy.

She looked down at some papers. "I can't remember who the latest consort is, or was, Pat something."

Breathed easier. Old business, the inflation of rumor.

"Kirsten, I've been thinking I want to expand the profile, into two parts. For the September and October issues."

She studied me, to see how I'd skipped past her point.

"Well . . . do you have enough? I don't want gush and film-school drivel."

"There's enough. Beyond this film, and filming, there are his earlier films and themes, the way he works. In this case, I would detail how he transformed John Trevelyan."

Thoughtfully she considered this. "And his marriage and his women . . . By the way, I'd like to meet Trevelyan, too. I trust you haven't forgotten."

Holding my gaze, I permitted my eyes to dull down. She glanced away. "Also, the question as to how he's holding up. Loomis. There've been rumors about his health."

"Fine."

" . . . If you're going to expand it, there's got to be the whole bit, you know. The personal side."

"I haven't pressed him on those things. I don't think there's anything particularly fresh about it."

"Well yes, nothing new under the sun—but here is a man making movies on moral themes, about other men who stumble, while he's taking women to bed. I'm not going to swallow that charade."

"That's something of an overstatement, but in any case why reduce the whole thing to sex?"

"Not reduce. Just the complete picture. The entire thing. Whether or not you admit it, most of us spend a fair amount of time thinking about it. Did you talk to Pat . . . Eliot, is it?"

"Not about that."

"Well, perhaps you should. And others."

"I don't want to betray a trust."

"Trust? . . . Which trust is that?"

"Analyzing his love life is not the point here."

"No? Perhaps not the focal point, but a subtext. Chrissy dear, haven't you caught on? You were married. Men do all they can. With very few exceptions. It's what they're built for. And successful artists are the worst, as for some reason, women help them, by throwing themselves at them, to be sacrificed. Don't pretend you're going to close your eyes."

"You don't want to sink to talk-show level, do you? Particularly as it would distract from what's most unique about him."

She raised an eyebrow. "It casts light on the rest. It affects the rest. And I'm not in the business of protecting the trespasses of those who exploit their chance-gifts of one talent or another. Your job is to present the complete picture, and make it interesting."

"Complete but focused, and focused somewhere above the lowest common denominator, is my understanding."

"I think you know what I mean."

I let the debate subside, despite internal grumbling. Kirsten agreed to two parts, so long as I included details which I had promised David I would not. Fortunately there's time to figure something out.

When she'd left, I spun in exasperation, staring out the window—only to discover my own partial reflection, a bit of hair, a cheek, an eye-fragmented, unconnected . . . What is she doing, that woman in the window?

Tonight, fortunately, we began our tutoring program. Melissa had arranged for half a dozen volunteers from other magazines to join us at six.

But the local schools, which promised us dozens of students, sent us a total of four—for the eight of us. Two tutors per student. On the one hand, ideal.

At least the responses from these four were encouraging, and we urged them to bring others next week. I volunteered to call the schools back, to try to light a few fires.

At home, exhausted, a letter in my box lifted me to my aerie.

Dear Christine:

Watched the sunrise this morning, an hour ago, as the entire sky grew yellow and soft with cottonball clouds. Dark flecks, then flocks, of birds: crows, hawks, thrushes, larks wheeled, flitted across the arc above me as I stepped out my door. Glimpses of the earth's beauty, as if I—this one eye— were present at the creation, this day in June.

If the world were as perfect as this, I would have been born ten years later, for you. Or ten years earlier for my work, awakening into the great flowering of filmmaking. But instead I find myself on a periphery, flailing to achieve what I can, without any clear sense of what it means, or contributes, beyond my own mixed satisfaction.

Fortunately perhaps, there is little time to dwell on this, as I stand in a rushing stream, spending most of my energy trying to remain upright and hold my ground. Things go well. John continues to improve, and I continue to marvel at Mandy's influence. My one eye holds, and seems to be enough. The other, it seems, is finished.

I hope you will forgive my silences. They are not because I am not thinking of you, not because I am not experiencing loneliness. As you wrote, so it is for me. From time to time during the day I turn around looking for you, expecting to see you, as for a week I did.

Your letter lies open on my desk, next to my script. I reread both, hoping the aspirations in both will soon be fully realized.

With love,
David.

So. We cry the same notes, two lovers in boats . . . carried where? I will call him.

Dialed, then waited while a woman at the motel office connected me to his room, where another woman answered.

"Uh, oh Pat . . . Hello, it's Christine."

"Oh hi . . ."

"How 're things? How's the movie going?"

"Fine, good . . . Just a moment . . ."

A muffled exchange, hand over the mouth piece. Felt my own tension tightening.

When David got on, he didn't sound free to talk, or be himself, beginning with some impersonal chat about the production, "We've been at the club all week. It's lovely now. You should see it. We've got it painted and set for opening night."

"David . . . do you remember the letter you wrote?"

" . . . Of course."

"Full of feeling."

"Yes."

"So, can't you ask whoever's in the room to step out for a few minutes?"

"Hold on."

Again the muffled phone, indistinct voices. Faintly I heard a door squeak open and clump shut. "Sorry, Chris . . ."

"David, I don't mean to be . . . but on the other hand, if our letters are to have any correspondence to . . ."

"I agree. I'm sorry. We were working on a scene, trying to wrap it up." A silence.

"So? Have you . . . wrapped up?"

"No . . . A few more lines . . . But generally it's going well. I'm managing quite ably . . . as I wrote . . ."

"And what does Pat say?"

"Pat?"

"Yes."

" . . . What do you mean?"

Is it significant that he didn't pick up on this, as he formerly did? "Should I not have called?"

"I'm sorry. It's just that, well, we were into the scene . . . But no, I'm glad you called."

" . . . David . . . Kirsten okayed a two-part article, for September, October."

"Oh? . . . Good. Two parts . . ."

"It gives us a little time."

"Yes, time . . . Thank you."

" . . . David, have things changed?"

" . . . It's been a long day. And my mind's crawling home. My eye, even the good one, is tired. It aches, and I've been living nothing but the story, the story, the story . . . *Got* to get it done. Get some rest. Can barely focus on anything else. I apologize, Christine . . . Christine . . ." His voice trailed off.

"David, you okay?"

"Yes, just tired, exhausted."

"I can understand . . . And yet talking is what bound us together, what we've done best."

"I know . . . Unfortunately it's not a good time. You know the litany: the scene, meet with Rudi and Graham, notes . . . Listen, could I call you over the Fourth?"

"I'll be in Amagansett, with Kate."

"Give me her number."

I did. And we struggled to exchange a few more words, before hanging up.

Could not believe the chill or the distance. The intervening miles stretched out, beyond physical reality.

July 2nd

Eyes achy and thick.

Whether for vengeance or dramatic necessity, I crushed Eiley's romantic hopes, for one of her client writers. Neil Loam, was his name, washed into town by the tide and the river, the type who's ever a taker and never a giver. Bent on making it, the cad led her on, and she never noticed, until he was gone.

After work, we escaped to the sea, to Amagansett we went, to Kate's house a-singing, leaving once more the city behind, weaving the lanes of the L.I.E., streaking east in her shiny Toyota, out past the pines, to the edge of the dunes, faster and faster we flew.

"And what about him? What have you heard?" she cried when she could hold it no more. "He must be going mad, kicking himself."

"'Fraid not, with the movie, daughters, divorce, and other . . . problems."

"But I don't understand. You said you two seemed like one—talked about everything."

Glancing at her, with her eyes to the road, I saw nothing would dislodge her plans for me. "Kate, I wish it were even remotely that simple."

In time, she began to accept that things would not be resolved for a while, and our conversation moved over to other subjects, motherhood among them.

Arriving, we unpacked, then raced to the beach, where I dove through the waves for a late-day swim—finding the froth, the thump of the waves, their enveloping hold, the perfect release.

And it seemed, over the next several days, that once again I'd made the right choice: working on their deck in the morning, then gardening, or swimming, or shopping with Kate after lunch. Afterward, dinner or a party with Larry. All in all, it proved entirely distracting, if not perfectly freeing.

I even began to consider again leaving my aerie, as it now seems more shackle than inspiration. On the other hand, I wondered if I had not entered a frame of mind where I am simply running.

One thing was unambiguously clear, however—he never called.

July 6th

Early morning on my terrace sipping coffee, felt remarkably light, defiantly free, free without fetters, in life, and in work.

At work, Kirsten stopped in with lists for Paris and to compare notes on the weekend. "I was in Southampton, with friends, but I'm afraid we never made it to the beach. No time. But how was it? It seemed rather cool."

"It was lovely and sensual, and I did a good bit of work."

This seemed to puzzle her, but she turned to move on, "Well good, we leave in a week."

July 8th

Home from work, found the awaited letter in my box.

Dear Christine,

I'm afraid our last call left neither of us happy. And the

fact that I was unable to call you over the 4th—as we worked throughout to make up for time lost—only compounded that unhappiness, at least for me.

Under this cloud I will not unnecessarily repeat a description of how the hours and days go up here, save to say that the filming proceeds well, as we move into the last stretch. I hope that the end will in some measure justify all the time spent, and time apart.

Alas, added into the mix are some difficulties which Kath has unexpectedly thrown up. These things, as you know, are seldom neat.

But all of this distracts from what I must attempt to somehow explain. With our multiple sharings, I can truthfully claim there is no one I would rather be with more than you. I have looked at our separation as a temporary one, created by commitments which pre-dated our discovery. (Candor nudges me, however, to remind you that at this point in my life, work is not of secondary importance.) And yet I earnestly look forward to our reunion, if that will still appeal to you.

You may think me weak, or duplicitous, then, when I attempt to explain that my physical condition and emotional state have lead me, at the end of these long days, back, temporarily, into intimacy with Pat. For each it is a haven against disappointment and strain. Her recent beau has signed off, unable apparently, or unwilling, to wait out her long absence from the city.

My excuse, if you care to know it, is simple. I need, and want, someone to embrace, and who will embrace back, at the end of these uncertain days. But by implicit understanding, this will not last beyond our work up here in the woods, although our friendship will.

I am sure no one—few women certainly—would understand and countenance this. And yet somehow I think, or hope, you might. And part of that hope rests on your understanding that there is no guarantee that I will ever literally see you again. The darkness may descend at any time. And with that prospect daily above me, I find I cannot but reach for and cling to those moments of still visible, physical closeness which remain possible, with someone I have long known and cared for.

I can only hope that this does not horrify you and compel you to crumple these pages. Perhaps when we both return to the city, we might make a new beginning under freer circumstances. That is one of the hopes which now sustain me—another being that I will indeed be able to see you when we meet. So far, one eye holds.

Despite all this, it is not a lie that I think of you daily and wish I could see you, even as these conflicting developments are equally insistent. You will always be the star in the sky for me, for now out of reach, but one with whom I have shared, and may share again, the silent joy, and sadness of our stumbling, uncertain work.

Thinking of you makes me smile most deeply, and if the request does not seem too unbearably discrepant, I would most deeply rejoice in hearing, at some point, from you, when you have digested these poor thoughts.

Most truly with love,
David

July 9th

At first, it had seemed . . . removed, unreal. Whose words were these? Why sent to me? . . . But slowly those words came blurring, bashing . . . They seemed to undo much, if not all, that he had professed . . . How could one trust him, if he was so . . . needy, a slave to the moment and appetite? . . . Did this confirm Kirsten's splenetic accusations about his reputation?

Scuffed around my aerie kicking things, then out onto the terrace, seeing nothing . . . wondering how to properly take this, the hurt, the disappointment, the distaste. And what loyalty do I owe him now? . . . May I not now write all I know? Would, to do any less, be a white-wash?

July 12th

Days, heavy days, have disappeared into my desks, at work and at home. Leave tomorrow. Yet have not begun to pack. The prospect barely stirs me, as I bend to consider re-casting his profile.

Kirsten blew in and out all day, dropping off items to read about the partnership and the Parisian publication. She kept hinting at the substantial role I will play, but though I listened and watched her closely, this prospect hardly excited me. Indeed it felt distant and wrong. And yet, is this other thing, David's excusing so much on behalf of his work, a warning to me that I may not be sufficiently clear-eyed and cool?

After lunch, a phone call from a Dr. Ismerlian, Metropolitan Hospital. "Christine Howth?"

"Yes?"

"Uh . . . Ms. Howth. I, uh . . . Sorry, here it is. We were wondering if you could possibly come here to identify someone."

"Identify?"

"Yes, an older woman . . ."

" . . . A homeless woman?"

"Yes. I'm afraid we don't have a name."

"How is she?"

" . . . I'm afraid . . . I'm sorry to have to report, that she died a few days ago, from pneumonia. A janitor found her only yesterday, curled up in an alleyway . . . We found your name in Social Services. I guess you called, said you'd been looking for her."

Mind fell blank, again, as if gently filling with snow.

"Ms. Howth? . . . Any chance you could come up?"

" . . . Yes, okay."

When I arrived, the doctor was paged. An intelligent, solid, dark-haired woman, she led me down several levels to the morgue, which was more horrifying for its dank, institutional airlessness.

A stainless steel table was wheeled to us, on which lay a bag such as one sees on the news, but barely filled. I closed my eyes as I heard the low whine of the zipper teeth slowly giving way. When I forced myself to look, it took a moment to make out a human face—so desiccated and diminished—but it was she . . . accompanied by the faint whiff of preserving chemicals, an eddy of unnatural substances.

Cold returned, winter's cold. I glanced at the doctor, whose face had softened.

Looking away somewhere, remembered her living, bird-like face, in the park, in my apartment, gazing up, blinking, alive.

What is this 'living?' In Father, Mother, in her—here one moment, filling a room, an hour—with movement, thought, yearning, and then no more, gone . . . . More than lungs pumping, more than a pulse or plasma . . . more than consciousness . . . A system, a galaxy, finite yet with potential . . . Felt my lungs leak. Did not inhale. To join her? And them . . . ? But then a cough and a jab of fear got the bags going again.

The doctor asked me what I knew. I put out a hand, to the icy steel table. Its cold snapped through me. Missed another breath, wheezed. The doctor offered a steadying hand on my shoulder. Briefly I told her our sad story, beginning with David's encounter in the rain. We knew next to nothing beyond her presumed name, found in her pocket. She said but a single word to me.

The doctor ran her eyes over the stone floor, then tried to comfort me by saying that Eleanor suffered from a number of problems, and there was little anyone could have done to sub-stantially improve or prolong her life . . . Her life . . .

Although I found I didn't quite believe the doctor, neither could I think what more might have been done, beyond finding her a last home.

Dr. Ismerlian asked if I knew of anyone else, who should know or would care.

"Only Mr. Loomis."

" . . . Would you two want a funeral?"

"He's away, working . . . I'm leaving tomorrow for Europe, for work." I looked at the doctor jotting this down. Her mind had moved on to the practical—undoubtedly necessary if she were to persevere.

She glanced up, nodded faintly. "We can take care of it. A service."

"Will you?"

Her eyes affirmed this. I turned away a little. Should I stay, and fly over in a day or so?

Perhaps Ismerlian read my thoughts. "There's no reason to stay, unless you want to. After the service, we can have her cremated. There's a city plot, for her ashes."

Eyes closed again. A passing dizziness. Not quite sure what I felt, or thought . . . Realized any gesture on my part would be for me . . . Kirsten would be annoyed. No point in calling and distracting David. My decision alone . . . Finally accepted that it would please my heart to stay, to say goodbye properly . . . even as my head urged me to go, get on the plane. Have mourned enough lately.

"You needn't decide now. Call me tomorrow, Ms. Howth."

Yes. "Thank you."

Found myself crossing ninety-sixth, over to the park and down past the Met, the great mausoleum which holds the past, and the best of our making. Walking helped. The sun felt gentle and warm as I descended the paths. Realized that to return home would be to slip under a shroud. Near work, on Third, stepped into a coffee bar. Bought Colombian and a scone, slumped on a stool, watching people passing on the sidewalk . . . as she no longer does. Was my sadness for the innocent-seeming, near-animal existence she lead, the lost potential? Or for my own losses, and mortality?

In the office, sought out Ben, to tell him the news. There was no particular reason why he should care, but he reacted kindly. We looked at each other with helplessness. Although I could not cry, I was aware of a moist, shrouded weight inside.

Decided that yes, my inclination was to be followed. I could not leave without something. Called Dr. Ismerlian, and asked what was possible. She explained their services in the hospital chapel.

"Tomorrow?"

"Probably. There's usually time."

She transferred me, and I scheduled one for three o'clock. And then I informed Kirsten. Her face turned stony, grew red, seemed about to burst. I repeated the story, the paltry circumstances. She rasped, "Christ! Just what I need!" And spun away. But peering back, she saw my resolve. Shook her head. Then inhaling deeply, shooed me out, to Billiam to book another flight the following day.

I called David's motel and left a message with the operator about Eleanor's death and service tomorrow.

Near midnight the phone rang. In bed I tried to imagine what might be said, but chose to let the machine pick up. And did not rise to listen to the message.

July 13th.

Saw Kirsten off from the office. She was not happy with me, but understood not to pester me—leaving only a packet to study for the Paris meetings.

I hung around the office, able to half-concentrate, scribbling thoughts. Melissa sat down for a while and asked about Eleanor. We discussed homelessness in a disjointed way, and I arranged for Ben to take my tutorees while I was in France.

And then I went up to the hospital.

She was in a casket, her forehead and nose prominent. It was difficult to look closely, but I forced myself. Her eyes and mouth were sunken, her body tiny, almost lost in the casket. Perhaps it was a mercy to be lifted from her life—I don't know.

I touched her hand—cold, rubbery—then stepped to the front pew and sat. Tried to make thoughts come, prayers. Remembered only a few words which fluttered down into my head, " . . . the snow falling faintly through the universe . . . upon all the living and the dead."

Yes, upon all . . .

And yet how unequal the snowfall. Some are given eulogies and tears. Others are all but forgotten. About some we know so little, almost nothing of their inner conversations and hopes . . . what thoughts might come as they curled up somewhere against the cold.

July 14th

On the evening plane. Kirsten bumped me from First Class, with her, to Coach. Which was fine. I had a window and an empty seat next to me. A relief to settle in. Turn my mind away, as he, evidently, does. Something to learn, after all those words of his, this selective focus. Probably one should devote oneself to an art only if it is absolutely necessary. Creating seems half a sham: papering over one's life and loves, exposing, manipulating, dismembering—pale invention, leaving too little time for life itself. At least work at the magazine brings me in contact with interesting people, fills a prescribed portion of the day, and pays the bills. What then do I hope to achieve in devising Eiley's story? A tale of a daughter and her mother? A warning against wasting life? Will Eiley's individuality carry it? Fortunately the wine they brought washed these thoughts away.

July 15th

Daylight and wisps of gray clouds, through which came glimpses of a rich green carpet—over which knights in heavy armor galloped to their deaths at Agincourt.

On the final swoop down, held my breath.

Taxiing through suburbs, saw they now look like ours, sadly. Even Frenchmen do it, soil their nests.

Little visual delight, until we reached the old city, bumping over narrow cobblestone streets, gliding over the graceful bridges, passing under smirking gargoyle gazes from gothic parapets. Isle Saint Louis. Horses' hooves clattering. Kirsten's tiny, immaculate hotel, a museum. See why she chose it. A doll's house, a fantasy she's secure enough to enter. As I was led to my room, it was up and into the 17th Century. Tiny lush rooms, with ingeniously designed, Lilliputian baths.

She had left a handwritten note welcoming me and directing me to meet her for lunch at the offices. As I never sleep on planes, part of me wanted to sink onto the bed, while part wanted to run out into the city of light.

A cab took me across the river to the Right Bank and the Rue Montaigne office, and I saw that this cityscape does not forget the land, but remaining connected, crowns her.

Upstairs: "Bonjour, bonjour, bienvenue, Mademoiselle Howth." Kirsten all but bowled me over with a hug, then introduced me to Antoine and Nadine, the publisher and editor of *La Rue*—in their forties, chic and sharp. Behind their smiles, they watched closely, to see whom Kirsten had brought.

Lunch was light and exquisite, and while we ate, Antoine summarized, bringing me up to date on the merging of the two magazines, whose purpose is to pool resources, reduce costs, and gain a window into the other world and market.

After coffee, introduced to Katerine—"comme tangerine," she lilted, then laughed. She was assigned to show me around and help me with my French. Her hair was beautiful and dark, her face round and pretty, like Françoise, a perfect Parisienne.

Katerine led me on a tour, beginning with the art department arrayed in floor-to-ceiling brilliant color prints interspersed by those in stark black-and-white. The men and women working over desks looked up for a moment with mild curiosity following Katerine's introduction. We moved on to editorial, layout, and commercial space. Pleasant nods . . . Bonjour . . . affairés . . . mesdames et messieurs.

I followed Katerine down the sweeping marble stair and out onto Rue Montaigne, where I glanced into windows, curious to compare them with Madison Avenue's. Here, not the wild panache to overwhelm the eye, but more subdued, with one item highlighted to entice.

Crossing the river, as I gazed at the city stretching low along the banks, our conversation tripped amicably back and forth. Having been told that I am a writer, Katerine asked if she could read Eiley's story. Flushing, I made excuses, and wondered if it would translate at all.

To my inquiry, she told me she lives in Montparnasse, with her boyfriend. At *La Rue*, Antoine and Nadine have promised that she can move into editing. "Mais, ils n'ont pas précisé la date!" she said, voice rising with light exasperation.

We walked to Musée D'Orsay where we stepped back into the 19th century—gliding up and down its stairs, among its paintings, sculpture, and furniture.

Later drifted through the narrow side streets of the Left Bank, stopping in a small square along Rue D. Furstenberg to listen to a student string quartet. Each block, each store, the Parisians themselves, offer style and detail to delight in. They shape, at least, the exteriors of their world.

In late afternoon, my head ringing with the French I strained to understand and fumbled to find phrases in, I heard myself cry, 'Enough! Must sleep!'

"Merci, Katerine, pour votre hospitalité et votre amitié."

"Mais, Christine, c'était avec plaisir. Bonsoir. A demain."

"A demain."

Crawled back to my isle and up to my room, curling onto my bed, to rest before dinner with Kirsten et ses amies.

Eyes closed, I floated above the roofs and graceful domes, through silent early evening. Where had she landed now? She who has been running, searching. Pulled a blanket completely over her.

A knock at the door. An older, bent, woman unhappily informed me, "Le téléphone, mademoiselle."

I followed her down the winding stairway, her every heavy step followed by a breath.

The voice in the phone was not, however, Kirsten's.

"Christine? Bonsoir, c'est Laurent. Comment ça va? Welcome to Paris."

" . . . Laurent? . . . Hello."

"I'm glad you've finally come."

"Yes . . . It's a wonder, to be here."

"I spoke to Kirsten, at *La Rue*. She said that your hosts, Antoine and Nadine, are taking you two to dinner, along with Gérard and a few others. And if you like, I might join the party too . . . If it would not make you uncomfortable. It is up to you."

I felt some hesitancy.

"They are all known to me, Christine. It need not be a big deal, as you say. If you are uncomfortable, perhaps we could meet another time."

"No, I'm sorry, Laurent—I'm half-asleep—but that would be fine. To meet there."

"Très bien . . . You know that as Kirsten has spoken highly of your writing, I am hoping to read some . . . But, well, I will pick you up at eight. Yes? I know your hotel."

"If it's not trouble for you. I can easily take a cab."

"Mais non, I will come. A bientôt."

Now awakened, wanted to see, to explore my neighborhood, and so wandered out through its tiny streets, peering up at the crooked buildings, through the still air of the little park, at the gray-green Seine sliding by, and at the diminutive couples strolling, trailing faint echoes of their footsteps.

By eight, had showered, dressed again, and was downstairs, stepping back outside into the blue light and nearly empty street. The straggling tourists had retreated to their hotels. A few Parisians strode quickly by hugging the walls. One, a man passing, stared at me. I turned a cool Parisian cheek.

Finally a figure in the dim light came gliding quickly, armored in a long raincoat. We bowed, eyes peering up, searching. Hands reached out. He leaned to kiss both cheeks. I looked away. My heart was racing.

We walked to find a cab. He asked how I was, how the Loomis article and Eiley's story were going. I was not happy to recall. Nor delighted by suddenly remembering that he has a wife, and children at home. But before I could ask about them, he leapt to talk about the merger.

At the restaurant, they greeted Laurent as a colleague, and our group was an even dozen. In addition to Kirsten, Gérard, Antoine, Nadine, I spoke with Jacqueline, François, and Maude—all alert and friendly.

When the hors d'oeuvres were served, all conversation converged over them, discussing tastes and textures—so noticeably different than our new world versions. Fish, mushrooms, pastry shells, relishes. Gérard and Antoine beckoned the chef over to compliment and inquire, but the details were exchanged too rapidly and idiomatically for me to catch.

Antoine asked us if New York remains in decline, and whether crime is still a danger. Kirsten was eager to correct this, "Not at all. Everywhere there are signs of revival; the economy 's back; crime is down. Oh no, not at all." And Laurent elaborated, "New York est une dynamo, Manhattan, au moins, visibly infused with energy by the newest arrivals."

Nadine asked about Eiley's story, suggesting some interest. I tried to give her a sense of what I'm attempting, and Laurent, I noticed, listened as he spoke with Maude.

I heard Kirsten confide to Antoine that my role with the magazines may bring me back to Paris for a considerable time. With this my heart skipped a beat. I felt the tug of opposing futures. The possibilities here seemed alluring, the realities coolly uncertain.

Later, Laurent and I said goodnight to the rest and stepped out for a walk around Le Marais, not far from the restaurant. He told me of his publishing business, and asked me to tell him more about Eiley.

But I decided it was time for the other, deferred discussion, and asked, "Pardonnez moi, Laurent, mais comment va votre famille? Votre femme et vos enfants?"

He was surprised, although not entirely. Glancing at me, then around at the square we'd entered, and finally at the walk ahead, he replied carefully, "Toute la famille va très bien, merci. Nous sommes mariés depuis dix ans maintenant. Nous sommes . . . des amis . . . We have three children, two girls and a boy, a darling boy, four years, who unfortunately suffered problems at birth . . ."

Our eyes met carefully. He glanced away. "He is . . . a very sweet boy, sweet but limited, I'm afraid. He will never learn very much. He will never be fully independent. And I cannot, could never, leave him. He is . . . we are all bound, in a way. He's a good, kind child, and my wife, Nicki—Well, we have agreed to do what we must, together, which is not a hardship; we get along; but it is, I realize, an even heavier burden for her." He breathed, "And so although some of the joys between us have gone, we live together and help each other."

Squinting ahead, he looked down. "Sometimes I think of all the things he will never know . . . bien évidemment, ses attentes sont moindres." Laurent's shoulders slumped slightly. "It is hard for Nicki, for both of us, to look into his eyes."

Though I turned to see Laurent more clearly, his eyes remained staring at the walk.

"And yet the life he knows is not so bad, with your love," I ventured.

Considering this, he moved his jaw, but displayed no signs that this afforded any relief.

"So Laurent . . . what do you want for us?"

Now he looked over with an even gaze. "A book to read and publish maybe . . . A woman with whom to talk about things that lie outside the home . . . To spend a night, several . . . To feel alive again in ways that . . ." Although his thoughts fell away, his eyes, taking me in, did not waver.

I was surprised, that I was not offended. Perhaps it was his straightforwardness. "I'm not sure that I, or my book, are exactly what you hope for. The book is not finished. It needs much work."

He seemed unconcerned.

"I'll say this, Laurent: you are direct."

"I will tell you what I remember. I remember our goodbye in New York—an intensity never experienced before—unique. And it is my belief that it still lives."

A twinge of that faint memory carried me off from any sense of time. Eventually, I suppose, I heard him breathe.

"You need not decide immediately. Tell me instead about David Loomis, whose last two films I have admired."

I felt myself start at this, as it remained something I was not eager to recall. I gazed around the square we were slowly circling. " . . . Well . . . I have completed my interviews, and observations. Now I must write it up."

"And what is your estimation of him?"

"I'm not sure . . . Recently I was disappointed, personally, by him . . . But I can say that he is a . . . mixed man . . . a good director, but an often absent, uncertain father." I looked at Laurent, who seems not to be. "He is something, I suppose, of a puppeteer, pulling strings, frequently . . . an illusionist, and idealist . . . Alas a bad driver . . . a guilty moralist . . . a meta-physician pondering . . . self-absorbed . . . indiscriminate . . . Yet the actors, and the crew, like him, admire him . . . But all together . . . I don't know . . ."

Laurent was watching closely.

I shrugged, "I don't know how to fit it into one piece, and weigh it."

He laughed a little. "Au contraire, I think you do."

When I found his face, he was smiling almost slyly at me, and although I tried to sound cool when I summoned a few other things to add, I'm afraid I could not entirely hide the emotion.

We strolled on, and shortly, when I peered over, he now seemed quite different to me, having divulged his son's affliction—certainly more the father now, and perhaps husband. Turning, as if he'd heard my thoughts, he reached out for a hand, which I gave him.

July 16th

The next day I worked with Katerine and some of the others. At the offices, Nadine and I reviewed copies of *La Rue* and *Avenue* and discussed how translations might go. We discussed which types of articles and stories might travel well, in both directions. But Kirsten was seldom to be seen, and in the late afternoon, Katerine and I worked on my French.

I asked Katerine if she was happy with her boyfriend. Matter of factly, she paused, reflected, then allowed things were okay, "Ça va." I asked if she hoped for something more. She looked at me with some surprise. "Peut être, mais, c'est un rêve Américain, Christine. To believe there is some heaven on this Earth."

I was surprised that at her young age she was so certain, and so resigned.

July 17th

In the late afternoon, Laurent came to the office and together we went up into Montmartre.

"Christine," he asked, "do you think you could work and live in Paris, for a time?"

"Is that what they are thinking?"

"Something of that, I believe. Obviously they must consult with you."

"What specifically would I do? Did they say?"

"No, I assume what you do now, no?"

"I write now, collaborating on stories and articles."

Eyes met, as I imagined this life, imagined an apartment, dark with great mirrors reflecting the outside light, and roofs stretching out beyond, and the cafés, and the office.

"So? What do you think?" he wondered.

"Maybe. I have been looking . . . for something new, for something right."

He studied me seriously, and indeed I wondered how truly open I was to this.

We walked up through Montmartre and north to the neighborhoods beyond, entering a world left behind, caught in mid-century: Boulevard Colcouquot and others, where the architecture is graceful and muted, along with the atmosphere and people. The dying light enhanced this feel, as slowly we returned along the winding streets and stairs and pocket parks of Montmartre, away from the touristy center. I was moved, and tried to imagine that this could be my world, the right place for me, for a time—where I might expand, and focus in on what I want to say, or write. I found myself clinging to his arm, so that he had to bring me along a little. Alone on a stairs, we stopped and looked ahead, down over the darkening city. I was aware of some insistent pulse, some anticipation. Imagining myself living here, I felt that I was soaring out over the stairs, and city—then saw that his face was near, watching. We studied one another, taking in each facet. Then leaned to kiss—sweet . . . eager. It did not end, but went on for minutes it seemed. Alone in a city where I was unknown, in a time unconnected to anything, it might have been a life unto itself.

When we walked again, he asked quietly, "Christine, would you come to my hotel?"

I looked at him, his brown eyes, his fine Gallic nose and lips.

"It is a very nice one," he added with some bemusement.

I felt myself smile. "Modern? Period?"

Faint smile. "Restoration." The dwindling daylight was reflected upon his cheeks and in his brown eyes. I found myself, or rather lost myself, in the softness of his skin—surprising for a man. Wondered if his wife notices anymore.

"Christine?"

"Yes?"

"Would you come with me?"

"I am thinking."

An indistinct tremor flickered in his cheek. His brow creased just noticeably, at this hesitation, at the possibility of rebuff.

Because, at that moment I had no one to answer to, no one I was tied to, no one who cared what I did, it was not so difficult a decision. But I wondered what it would mean, if anything. "Laurent . . . D'accord, je viens."

His hotel was all the expansive elegance that ours resisted. Endless rooms off the lobby, countless bouquets in the empty halls. His suite was equally large and graceful, seemingly all in satin. After he opened a bottle, we talked for a while, finding a certain pleasure, or amusement in holding back—a taste shared, raising the ante, in our glancing smiles, fleeting touches.

By chance he happened upon a radio station playing a Viennese waltz, and he took my hand. We danced, but I no longer remembered the steps, and could not keep up. He suggested we take off our shoes, to move more easily. Bending, we kicked them off under the chairs. It was so freeing to be on my toes, feet in the soft carpet.

In the midst of a turn, he leaned to my ear and whispered, "J'aimerais te deshabiller. Tu permets?"

My French failed me, a laugh caught in my throat. I swallowed, not to choke. Closed my eyes, smiling, amused, holding him. But he carefully released himself from my arms, hands, and turned me around. Fingers pushed my hair aside, tracing my neck. Necklace unclasped, lifted away, as I was held between delight and uncertainty. Yet could not remain forever still, and so turned and pressed into him. Wanted to hold and be still. But he pulled back, turning me again. Sleeve buttons opened, a gentle tugging my blouse down along my arms, which rose as his fingers trailed over my back and shoulders, plucking and playing. He released my bra, sliding it off my shoulders, to the floor. Wanted to turn to him, but he embraced my waist restraining me. I felt his heat through his shirt. Soft hands, then nails moved over my stomach, tracing, stirring me—was barely able to breathe. Things began cascading, as he was kissing me. Reached for his shoulders, and we were sidestepping, dancing, to and down onto the satin spread.

Skirt unbuttoned, slipped off. Hot hands, urgent fingers, curling unaccustomedly, all gently stirred, squeezed. Heard myself inhale deeply, felt myself rising to him. "Laurent . . ."

But he slipped away, kissing me. Heard the rustle of clothes, then he was next to me on his side. I felt his weight gently descending—wanted his mouth—eyes rolling back, sliding, surging, out over the city, soaring . . . then falling, tumbling, away . . .

Darkness. The tick of a clock. Could not move. No need to. Eyes shut, away from flickering fire, into darkness.

In time he moved off, shoulder to shoulder. Lips brushed. Mind groped.

Moments seemed to pass. He moved, half on me again, chest to chest. A long kiss. Yes, without end.

Morning. Light at the edges of the drapes. He breathed just audibly next to me. I rose and held my breath, motionless as the drapes, then slipped to the bath.

In the cavernous shower, questions streamed, beat upon my brow. I wiped them away, and stepping out, wrapped his magenta-streaked robe around me.

Awakening, he ordered breakfast which shortly was wheeled in. Juice, coffee, croissants, fresh fruit. We settled down on the couch in the semi-light. The same questions attempted to return, but were firmly spurned as I sipped coffee and tugged at a fleshy croissant.

When we had eaten, he stood and drew me up to him and led me quickly back to the shower where I was disrobed and pressed against the cool tile. The warm water ran down between us. He was touching me, and I felt my knees go weak as I knew I wanted him again. Arms around him, he lifted me and pressed me against the wall now warm and wet. All was streaming, flowing. Voices, our voices, could be heard above the water spattering, before the final cry, when we stumbled out together and sank upon the thick bath rug.

Eventually, when we had dressed, we went out. Walked through the Tuilleries, past La Louvre. Arm in arm, without words.

July 19th

Another evening took us to Montparnasse and a choral concert in a lovely Byzantine church. French songs and early hymns lifted me up and through the unusual, circular, pillared nave, and beyond, into the apse. From our seats, the female soloist was in silhouette, head back, arms rising and spreading, her voice clear and strong and lovely—something that was, I think, the most perfect embodiment of the spirituality of which her songs spoke.

By chance we encountered Katerine, at intermission, with her friend, Philippe. He was tall and thin, with lively eyes—a student of philosophy. And Katerine looked much more happy than her own assessment led me to foresee.

Later, Laurent and I walked hand-in-hand through the Left Bank.

"Laurent, the singing moved me, much more than I expected."

He smiled faintly, through some thought he had.

"May I ask you something, Laurent? How did you come to live as you do? Did you plan it, or did it just happen?"

With his Gallic pout, he refocused his mind on this.

"My uncle was in publishing. I thought I would like it. It seemed a noble business, creating beautiful, worthy objects."

"Have you ever had second thoughts? Wished you'd tried something else?"

A second, pensive pout. "No, not seriously."

"Did you ever think of writing?"

He laughed, caught by surprise. "Mais non. I have not the talent, nor the patience." Glancing at me he wondered, "Why do you ask?"

"I fear it's not possible to write seriously and live a balanced life."

He seemed surprised. "Depends, no, on who you are. And what and how you write."

"It appears, to me, that writing fiction takes all my energy."

" . . . Well . . . But Kirsten, as I told you, speaks highly of your writing."

"I can't quite imagine how she sees it; our tastes are so different."

"Would you want me to read your manuscript and give you my opinion? I read and have read many books."

"I would not hesitate, if it were further along, but it stumbles so."

"I have read works in progress, frequently. Even in English." He smiled lightly, kindly.

"Well thank you. I also want to ask you if you think I'm foolish to hold this job, as I try to write. Should I do one or the other?"

"Not necessarily, though only you can truly answer for yourself."

"I fear two things: if I throw all into it, I still may fail; and if I do not commit entirely, I may fall back into the closed world from which I've recently begun to emerge."

He reflected, before looking carefully at me. "From those I've known, and read about, many writers feel they have no choice, but to do what they do."

Yes, I thought. I suspect I have not quite reached that imperative.

"Perhaps, Christine, you should ask yourself how strong is that need in you."

"I have. And the answer, I guess, is strong but not consuming. Particularly as I fear my talent is modest, at best. I wonder if I can produce anything that will . . . please me."

"Some devote years to learning the craft."

"Yes. That, I think, I'm prepared to do."

"It is a gamble, of course."

"Yes."

"But those who must are not dissuaded by that risk."

"No . . . I sense, I fear, that despite my doubt, nothing else will be as compelling."

"Then perhaps the only way to resolve it is to try."

"Devote everything?"

He opened his mouth to answer, smiled shyly, then studied me again. "Again, only you, Christine, can answer . . . Nicki and I found the plans we made were bent by circumstance. We do not live quite as we thought we would, though we manage. You on the other hand are unusually free, it seems."

I felt myself breathe involuntarily, deeply. "I think I must try."

As our eyes met, his smiled, as from a distance, but in support. Then he asked, "What does your friend, Loomis, say?"

I recognized that I now felt detached enough to consider it. "Maybe that like Freud's counsel on love, there is no advice."

"He certainly has continued telling his stories."

"Yes. Sometimes it glows in him. Other times, all the faults he finds in his films, and himself, haunt him and leech out any satisfaction."

"But still he works."

"Making one after the other . . . Filling some need."

Laurent, I now noticed, was now watching me closely. "You are involved with him?"

"We were, a bit, but time and clarity have shattered it." Out of the corner of my eye, I saw that he nodded and looked away.

We walked silently for a time, before I sought and took his hand and brought it to my lips, then held it to my breast, thinking that in many ways here was perfect physical union, kindness, and comfort.

In the remaining evenings, Laurent and I enjoyed each other, but never again quite reached the intensity of that concert night, nor of our first night in his hotel, try though we did. Despite our physical openness, and harmony, it was as if our minds were drawn elsewhere by some other intensity.

He read some of Eiley's chapters, and attempted to be encouraging, but I saw that much more of the sweep of her story was necessary for him to judge or consider publishing.

"I like your voice. And the story," he said. "It is fresh; it pricks and captures me. But I will want to see more, and to go deeper."

"Yes . . ."

Despite this falling off, Laurent showed me a Paris I would not have otherwise seen and in which I deeply delighted. For a short time, I lived the life of a Parisian. At the end, we agreed to meet when work or travel permitted, in New York or here. Indeed saying goodbye I felt a physical longing, even as the rest had lost some of its urgency and excitement.

Only over the last two days did Kirsten make time to meet with me. "I apologize, Christine. Yet I trust things have not been dull for you."

"Nor for you, madame."

Our eyes lingered on the other.

"How did it go with Gérard?"

"I'll get into that later, but we want to continue spending time together."

I bowed in happiness for her.

"That means, more time over here. So that I will have to make a number of arrangements. And one of them is the possibility of having you come back here, for an extended stay, to essentially represent *Avenue* in this office, for the initial phase. And of course to learn this side of the business." She smiled briefly, behind which she sought my reaction. I put on my poker face.

"But my ultimate purpose is . . . to find someone who can help run the magazine, in New York." Narrowing her eyes she looked more closely. "And I'm thinking that person may be you."

Though I saw it coming, still it chilled me. "Oh? . . . Really? . . . Well, thank you . . ."

Perhaps she saw my ambivalence, or perhaps she didn't, as possibly she didn't want to. Or maybe it was impatience, or her own thoughts. Anyway, she rushed on, "You can write and can judge whether others can. You pick things up quickly and get things done. You'd be surprised how many in our office can do neither . . . While I understand there are some differences between us, I feel we're sufficiently on the same wave length. Of course there would be a trial period. We'd work together, quite closely. And eventually, when I'm over here, you'd be overseeing things in New York, something all this new communications business makes possible."

As I knew she was studying me, I tried to hide my uneasiness. The fact was, I realized, I'd been leaning more and more the other way.

Finally detecting something of this, she adjusted, "However none of this will begin until the first of the year, so we have time. But give it some thought, serious thought. It's really quite an interesting job; the variety is unsurpassed; it's never dull; and you would be paid handsomely, very handsomely. We'll talk, from time to time."

Evening brought our farewell dinner, and I quite enjoyed talking to Antoine, Nadine, and François, now that my French was more serviceable. And yet I realized that there was something ultimately remote about the conversations. As Kirsten's protégé, they treated me well enough, and were polite, indeed interesting, but they kept a distance, revealed nothing personal.

Alone in my tiny hotel room, turning back the covers—Laurent, I imagined, was already home—I visualized all these intersecting paths, each extending beyond the horizon. With the year's losses has come a sense of impermanence, and from that, a desire to both explore and to burrow into something whole.

I realized I'm fortunate, even to be able to consider this. Yet given this luck, I must not waste it. I have seen, through his whole mixed story, what David gains from work, joining his entire being, animating his every fiber.

In the morning, Kirsten returned early, and we packed, talking between our adjacent rooms. And then one of the office staff from *La Rue* drove us to the airport.

As we made our way through the city, I thought of Laurent, and somehow felt our closeness in the bronze light reflected by the windows of the older buildings, and in the cracks and stains on their facades—the cost perhaps of their silent witness to the centuries of man's insistent writhing. And while I recognized that thrill of our closeness, and something of our friendship, would probably fade, as the seasons do, I was no longer doubtful . . . that things were possible.

July 22

Summer haze envelopes all I see. The grays of the sky, buildings, and river are one. Upstairs, my apartment is dim and still, as I put down my sagging suitcase and inhale. It feels heavy to be back. The future, facing Kirsten's offer and the direction of my life, hangs unhappily at the center of what seems a maze. Paris is already a faint halo back through the night, although the memory of Laurent clings along my entire length.

At my desk, I stare down at Eiley's pages—drafts. Unable to draw in a full breath.

On my machine, a message from Martina, for David, asking me to call when I return.

July 24th

Call the office, telling William I won't be in. Haven't recovered.

"Hey, tell me about it. Jet lag's a bitch. Shall I put you through?"

"No. Just tell her I called."

Sat down wearily at my desk, holding my pen. Only to find that nothing would come, until finally bits and pieces began stumbling forth, and I crawled after them.

> Now she rose and walked to the bedroom, and pulled out her large suitcase and heaved it onto the bed. She emptied the blankets and sheets it held, and groped around in other bags and boxes for an assortment of clothing, and stuffed them into the bag. She found her raincoat, put it on and packed several books.
>
> Then she wrote him a note.
>
> My dear Karl,
>
> I apologize more deeply than I can here express to you, but if I attempted this in any other way, I wouldn't have the strength to carry it through. I need to leave, get away for a while, knowing neither where nor how long. I need to find

out what the possibilities are. Need to feel, at least briefly, the nub of life. Yes, I laugh a little, too, but it's what I feel, and can no longer deny.

I do not mean other people, Karl dear. I could find no one better than you. But mean maybe some other way of living, maybe other priorities, other means of reaching into life.

This escape may last a day, a week, a lifetime.

I will write you. I don't know where I'm going. I know it's thoughtless of me, but I fear there is not, at this moment, enough of me sufficiently alive to give you. This is not your deficiency, but mine. Try to understand that it is the personal craziness of a Yankee girl cast into the wrong world and still unable to identify exactly where she should be.

Love, Eiley.

She left the note on the floor where he would see it when he walked in. She left the lights on, and the radio playing the ever-modulated WQXR announcer. And she went out, hurrying so that she would not run into him, leaving through the back way, and hailing a cab.

August 1st

Outside the continuing humidity transforms all into an underwater world. I hide up in my cooled cell, crossing out pages and pages of Eiley, passing on to her the new sense of things I have brought back from across the ocean.

At some point I became aware that the phone was ringing, that someone was reaching through the summer heat to my bubble.

"Christine . . ."

" . . . David . . ." Although not entirely unexpected, I was not prepared. "Hello . . ."

"How are you? How was Paris?" Uneasiness wavered in his voice, as well it should. And yet I recognized that most of my anger and hurt had been released in Paris. "I'm fine. Paris was beautiful, stimulating."

I heard a just-audible expelling of relief. "Good, I'm glad."

"And how's the movie, and you?"

"Finished, thank God . . . the filming anyway."

"Congratulations. But what about you?"

"Experiencing the joy of reprieve, as you can well imagine."

I could. Yet in the silence that followed, perhaps we both wondered where to go. He, of course, owed at least an explanation.

"Chris, we need . . . I need, to talk."

"I'm not sure there seems to be much connection between all our talking and what happened."

"I understand, but I'd like to explain, better than my letter did, what was going on."

Yes, but did I want to go through it all again? "I don't know, David, what really could be added?"

"Well . . . we must talk, if we're to have anything at all."

"Maybe that's my point. I'm not sure I want to get into it again."

This, I'm afraid, silenced him. But in the intervening quiet, I cannot claim that my feelings did not lean toward him.

"Chris, don't you think we owe ourselves a new start, under clearer circumstances? What we had was not so easily replaced, if replaceable at all."

"I'm not so good at compartmentalizing."

"But you knew better than anyone the situation."

"Pat knew, I believe." I heard him breathe, even as I felt that bruise growing tender once more.

"You accepted nothing of what I wrote?"

"David, we may simply be in different places, wanting different things."

"Of course. We were. But now we're free to reshape things."

This, still, was not something I was at all sure I wanted. "Possibly, David. But possibly the time for that has passed."

" . . . Oh Chris . . . One does not find what we had."

Not exactly, I was thinking. Yet we both found something, didn't we. "David, I thought you were going to take some time off now."

Another breath expelled quietly, at my sidestepping. "I had hoped to, but now the distributors need a print by early next year, and we've got to get cutting, get the music set, the sound effects laid in—everything . . ."

"And how's your eye?"

"Much the same. I've seen my doctor. We may try some different things."

"Medicines?"

"Yes. But listen, couldn't we give it a try? It seems such an utter waste to let it slip away . . . just die."

"I . . . I don't know. How could I believe . . . ?"

"You were there. You saw everything."

"I had thought so. But as I said, I don't know whether I want to return to all that."

"Chris . . . I'm asking."

Something in his voice struck me as exposed, unrehearsed. Something in his tone caught me. "David, I don't know . . . Maybe . . . I mean I'll try to give it some thought, but . . ."

"I'd appreciate that . . . Would you call me, when you have? . . . I'll give you the number."

"Do you understand my hesitancy?"

"Of course."

Did he blurt this out too glibly? Or was it relief?

When I hung up, I felt some annoyance that I had agreed to open it again. And felt even more annoyed, when trying to return to Eiley, found that I could not put it aside.

August 5th

Maybe it's been the heat, but the days have dragged on at the office. I've found it difficult to concentrate, particularly on the new article Ben and I are attempting. My head 's felt clogged, my entire body on-hold. At home, I've tried to follow Eiley running fiercely down one wrong trail after the other. Sometimes I catch sight of her, a stray cantering through the alleyways, nose to the ground, following some scent.

August 7th

Have concluded, finally, that I may only be able to clear my mind by going to see him, and separating what's real from what's imagined.

His editing suite lies at the edge of honky-tonk, or what remains of it, at 51st and Broadway: the strip of lights, the arcades of video games, the fast food and cheap goods—at least until the corporate giants, already among them, complete their erasure. It's also the edge of the theatre district, where one holds one's breath in hope of being drawn into something truly moving.

Upstairs, I was lead back to the cutting room where I found him perched owl-like upon a stool staring down at a scene on the editing machine. When he turned, he was much as I remembered, though tanned from outdoor days, and bent, it seemed, around his chest. Hastily he put out a cigarette and came warmly toward me, although he must've noticed I was restrained. "Thanks for coming down." Embracing, I leaned stiffly, holding off feeling. He introduced me to his editor, Jeff. Between them, on the screen, stretched a hazy panorama of the gray-green Adirondacks.

He pulled another stool forward for me to sit on and peer over Jeff's shoulder. As he did, I saw that he'd lost weight. I tried to see into his left eye, but it was shadowed by his brow.

He asked Jeff to roll the scene. The blanket of ancient mountains jerked into motion, and we swooped into the deep uphill woods, through dark and darker shades of green, over moss-covered trunks and earth-brown rocks and roots. Descending and ascending over the forest floor, the camera winged rhythmically down, then up, through sunlight and shade, the vantage shifting almost imperceptibly between Stephen's and the tracking shots of him jogging, puffing, diving. It was beautiful and more stirring than I remembered, or could have foreseen— all swaying and swimming. Stephen had become a creature of the deep wood, a centaur, seen fleetingly, sometimes in slow motion, his face marbleized by the mottled light, ursine eyes moving fiercely, heavy with intent.

As the effect accumulated, I felt a flow, then a rush, of joy for David. If this was representative, he'd done it, taken a step beyond his other films and transformed this small-town story into something multi-leveled, and maybe mythic. Stephen was a creature groping for understanding and contribution, struggling to find his stride, find a purpose, survive—inspired yet learning to compromise, limited yet aware, realistic yet hopeful—climbing slowly, crevice by crevice, knuckles nicked open, bleeding as he scrambled on.

Glancing at David, I found his head turned to favor his good eye, arms folded across his chest, as he watched with attentive stillness—a weightless yet uncrushable shell.

When the sequence ended, Jeff stopped the machine. The two conferred on what might be changed or tightened.

And then, turning, he asked, "So, do you recognize it?"

"Of course. And yet you've altered it. Made it something strange—not just another pretty scene, but a mix of ferocity, turmoil, and hope."

He looked closely at me, perhaps wondering at my words.

Then he asked Jeff to thread another scene, and while Jeff was occupied, he told me in a low voice, "You know, Mandy 's gone out to L.A. with John." An eyebrow rose, his mouth distorted.

"Oh dear . . ."

He looked involuntarily away. "She claims he's going to get her a job on his new film. I tried to warn her, stop her, but . . ."

Poor girl, I thought. How soon until she's dumped and sent reeling back across the country on the red-eye. And as if David understood my thoughts, he faintly nodded.

The next scene was set at the club, where Teresa had come out to see about the jobs advertised in the classifieds. John, to my grudging acknowledgement, so inhabited Stephen that I found him entirely credible. Or maybe it was time and distance. On the other hand, Teresa's flinty diffidence was more difficult to accept. I kept muttering to myself, "What's your problem, girl, what's your problem?"

She stood glancing around at the club's interior. "When you gonna get this place ready?" she asked. "When's it gonna open?"

"Soon. Soon as I can."

Teresa's skeptical glance took in the unfinished details. She didn't bother hiding her doubt. "I'd say it needs a paint-job, for one thing."

Nodding, Stephen surveyed the place, then offered to take her on a tour of the bar, stage, kitchen, and dressing rooms. Their glancing appraisals of one another belied their coolness. Their situation was, familiarly, that they had few others to answer to—but with many fewer alternatives.

Near the entrance, he stopped and inquired carefully, "You were, uh, married to Bayard, weren't you?"

"For three long years . . . Two girls is what I got out of it."

"Sorry . . ."

She shrugged it off. "Don't be. I love my girls. Don't make the mistake of gettin' that wrong."

I glanced at David and discovered that though he faced the screen, he'd closed his eyes. I wondered if he was listening or dreaming, but saw his fingers tapping out odd rhythms on his leg. In front, hand on the control, Jeff watched without blinking.

It was nearly ten before David and I made it out to a Seventh Avenue restaurant, mostly empty, and settled in behind a large table. He ordered a scotch and filet, and I, a glass of wine. We looked at each other in the low light.

"Those scenes were good, David. Beautiful."

Appearing not to have heard, he sipped his drink and seemed to be formulating what he wanted to say. "Chris, I felt derelict when I heard about poor Eleanor. I should've taken her home that evening . . . although I felt I couldn't sacrifice Marnie, or my work." He stared into his drink, his mouth stretching wide with discomfort. "Guess too often, when it comes down to it, work gets the nod."

Silently I agreed, wondering how long he had acknowledged

this. I tried, however, to ease his self-accusation, "The doctor at the hospital told me that there was little we could have done."

He glanced up—good eye strained, weary—then looked down again. For some moments we were silent, before he again found me. "Should I try to explain about Pat?"

As our eyes took in the other, I was not sure I wanted to hear. I sputtered, "That phone call to your room, with Pat there, stung . . . stung quite a bit."

He reflected, then acknowledged this. "I'm sorry . . . I was exhausted. I'd reached the point where I could only keep one thing in focus at a time. To concentrate on anything was an effort." Brow creasing, he glanced at me, then out across the room. "But before that, I'd felt uneasy, guilty toward you, with respect to my growing limitations . . . Whereas Pat and I have long recognized our even greater limitations, and have accepted them. If we occasionally go beyond that, it's, well . . . physical need, or sympathy—however difficult for others that may be to accept. It's helping one another get through. I'm pretty sure she saw my divorce coming long before I did, yet was always ready to offer encouragement or just listen. Our friendship comes out of our work. She gives me the actor's view, of a scene say, and I try to explain what I need."

From within his vulnerable eye, he peered out to see if I understood, and I suppose, in some place, I did.

"Whereas Chris, you and I—I thought—were two of a kind, of the same egg, cut from the same cloth."

I felt myself wincing, wondering how this could be true. "If that were so, how could we . . ." Yet I was interrupted by a flash of Laurent's face. "Why . . . would we have gone off so easily?"

"Circumstances, don't you think? . . . The movie, Kath and me, the girls, your work . . . And as I said, I felt wrong, sometimes, drawing you along after me."

My brain seemed to reject this, choke on it. Too much . . . not credible . . . I wondered if his mourning Eleanor, and perhaps Kath in his intermittent way, were, in reality, mourning his own incapacity to commit to anyone—outside his work. I wondered if

Stephen too suffers from this, as his feelings for Teresa surge, then waver.

David ate a little, carving his filet fine, and we sipped our drinks as our eyes and minds wandered. When we spoke again, we circled around the future. I can't say I knew what I wanted, even as I felt my eyes blinking, trying to clear. We eventually decided to see each other when time allows—his time. He maintained that his life will change when the film is done, and while I didn't place great store in this, I could not pretend that I was entirely indifferent.

I wondered about escorting him back to the hotel he had just moved into—his belongings packed and placed in storage, living out of a suitcase. We walked together for several minutes, before I asked him how to reach him, but he could hardly think. "Oh . . . well, call the editing room, or Martina, or the hotel. If I'm tied up, leave a message. I'll get back."

Over doubts and a feeling of distance, I leaned to kiss his cheek, offering encouragement as much as anything. When he returned it, to my cheek, his lips were dry and thin, his breath sour.

As we turned to our respective cabs, I felt a stab inside and swung back, to see him bending, disappearing into the dark doorway of his cab. I called, "David!" But his door had closed.

August 12th

At the office, intermittent despondency weighs upon me, sometimes bringing my writing to a halt, as I picture him curled on his editing stool, or alone at night in his hotel room, barely able to pull back the covers. But other images come back too: Paris and its prospect of a new life, the excitement of the unknown, the elegiac Parisian neighborhoods, somehow reminiscent of the world when I was young—and Laurent, too, in the shower, or expressing the melancholic joy he feels for his son.

Yet piled on these: my own decisions, Kirsten's expectations, and up in my aerie, Eiley waiting for the insight which our joint experiences might be expected to unlock.

Aug. 13th

Melissa came in during the afternoon, to give me her reaction to my first installment—a meeting I scheduled when Kirsten was out of the office for two days.

"Well, Chris, let me say that unfortunately I found his reputation more interesting than what you wrote about him."

"Oh-oh . . ." Ready for mild criticism, I saw I'd better brace myself for something sharper.

"I cannot help but feel, Chris, that you've written an apologia, skipping past his problems to praise his art."

"But it's his work, his art, that I'm looking at here. Not the other things."

"I'm afraid I also found it a little pedantic. But foremost, our readers, and their advocate, Madame K., will want the artist, above his art, stripped bare, front-on, warts and all—With only a side-order of ideas. You know that, Chris. At the very least, Kirsten will want the gore about his love life." Melissa arched her eyebrows, mildly incredulous that I needed to be told.

"But Melissa, understand that he's devoted his filmmaking to the exploration and dramatization of choices in life."

She held up her palms to me. "Hey, I'm just warning you of the approaching storm."

"Is there nothing you think I can counter with? If we eliminate the discussion of his ideas, we eliminate what's valuable and unique about him, and the piece."

"I don't know, maybe you can bargain for a few lines of ideas, with paragraphs of gossip."

While I saw that she was only half-serious, her prediction about Kirsten's reaction was deadly earnest. I tried arguing that those interested in Loomis's career would not be seeking gossip, but Melissa was unswayed, "You know she's not going to be satisfied."

Facing the prospect of rejection, I rushed to insert a few changes, in the beginning, to draw the casual reader in, before more substantive issues were introduced.

As I sat rereading it, a guy called, saying he was a friend of Josh. "Was wondering if you'd care to get a drink? Josh said he thought we'd enjoy meeting, and he'd be glad to vouch for me."

What? At first thinking 'no, no, no', I abruptly reversed myself. We met after work in a bar on Lex. Nice enough, attractive, but turned out he doesn't read, much beyond law briefs, *and* he plays golf. What would we talk about, if our paths ever crossed at all? No, not the match of which I dream, having witnessed several such marriages, having lived through my own. After two drinks, I think he got the picture—perhaps as I was describing David's labors, and wondering about lifestyles and their costs.

Need to call Josh, to explain, and ask him what the hell he was thinking.

August 20th

We've talked on the phone, but each time was brief, limited. Yet, in the summer heat, I've found the hurt I ran into in July has nearly baked away. And his voice, I'm discovering, keeps re-playing in my head.

When we met, after nearly two weeks, it was in his hotel bar, at ten. A quick drink and he wanted to walk. "Get outside. Move a little." His stiffness from hours of sitting was evident—as was mine, I've recently noticed, from hours at my office desk. And though he smiled, he could not hide the strain on him. We walked along Fifth, in the fifties, with a smattering of tourists, and several of the lost ones.

"So, how's the editing going?" I asked. "Where are you now?"

He looked up at the buildings. "We're working on the town meetings, with Sam, Stephen, Harvey and so forth."

"Yes, I remember. How's it going?"

"Okay. A few problems."

"May I ask you what they are?"

Lightly he brushed his fingers across his eyes to push away a hair. We turned into Rockefeller Center, and down the flowered promenade. "In a few cases, the best acting takes aren't the best camera-takes. We've been playing around, and have had some of the rejected takes printed, so that we have more options to cut back and forth between. But it's more cutting than I intended."

We paused and gazed down at the tables set up where the skating rink lies in winter. His thoughts, with his good eye, seemed to wander. Without introduction, he suddenly confided, "I was thinking I should spend a weekend with Marnie—go somewhere. Lately she's come down to the editing room, and Jeff's been good with her, showing her the process, letting her run the Steenbeck."

Hearing about Marnie brought back the entire cast. "Well, that's a step. No?"

He nodded from within his thoughts, gazing down at the mostly empty tables. I wondered if Marnie would feel this increased contact was a significant improvement. But then I had something I wanted to discuss with him, and when he turned back to me, I took the opportunity, "David, I've finished the first segment of your profile. And turned it in to Kirsten."

He appeared at first to have forgotten, but then some dark inkling suffused his eye, visible in the top half of his glasses.

"In the second part, I've been thinking that at some point I'd like to mention the eye problem."

For a moment, he did not move, then spoke without looking my way. "And why is that? Why would you like to?"

"It's part of the story, part of what you've overcome."

Slowly now he found me. "Are you asking me, or are you presenting a fait accompli? We had an agreement."

"I'd like to know your thoughts."

"I'm sure you do know them. I'd prefer you didn't."

"But the profile is about you, and that, unfortunately, is part of the story. It hasn't held you back, and I wonder now how I can credibly ignore it."

"But there are other things you have ignored presumably, such as our relationship. So why this? Particularly as this would extinguish chances for future movies?"

Was this so? . . . Yet I knew I had to press him. I had to have something to throw Kirsten. "But quite clearly you're functioning. You've finished the filming. You've made it."

"I thought I'd described to you the people I must work with, the bankers and the distributors."

"But shouldn't this film be a testament? You've said it may well be your best."

He turned away, then back. "Christine . . ."

"What harm, if it won't affect you?"

"Because it will. This business is based on perceptions. Mention of it will freeze up financing and distribution agreements. Projects will dry up over night."

We studied each other, recoiling from frustration and disenchantment.

"David, my problem is that Kirsten may go ahead and insert some personal business, no matter what I do."

His eye flickered away, then snapped back to me. "Nonsense. You have leverage. You can take a stand, simply refuse."

"I don't have leverage. She doesn't care."

"Threaten to leave."

"She wouldn't be happy, but she wouldn't budge. There are literally dozens with whom she could replace me."

He looked down, dismissing my contention with a scowl.

"David, for my own part, it's been so affecting watching you fight past all the difficulties. Don't you think something of that should be in there?"

"At the cost of ushering me into retirement? Is that what you want?"

"Not at all. But won't the story get around anyway? I think Kirsten's gotten wind of something. Isn't it better to set out the real story?"

"Listen, I'm too tired to debate you. I told you what will happen. You'll essentially end my work." He was staring darkly at me. "I ask you not to."

Okay, but I had to again warn him, "Unfortunately she has final edit, and she'll add whatever she wants."

Now I heard him growl and saw him look up to the sky which was but a hazed cloud of light. "This whole thing was a mistake."

Despite understanding his anger, I found it wounding, and turned away.

"Christine, don't tell me you don't have influence. She's clearly grooming you for something. Explain the reasons to her. She can't be so unreasonable."

Without meeting his gaze I told him, "She doesn't see these things as we do. The magazine and its circulation come above all else. She claims the competition, for advertising dollars, is just too tough."

"Well, I'm sure you can make it clear to her, if you put your mind to it. Point out to her it'd be a death sentence."

I stared down at my shoes, whose color I could not make out. I felt stymied, unable to find accommodation or solution. Surely there must be something we'd overlooked. "I'll try. I'll do my best."

His eye moved over me, heavily, unhappily. "Keep in mind the repercussions. With these people, it's open or shut. And once one pulls out, they all do, like sheep."

Back at his hotel, after an all-but-silent return walk, we parted with rather tepid good nights. The averted looks and cool peck on my cheek served to maintain the pall.

At home, I tried to understand what had happened, how things had fallen once again. It was, of course, the threat to his work. But why had we found no compromise?

With Labor Day approaching, I wondered when there would be time to work this out. I tried to think of some formula to call him back about, but he, I realized, felt he could not accept compromise. As I stepped back into my apartment, I wondered if I had picked this fight intentionally, even as I knew that under everything lay Kirsten's diamond determination.

August 26th

Kirsten called me into her office. Dashing off the end of some memo, as I pushed in, her head was down, but when she looked up, I saw that while outwardly composed, she was quaking at the margins. Sitting down before her, I summoned my composure. Her eyes darted sharply over my face, her upper lip twitching. She then looked down at several pages before her. "This, this Loomis segment, is simply *not* acceptable. Your treatment of Loomis's marriage and women is just nothing! I mean I was under the distinct impression that I had laid out exactly what I needed. And then you go and give me nothing. I don't get it."

Having waded through this debate before, I felt there were ample places to begin. My eyes moved over her face, in order that I might decide.

She looked down, calming herself, smoothing her skirt over her lap, before her head jerked up again, and she snapped, "It's dull, it's lifeless. And now I'm going to have to re-do it myself! With no time!"

We stared at each other—she steaming, I attempting to clear my head.

"Christine, I'm moving up the due-date for Part II of Loomis. I want it when you return from Maine."

I blinked in acknowledgement.

"I hope, indeed I direct you, while you're in Maine, to give some very serious thought to all that I've taught you about the magazine. Our survival here is never a given, but must be earned with each and every issue. If we bore readers, they'll desert us in droves, as will our advertisers, and we will be out on the streets! There will *be* no magazine. Do you understand?"

I indicated I understood. But she barely waited. "I see you wanted to protect him, but at the cost to, at the embarrassment of, the rest of us?! Are you mad? Do you not know where your loyalty lies?"

Fairly certain she didn't want a response, I waited, dry lips sticking as they slid over each other. And I was right. She sputtered out, "I have offered you an opportunity that few other people will ever get even close to, that others would kill for! Do you realize that? And you want to toss it away for some passing fling, with a fragile, philandering filmmaker.

"Well, you'd better damn-well make some time up there in

that cabin to re-screw your head on right! Or you'll be living in some flop house with your brother."

Aware that my own anger was nearing the surface, even as I heard a voice cautioning me not to vent something I'd later regret, I pulled myself to the edge of my chair, trembling, ready to bolt. But she, under no such restraint, took my pages and pitched them out in my direction. Some floated gently down upon me. Others scalloped unhurriedly down onto her rich red Persian rug.

Aug. 28th

Called David at several places, but never reached him, and he never returned my calls. I have wondered if our spiraling apart has resulted from my own professional obtuseness. Should I have never presumed to consider his work? Particularly from the vantage of the commercial vessel to which I've signed on.

Over this month, what I have concluded is that my view of things falls consistently between these two camps, his and Kirsten's (the ideal world and the real, commercial one, perhaps) and that I underestimated the tenacity with which each holds to his or her views. So where does this leave me? In limbo, stuck in my own fear and rigidities? Or will I be able to adapt, flesh out, and defend my own priorities? Laurent contended that I alone will know whether I need to take this gamble.

Yet, while I am aware that it is change toward which I am leaning, I cannot help but wonder where it will take me, and what the costs will be. What I *am* sure of is that if I am to pass through this window, it must be soon. It is my hope that the coming hiatus, up, for the first time since he died, to my father's cabin, will provide the quiet and clarity in which to make a decision.

Maine retreat—Labor Day

Pulled myself out, stiff and sweaty, from the panting hamster, the hot red roadster, both of us grimy from our ten-hour grind. Stretched over knees to ankles, then slowly straightened, catching a flash of pale afternoon sky. Feel disoriented that I am suddenly way up here, removed, alone.

Squeezing in again, proceeded slowly, glancing out through the dwindling light and shadows for Father, remembering his deliberate gait, and endless puttering—a silent forest creature.

Blending with the light, the gray cabin came slowly into view through the trees, and as I pulled into the circle, I stared out at a year's changes: forest offerings, a dusting of needles, leaves, twigs, branches.

Should Father have been buried up here? Where he was most at peace? . . . No, better at Mother's side in Westchester.

Turned to the simple tasks: unloading, turning on the electricity, placing the perishables in the refrigerator, opening windows, though the day is nearly done. Considered a quick swim, urged on by my mind, but my body shivered as I stared out past the long shadows reaching over the gray black lake.

Sat instead in the rocker on the porch for a time staring out. The day's last breezes have left the trees. Summer's gone. Fall awaits in the hills around.

Morning

Crows carping above the faintly whispering wood. Bright, thin light out upon the lake, not yet illuminating the cabin or me.

Made my breakfast and carried it on a tray, carefully, bare-footed, stepping down to the lakeside, over the cool pebbles, the soft grasses, watching for the razor edges of splintered shells.

Went for a swim, out into the flat blue lake. Hardly a ripple.

Later drove to the local store at the crossroads. Both Eatons were there, behind their counter, players awaiting the curtain's rise. Amy and Emmet, now in their seventies, extended cool, enclosing handshakes. Condolences concerning Dad, whom our neighbors, the Burts, had called about last March.

They asked about Luke and learned more of his sad story from my stumbling detail than Father ever told them. They seemed

confused and saddened, and asked if he would be coming up—
not quite able to grasp the limitations.

They told me the Burts had left a week ago, and that there are
rumors of a development of ten or more houses at the far end of
the lake, which, though they stand to gain financially, they oppose.

"The world is fillin' up too much," exclaimed Emmet sadly,
his eyes drifting over the counter.

"Course where you live, that's the least 'a' your problems, isn't
it?" offered Amy.

"We went down there once, in the '50s . . ." he recalled. "Was
crowded, and hectic, then."

"I hear it's changed," she noted with a doubtful, worried
expression, to which I nodded.

They told me they believed Father had been one of them, a
New Englander, out of his element in the city. "He shoulda moved
up here. His spirit was here. Might be alive now, if he'd . . . But
not s' many people have time for the woods these days," Amy
sighed. "Including us." They laughed with blinking reflection.

"How's the place lookin'?" Emmet asked. "We drove over 'a
month ago. Seemed in tact."

As we packed up my purchases, I noticed they still cared for
each other, listening, responding, laughing, hands brushing over
arms or hands. And though they live only behind the store, a
modest life, they seemed happy. Their son and daughter have long
since graduated from the University at Orono. He's a lawyer,
married, living outside of Portland. She, Alice, is divorced, and
now teaches art on Deer Isle in the summers, elementary school in
Brewer in the winters. She was a year or two older than me, but we
played together over several summers before adolescence and its
divergent routes carried us apart.

So I took my supplies back to the cabin, and a routine, of
sorts, was established: breakfast, swim, and write. And when I
could write no more, usually in mid-afternoon, I turned to chores,
or to walking through the woods.

Made several trips, to Swans Island, and to the bottom of Deer

Isle, to Eiley's town, Stonington, a fishing village, now half filled with art galleries. Houses irregularly perched upon a hill over the harbor. Fishermen on toothpick docks unloaded crates of lobster and fish dragged from the bay's bottom.

On David's piece I worked with a strange heaviness. Although I could picture Kirsten's damming eyes, I found I could not describe his affliction, and end his work. Finally I decided, or rather, finally I listened to what I'd long known was important to me: that he's directed men and women in moving stories of life and thought and beauty, in portraying the mixed human story in these late years of this passing century.

FALL

September 20th

A cool dryness had settled over the coast and its lake-filled
wooded plain. She had stayed up far longer than she'd planned,
held by forces she could not quite name, not completely anyway,
for certainly one was the place itself. And yet it was also the local
changes in the season which prevented her from fully rooting in.
The red and yellow patches upon the hills were nightly stealing
closer to the shore.

She called down to her office, leaving progress reports for her
boss. Called Kate, who groaned that growing she might spill out
any day or week now, though the due date remained November.

Mailed down the second installment of his story, omitting
any report of eye affliction. Her boss may well erupt, but she had
made her choice. No word so far, via post or phone.

Childhood friend, Alice Eaton, stopped by on the way inland
to Orono. The two looked closely at each other, seeking every
change. Alice expressed wonder at C.'s slowly birthing novel—
something Alice often thought of doing, but never dared. She writes,
she said, but said not what. She asked of brother Luke, and after
hearing his sad tale, said of her students, "Oh Christine, if you
could see their faces, their potential already stifled. I try to give it
back, but it's too late for most—so dear, so needy. There's something
wrong with our taciturn New England way, too contained, too
hardened to offer a hand to the lost ones, the bruised or
unawakened."

This they talked of, and other things, and she invited C. to
stop by Brewer. Yet perhaps both saw that this was not where C.
needed to go. Alice understood, C. thought, when by her car she

said with a nervous, complicit smile, "Oh you and I, Christine, have miles to travel before we sleep."

And indeed the cool air and slipsliding leaves turned her mind to home and work, certain now that she should pursue what she'd begun, rather than turn aside for the boss's plan, and certain that it was time to move out of the aerie, downtown, into a more lively stream, where less formality and more openness call out the humanness, the unexpectedness of life, in those narrow streets, and buildings on a human scale. She'd had, she saw, a run of the rich, jetting life, which was not without its charms.

In preparing the cabin for winter, she realized that she could not foresee when she'd be back—a thought which brought a cry, standing in the dining area, gazing through to kitchen, one way, and to living room, the other.

Sept. 22

Time, never pausing, deposited her back in the office. And as if she needed confirming, the staff's forced smiles and wide-eyed concern—Melissa's in particular—portended the accounting with Kirsten which must come.

Ben, at least, had forgiven me, and greeted me with a hug, sincere if restrained. And to my inquiry about Kirsten's state of mind, he exhaled, "Oh, ho-ho-ho! Has she been peeved! Beside herself. You, on whom she was so much depending, stayed away, as she saw it, blew the magazine off. Vengeance's burned in her eyes. I'd dodge her for as long as you can, let her simmer down."

"And on the profile, did she say anything?"

"That you had willfully withheld the truth, about his eyes, I think it was." Under his copper curls, Ben's cobalt eyes searched out what I would do—first with concern, then gleaming with expectation. He extended his hand, fingertips gnawed and pale, which I took.

"Whatever comes, Ben, I'm happy with my decisions up there: not to wound Loomis, to devote my talents to some good, to see where I can take my writing."

His broadening smile sent his freckles purling. "I hear you, and I applaud . . . but uh, I, uh, I only hope she hears you."

I appreciated his kind wishes.

"And Chris, I admire you," he added, his lined brow suggesting some awareness of the difficulties ahead. "Because I hope someday to launch out like that myself."

I reached and touched his shoulder, before we waved and backed away. Alone, I weighed his counsel for some time, before deciding it was my responsibility to explain, and face the repercussions.

Approaching William's desk, I asked if she was in. Almost comically, he unknowingly mimicked what must be her contorting anger. But then motioned me on, to get my comeuppance.

At her desk, Kirsten glanced up from a page she was reading, took me in, then returned to her page. The first lash, I assumed.

I stood watching her, until when no further response seemed forthcoming, I side stepped to a chair and dropped into it. She ignored the thump, until, ready and blinking heavily, she looked unhappily my way. Deliberately, almost theatrically, she inhaled. "Nothing . . . you've done lately has been adequate."

"Did you have a chance to read Part Two?"

"Let me finish, please." Eyes flashed. "To stay out, playing Nature's child, never to consult, to leave no phone number? You came within a hair's breadth of being summarily fired. And it still may come to that."

"But I did call! And left a number, and left my mailing address. And sent in my work, early."

Her eyes enlarged, emitting flashes. "Not while I was in! . . . You think that's enough? To leave it at that? Who the hell do you think you are, making me chase around after you?"

"I also needed the time, to think through a number of things."

"I don't give an agent's ass about that. You do that on your own time, not when I'm waiting to hear from you. I'm paying you a professional salary, and I expect you to act like one . . . As for Part II, it is, once again, only half the story! Which I cannot believe, after our discussion. Are you trying to thwart me or are you truly obtuse?"

"I'd like to explain."

"I haven't finished! Your fate here is hanging by a thread, and at this point almost nothing you can say will have any bearing. Do you understand?"

"I do, but I needed time to reflect on your kind offer." This held her for an instant, allowing me to quickly insert, "Concerning Loomis, I had wanted to write an account of his problem, but he pleaded with me not to, as it would effectively end his career."

Her dull eyes hung without life or sympathy. Slowly she reached to her side for a newspaper clipping attached to a legal sheet, brought it before her, and read,

> "*The Glenn's Falls Courier.* June 24th. TRAPPER'S LAKE MISHAP. Movie Director David Loomis evidently lost control of his rented car while driving back to his motel after a day of filming. The car skidded off the road and down an embankment, narrowly missing a drop of one hundred feet, before being cradled by several trees. Neither Mr. Loomis nor his passenger, C. Howth, a journalist from *Avenue Magazine,* appeared to be hurt."

Kirsten glanced up with meaningful disenchantment, before continuing. "Same paper, two days later.

> DIRECTOR MISSES FILMING. Director David Loomis presiding over the filming, in and around Trappers Lake, of the movie, "The democrat," did not appear on the set today, apparently recovering from an automobile accident the previous evening. A spokeswoman for the production company denied that there was any truth to the rumor that the director has lost his sight. She said he is expected to resume work soon and would complete the picture."

Once more she looked up at me. "A local paper writes it up, and not a mention in your piece?"

"He returned to work after missing a single day."

"Word has it he's nearly blind."

"Not so."

"Well there's something to it. Rumors like that don't rise out of thin air. And in any case, you didn't refute them. Surely you were aware of them."

"Kirsten, he pleaded with me not to open this Pandora's box."

"Nonsense. And who are you to jeopardize the reputation of this magazine—on which we all depend for our livelihoods?"

"The subject was his filmmaking. Not . . ."

"Don't tell me what the subject was. The subject was David Loomis. This is not some academic exercise to keep some film school professor employed. This is real life, and you are here to report it. People want to read about people. You failed to provide an accurate portrayal of your subject. And this failure is not only inexcusable in itself, but is doubly so because I had to turn aside from my work and correct all your omissions!"

"Journalists have a moral responsibility."

"To tell the truth, the whole truth, and nothing but the truth."

"Even if it will destroy the very subject of their reporting? The press has held things back in the past."

"We are not a headline, we dig beyond the headlines. Neither do we control his career, which, if this film sells any tickets and is even half as good as you seem to think, will continue quite handily. He will make other films, even if he *is* blind. Look at Woody Allen, the little schlemiel."

Seeing no parallel, I tried to push past. "I made a choice: I felt I couldn't ignore his wish."

She studied me for a moment, then looked down at her curled fingers and their nails. "Maybe I misjudged you."

I ignored this calculated comment. "Kirsten, concerning your generous plan to install me as your assistant . . . I've thought about it . . . I'm flattered that you had that confidence in me; indeed I was overwhelmed, but I believe now that it's not something I could do well, to the best of my abilities. I would prefer to remain on as a staff writer."

Kirsten's blank gaze slowly rumpled into anger. She moistened her puffed lips, pressing them against each other, then swiveled away in her chair, before turning her head back to me. "I'm not sure you're the writer I thought you were, either."

I knew she liked to turn the screw.

"Please leave me now. I've got things to do, including think about all of this."

Slowly at first, then rather quickly, I pushed myself up, and walking out, realized I felt quite unruffled by this. Passing William, I asked for a copy of the revised first segment. He told me he'd bring it in as soon as possible.

Back in my office, at my desk, I swung my chair around and stared out the window. Indistinctly, figures in the building across the avenue, were sitting at their desks, calculating, conferring, reflecting upon their futures. These are the individuals I pass at rush hour, rushing to their desks, floor after floor of them—all of us filled with importance and purpose.

William knocked and wordlessly deposited the requested copy. Its authorial initials were, in order, K., M., CH. But I found its paragraphs were mostly mine, except for several slithering rumors about his marriage and women. Among the names I recognized: only Pat's.

For some time I sat. Then bugged William once again to ask Kirsten what project did she wish me to start.

"Hold on," he said, busy, out of breath. After several moments he came back with, "Your résumé."

"What?"

"She said, 'Your résumé.'"

A silence. I heard his low uncertain laugh as he said hello to someone arriving at his desk. After a muffled exchange, he spoke confidentially to me again, "Christine, uh, she may be feeling a little pissed—piqued, as she says. I know she's not happy with your profile. But it's good for her to vent, you know, get it off her chest. By afternoon she'll have recovered. Just, uh, work on something . . . you know . . . whatever."

Hanging up, closed my eyes. Imagined David, hearing this.

Pictured his fury and dismay, before my mind jetted out to San Francisco, where Eiley wanders the hills and neighborhoods. Should I soon follow? What value midwifing stories, if the story teller's life withers in the telling? There are less taxing ways to pay the rent. On the other hand, what value a comfortable life if it does not address the essential questions, and lies unexamined at its core?

But are these the only choices? Could David have done other than he did? Tended to his craft, and his family too? Or is it probable that genius is aberrant growth, unnatural focus, oozing out of human imbalance? So that once he latched onto his track, driven or pushed to tell his stories, once he'd found balance and meaning, he could never step away. And now . . . at some corresponding crossroads, what is the case right here?

Evening

Called Kate. Found her ready to explode. "Chrissy, I had no idea this would be so all-consuming. I mean it's impossible to concentrate on anything. The little thing must weigh a ton; it's impossible to get comfortable. God! I wish it'd come tomorrow. And by the way, what God dreamt this up? A cinch he's no woman. And Larry's never home, working night 'n' day. What is this? I've started wondering if he's seeing another woman . . . Listen to me, giving myself a fright. When he's here, he's fine, we talk, but he keeps staring at my stomach, reaching out and exclaiming it's harder than a basketball. A basketball?! Why? Who cares? It's a baby! . . . Sorry, Chrissy, sorry. How are you? Why don't you come over for supper. I'll order something in."

At her apartment, I examined mama-to-be, touching, tracing her tummy, listening to its ocean, then to her, about this experience which is largely hers alone. Tried to picture a little thing swimming, tumbling in a watery world.

Eventually, when she calmed down, she asked, "So, how was Maine, after we spoke? Tell me what you did. And what's going on with your job? Is Kirsten being a pain?"

"Oh, Maine gave me more time to think. And I got some

writing done, and got outdoors, exploring, working around the cabin. You have to come up some time, with the baby." Perhaps we both heard the omission of Larry, realizing, rationalizing, it's not for him.

"As for Kirsten, she hit the roof, that I wouldn't deal in all the dirt."

"The creep."

"And I told her I didn't really want to be her assistant, that I want to try to write."

Concern rose up across Kate's face, as clearly this was not what she would've done. "You sure, Chrissy, about that?"

"I think so."

"Well, Kirsten should at least be happy that you figured it out now, rather than a few months into it. And what about David?"

"I haven't seen or spoken to him."

"Still? . . . Why not?"

"Well, his work, and his disenchantment with me over the profile. Kirsten added private details, about his marriage, and affairs."

"Affairs?" She chewed her lip. "Really? . . . Well . . ." She glanced uncertainly at me, then swallowed. "But shouldn't he have understood about the magazine, that it's her toy?"

"He didn't believe that I couldn't dissuade her."

She frowned. "You know, I can understand his reluctance to have it all revealed, but, on the other hand, you should remind him that he's in the public eye . . . and anyway, no one's going to remember this stuff beyond a week."

"He said the bankers and distributors will, the people who finance his projects."

Her face flushed at not having thought of this. Then her eyes and attention fell away. Although she tried to fit all of this together, clearly it lay even further beyond her shores right now. And in a way, how could I blame her? Next to her baby, it seemed removed from life itself.

"Kate, just to pass on one final goody: Kirsten said she may let me go."

"What? You're kidding. Why?"

I felt myself stutter slightly, sifting for the right words, brain straining to hold its cool.

"Because you're not willing to ruin the man's career?"

I breathed and looked away.

She scowled. "I always said she was a hard-ass. But how can she? You're the only good writer she's got. Do you ever read those other columns? They're a joke, the simplest of ideas and prose, for simpletons. Hey girls, listen up. . . . How can she? She must know you're the only one. You said she's not stupid."

I watched Kate's forehead grow pink with indignation. Dear Kate, long my sole defender. Told poor Father a thing or two about skulking Richard, whom he thought I was crazy to divorce.

"I'm serious, Chrissy. Am I right? Shall I call her?"

Laughed. "I'd love to listen in."

"I will. Wake up, you pandering bitch, quit threatening the only writer you've got. Are you out of your gourd?"

Eyes lingered, then lightened.

When supper was delivered, we dismissed these troubles and talked as we had not in years, about old friends and schoolmates. Hours passed as I relaxed deep in one of her arm chairs, while she lay on her couch, rolling, sloshing like the sea.

At the end, as I was leaving, we embraced and I told her how lucky I was to have her as a friend.

"Hey, me too!" she cried. "I need it more than ever, to sometimes get out of myself and away from this baby business. God, let's both remember we need these breaks . . . And hey, don't take shit from Kirsten!"

Sept. 23rd

This uplift lasted until I reached the office, where, before I sat down at my desk, she summoned me in once more.

Calm and business-like, she welcomed me cordially, that is to say, with artificial graciousness. As I sat, her narrowed eyes ran over my outfit, remembering it was one we bought together in

Paris. She appeared still pleased. And as I had then, I thanked her for her good taste, even as I saw her eyes were refocusing on the business at hand. "I've given the things we discussed yesterday some thought, and have come to a conclusion, which is not personal in any way. Indeed I'm sure we'll remain friends, and I'm sure you have a wonderful writing career ahead. But I need to do what's best for the magazine." She waited for my reaction. I managed to keep all well contained.

"I want you to take a month off, an unpaid leave: time to sort out, further, what you want to do. I assume you have some money now, to tide you over?"

I heard, then felt the rush of implications. I began to voice a question. "But . . ."

"I want you to think about the magazine, both as a writer, and also as an assistant to me. I know you said you did that in Maine, but I believe some further reflection is warranted, for your benefit, and mine."

Despite anticipating something of this, I was stunned. Maybe because she'd taken it out of my hands, for the actual idea was not so bad.

"Finish up Eiley's story," she continued. "Do some other writing, possibly to submit to us, if you wish. And then in early November, we'll talk and see where things stand."

I looked at her. "What about the upcoming month?"

"We have your profile." Her face now hardened into stone. "I think you need time, to decide what's important. It's my feeling you'll thank me in the end."

"But I feel I should see the Loomis piece through."

Her gray eyes seemed to disappear beneath her lids. Coldly she gazed at her desk, then me. "Look. As I was saying, I want you to reflect on what the magazine and I need. I've been in this business for a long time. I know what it takes to survive. If you're going to work here, I'll need to see that you understand that, or at least are open to learning. For one thing, we can't allow our writers to set new ground rules with each issue."

Watching her, I felt we were both retreating from any hope of accommodation.

"So, that's all, for the moment."

"Well . . . When do I start?"

"Immediately."

I glanced down as I slid forward to stand. "There's no reason not to continue with the tutoring program?"

"None at all. That's your project, Melissa's and yours."

I looked again into her face. It remained unmoved, and I found myself thinking again, yes, this, evidently, is what it takes . . . But is it what I want . . . and believe in?

And so I left, cleaning out my desk, saying goodbye, as an employee anyway, for a month or more, to Melissa, Ben, and a few others. They seemed more taken aback than horrified, although I realized their innermost thoughts remained unspoken. I tried to reassure them that it was fine with me, and that I looked forward to the freedom. And yet I sensed, with every word, a distance was already opening.

At home I fell face down onto my bed, and lay motionless, to allow the shock to dissipate. In time slept deeply, and in the late afternoon, rose and sat down to Eiley.

> Hunched against the damp sea air, Eiley slumped along Judah street, hands wedged in faded jeans, glancing ahead out over the gray Pacific. Jobs were not materializing, surprising this hot New York editor—yet also pleasing her. She'd half-expected doors to open wide. How could they match her brains and energy? But that would've been too easy. So now, on this new coast, to find it comes with its own challenges and values was a riff.

> The café joggled into sight at the corner. The Quarter Moon, shelter for reduced, indeed slivered, expectations. Sip coffee, chew the fat with Denise or whomever. Yes, sit and sip, wait and think. Let the good times slide, till something breaks.

Sept. 24th

Realized, at some point, that I should warn him, explain that my efforts to shield him had failed, and landed me out on my ass.

Called the editing room but was told he'd taken a few days off. Seemed strange. Fear raised its head. Hoped he hadn't stumbled.

Called Martina, and heard in her voice a new reserve, as she told me also that he was taking a few days off.

"To rest?"

"Well, yes . . ." But guarded, she added no more.

I left a message asking that he call me, at home, as I had several things to tell him. She said she would, but I realized she, along with him, by now had probably read the first segment, and both saw me as Delilah.

Sept. 25th

Waiting for his call, I ran my lines numerous times, trying to explain, but ultimately falling back on Kirsten's banishment.

Yet when the call finally came, it didn't work out as envisioned.

"Christine?"

"David . . ." In the momentary silence, I heard him breathing, perhaps wrestling with his anger. "I have several things I need to tell you."

"I read the first installment, Christine. I thought we had an understanding. I thought you were going to do something."

I closed my eyes and put down a hand to steady myself. "Yes, David. I tried, but Kirsten wouldn't relent. She wrote the personal parts herself."

" . . . I find that a little hard to believe."

"She's put me on unpaid leave."

"What? . . . Why? Because of the profile?"

"In part."

Another grunt, then silence. I imagined his mind pacing wall-to-wall.

"I don't understand. What does she think she's doing? What does she get out of all this?"

"Sales, she claims. She's furious at me for not having written it for her. On top of that, I told her I didn't want to become her assistant."

He breathed, "Well Christ! I can see why."

This helped a little.

"But this is unacceptable."

"David, I'm afraid there's something else. Kirsten's going to print something about the eye business, in the second segment. She got a hold of reports in an Adirondack paper."

"You're kidding."

Alas I could utter no refutation.

"Tell me you're kidding."

But I could not.

"Do you know, I mean, do you know what this means?"

"I know. I tried to change her mind."

"This could end everything. I may never work again, never get financed again—finished . . . Is that what you wanted, Christine?"

"David, really, I tried to skirt it, but once she got her talons on those newspaper stories . . ."

I heard him groaning, drawing air. "I can't believe . . . I mean who *is* she? What does she want? To ruin people? . . . You know I'm not the only person who suffers from this. Did you happen to mention to her that I have two daughters?"

"I think she knows."

"Listen . . . I've got to talk to her. There's gotta be a way to get her to back off."

"I tried. She doesn't bend."

"Well, she can't do this," he sharply warned, "or she'll find there are repercussions. I'll expose her, reveal her rag for what it is."

"I tried to reason, but found I don't have much clout."

Silence again, before he loudly exhaled, "Christ! There's gotta be some way . . . I know people at other publications. This is just rumor-mongering, and I'm not going to be undone by some bitch selling that!"

"David, do you really think it'll have such an impact?"

A sardonic laugh caught in his throat. "What? You think I'm making it up? The idiots at the banks, the distributors are always looking for something to spook them, to hang a 'no' on. This is perfect."

We were silent for some moments, until he rasped, "Listen, Chris, you must know how to get to her, what might work. Can you meet me tomorrow, to figure something out, say around seven?"

"Yes, I guess. Where?"

"285 Vestrey Street. I can't believe you allowed this. Didn't you think things have been difficult enough?"

"David, I feel horrible, but I never thought she'd override me, and take things this far."

"Well you should've damn-well made the risks clear to me."

"I would've, if I'd realized."

"Well, put your mind to it. We've got to come up with something, some means, some strategy."

But before I could express the likely futility, I heard him mutter something and heavily jam down the phone.

My head spun. I closed my eyes. Then felt for the phone, to call William to request a copy of the final second segment. He mumbled something about not being authorized, and that Kirsten was out of the office, before he switched me to Melissa.

"Hi Chris. What's up?"

"I want to get a copy of the second Loomis segment."

Silence. "You know it's put to bed."

"Yes, but I never saw the final version. I understand you worked on it too. How'd you think it came out?"

Another pause. "Okay."

"That all?"

"He's more intriguing than I thought . . . though typical in some ways. His movies are well-done, but pitched to men."

" . . . Maybe."

"I can't say they deeply interest me."

"No? Well, would you mind, could you fax me a copy?"

"What's your number?"

While of course she has a right to her point of view, still her narrow-mindedness, her ennui, irked me.

When shortly it creaked out, I felt my face flush, at the innuendo, at their running with unsubstantiated stories. Embarrassed for them, and myself. Did neither check anything? Did neither consider the repercussions? Did they not care that the tone of the article suddenly and diametrically shifted?

At the same time, I wondered if it were so likely this could snowball and end his career. I covered my eyes, turned in circles, then stepped out onto the terrace. What should I have done, once I saw Kirsten would rip it from my hands? What would Eiley do? . . . I'm afraid I knew.

Morning

Sat on my couch and scribbled protests and threats to Kirsten, none effective with my lack of leverage. A call from Josh interrupted invectives. He happily announced he'd found a downtown apartment for me, their recently renovated company brownstone in Chelsea, on West 22nd, between 9th and 10th, furnished, reasonable.

I kissed him through the phone and said of course I was eager to take a look. He explained that his company shares it with several others for out-of-town business clients and that from time to time someone would stay there, but I could rent one of the bedrooms and essentially have the run of the place.

In thanks, I told him the least I could do was take him out to lunch, later in the week. Accepting, he proposed that afterward we walk over to take a look.

Evening

Around seven, I cabbed down to Vestrey Street through descending darkness. As we neared Canal, I felt anxiety returning and braced myself, against the lurching, and the coming anger. The winter months, I saw, were settling in.

After paying the driver, I turned to scan his building, originally built for business, now a townhouse. It stood oddly open-eyed among its unclean, darker, sightless, commercial cousins.

David answered the door. For a moment we looked at one another. His good eye stared out darkly and unhappily at me, before he stepped back to allow me in. As I moved past, I noticed his face was gray with unhappiness, and that his hair had grown longer, sprouting gray tufts over his ears and tumbling softly over his brow and collar.

When I turned to face him, he hesitated before forcing a perfunctory nod. "I appreciate your coming . . ."

I looked more closely. He seemed oddly uncertain what to do next. He cleared his throat, turned a little. "Maybe you'd like to see the place, take a look around."

"How's the film? Jeff said you're pleased."

He breathed just discernibly. "It's getting there."

"Have you gotten any rest?"

A meager smile. "Rest? . . ." Reaching for my elbow, he murmured, "Come on," and turned me down the hall. "The fellow whose place this is, is a long-time friend, taking a year in England. He asked if I'd house-sit." His lower lip pushed up. "Like sitting-in, I guess."

Glancing ahead, I saw the hall glowed with a cool shine. When we reached the first room, he announced it was the parlor.

"To parley what?" I wondered.

"To parley his talent into cash. He makes commercials."

We leaned in to gaze at the spare, modern space, and I stepped in to better see, circling around its iron and canvas chairs, off-white loveseat, and corner desk, all spot-lit by diminutive track-lighting. The brick walls were adorned by glowing black-and-white photographs, of striking ethnic faces, long, pensive, vexed, melancholic.

"A museum, it seems. Not for kids," I ventured.

"No, he does his business here. Meetings. He has an office upstairs . . . but come."

He led me into the dining room adjacent to the parlor and then downstairs to the kitchen where a bottle of Shiraz-Cabernet and two glasses waited starkly on a long marble-top table.

"Chris, I've been wondering where to start." He took out a corkscrew, and leaned into the insertion, emitting a faint groan at the first twist. I waited as he grimaced under the force needed to extract the cork, which gave way with a subdued, hollow pop. He glanced at me, distractedly smelling the cork. His bad eye, I saw, was clouded and remote, behind the smudged left lens of his glasses. As he poured, his brow bunched in searching. "I've thought . . . I suppose if we'd stayed in closer touch, I might've caught on, and we could have headed this thing off . . . Still, I don't quite understand how it happened."

"Again, David, I didn't think she'd insist. I didn't think she'd strong-arm me . . . Guess I didn't think it through."

He looked at me, blinked, then handed me a glass. With a contorted, perhaps ironic, expression, he clinked my glass. "Bonne santé."

Following pensive sips, I told him, "I re-read it, David, and I have to believe most people will see the speculation and rumor for what they are."

Head tilted down, eye reaching up, he studied me. "You've seen the second segment?"

Avoiding his trembling gaze, I confirmed this with an unhappy nod. "She's put in whatever hearsay and stories she could find."

Forcefully he wrenched himself around, crying out, "Why, in God's name, did I ever agree to this?" From behind his bent back, he snapped, "This is precisely why I haven't done these!"

He half-turned, and I saw his eye glaring into his glass, and felt the pounding implications. I attempted, "Is there no hope the film itself will counter all the stories and rumors?"

Slowly rotating his head and neck my way, he took me in, his face distorted with disgust. "I should've known and been more careful." Unhappily he exhaled. "Listen, I was thinking, what if I call her? Invite her to meet me, show her that I'm functioning?"

Over a distant cry inside I told him, "It's too late."

"She would see the errors in the piece, and would have to correct them."

"It's at the presses."

He frowned. "They could print an insert, a correction, a retraction."

"But if she met you, she'd report everything. She'd latch onto your bad eye like a pitbull."

"If I did it at my office, in low light, at my desk."

"Maybe . . . if it were not all too late."

"What *is* this? You can't just give up! Never, never give up! I'll get some other magazine to refute it, with pictures and interviews." Yet glancing over, he saw my doubt. "Don't worry, I'll think of something."

"I'm only worried that stirring things up will make it worse. She'll come back twice as hard."

"What? You don't expect me to just lie down and take it, do you?"

"Sometimes ignoring something is better. You can refute it to the people you need to. They'll see "The democrat.""

He half-growled, half-groaned. For some moments, we stood motionless. Then after throwing down his wine, he bent toward me, curious it appeared, to see if I expressed any anguish or remorse. His face swayed before me, until he straightened, and slapping the green bottle into his hand, spun and hunched out of the room.

With a spiritless glance around the white-tiled kitchen, somehow Dutch in its hard, clean spareness, I followed him into the hall. We passed a laundry empty of clothes or linen, a powder room seemingly unvisited, before coming to French doors through which, he announced, one can reach a garden. Blankly we stared at the glass panels emptily reflecting the hall light behind. I bent to peer out into the night. Stepping stones, barely visible, arced away through grass toward pebbles and graceful, shadowed shrubs crouching around sizable boulders.

"A serious garden," I whispered uncomfortably, my mind unable to really attend.

"Neither designed nor frequented by my friend."

When we straightened up, our faces closer now, his seemed swollen and misshapen, but his voice sounded less angry, "All things need tending to. One cannot leave them to others."

Somewhere, in this dully painful stab, I wondered if it helped him to take responsibility, assume the burden. I stared at him as I tried to discern what lay where. But he spoke first, flicking a glance my way, "I remember, before I asked you to stay longer up there, that I had warned you away." He all but closed his eyes. "I should have followed that first intuition."

The impact came penetrating in slow motion. I seemed to fall a half-step back, then saw he was preparing for more. "Upstate, after you'd gone, as I think I said, I didn't know if I'd see you again, ever . . . or see anything. This, coupled with the strain of pushing the thing ahead, blindly, fearful that I would let down, give in, permit it to be less than it could be, was something which grew increasingly unbearable. At some point, I simply needed something, someone, to put an arm around, to take the weight off, someone to restore a feeling of self, and life."

I found I could not quite look up. "Yes, you said."

He turned partly away, folding and unfolding his arms. "A weakness, yes, but not the worst, I think . . . I was not ready to give up . . . all physical connection. I don't think love dies. Not in me, at least. We'd had that, Pat and I, though we'd come to recognize it was limited, not quite right. But when I tried to imagine what lay ahead, it frightened me, froze me—nearly stopped my heart. When solitary darkness comes, as seems certain, life will be different. Those things which stir me most will be gone: my work, my daughters, the beauty of the world . . . you . . . Each a terrible allure, a dependency . . . I want to cry out against it, scream: I hate it! Just hate it!" And as he hurled this out, he wrenched around, writhing, head swinging, before adding in a biting tone, "No doubt you and others think I twist and rationalize about Kath and Pat . . . and undoubtedly, there is some. But over the years, it was more than that—much more—as you, in your own life, and marriage, must be somewhat acquainted with."

Faced with his sad, curled figure, I mumbled, "I feel bad, David, about these misunderstandings . . . Time has not been kind to us." As he turned slowly back, I confessed, "I guess I thought you turned to Pat out of anger, and maybe appetite, but now I see more clearly what weighed upon you."

Slowly, darkly, he took me in, with his bloodshot eye. He scowled, then breathed. "I cannot claim there was no anger, in the dark of those days, when I felt I was running a half-step ahead of collapse and failure . . ." His voice faltered. My moist palms joined, pressing against each other. His breathing emitted a faint wheezing, as if cries from a distance. At length he seemed to grope, "So, what . . . what now? . . . Will this latest thing tear all apart irreparably?"

Though I scanned his face, my mind was flying elsewhere, anywhere away. He turned to stare heavily into the reflecting doors, until he offered, "Maybe time, and talking, will lead us back, though time itself remains a problem."

I looked uneasily around. "I must confess that through all this, despite trying to re-direct my thoughts, I find they always circle back to you." Watching closely, I saw his expression slowly soften. He murmured, "I find myself increasingly aware of what I cannot offer."

"David, you will rebound. But this time, allow me that risk."

Deliberately, he studied my face, until his pondering appeared to shift. "You know the accident was a greater blow than I first recognized. It lingered, gnawed, injected doubt, even into my ability to see clearly. Which opened doors to fear."

I reached out and touched his arm. He peered awkwardly down at my hand, then motioned for us to continue our tour. Heavily, we turned and moved back to the stairs. As we trudged up, he turned and growled, "Christ, you know despite all this . . . we must keep talking."

I nearly missed a step, then stopped and tried to find his face, but in the half-dark could make out only his dim outline. I sent up an uncertain smile, but he may have been able to read me no better, and so resumed his climb. Bent and conflicted, it seemed, he lunged for some brighter subject, calling back, "Chris . . . what will you be doing, now, with your time?"

For a moment I wondered at this shift, then weakly offered, "Eiley . . . Pushing her on, of course . . ." My moist hand squeaked as it rode up the banister. My spinning thoughts merged, then flew apart. I closed my eyes, and climbed by feel.

Reaching the third floor, he paused unsteadily to catch his breath. I reached out to him, gently urging, "You must get out walking more, after all these weeks inside."

"All these indoor places seem like prisons now," he exhaled, then gasped for breath. When he straightened up, though his demeanor seemed less dark, his condition seemed weaker. But he led me on, stepping into a long living room furnished in a softer manner than the parlor, with wool fabrics and tasteful prints and paintings undulating along the walls.

"This is nice, David, although not so terribly unique."

"I'm sure he had someone decorate it. He's divorced. His wife lives uptown, near you. His kids have known Mandy and Marnie for years . . . By the way, Mandy's back."

My eyes, which had been scanning the room, now looked back at him. I tried to picture old Johnny.

Without looking my way, David elaborated, "Of course he dumped her, as we foresaw. I can't tell how great the shock was; she won't let me see, though Marnie's heard her crying in her room . . . She put a lot into it . . . Maybe the experience will help, in some way. She'll start again at Columbia next semester. Just pray it hasn't cracked her confidence."

I remembered John's speech extolling her. Part of me had hoped then that he believed it, and could grow. Now I could only shake my head.

Turning back to the room, I moved slowly around, taking in the art, two walls of women mostly: physiognomies, bodies, lines, curves, shadings—sketched, printed, painted—a sorority gazing warily back.

David sat on an ottoman and refilled his glass. I stood watching, hoping he would not drink too much, wondering how it mixed with his medicine, and sniffing, for the first time, the residue of cigarette smoke.

I drifted into the adjacent room, his friend's office, a spacious, yet busy room, reminiscent of David's office, with scripts, storyboards, and film and tape cases neatly organized—the one room that felt lived-in. "Did you two meet through filmmaking?" I called.

He came to the door. "Years ago."

"How did you end up going in such different directions?"

He paused and stared down into the past, it seemed. "He could always make his way in any circles. He likes the business of it, making money, as well as the craft. And he prefers the shorter, intense productions, a week or two, and the regular checks."

"He lives here alone now?"

David's cautious glance suggested otherwise, that his friend was not alone, had a girlfriend. I felt my head tugged away.

David sighed just audibly. "In one way or another, most of us are such unpredictable air-bags, ready to deploy prematurely with a bang—dangerous to ourselves, and others. One wonders how our city, and civilization has reached the level it has."

"Restraint and sacrifice. Isn't that your prescription for Stephen?" I asked with a muted jab.

"For some." He briefly smiled, then searched across the room. "We are each so many things, all stirred together . . . A strange infinity."

Yes, I acknowledged to myself, quite beyond understanding. But he, I noticed, had begun moving away, and glancing back, motioned for me to follow.

The last room on this floor was the master bedroom and bath, simply but richly decorated in browns and beige and maroon. While he stood by the door, I entered, toured, peered into the spacious bathroom, reminding me of a similar one not so long ago. On the door's hook, I saw a woman's silk robe . . . Quickly I moved away, past the bed, past David, noticing that he stared there too.

I led him up to the final floor. Here skylights transmitted the city's glow, into which we climbed. The first room combined library with guestroom. I scanned its walls and shelves, reading titles: the usual best sellers and histories, but also art books and film books, and one shelf holding Mandy's things.

David leaned against the door. Our eyes met and fell away.

"Maybe this is enough, David."

He understood, and slowly we descended to the living room, where, when I'd seated myself on the sofa, he asked, "Are you hungry? Shall we go out? Order something in?"

I studied him. "Does it bother you, what your friend's done to his family?"

His mouth opened. "Of course . . . In many ways we were close, as families. The kids played; I like Polly . . . but even before the divorce, he no longer joined us as much. Yet I am not the one to criticize."

Nervously, ready to dart away, our eyes passed across the other. "David, I wonder if I'm any different from the owner of that robe."

Slowly he moistened his lips, but did not reply. I allowed my eyes to run back over the room's decor, as I tried to make sense of our fluctuating feelings. Do our emotions, our needs, our insecurities drive all . . . or is it the wine?

He asked if I wanted another glass, and despite recognizing that it would further muddy things, I held mine out. But he had to return downstairs to the kitchen for a second bottle.

Wearily I sat and clumsily made another effort to sort things clear. Had my too-facile acceptance of this project subverted it? Did the accident set all tumbling? Or did his affliction? Where to begin? Things swam unintelligibly before me, and I could extract nothing but a sigh.

Puffing back up the stairs with a bottle and new glasses, he collapsed down next to me on the sofa and poured each a good bit. As awkwardly we clinked glasses, the thick pillows tipped us together. "So David, you were right. We need some food."

Carefully he sipped and savored. "Well, there are several places not too far away. What's your preference?"

"Something healing."

"There's a good bistro a block or so . . ."

But instead of moving, we lifted our feet up on the coffee table and continued our sipping. Shortly I asked, "Shall we go?"

"Absolutely. I'm nearly done." But neither moved. Soon I found my whirring head resting on his shoulder, and shortly his head slumped against mine. Although sipping wasn't easy, we managed. Time passed, I don't know how much. Perhaps we dozed. At some point, I awoke, hearing my tummy drumming like a tympanum. "David, wake up. The evening's passing. The kitchens may be closing."

He coughed as I pried myself up and away from him.

"Can't move, right now," he moaned. "Too much wine."

Standing, looking down, I saw indeed he could not, and so I stepped away a little to think. Considered descending to the kitchen—old patterns—but this time called out to a nearby deli, and surprisingly, after not too great an interval, roast beef sandwiches on rye with Russian, cold slaw, and coffee adorned the table. Somewhere a grandfather clock struck eleven, drawing forth long-buried memories of grandparents and childhood. I nudged my slumbering companion.

When he was revived by food and coffee, we skirted our issues and talked of his neighborhood, where artists, Wall Streeters, lawyers, and light industry, exist shoulder-to-shoulder. An unusual mix, he thought, yet with little intermingling.

When we noticed midnight had come and gone, he urged me to stay, "You can have your choice of top floor bedrooms. I'd offer you the master bedroom, but I've already dirtied the sheets."

"A convenient story."

"Take it, then. Whichever bed you wish, take several."

"No, I prefer being on top, top dog."

His good eye slid my way, narrowing. But then, over my protestations, he struggled up to my floor to make sure I had towels and blankets. By the stairway, we said goodnight, hesitating, then leaning into a soft kiss, not quite on the mark, misguided by memories and too much Shiraz.

Opening a window, I felt an overwhelming heaviness drawing me to bed, while a faint wooziness spun out a sensation that this top floor was higher than my aerie. Far below, it seemed, the city slept, its horns and motors muted. But through that quiet, I heard hurrying footsteps out on the street, echoing over cobblestones, and then a cry—anguished, I feared—reverberating off the brick and stone. I rushed back to the window and pushed aside the curtains. Below all was yellow-lamplight gloom. Nothing moved, no sign of life. I searched, then re-drew the curtains, crossed the room, and slipped under the sheets, tugging up the comforter.

Morning

Early light revealed him standing, bending, near my head.

"Couldn't sleep. May I crawl in?"

'More sleep!' cried a voice, but I couldn't send him away. Soon his starchy p.j.'s were scraping the unprotected spaces between my underwear, and he was nestled against my side, face buried in my hair. For a long time, we were motionless, and in that warmth, I drifted.

Later, with my head now upon his shoulder, he warbled lightly, "The eyes, the eyes have it. The eyes are all. Gavel gavel, cavil not. We watch in undeniable delight, while we can, aware that the tide is flowing out, aware that the visual abundance renders a heaven on earth. What an incredible torrent of intricacy and variety and beauty—beyond comprehension . . ."

"Nearly as inspiring as your revival," I mumbled. Leaning my head back, I could partially see his face.

"I feel reborn," he confirmed. "How could I not be?" And he gave my arm a gentle squeeze. With a sideways glint, he sought my hand and brought it to his lips. "We talk; we listen; we discuss; we look; and when this project's done, what riches we will share."

We fell silent for some moments, before he slipped his arm round me, and shortly slid his other hand across my bare stomach.

At length we moved together, freeing my mind to float above our bed. In truth, I don't know whether I dreamt of making love, or making love, did dream.

When at length I deeply inhaled and turned my head to see, I found him gently breathing at my side, a peaceful light upon his face.

At midday, when we'd risen, showered, dressed, and eaten, we stepped out into a crisp, cool day. David quickly zipped up his heavy jacket and put an arm around me, before we headed south down Hudson to Chambers, then to the river and the graceful promenade.

We squinted out across the Hudson's placid pewter surface. "Poor, exploited New Jersey," he breathed, "all but buried under miles of pavement . . . transformed utterly from what Burr and Hamilton knew when they met to settle. How much can we alter, and still believe healthful balance will not be altered too?"

Our gazes traveled along the water front, over the unbroken line of shapes spiking the skyline. But then I noticed David's brow grow dark and his mood change. I saw him form a fist, raise it up, then strike it down, "Damn! Damn!" He turned to grip my shoulders, his face growing red and fiercely lined.

"What, David, what?"

He winced, recoiled, as from a blow. "Your boss, your fucking boss! . . . How will I save it all?" His eye narrowed to a slit, giving off a glare gray and cold. Then bending, he reached around my legs and hoisted me over his shoulder, then staggered toward the river. "David? What? What are you doing? David, please . . ." He did not stop but struggled on, lurching dangerously near the rail. My hands gripped and re-gripped his coat as the wooden rail tottered into view. "David!" He began to lift me higher. Was this a joke? Did he really mean to throw me? My arms embraced his head, my hands dug into his collar. The cement walk and railing pitched at the edges of my sight. Wrenching around to look where he was going, I saw the pastel sky yawning crazily above, while silver slivers of the river flashed below. Fear now clamped my stomach. My pant leg caught on the wire fence and ripped, upsetting his balance. He skidded, feet flapping against the gray cement. My fear bulged, then burst. "David! Don't! Stop it! Have you lost your mind?" My heel raked the wire mesh and slowed his lifting. "This won't save it!" I cried as he tried to heave me over.

Thrashing, I clawed his coat. "No, David, no! Stop!" His arms were trembling. I felt his body shaking. My desperate struggle sent him reeling back a step or so, where he seemed to slip and sink, and suck in air. His strength, I felt, was draining; his poison seemed leaked away. "David, let me down! A counter article is the only way to save it!"

Swaying now side to side, then bending forward, he released me and lunged for the rail himself. I backed off a bit, bending to fully breathe. He leaned panting, nodding, "Yes . . . okay . . . sorry . . . I know someone at the *Times*. I'll ask him; I'll steal a march on her, take her down a peg."

The sudden force, the terror—the craziness—left me emptied. An entirely different man. Should I run, escape, save myself? Instead, I forced myself to look closely and found him nearly doubled up against the rail, gasping. Needing its support as well, I came forward and put out a hand, and stared, trying to make sense. What was this? What had set it all in motion? Had the pressure cracked him? . . . And how much was my part? Why had I not seen the repercussions? Had I willfully averted my eyes? . . . With such uncertainty pressuring him, should I not have foreseen that my probing would breach his skin and release all restraint? . . . Or had I stumbled upon another flailing, fabricating man? . . . Now as I stared, I recognized that it was no longer fear that trembled in me, but cold doubt as to who lived within that frame.

When I looked again, however, I found him staring at a single pinkish cloud above the river, one neither crisp nor clean like those in Maine. I saw him close down his eye, straining to see it clearly, and in that concentration, he seemed to reclaim control. "You know," he said, without looking at me, quite as if he'd forgotten his madness and his fury, "my family, my mother's father and ancestors were merchants here, working up the river to Albany, for much of the last century. And I, their beneficiary, have thought that I trade too, though for something quite other . . . but maybe not."

He faced away and began to unsteadily wander off, back along the way we'd come. I hesitated, then followed at a distance. What to do? Had this been a mortal blow? Would further outbursts surface, erupting through the cracks? The imprint of his grip around my waist, though fading, evinced the hidden strength and determination that daily drove him in his work. Would it be better if I left him alone? . . . But watching him, shrunken, unsteady, I found I could not. And so, slowly I walked after him, my fear snatched up, for the moment, by the rising, whipping wind.

When we'd staggered home, he dragged himself upstairs and lay down on his large bed, falling, retreating into sleep. For a short time, I watched him, wondering still, before stepping silently downstairs to the living room to stare at the paper.

Should I leave him to Pat and others? Was this not the final straw? Yet, as the minutes ticked by, again I found I could not.

When he awakened and came down, we made tea to warm ourselves in the cold house and sat facing one another across the kitchen table. "David, are you feeling any better?"

His mouth opened, then wavered. The question perplexed him. "Yes . . . I guess."

"I have been thinking . . . that if you could promise me . . . if you believe it will not happen again . . . I would be prepared to put it behind us."

Puzzled, he appeared to turn it over. "Yes . . . I apologize . . . but I was not angry at you . . . so much as angry at your boss and her attempted assassination."

"But then why . . ." I began, "did you lift me up?"

Still he appeared bewildered. Was it his memory of the struggle, or the question of attribution, that appeared to confuse him? Where to lay the blame? Unsettled, he seemed to seek my reaction. And so I asked, "David, what am I to make of that episode?"

He searched the room, before turning back to me, again for my interpretation. Yet when he found my frown and read the firmness of my feeling, dismay clouded his cheek, lined his brow, and his gaze fell. "I don't know . . ." His lips trembled. I heard him catch his breath, before he whispered, "Sorry." Blinking, he appeared to replay our scuffle, then asked, "What should we do?"

I did not know what to say, glancing at him uneasily. Tumbling in my mind were the clouded beginnings of our succession of mistakes. "David, I guess we both have things to apologize for."

With an effort he found me, and nodded, and looked away. "For my part, I'm sorry."

I, too, uttered my regret. Yet something seemed too quick, too easy. Our words were outstripping difficult reality. Nonetheless, somewhere, my intuition pronounced it over, and studying him, I judged that his remorse was sincere. Certainly I knew I did not want to replay it ever again.

He returned to sipping his tea for some moments, then lifted his head. "Chris, if we could forgive, if you could . . . could you stay another night or two, before I must return to the headlong schedule, for another month or so?"

Unsettled, and, at the same time touched, I felt myself vacillate. Could each put it behind? Had he changed his view of his career? Did he no longer fear its end? "Maybe we should each think it through."

"Maybe . . . but I'm afraid I'm sure of little else."

"You claimed the profile would be your death . . ."

He looked away, his now pale eyes motionless in reflection. "No, no . . ." He studied me carefully, then expelled, "I must find a way to get past it, as, to an extent, you and I already have. I'll show the *Times* fellow that I'm alive and kicking. The next month will be hard, but thereafter, I think, things will ease."

Perhaps discomfort shoved my mind back in the direction of work. These interruptions of Eiley have required days to regain momentum. The old question resurfaced: is he the wrong distraction? Or is it, as I'd thought months ago, the connection of a lifetime? "David, I wonder if we should allow some time for things to heal . . ."

His frowning, imploring gaze bore into mine. "No . . . I must, I want to, see you, while I can. Could hardly bear not to . . . It will be limited, on the spur of the moment. I can never tell. As you see, I'm a prisoner of my own making. I apologize for losing it, by the river. I hardly knew myself . . . But maybe, as you say, if the film is good, maybe all these doubts and things . . . will fade."

I stared into my tea, watching its different shades slowly merge. I realized that what I could not do was abandon him, even as our betrayals continued to flay inside. And therefore, what unfolded, as if in something of a dream, were two more evenings with this borrowed man, in his borrowed home; another walk, this time down around the Battery; excursions out for food; we read to one another, considered Eiley's middle stages—he had more insight than I was at first ready to accept, and more than I could return. But together it helped to dissipate the fears and anger, and showed us that, evidently, resiliency is something else we share.

October

Cold Canadian air has blown away the tails of summer, I saw, as I stepped out to buy a copy of the magazine, to read David's story as the public will. The section they redid stood out like gouges into glass. The only saving grace: the account of his affliction comes near the end, and they've resisted lurid headings. But still it subverts the intended focus, his ideas. And while Kirsten does not expressly suggest this was his last film, that implication hangs there, swinging slowly above the pages. And I am left confronting my undoing of the very one I'd thought to praise.

All this sent me under something of a shroud to lunch with Josh. In a faintly grimy health food joint off Sixth, I described to him the strands of Kirsten's web. "When she feels the vibrations of other views, the unfeeling bitch binds and bites whomever's in her path and wields her tongue like a whip."

"Hey, I know," he nodded grimly. "Remember, I worked for her a while back." He shook his head. "It sounds as if the personal detail was unnecessary. We have so much coming at us, these days, that it all becomes a blur. Maybe it's the business that drives us all a little nuts."

"The business or its types?"

"People's high ideals, bent by grim reality."

"Gouging to survive?"

"Surviving in the manner to which they've grown accustomed. Anchored to the bottom line."

When my questioning expression wondered if he included himself, he was quick to confess, "Oh yes, right here as well. I no longer want to live the threadbare writer's life. And certainly Betsy even less. It's not an easy road you've chosen."

"The conventional wisdom. And yet so many try. For the moment, however, this road has left me sublimely free."

This raised a sudden qualm. "By the way, you have the bread for this place, right? The rent, I'm afraid, can't be gratis."

"Don't worry, Dude, I'm flush for several months."

He smiled. "I have some jobs, some decent destinations." His eyes half closed. "Down Mexico way, if that grabs you?"

"Thanks, Josh, again. But not right now. Maybe in a while . . . But how can I thank you for all this?"

His eyebrows arched ahead of a rakish smirk. I smiled as I shook my head and reached for my tea.

After lunch, we headed over to 22nd Street. Crossing Ninth, I discovered the block was all but perfectly restored to its original, tree-lined harmony, with rows of houses all alike and facades of grace and beauty. How to explain the good fortune once again visiting me? Was it the seesaw continually tilting?

Inside, the house was decorated with striking art-deco pieces and antiques from the early century—someone's feminine touch, I'd all but bet. Airy, high-ceilinged downstairs rooms, including several to write in, while upstairs more intimate spaces with ornate dressers, porcelain sinks and iron tubs, all in beige, pinks, and yellows. Though clearly it was a showcase, I told him I'd have no trouble settling in, delivering me, as it does, to the neighborhoods of which I've dreamed.

When I called to inform the management for my aerie that I'd be leaving, the agent could barely contain his glee, for now he can raise the rent beyond the roof and collect another fee.

"So, by November first, I'll have flown the coup," I told him. "Happy Halloween."

"What?" His labored breath stopped altogether, then he grunted, before I dropped the phone.

Carried by this prospect, I buried myself in work through days lost in the calendar. Over and over I visited Eiley's efforts, and page upon page was pushed upon the heap.

David, however, slipped out of touch—his schedule, I assumed, and not his rage. Martina explained he's ever running between studios, cutting rooms, effects houses, music recordings and film labs, as well as the frenzied assembling of a trailer to pull the people in, not to mention selecting stills and graphics for the campaign. "A marathon, each time," she said, "without, I hope, that end."

A week disappeared, then two.

I called, but he was never there, and so once my daily duty was done—this writing that first feeds, then wrings me out—I turned to organize and pack. What chairs and bureaus Father left, I'll store for some future place. Surprisingly I found I liked this feeling, of being, as of November, free to skip above the encumbrances, and dwell within the mind.

While picking through my things—old utensils, wedding plates, doilies, vases, moth-balled clothes, and blankets—I wondered if Eiley would simply pitch them out. Lifting and turning the china and silver, feeling their bony weight, or draping the faintly yellowed fabrics on my arm, I recalled the faces of those who'd used them. And I thought of David, wondering if he'd left such things behind.

This week at tutoring, one student, a Mexican woman, did not return, and when I asked another who knew her, she had no answer. Swallowed by the sprawling city, we supposed—a fate I've had some acquaintance with. And although she was replaced by a Guatemalan and a Russian, I recalled her haunting eyes, which seemed to look into my life's empty quarter, despite our wholly different spheres. I wondered how she'd find what she wanted, without the necessary words.

One evening, as I was boxing books and summer clothes, Luke

reappeared. No explanation of his silence or whereabouts, nor any questions asked of me. Nor any interest in the food or drink I offered, before, as always, he headed for his room, until I mentioned, "Luke, I'm leaving, moving out."

He stopped and slowly turned. "Moving? . . . Why? Because of me?"

"No, not at all." Yet looking, I discovered resentment in his eyes. "To live in Chelsea, for a while."

"What d' you mean?"

"A kind of house-sitting, at least till Spring."

"In Chelsea? With all the gays?"

I looked and shook my head at his diminished, fearing brain.

His head now fell. "What about my stuff? I suppose . . . suppose I'll have to find another place."

"No, I'll be storing my furniture, and most of Dad's, but there's room for your things at either place."

He found me once again. "When do you . . . ?"

"The thirty-first."

He heard, then looked away, then turned once more and continued to his room.

Family, mine at least, has never meant much intimacy, not since Mother died. Thin connections persisted for purely formal reasons—connections now down to one. I don't know quite what to make of, or do with, Luke, though the doctors have said their piece. But when shuffled in with David's conflicting needs, it occurs to me that freedom may be best these days, in place of futile ties.

When Luke emerged to leave again, I asked him where he was living, but he declined to say. I gave him my new address and mentioned I'd have the same number. He looked at me strangely, as if amused by this sisterly gesture. But when I blinked and looked carefully back, he scowled and turned away, stepping over to the door, and slipping through it without goodbye.

Free once more, I dialed David, but still he's never where he's meant to be—in headlong flight as his schedule dwindles down. Alone instead, I took his cue and tied myself to my desk.

Turning the key, Eiley pushed into the partially furnished Oakland office. Vacuum-like Sonoran dryness sucked her on, past minimal furnishings piled along the walls: a government-issue metal desk, some matching fold-up chairs, three shadeless lamps, a dusty couch, and peeling paint. By the window, she surveyed the place, then padded slowly like a cat back across the room to settle in a swivel chair. She ran through all that'd happened, the various stops along the way. She pictured Roy, who'd simply wandered into the Quarter Moon Café one day. They'd started talking and had not yet stopped.

What had changed was now she knew what she wanted: stories by herself and others, stories to explore mysteries like her mother, to reflect what thoughts her mother might've had. She knew she also was ready for closeness, and Roy, when he wasn't tapping at his keyboard, gave her that. They communicated silently in their hiking and sharing books—odd mixtures that they were. He, the solitary biker/hiker/techie, had shown her through the northern California sequoia stands, temperate, moist, and out of scale . . .

All's arranged, bags and boxes packed and taped. Tomorrow brings the movers and the move. I fingered my long-time keys in my pocket, wondering if I erred—then reminded myself to drop them off at the desk, and say goodbye to Frank and Tony.

I sat up through the hours, watching minutes inch into the dark. I called him twice, but he wasn't in. I'd hoped to spend this last night with him—another sentimental whim.

Instead I tried to recall the few connecting moments through the years. Alas he dominates those scenes. His story beats so strongly that I can now flesh no other men. The truth is that, with a song sung ardently, nothing else can compete. He said it once himself: that once it's tasted thoroughly, it can never be put back on the shelf.

I walked out on the terrace. The wind stalked and snapped my coat. I stared at all the lofty glowing towers, my jeweled and silent neighbors for this time—my lovely views. I looked to deeply plant these lasting symbols of this sequestered life, that's ending now, with Father's year. It had seemed so perfect, these heights above the din, but had kept me from unlocking the essential self within.

I witnessed every hour, though they proceeded at varied pace. I breakfasted with the sun, then fell asleep as it moved across my face. Then started, rose, and moaned under final preparations, stuffing a few last items into one last box, before the movers bared the place.

They came at eight. All went quickly, smoothly. In fact they told me, compared to most, I had hardly any stuff. "Hey lady, whajado? Heave it off the roof?"

By two, they'd trucked me down, and left me standing with my bags and boxes. The only item I'd forgotten was the ring of keys I'd meant to leave, which now I fingered in my pocket.

November

Pleased with having stashed my stuff, and with this new world, and at holding my ground with Kirsten, I found I could barely contain my joy. This completely different place, like some hotel, is as ornate as my old was spare, and so immaculate that surely there must be a cleaning service, a maid to dust the stair.

Chose the library's great desk facing north on which to lay out all my books. While glancing through the picture window into the leafless garden, electric is what I feel—a charge that change has fed. The question is how to best apply the spark.

Tried David. But he's remained successful at staying out of touch, which I understand—otherwise he'd get nothing done. Yet it left me with an ache.

Called Kirsten, after I'd tried all his phones. An appointment at five was made. Walked up past Macy's, then east to Madison, passing some of the homeless in the shadows of the office buildings. I could not help notice the discrepancy between how well we do with things, and how poorly with each other.

Staring out her window, Kirsten turned to greet me, "So how was it? You get lots done?"

"You know I've moved?"

Surprise lined her face. "No-o, no one told me. Where?"

"Chelsea, West 22nd. Josh offered it to me, for a time."

Her mouth fell open. "But why?"

"I wanted to be nearer people, and pay a smaller rent."

"Is that nearer Loomis too?"

"That as well."

Nail to tooth, she pondered. "Josh, I remember, was always fond of you."

"Some fantasy he keeps. We dated years ago."

"I've met his wife, somewhere, but can't recall the face." She dismissed this with a wave of her hand, and her gray eyes slowly lightened. "Well I have some news as well."

"Well good."

"Gérard and I will marry, in the Spring."

My turn to feel the shock, to feel time for an instant stop. "Why Kirsten, congratulations!" I sprung up and over to her, and she graciously allowed a hug.

"The wedding will be in Paris. We'll be spending a fair amount of time there, there and in Provence."

I pulled back to look. "This certainly is a surprise. I saw in Paris that you two got along, but this is a major move."

She nodded, turned away, and sank into her chair. "It is. But we do indeed get along. He's bright and dear and funny—the right one, at last, for me."

"Yes, yes. Well again, congratulations. I wish you all the best."

She eyed me carefully. "And what of you and Loomis, to whom I've not yet been introduced."

"I barely see him myself."

She understood, saying, "The directors I've known, I'm afraid, are all like that, married to their craft, and not their wives, or their revolving mistresses." Again a doubtful stare. "I hope sometime you'll find the happiness that has eluded you."

"Well thank you, Kirsten."

Her eyes fell to her desk. "And now, what have you concluded from your month of reflection?"

Although I assumed she must have guessed, I saw she wanted to hear it from my lips. "Despite the generosity of your offer, and your kind confidence in me that it implies, despite my wish to help you, as you have so helped me, I cannot pretend my heart would be in it. I wish there were some genuine way that I could whole-heartedly say yes."

"So nothing's changed?"

"I looked as deeply as I could, but found my heart was set on writing. I need that way out, and in."

Her eyes narrowed as they watched. Her mouth pursed, as around a slice of lemon. "Well. This is as I suspected. I merely wanted to give you one last chance."

"Thank you for your patience and support."

She inhaled and sat up straight. "I've brought in someone new, and will begin to acquaint her with the work. She'll need to take your office. You'll have to share with Mary Oester."

I bowed my head which was spinning with relief.

Her eyebrow rose, nudged by something less agreeable. "As for your wish to continue writing, I want to make one thing clear: you're not the editor here; you don't decide on policy. If that's something you want to do, you'd better find another job. Is that crystal clear?"

Shaking off her over-kill, I bowed again. For the moment I would acquiesce, and when I'm ready, leave.

"And allow a word to the wise. One doesn't sleep with subjects, at least until the piece is done."

A faint smile this time. I wondered if she had any inkling of all that's unfolded.

"So for a time I'm putting you on a kind of probation. You will have to prove you've learned the lesson. Of course you'll lose some pay. I don't know exactly what it is, but it's probably good you've moved." With this she breathed, but our not-completely-happy eyes did not release the other. Then, however, her expression softened. "As for our last two issues, they've sold surprisingly well.

Loomis, it seems, is a substantial draw. He's caught our readers' interest. I think that although his name is known, he exists in the public mind as something of a mystery—something which you caught well. So together Chris, you see, we gave them what they wanted. On that you must agree." She peered closely to see if I was in accord.

I forced a reluctant smile. "If integrity is no great matter."

She seemed to have not quite heard, or take it fully in. Engaged by her own thoughts, she rose to exchange one more hug, during which she whispered, "Oh, by the way, our wedding will be very small, just a few business friends and family, and of course his kids,' so don't be insulted at no invitation."

Once more I smiled away her concern, as she leaned back to study me. She added with frowning puzzlement, "In a way it's a shame you couldn't work out something with Laurent, although I acknowledge there were problems. But I thought your interests fit hand and glove."

Silently I pushed out one more smile at this thought on my behalf. And then reflected that for all the time Kirsten and I have known each other, our understanding has not deepened very much.

At home, I wandered my new floors, so different from my aerie. More space, and yet it feels more confined and intimate. Perhaps it'll help me focus thoughts, where the aerie set them free.

When again I could not reach him, I sat to write a note.

> David,
>
> It's no fun being out of reach. It raises fears, reopens holes that connect back through the years. But there's no one else to talk to, as we do, funning, punning, arm-in-arm puzzling what to do and how to be. You embody the possibilities in life, the range of things, and remind me that existence need not be merely endured, but can be stretched and celebrated. You remind me that there can be one who can imagine one's better side, and share one's hope and share the beauty in the world. You remind me that there have been few—in a word, none—who have seen, let alone even

looked, into my yard. This spirit would prefer not to wait too long. The year's already mourned too much, and I have no wish to slip again into that icy state of being.

With love, C.

Night

I leaned over my desk, to see where Ms. E. would go, as one evening she talked with Roy. Somewhere along, the phone interrupted, and it was him. "We have, at last, a screening scheduled. Can you believe? I've reached the closing stretch."

"Oh David, good, that's very good!"

"It's on the 22nd, at eight o'clock. 55th and Sixth."

"Got it, and congratulations too."

"After this unending trek, the end's in sight. All the blocks and pieces are pried into place."

"You must be relieved, and very pleased."

"I . . ." But a deep, heavy cough cut him off, followed by shallow gasping. "Sorry . . . I kiss the air, the sun, the moon, and you, real soon, I hope."

"Why not now? You don't have a cold, do you?"

"No, but I'm done, cooked. I'm nearly crawling into bed."

"I could rub your back."

"Yes, but I'd never know. I'm all but slipping into sleep."

"So when?"

"Before I crash, tell me how you are?"

"Buoyant . . . desperate."

" . . . Well, Saturday, then. Saturday afternoon and night. I have something in the morning. Mandy and Marnie will be here for the weekend, but they're mostly with their friends. So, will that be good for you?"

"If I must wait . . . You okay? Sure you don't have something? Your voice sounds bad."

"No, listen, I've made it. That's the thing. I look back through all these months, through the days of dread uncertainty, and now I tell myself, it's done!"

I closed my eyes.

"And soon will have time, Miss Chris, for us."

My eyes stayed closed, warding off habitual fear.

"So, let me go, and sleep, the sooner that I'll see you."

"Saturday."

"Good night."

I heard, I think, a faint kiss, but in the silence he was gone. I pictured his face, his intensely glowing eye.

Weekend

Have looked forward to sauntering down, in bracing air, through the Village, Soho, to his street. But with my coat pulled up one arm, the phone pulled at the other. Should I slam the door and let the machine do its thing? Yet it might be him calling with yet another delay, something unforeseen. Torn, I cried out, "Ohh, for God's sake! Hello!"

"Christine? It's Larry."

"Larry? What's . . . How is she?"

"It's started, the contractions. We just brought her to the hospital. She's hoping you'll come up."

"Of course. Just have to make one call. She's fine?"

"Yes, anxious, a little worried, but ready."

"Lenox Hill?"

"Third floor, Maternity."

Slumped into my desk chair. Just when . . . But I dialed and reached his machine, explaining, promising to call when I can, when it's over. What else? A kiss. Hoped the girls weren't standing over it, staring down.

At the hospital, I found Kate sitting propped up in bed, floating somewhere within a white, impersonal gown—a sight both dismaying and comical. We embraced lightly to avoid disturbing the various lines and tubes running in and out.

"God Chrissy! Can you believe? At last! I'm so glad you've come. Sorry to drag you all the way up here."

"Are you kidding? I wouldn't miss this for the world. How are you?"

"Relieved. I can't tell you how much I've been looking forward to this. Both to see the little thing, and lose this baggage."

Kate was keyed up. Her chattering flew in all directions, without transition. I hung on as best I could, while Larry took the chance to run out for something to eat.

Sometime after three, contractions increased, and she, growing more uncomfortable, turned and halted our conversation with groans and deep breathing. At one point she leaned sharply back, then bent forward with a shout. I took her sweaty hand, but writhing, she pulled it back.

From somewhere across the room, we heard a nurse gasp, "Oh God, the heartbeat?" This brought other nurses running, then doctors. It seemed the baby's heartbeat had disappeared from the monitor. Maybe Kate's sharp movement had disconnected something, but they couldn't get a reading. There was much rapid checking. The doctors explained they could take no chances, and prepared to wheel her upstairs for a Caesarian, to get the baby quickly out and breathing. Kate cried out, "But I don't want one. I've never had an operation in my life! Larry tell them! Stop them!"

Larry tried to question the rushing doctors. Was this necessary? But they kept repeating they had little time, and soon we were all heading for the elevator.

Upstairs, outside the O.R., Larry, then I, gave worried Kate a kiss, before she was wheeled inside. We were directed, with minimal assurances, to wait in a drab little room.

Poor Larry paced back and forth, muttering. I tried to tell him Kate was a battler and would come through fine. Though he agreed, it gave him little solace.

But after not too long, having leafed through months-old magazines and stared out the sooty window at institutional roofs and walls, I saw a nurse come out for Larry. "Mr. Miller?" Sprawled in an armchair, forearm over his eyes, he peered up warily.

"You have a lovely baby girl, and your wife is doing fine. I'll take you in."

Relief passed through him. He closed his eyes. Then rising together, we threw our arms around each other briefly in a fumbling, awkward hug, before he hurried off.

Not long afterward, I was allowed in, to see little Christina—for such was her parents' choice—and found her Mom groggily glowing, the tiny thing at her breast. Bending over, I saw how cute and wrinkled she was, dark-haired and looking more like Larry.

I gently embraced and kissed dear Kate, who seemed deeply satisfied, having done her maternal duty and launched another life.

After another hour, Kate passed out—for the night, the nurse predicted. And little Christina was swaddled and returned to the nursery, in a row with several other tiny bundles.

And so with a final hug to Larry, who was only slightly more alert, I left them, slipping him David's number for tomorrow. Downstairs, I called David, but Marnie answered and informed me that he was sleeping. I asked her to tell him I called, and that I'd call again in the morning, and that my friend had a lovely little girl."

Her high-pitched, "Oh neat," was followed by a grunting acknowledgement that she'd relay the news, and finally by our terse goodnights.

Sunday

The image of the tiny face lifted me lightly when I awoke late the next morning. Called Kate to hear her voice. "Hey, Mama, how are you all?"

"I just sent Larry home. He stayed all night, which was so sweet of him, but we two were sleeping dead out."

"How's the little thing?"

"Oh, she's right here feeding silently, happy as a clam. It's just such an indescribable feeling . . . this little family."

But her assertion aside, she spent the next thirty minutes describing just that indescribability. Then asked if I wanted to stop by. But I reminded her that I was hoping to see David, and with that she rushed me off the phone. "Oh, go, go, see him. Tell him you want a baby, a baby girl. Tell him to come see sweet Christina."

"He has two teenage daughters."

"Oh God, that's right. But you don't! He's got to get you pregnant."

I laughed and sent Kate a kiss, and told her I'd see her in a day or two.

Calling Vestry Street, I reached Mandy and asked her if it was okay to head down. She said her dad was still sleeping, but she expected him to soon be up.

Following my planned route of yesterday, I meandered through the Village and Soho, and it was Mandy again whom I met when I rang the bell. We exchanged not-quite-comfortable greetings, as she avoided my gaze and ushered me in, announcing quietly, "Dad just got up. I told him you're here."

I tried to see her face, but she turned away to lead me upstairs. I called ahead, "I hear you're going to pick up at Columbia again."

Not turning, she corrected, "Not until January."

As we reached the living room, creaks on the upper stairs preceded David's arrival. Mandy quickly disappeared back down, and I turned to find him descending, his skull more prominent than ever, thinner, paler. "David."

He wore a jacket, which seemed oddly formal and contributed to an air of change. Extending both hands to enclose mine, he pulled me gently into a light embrace, murmuring, "You have the glow of having given birth." Our cheeks gently touched.

"It was a Caesarian."

"A healthy little girl, you said?"

"Yes. So tiny, so serious, so cute."

Smiling, he surveyed me. "It's so good to see you. Sorry it's been too long, though it was me who suffered most."

"No, Eiley and I have both been thinking about you, from our exiled vantage."

With a wan smile he looked at me. "That's sometimes what writing takes. It's not for everyone."

I studied him, wondering what he meant to tell me, before I rushed on, "What we concluded is that you and I need to take a trip."

His gaze passed over me, then seemed to drift off. "Yes . . . but first I must take the girls, perhaps over Marnie's Christmas break."

"Again? Putting me off? What is this?"

He found me, and his hand reached out, not quite all the way. "Don't worry, we'll go, when there's more time. Over New Year's, I've been thinking, if that's good for you. But I need to spend some time with them. In truth, the divorce has been a heavier blow than any of us understood. We three need some time together. I depend on you, above the rest, to see this."

Manipulation? Or too familiar truth?

He turned, to move toward the couch. "Will you come and sit?" Slowly I followed.

"Mandy, I think, and Marnie are making brunch. Will you have something? Some coffee at least, if you've eaten?"

We settled down next to each other. A fire played in the fireplace, into whose flames I stared. His hands felt for mine. For a time we rested, suspended once more, it seemed, between joy and our recent past.

At length he uttered, "If not for the need to finish up, and pay the bills, how little important work now seems. I'd like to sit like this for months."

"David, you could no more sit like this than I."

Slowly he shook his head. "No, nor do I have the time."

I heard four footsteps on the stairs, and the two daughters dear arrived with trays of food and drink. I stood to greet Marnie, but she, like her sister, did not meet my eyes. Yet neither did she exhibit her former pouting disapproval. Indeed she seemed faintly lost or untethered, and like her dad, had grown unnaturally pale. I felt a twinge for her, and a second one, when I noted that she'd put on weight. A sign of sadness was my guess. A chubby school girl hiding under layers. It's good he's going off with them—good for them.

We four tried to talk, but it was a halting effort, and David was too tired to fill in the gaps. At the end, when we three women carried things back downstairs, I took a moment when we were alone to ask Mandy, "How was California?"

A sharp, frowning glance was thrown my way. "How was it? I think you know. I got shafted." Surprisingly she laughed a high-pitched sardonic laugh, then blushed and turned away, to wrench on the faucet. "He changed a lot, once we got out there. I guess it was all the women, actresses, parties. He talked a lot about you." Our uncertain eyes met and scanned the other for reaction.

"I think you freaked him, unsettled him . . . In many ways he's still not totally confident. I think working with Pat did the same, and with Dad too. Dad lets you know when he's not happy. John, I think, felt everyone was judging him. I think eventually I got lumped in there, with all the rest."

Now she faced me and studied me as I scraped scraps into the garbage. "Why did you hook up with him? Just for the profile? I mean you two are so different."

Breathing out, I laughed once to myself. "Good question . . . A case maybe of opposites attracting. After my divorce, I didn't have things, well, quite together."

She looked down.

I added quickly, "Of course, he is attractive. And when he relaxes, he can be charming, in his mid-American simplicity—not much ambiguity there. And sometimes he can be quite funny."

She sought my eyes, exhaled, then moved slowly toward the fridge, before glancing down. "Dad's not in good shape."

"I know." I felt the old fear returning.

"He needs to just vege out, I think."

"I've wondered if he should see some other doctors."

"I'm going with him to see his doctor this week."

"I'm not sure he's told me the whole story."

Sucking on her lip, she peered unhappily at me. "Why? Why

would you think he would? After—I mean, why did you write about him, and Mom, the way you did?"

I saw her eyes accuse me, and I felt for her. The tearing of the family. Inside, I felt an anguished cry. Then tried to explain, "It was never my intention to include his personal story. In fact I wrote none of that. The editor, put it in, against my objections . . . I'm sorry."

"Why didn't you tell her not to?"

"I did. She wouldn't listen."

"Well, who told her about all that?"

"Some she found in an upstate paper, some was gossip and rumor, some came from what I hinted at."

Her head tipped into thought. Slowly she turned away, then pivoted back, looking unhappily at me. "It seems to me you should have quit."

"Yes, although that would not have changed a word."

Her expression grew heavy as she eyed me. "Well, would you do us a favor?"

Although I suspected I knew what was coming, I indicated I would.

"Don't ask him for too much, before our trip. We want him to be well rested, for once."

I nodded, as the floor seemed to sway. The repeated request, the recurring separation—something Mandy and I somehow share.

When we had cleaned and loaded up, then returned back upstairs, the two sisters disappeared.

"Shall we take a walk?" I asked him, standing near the fire, warming hands.

"Not today. I'm sorry, but I don't have the energy—feel already I need a nap. But we'll have time. I want to see your place."

"So what shall we do?"

"Now? Or into the future?"

"Both."

He fell into reflection, then winced as he tilted his head.

"Stiff neck?"

Gingerly he nodded. "Must've slept on it wrong."

I moved to him, bending down and turning him a bit, to rub and knead his neck. His faint groans suggested I'd found the offending spot. "You should be available regularly," he sighed.

"I am. The question is, are you?"

"Soon, soon. We have walks to take, plays to see, dances and music to lift our dreams. What do you think?"

"Mm, much to do."

"And trips to take."

" . . . Yes."

So, despite his fatigue, and daughters somewhere around, something of our old caring returned. I pictured us walking on a beach perhaps, or maybe writing something together.

In time, the Friday screening came. While I thought of inviting Kirsten, to introduce her, now of course, too much ill will existed. I did ask Ben, but though eager, he was busy, and so I walked over alone after a long day. The screening room was on the street-level floor of one of the newer office buildings along Sixth, and it was Jeff I met first, in the plush, red velvet antechamber. I asked if he was excited to see it with an audience. His brow rose as he considered this. "Well yes, but this is also our first opportunity to see the entire, fully mixed, color-corrected print with all the effects."

"Are many changes likely?"

"Undoubtedly some. Things always look a bit different on the big screen."

"And what's your sense? Is it where you want it to be?"

"Hard to say. I know David's feelings have fluctuated lately."

Before I could ask why, Graham appeared, trailing and introducing, "Marty, Marty Berg, our producer."

Shaking hands, I found Marty trim, dark-haired, athletic—a tennis player, judging from his edgy springiness. His negligible reaction to me suggested he hadn't read the profile, and while he smiled and said the proper things, his eyes scanned the arriving crowd for the necessary names.

Debbie and Rudi now filled the space Marty vacated. We greeted as if best-of-friends. Indeed I wondered at it. Had they too not read my piece? Was their enthusiasm for the finally finished film, or were these their screening faces?

Behind me, a woman's voice uttered my name. Turning, I discovered Pat looking rather intensely at me, her face floating above the darkest black. Surprisingly she gave me a quick hug, and confided with feeling, "I need to talk to you sometime."

"I'm back at the magazine most days now."

She squeezed my hand and moved away to a rather striking-looking man in a modish leather jacket.

With time to gaze around, I saw that perhaps only John was conspicuously missing from the cast and crew. As people began to filter into the theater itself, I spotted David arriving, in earnest conversation with two gentlemen, a European-looking fellow roughly his age, and a younger man, the *Times* reporter, my guess. As I waited for an opportunity to step over, I gathered the older fellow was composer, René Auberge. David, now seeing me, held up a finger, while at his coattails tagged Mandy and Marnie, heads slightly bowed, reluctant to peer around. I slid over. "How are you two doing? Excited, after all these months?" And yet, in the instant I spoke, I realized that for them the film may seem the blade which halved their lives. But Mandy swallowed and artificially brightened a bit. "Yes, I'm eager to see it." Her eyes fell away, though, perhaps fearing that I'd think watching Johnny would be painful for her. I touched her arm, then turned to Marnie, who, as ever, avoided my gaze.

Gamely recovering, Mandy asked, "How's your writing going?"

I shook my head. "Frustratingly slow."

"You're still at the magazine?"

"Back at, after some time off." Mandy, at least, did not appear to see me as the evil witch.

David now turned to us and introduced me to René and the *Times* man, whose name was vaguely familiar. He then lead us all in to our center-row seats, ushering in Marnie and Mandy, then following himself. I urged the reporter and Mr. Auberge to slide in ahead of me. Seated and waiting for the lights to dim, René whispered that various distributors were in attendance as well as several other possibly sympathetic reviewers. He then leaned discreetly closer. "I understand you're writing a novel."

I cleared my throat. "Isn't everybody? But struggling to is more like it."

A serious nod. "Don't worry, you're not alone. Every mode of original expression is a struggle, at many levels."

"I wonder if it's merely desperation."

He smiled and whispered, "It almost must be."

"In composing too?"

"Oh, alors," and he rolled his eyes. "I must practically whip myself to extract anything new out of me." And he laughed.

"I liked your scores for "The Kestrel" and " . . . Daniel . . ."

"Oh, well thank you."

"Particularly "The Kestrel.""

"Yes, that came out well. However, few people have, I think, appreciated the complexity of both men, and the sympathy David expressed for them. He portrayed the difficulties so finely."

The lights now dimmed, and the curtain opened. The leading actors' names faded in, and then the title. A hundred fleeting memories flew down from that northern wood.

Before us, a brown, gray, exterior wooden wall appeared, and Stephen's grizzled, dispirited face, moved into frame, as he leaned back to look up into an overcast sky. "Should be snowin'" he muttered to himself, "coverin' the town." He allowed his gaze to fall back to Main Street, where a few slow-moving residents rocked along the walk, and finally out over the gray, uninviting lake where sky and water merged.

Across the street a young mother, Teresa, shepherded her two young girls along the sidewalk. Stephen and she noticed each other briefly, without acknowledgement, before their attention was drawn to the diner where three older men, pulling on coats against the chill wind, conferred and dispersed. Harvey, I recognized, was among them.

A call came from behind, "Stephen." He turned, to find Sam the mayor approaching. "Got an idea for you, amigo."

Unmoved, Stephen waited.

"Peter Rodino's leavin'. Got a job down in Glens Falls, freein' his spot at the garage."

Stephen didn't react at first, then nodded faintly.

"I understand it may not be the cat's meow, but, Rick pays at least. It's better than nothin'."

"I've been thinkin' about leavin' too, Sam, like Peter."

Sam frowned, and shook his head. "No-o, Stephen don't. If you go, who'll be left? You'd leave me here with Harvey and the crew, all bitter as bitter root. No, don't do that."

Stephen shifted his eyes to Sam. "What am I gonna do? . . . Besides, Rick and I don't see eye-to-eye." He glanced up at the withholding sky. "It's time for me, time to do somethin'."

Sam's gaze fell to the ground for a moment, then slowly rose as he shook his head. "Yeah, I'd like to go as well . . . if I could."

Stephen looked over, found him, felt a pang for Sam.

Sam inhaled, then expelled, "Being mayor sounds good, until you put on the chains."

Their eyes met and held, wondering about choices and feeling for the other.

Watching, I forgot that this was David's film, or that these were actors. It just flowed forth, unfolding with a terrible poignancy, barely allowing time to breathe. And, as lovely as the Adirondacks were, it was the New York segments that surprised me and tugged my heart. The monochromatic streets and rooms, Stephen's slow, inexorable searching, failing, block by block, walking past silent buildings, desperately seeking un-skilled work which paid enough to keep him here. His determination became obsession and turned self-defeating—to extract something from the city, from those unsmiling bosses he attempted to buttonhole.

Confining himself to bread and milk, staving off retreat, and thus in a weakened state, he was swept up along Sixth, that afternoon, into another state, out of which he found something to take home. Sitting there, I wondered how true this was for most of us: needing some jolt, or hitting bottom.

Yet even at the end, in Stephen's and Teresa's triumph, the

fragility of things was apparent: the opposition to the club may rise again; the club may fail financially; Stephen and Teresa may slip apart, once the glue of their common struggle no longer binds. For what could match the intensity of that fight? Indeed as their two tired faces stared out upon their crowning evening, some awareness, I thought, blurred their sight.

As the final shot faded, I tried to clear my eyes before René turned my way. Fortunately applause put this off, crescendoing until it pulled David up, bowing, calling, "Thank you, thank you, thank you all." He then waved the others up as well to acknowledge their contributions. René stood eagerly, not in the least shy to share acclaim. And in the commotion, I stole glances at the faces watching David, some beaming, eyebrows lifted, some curious, some wiped after their own long days.

When the applause died down, we filed out of our row into a gathering of friends and colleagues. The inner group slowly spiraled up the aisle, including at different points: Rudi, Graham, Marty, some of the banking people, and the distributors. Marty, in particular, shaking hand after hand, glowed with satisfaction.

I found myself next to Debbie who was expressing tearful joy at the picture and David's triumph—but who then whispered details of her new production, assisting Marty. To Peter and Dave I nodded, and when Jeff pushed by to confer with David, I managed to offer him congratulations. With a bovine smile, he touched my hand and lowed.

All this proceeded in stops and starts, up into the lobby, then out to the street, slowly throwing off members. I wondered how long David could continue finding and repeating gracious words, but at last we four stood alone.

Facing us, slightly stooped, his one eye dimly shining, he exclaimed, "Well, thank you each for your patience. If Lear were so well attended, would he have gone mad? How about a cab? My family for a cab."

Soon, in one, we were taking his daughters home to Kath's. In the front seat, I half-turned, glancing back. Mandy, excited by the film and its reception, spewed out little joys and observations.

David, aware of Marnie's quite other mood, tried to include her in the celebration, working his arm around her and pulling her close. She rested her head silently against his shoulder.

At 83rd near Park, we all climbed out, and unexpectedly David paid the driver. I'd thought we'd continue on. Good nights and plans for the following weekend were exchanged, along with allusions to their trip. The girls and I shook hands. Marnie forced herself to look at me. Closely I looked back.

And then it was only David and me.

"I want to walk, through our old neighborhood," he said, "as long as we're up here. How about you? Unwind after all that. Are you game?"

"Certainly . . . but David, the film was so moving . . . a crystal, reflecting, dissecting . . . everything. At the end it wrung tears."

"But the ending's hopeful."

"It's uncertain—their future and the club's."

He was bending slightly to find my eyes. He took my arm, and we began to walk. "What future brings guarantees? Yet their horizons are substantially brighter than they were. Together they have achieved something."

"Yet what will come?"

With some impatience he nodded. "Who knows? Knowing would undo us all. It's *not* knowing that keeps us reaching. Chris, Chris, let us enjoy our walk. I crawl on borrowed energy."

And so we walked to East End Avenue and then back along 79th. Waiting to cross First, I asked, "How pleased were you?"

"I was not looking to be pleased tonight, but to see what needs to be done. I made a list."

"Does this postpone your rest?"

"Not a lot, Jeff can take care of much of it. René needs to re-do a few things."

Time seemed to slow as we walked and gazed and reflected. Soon I realized we were nearing my old place, my aerie, and I told him I'd like to stop and say hello to the doorman on duty. And by chance, it was Tony, who called 'hello.' I introduced David, but the name meant nothing to him. I asked who's living in my apartment now, and he said the new tenant was planning an elaborate renovation and probably wouldn't move in for months.

"Shall we go up?" wondered David. "Take a last look from the terrace?"

Uncertain, Tony hesitated, "I don't think I have a key."

"Oh Tony, I still have mine." And I pulled it out of my bag. And so Tony let us up.

Without furniture, the rooms seemed smaller, lonely, with oblique shadows on the walls. But outside the night was cool and clear. A planet or star dimly hung above the city haze, and all the buildings shone as if they'd never noticed I'd left. We circled the terrace gazing downtown and west, then stood and held each other silently for some minutes.

I became aware that his eyes had moistened. He turned me away and buried his face in my hair. His body shook, two racking tremors. I twisted back to him to lean cheek-and-cheek, then lips lightly as well, until the sense of separateness disappeared. I felt a desire to be closer still and worked my hands inside his coat, but a gust unbalanced us, reminding us that the night was cold and that we were far from either home. And so we stood there, now brow to brow, trying to ignore the prying cold. More gusts swayed us. We tried to plant our feet.

Shortly, he lifted his head back, and I heard him mutter, "What? . . . Chris, has it grown suddenly dark?"

I leaned back to look, as some fear rose up. "No."

He breathed, then looked around. "Well then, something . . . something's happened."

Alas, though I feared I knew, I asked, "What?"

"It's gone . . . gone once more."

He moved his hands to my shoulders, to steady himself. I tried to see, and indeed found him turning his head, tilted up, futilely, one way, then the other.

"Chris . . . Christine!"

"I'm here!"

" . . . My God!"

For a moment he seemed to shiver, then coughed twice before

he muttered, "God, it's cold." He reached out a hand to feel for something, then slid a foot, without letting go. He closed his eyes and expelled a breath, a half-cry, then leaned carefully into me, as another gust shoved by. I braced myself to hold us both.

"Don't, don't move. I feel dizzy. I may be sick. I'm trying to find, trying to picture, those several faint stars I saw minutes ago, and the glowing buildings, and your face."

I stretched up on my toes to touch his cheek with mine.

He inhaled, then released it. "It may be temporary. Maybe not. I suddenly fear this roof, its height. Fear stepping off, or being blown. I shouldn't be up here. Will you lead me in, Chris?"

"Yes."

"Now I'm freezing."

Slowly, trying to quell my own trembling, I led him back in through the sliding door. There we held each other. I asked, "David, should we go to a hospital? Lenox Hill's not far."

"Shh, a hospital can do nothing now."

We didn't move. My hand lightly held his head to mine. "Do you want to go home?"

"Yes."

Downstairs, we made every effort to hide his condition from Tony, as I handed over my two keys, and thanked him, and shook his hand. And then David and I, as we did once months ago, walked to the door and out.

We took a cab, saying nothing, though my mind flew in all directions down the passing blocks. I cracked my window to let the cold air buffet me and dry my eyes. My hands clamped his.

At Vestry Street, I led him upstairs to the living room and couch, where he sat leaning forward, upright, turning his head, searching for light, before resignation appeared to progressively weigh him down.

"David? What do you need, what can I do for you?"

He opened his mouth, then closed it. He seemed not to know where to face. I stepped to him and touched his knee. His face tipped back, turning, cheek twitching. His mouth opened once more. "A scotch," he requested, coughing, almost swallowing the word. "Scotch and water. Liquor's in the office, first cabinet to the right."

Surprised, I went and poured two scotches with water, and returned and placed his in his shaking hand. Indeed I steadied his hold before I let go and settled down next to him. We sipped carefully, trying to understand what had happened, and why. It seemed an extension of the movie, a scene I was watching.

After not too long, he murmured, "The movie already seems both near and far—one second eye to eye, the next barely visible. A dream. Is it real? Did I do it? . . . Why?"

I turned my head to see him, but his head was turned away in reflection, and so instead I entwined his arm with mine. He finished his drink in a series of rapid sips, then held out the glass for a refill. Taking it and standing, I looked back. He waited trustingly, alone. I forced myself away. Clearing eyes, trying to inhale deeply, I found the taste of scotch evoked Father, his drink. Old tar. Not sure I wanted mine now.

At length, when he finished the second one, he leaned back. "Not much good for anything now. Empty, tank gone dry . . . Might as well pass out . . . or away."

Seated again, I brought my cheek to his and we did not move for some time. Eventually I led him upstairs, not without some deep, vague fear. Sitting on the side of his bed, he asked, "Will you stay?"

"Of course." Yet I was aware of a heaviness, part of which came, I'm sure, from the sense of having been through this before, but another part seemed new and grim, not unlike one of the movie's scenes of sullen, rain-shrouded Trappers Lake.

Beneath the covers, we lay on our backs.

"Chris? What are you thinking?"

"Oh, everything. About this evening, and your achievement."

"And collapse."

"The movie filled my eyes."

He faintly groaned.

"I don't think one could ask for more."

"As once I said, you should write publicity for us."

I nudged his arm. "You should be pleased, deeply pleased, with what you did."

"I was, for what—nearly an hour? Then it receded, as the bills came due."

I took his arm and rolled toward him to kiss his cheek.

"Thank you. You bring it back, make it immediate, worth thinking about. There are still changes needed. I'll talk to Jeff tomorrow."

"You said he can do most of them?"

"Once we talk. We spoke about this eventuality some months ago. I had to . . . but then I thought I'd made it."

"You did."

"I saw other things I would change, if I could, if there were time and money."

"I thought it was complete."

"There are always improvements possible."

We fell silent. Eventually I heard him breathing evenly. I listened and tried to breathe as he did—the last thing I remembered before morning.

When I opened my eyes, it was light, and he was awake, sitting up next to me. Hearing my stirring, he asked, "How did you sleep?"

I pulled myself up next to him. "Okay. And you? Any sign of . . . ?"

"No."

I inhaled deeply and pushed myself up further, discovering the covers pulled up to his neck.

"This is fiendish . . . perverse," he mumbled. "The only thing in my mind is fear's great pale face, standing right there, in my face." He snorted faintly. "In place of light."

I leaned and held him.

"Yes, that is best. Your touch."

"I feel I want to join you."

"What? . . . What tripe! I want to curse it with all my fucking might! Though I know I'm lucky, twice." He squeezed my hand and breathed, "It's suffocating, fright circling just below, while over me, a great, airless metal box has clamped down, immovably. In panic, I almost woke you."

"You should have."

"I managed to feel my pulse, calm myself. I still expect to see each time I open my eyes. And each time, the blow, the fear, the panic, sweep back in." With this, some force lifted him upright as he half-cried out. I pushed myself closer. He leaned his head against mine, recovering, panting. My hand felt and wiped his moist brow, soothing him. In time, this calmed us both. We lay back down again, heads upon our pillows. Shortly he said, "I've been picturing things: this house, its rooms, the movie, the editing rooms, my daughters, Kath, various blocks in the city, the park . . . Eleanor, her face . . . I can dwell on no one thing, but my now-pelagic mind swims on, as if it knows there's nothing more on which to feed."

I turned and touched his hair. This again seemed to soothe him.

"I was trying to imagine what to do, as I had first done months ago . . . Volunteer at the shelter, maybe."

"Or with our tutorial program."

"You'd have to teach me Braille."

"I wonder how hard that must be."

"Necessity would be the spur. Maybe I could help in a school reading program. The kids might spell the words they don't know. I wonder if I could write legibly on a blackboard."

"On a computer. You could write your poetry."

He laughed to himself. "I have no meter-making thoughts left."

"Oh, you do. In fact they might come more easily now."

His brow furrowed, before he faintly breathed. But then he jerked forward sharply, away from me, and thrust out a hand, swinging it in all directions as if to ward off some fearful thing approaching. Then he gagged, as if he might be sick.

"David?" I felt him inhaling with difficulty.

"Sorry," he managed. "Picturing everything . . . unable to get out . . . Shit, I may be sick." And he pulled himself to the side of the bed and leaned over.

I threw the covers off and jumped out as he coughed, then heaved. I grabbed a basket and ran around to his side. He heaved again, but it was dry, and he convulsed deeply once more, again dryly, after which he lay there panting, mouth open, brow moist, head tilted weakly.

I sat on the edge and placed my hand on his forehead and cheek, wet and cool. After a while, when his body relaxed, he decided it would be better to get up, rather than lie and ruminate. And so I helped him up and to the toilet, then the shower, then into his clothes. He called his doctor and left a message with the service. "Tell him this is David. I'm afraid the final curtain's dropped. Call me." He snorted, once again, lightly to himself.

He then called and spoke with Jeff at length about what was to be done—without any mention of this thing.

"I'll delay, Chris, as long as possible, so as not to jangle all their bells and get them fretting and calling."

He insisted on helping me prepare breakfast. "It's better if I do something, rather than sit and stew. In any case, I must learn how . . . must get used to this."

While we assembled our food and drink, he thought aloud, "I should call Mandy and Marne. Of course this means Kath will know . . . After we eat, how about getting out and taking a walk?"

After breakfast, we bundled up against the chill, gray day, and walked east and down through a world little known to me, back into earlier years, Little Italy, Chinatown, the Bowery, Wall Street, and the Battery, there along the water. The city felt deserted; the chill wind had swept the streets. Everything seemed gray and distant, except for David. I described the scenes we passed, described the sky, the gulls, the boats out in the harbor, and other walkers. A few snow flakes floated down out of nothing. David's face tilted back and allowed the flakes to land, and melt.

Returning to his house, we found he'd received a number of calls, including one from his doctor. I directed him to the office desk to return them, and in the process, he received several more, from Rudi, Pat, and Graham, each expressing his or her thoughts on the film and sounding out his reaction. Upbeat, he never revealed the situation. Rudi apparently urged him to make more of an effort to see me.

"Well Rudi, as a matter of fact, she's here now. We've just come in from a bracing, exhausting walk."

As he talked to them, and indeed throughout the afternoon, he reacted to his sight-loss with unexplained equanimity. Although I reminded myself he'd had months to prepare himself, to imagine it, and that he had experienced that short period of blindness following the accident, still his lack of mourning, self-pity, despair seemed odd to me. Had he locked it away, denying it? Or was it something else?

Later when we sat together, I wondered, "How have you been so strong about this?"

"As I said, I have you here, with me. You hold off the terror."

"I'm serious."

"As am I. When I was a child, I was afraid of the dark, unless there was one other person with me, a friend. Then it became a playland, an adventure. 'There is nothing either good or bad but thinking makes it so.'"

"I hope it's so."

"Hoping sometimes does as well . . . For me at least, fortune has brought me much—and the crowning piece is you."

I looked at him and found a mild sheen upon his face. And yet as we sat, his face changed, grew long and dark, and he brought his hands to cover it. Was it the face of fear again? Does he see that his work, and all that life, are past—the visual world shut off? "David, what is it that grips you?"

"The same reel of sorts: this year, my daughters, the movie, you, all in and out of focus. Nothing lingers, all rushes on . . . I wonder if Mandy will make films. For all I know of her, and we do talk more now—I've read some of her papers, know some of the books she likes—still I cannot know where she will go. How few do we ever really know, or feel know us, as we see ourselves. How few, these days, have time to reflect and talk. Money and things have taken over. I sometimes think you and I may be among the few." His cheek contorted with this thought. "Is he or she richest who is freest? Is he or she freest who has the fewest trappings? Sometimes I think it was the kids we chose to have—our joy and our burden, who we allowed to pull us apart . . . as together, they and work, left us hardly any time or energy for each other. Each grew hurt, and after time, there was no way back . . . But it is, in fact, more complex than that."

He rubbed his eyes, wiped his brow and face. "Or maybe one of the bard's questions hangs upon me: 'What is a man, if his chief good and market of his time be but to sleep and feed?' . . . I turned away from domestic life, which I confess I did esteem less and less. Felt compelled to, maybe could not have done other. Yet it is, I see too late, no less estimable. And somehow, despite all of these mistakes, you have appeared . . . The one price, however, for all of this is my daughters' faces, which suggest, strongly, it's not worth it, this work. Problem was, at some juncture, I felt there was no other choice, even as all was paraded before me, even as the Promethean costs were early known . . . What value a branch or stalk which but for a week does bloom? A match struck, flares up, burns out, shining light for some few seconds."

I slid my arm around him, as my mind replayed his speech.

At length, he breathed in deeply. "Tomorrow I must call them, and tell them. I think we must make the trip to Mexico in any case. I owe it to them, and myself, to have some undivided time . . . You know, it just occurred to me that Thursday's Thanksgiving. Are you free, to share it with me?"

With a swallowed laugh I asked, "David, with who else did you think I would?"

"Should we make a party? Ask a gang? Rudi would come, with his friend, Françoise. Maybe Pat, and beau. Jeff and his young wife. What do you think? Who has more to celebrate and thank than me? . . . Of course my daughters will split the day."

"That's fine by me. I told Kate I would visit her and little Christina."

"Christina? . . . Well bring them down."

"She has in-laws and her mother who need attention. I'll see them in the morning. But could hardly stay away for long."

He fumbled for, and took, my hand and brought it to his lips.

The rest of the day, evening, and Sunday shared this alternation between dreamlike affection and abrupt terror. Sometimes the tightening and horror came quickly upon him as we talked or walked, or I read to him. Other times the mood gradually shifted, as a storm slowly drifts up from the horizon. One moment, it was something to be accepted, lived with. Another, it was unjust fate, to rail against, to bitterly dispute, "Why, why has this happened? When there's so much left to be done?"

After Sunday breakfast and reading him the *Times*, he went back upstairs, to be by himself, to see how it was—to confront it. He told me later that he cried out, twice, yet not loud enough for me to hear. Twice he rose and tried to feel his way to the door, to get out. But stopped himself half-way, breathing deeply and wrestling bodily with it, trying to accept that this was now his world.

Unexpectedly, his darkness seemed to bring us closer. Our words hovered like transparent, deep-sea fish. Outside, time rushed by. We heard its turbulence, recognized it might crack the walls, but for now, all held together. Sometimes, feeling him next to me, as we lay silent, I imagined a tiny figure, half-man, half-boy, up on the roof, calling out, waving, strutting, dancing in the sunlight.

Monday

Morning brought clouded light. In the long tile kitchen, I moved slowly, making our breakfast, while he sat head-bent-down at the rectangular table. Sometimes found I could barely look at him. At other moments, I embraced him as he almost pathetically spooned the oatmeal I'd cooked. His hand shook as he lifted his black coffee. Its dark ripples filled the cup.

Yet beyond this, I knew I must get to the office. And when I mentioned it, he decided that he too would go uptown, to the editing suite. "Better to go and sit up there with Jeff, than remain alone here and slowly boil away. I will see what I can do. The news will get out . . . but, so be it."

Taxiing uptown together almost felt normal. His spirits rose, our heads swayed together as the cab jounced and swerved.

I led him through the editing rooms, past a lone young woman packing up the countless rolls for storage. Jeff was expected soon. Entering the main editing room, I seated David and searched for a pad and pencil for him, to attempt some notes. He said he wanted to think through the changes he'd been contemplating, wanted to run the film one final time in his mind.

"I'll pick you up after five, unless you head home early," I told him. Once more he did not know quite where to face as I bent to gently stroke his cheek.

At the office, Kirsten informed me that she was off to Paris for Thanksgiving, and then two weeks in Provence. She read her list. "Arliss will be our editor. I have some assignments for you, which you are to discuss with her, including: editing some of Eiley's chapters for us, possibly a piece on your brother's problems. Mental issues are hot right now, what with the recent breakthroughs." She sent me a pointed yet sympathetic grimace, presumably over the fact that Luke has not received this help. Her ignorance didn't bother me, and she danced on, "And another park piece, a winter's tale. Oh . . . and Loomis—I hear his film was quite a success. I'm sorry I couldn't make the screening. How did you feel it was?"

"Quite moving."

She raised a skeptical eyebrow. "Well good. Someone said that he, however, wasn't looking all that well."

"He's tired."

Another eyebrow raised, as this too she seemed to discount. But I paid scant attention. My mind was back with him, in the editing room, where he would be trying to picture, trying to listen to the scenes once more, before he let them go.

"Chris," she began, calling back my attention, "I hope you're not tying yourself to a spent horse, if you'll forgive the term."

I looked at her, my eyes heavy with distaste. I wondered if she's even aware of her jabs. Or is she simply seeking a reaction? Her eyes dropped down for a second, then returned. "If you want my opinion, you need someone your own age, someone you can grow with. Not someone who's reached his peak."

What could her intentions be? She sighed when she saw my receptivity was not all she deserved. Then inhaled and went on, "Well, I suspect it will pass in any case. It's not at all certain, I understand, that he'll be making more films."

"It's not his films that have drawn us together."

"What then? . . . His vision?" Her mouth and eyes fluttered, then went still. "Well, will you be having Thanksgiving with him? I assume your brother's not coming in from the cold."

They come in volleys, I see. She cannot stop. Perhaps Gérard will reign her in. "With David, yes, and my friend, Kate, and her new baby."

"Oh? Well again, I hope this is what you want."

I nodded, it was. She stood, and so did I. We shook hands. "Have a good trip," I wished her. "Say hello to Gérard for me."

"I will. We'll have lunch, or maybe dinner, when I get back."

"Love to."

She was already reaching for the phone as I turned away.

In my office, sitting across from Mary, I set Kirsten's list before me, and began to pull out Eiley's early chapters and my park pieces. But the phone was calling, and I answered.

"Christine Howth?" came a cry.

"Yes, who's this, please?" The voice I heard belonged to a middle-aged woman.

"I would like to ask you just one question."

"Fine, but who am I speaking to?"

"I have been wondering if, if you are pleased with yourself, for what you've done, wrecked a marriage, and taken two girls' father away from them. Are you? Pleased?"

" . . . Katherine?"

"Loomis, thank you. The name I can keep—an awkwardness for you, no doubt . . . But are you? I'd like to know. Are you feeling good about yourself?"

"Kath, I'm sorry. I know the pain of divorce. I went through my own."

"I'm not surprised . . . Heroic, truly. And now you thought you'd pass it on, share the feeling. How thoughtful."

"Did you want to talk genuinely?"

"Genuinely? You think what I'm saying is not genuine? How good you are, evidently, at deluding yourself. I guess you'd have to be, to do what you've done. But let me assure you, the pain you've caused my daughters is quite genuine. They are suffering, and have no father to turn to."

"Kath, I'm sorry for the . . ."

"Like hell you are! If you even knew what the word meant, you wouldn't be parading, wouldn't be smearing, your lies in that rag you work for—for the whole city to see."

"Kath, I apologize for those personal parts of the article, although they were not mine. Whether they're all lies is something else."

"You're a cool bitch, aren't you. Presuming to tell me what's what. How can you live with yourself? How can you wr-write such drivel and then look at yourself? That's what I want to know! How can you?"

"It was never my intention to . . ."

"Intention? It's all too clear what your intentions were. To confuse poor David, and humiliate the rest of us."

"Are you going to let me speak, or are you just going to vent?"

"Don't you get snooty with me. You've had your pulpit, for all the city to gape. Now it's my turn. You just shut up. You probably don't even know David's a sick man, in need of care. And to exploit him in his weakness, his defenses down, when he's preoccupied with another god-damned film, when he hardly has time for his daughters—to lure out his story, and I'm sure I know how you did it—sucking out all the family details . . . I mean, have you not even the vestige of a conscience?"

Unable to get through, I waited her out, as she huffed and spat. What sympathy I had felt drained away. Noticing that Mary was looking up wondering, I raised my eyebrows in sad exasperation, to which she sent commiseration.

"Are you going to answer me, Christine Ho . . . Hoat, or whatever it is? People are on to you, you know. They know how you work. I heard how you exploited that actor, corrupted him, so that he did the same thing to poor Mandy.

"As for David, he shouldn't be working. He needs rest, someone to care for him, rather than all you vultures stealing his very life. But of course I don't expect you to understand. What do you know of him? You're interested only in one thing. I'm going to your editor and tell her. I've got her name. I'm revealing your—the way you work, your methods, that you're a home-wrecker. And I hope she gives you what you've got coming. And then when you're out on the street, you try living with yourself, try facing your conscience, and then maybe you'll see what you've done, you, you, you . . . !" And the phone was slammed down.

I sat suspended between the unreality and the assault of her voice. I tried to imagine her woundedness, and sadness. Mary glanced up, unsure whether to ask or not. I pressed my lips and shook my head and looked down. How much was Kath driven to this, how much was she the driver? It's never simple, and indeed is impossible for outsiders to know the layers of unmet expectations and untended wounds.

Later I called Kate and replayed it. She too was stunned.

"The poor woman . . . Poor Chrissy. I can imagine how she might have slid into that . . ."

"Yes, I can too . . . David—I don't know the whole story—but he had Pat, and maybe another one or two, from what I gather."

"Well, it's a business where the temptations are right out there, isn't it? And of course, he's male."

"But not without conscience . . . and ideals . . . and fantasies."

" . . . I guess you're her scapegoat, Chrissy. Sounds like she can't accept it, and doesn't admit it predated you."

"The article must have torn it open. She had my ear, until she became quite unhinged and wouldn't let me reply at all."

"She's still bleeding."

" . . . Is it a zero-sum game?" I wondered.

"Where one's gain is from another's loss?"

"Mm.

"So it seems. But I hope that's not our world, yours and mine . . . although we've both had our run-ins, with men, and their appetites, their competitiveness . . . their pricks."

Not so happily I laughed a little. "The natural order, I suspect, which predates our wondrous species."

"Maybe. At what age, do you think, I should tell Christina?"

"About men? . . . Don't wait too long."

Later still, I wondered whether to report this to David. But decided it would only upset him. May mention it sometime. On the other hand, I felt I should tell Mandy, if I can find a moment, possibly on Thanksgiving. Kath needs some attention, and love.

For me, the week at work went by productively enough, but as I watched and listened to him, I realized that he was increasingly bowed by his darkness, by his inability to see his work, and finally by its drawing to a close.

Yet working with Jeff and René, finish it they did. He confided to me, however, that words are clumsy substitutes for simply seeing and cutting—bushels of words to roughly approximate. And yet it did get done, with mixed effects upon him. Completing the entire, hydra-headed thing relieved him of much weight and stress, yet because it will not come again—this major part of him—it left a critical hole. And while it freed us to talk about other practical things—finding him a cane, a dog, a counselor, writing together, learning Braille—he pursued not a one, perhaps because he was anticipating the trip with his daughters.

We spent the evenings at his house, where there were always calls to return. But we also got out to walk, or eat or have a drink at a café. This walking helped us both. It was then he described the fearful shut-in claustrophobia, bursting into terror, particularly in the night, when he awakened in a sweat, and I would hold him and try to tell him it was all right and that I was there. He said it feels as if he cannot get enough oxygen or that his heart will simply quit. It's panic, he knows, but cannot quickly quell it. I would hold him, and bring his head to my shoulder. We would lay together hands locked, or I would kneel over him, hands upon him, silently for minutes, waiting for the fear to release him.

There were moments when he relaxed and let his mind wander. At Café Noir one night, he asked, "Chris, why do we seem compelled to tell these tales time and time again? You would think they'd soon grow old, the lessons tiresome."

"They soothe us, divert us. They help explain the world."

" . . . Fill loneliness, and holes we find."

"Disappointments . . ." Looking up, I saw he held his head back, as if to avoid some thing which passed too close. "David, it will be good for you to take this time with Mandy and Marnie, in Mexico."

"Yes," he breathed, "Mandy and Marnie make a fine expedition to Mexico, with long-lost Dad."

"I meant it earnestly."

"I know. I just liked the hilly sound."

Reproaching myself for avoiding his eyes, I stared at them. Shadowed by the café's low light, freed from glasses, lids half-open, they seemed inert, dark smudges; they seemed mistakes, not connected to him. No longer were they part of this man I knew, nor the instruments through which he engaged life around him.

Thanksgiving

I went to Kate's in the morning, where the gathering was enlivened by little Christina smiling up at the adoring adult faces:

Kate's mother, the in-laws, a friend of Kate's from California who didn't want to fly home, and Larry, who's become quite the baby-holder, gazing down at her, making unending silly faces. "How many women would smile back at me for hours?" he asked me when he noticed I was watching.

"I know one other," I replied.

Glancing at Kate, he said, "Not always. Mama's not always so happy with Dada these days. She doesn't appreciate how hard he works."

Although I smiled, I knew he was skewing the dynamics. He could give up the extra hours and their bonuses for more time at home. But it's a choice he's chosen not to make.

Back at Vestry Street, it was Mandy who, as usual, greeted me at the front door, and I confided I'd like to talk to her privately sometime when she had a moment.

Soon after I arrived, Rudi and Françoise appeared, and I spent some time with her comparing memories of Paris, which she said she misses, even as she prefers the greater opportunity here. She has in fact decided to enroll in NYU's MBA program.

"And what of your husband?"

With a French shrug, she dismissed him, "Oh, he has his own life."

Pat arrived, trailing again her model-beau, by which I meant he's almost too pretty and maybe too young. I didn't see him talk to anyone but Mandy, who, under his glazed stare, broke out into unappreciated radiance.

When Mandy excused herself, I followed her down to the kitchen and caught her alone placing vegetable dumplings on a tray. "Is this a good time?"

Glancing up, she grew tight, her luster disappeared.

"Your mother called me last week at the office."

She nodded and waited.

"She was quite upset about the articles on your dad."

"Well, can you blame her?"

"No, I can understand."

" . . . How could you?"

"I went through a divorce."

Mandy seem unimpressed. I went on, "I guess my other point is that I think she's attributing many of the troubles to the two articles, and to me, and not to the underlying, long-standing issues."

She breathed and now slid the tray of dumplings into the oven. "Of course Mom's upset. We saw her earlier . . . But I mean Dad's always gotten stressed out by these movies, and he sort of resents it when she tells him. So he looks elsewhere for sympathy and support." She glanced at me.

"According to your dad, they tried to work things out, talk things out, but unfortunately it didn't solve the issues."

Straightening up, she checked the oven temperature, took me in again, then wiped the counter and sighed. "I don't know. I don't know if Dad really ever gave it a chance. He's always busy."

"He claims he did."

"In his mind, he did."

" . . . Have you spoken to him?"

She gave me a strange look. "It's a little late now."

"Not necessarily, not if there's something there."

A frown, out of which she asked, "Why are you telling me this?"

"Because your mom was clearly needy, was maybe even a little unhinged."

Mandy turned away for a glass of wine she'd set aside. "Look, I tried, but there's nothing I can do now. Mom has her problems, and Dad isn't any easier. He's not one to be persuaded, when he doesn't want to be."

I inhaled and turned away. "Is there nothing, no friendship they could hold on to?"

Again she gave me a strange look. "Why? Are you friends with your ex? . . . And I still don't get it. What do you, I mean, what do you want with this?"

Aware that my hand was trailing across my brow, I wondered if there was an answer. "Happiness, for each. I know both are unhappy."

"Still I don't get it. What business is it of yours? . . . And frankly, Dad seems okay. I mean despite his blindness, despite the fact that he can no longer do what he loves, he seems okay . . . mentally at least, which is just crazy. I've wondered if he feels he deserves it somehow, for neglecting Mom, or from the years of smoking. I'm not saying he does feel that way, it's just that he seems so . . . oddly at peace . . . Maybe it's good you two hooked up. He might really have lost it otherwise." Now she turned away again. "Probably today's not the day to talk about all this. Maybe on our trip I can bring it up."

"I think he'd like that."

Looking back, she frowned in annoyance, in confusion, before opening the oven door once more.

Upstairs, Jeff had arrived with his wife, and soon thereafter we all descended to the dining room and settled around the long table. Before Rudi carved the turkey, David stood, his trembling hands extending down to, and planting themselves on, the table. Eyes shut, he cleared his throat. "If this film we've been working on, is as good as it seems to me it is, then it represents an apogee in our ensemble work. And because, as we all know, so many little, as well as big, things can thwart a film, this apparent success we've achieved together must be cherished, by us at least, as a small miracle. And for that, I deeply thank you all.

"Rudi, my eyes for years, you became even more so. And in the future, you will have to be my dolly and my transport, if there is a future project. Blind man directs—as preposterous as blind Rodin sculpting, or deaf Beethoven composing. Or maybe Rudi, you will direct, and I will simply be writer and consultant."

"No-o, David, no," protested Rudi, too much.

"Françoise, I warn you to check your suitcase for stowaways before Rudi and you embark on your next St. Barts trip.

"Pat, you were the rock the story was emotionally anchored to. The down-to-earth personality, with which you invested Teresa, rooted all the rest—as did your friendship sustain me when I most needed it. Mandy, you'll forgive me if I thank both Pat and you for helping John be a better Stephen than he or I could imagine. For

Pat, this was not new, as she has long been a dear friend, acting as my internal seeing-eye for years before it became literally necessary.

"Jeff, you found solutions where I thought there were none. You were always upbeat and hopeful and willing to try it one more cut, even at ten at night. I hope your dear wife will forgive me. I promise I won't make a habit of it.

"My two wonderful daughters have been forbearing toward a dad who didn't always know when to stop. Perhaps my behavior will be a lesson to you both. Perhaps looking around here, at this table, you will see that there are different and better ways to live. When to concentrate and when to balance, being among the more critical lessons to learn. Watching your dad, you must already know that—must already know more than he. I'm looking forward to our trip together. I'm eager to learn of historic Mexico through your eyes and voices. And am eager to learn of you two, whom I have too much missed these last several years. I believe it can be a new beginning, for me. And from what I've heard of where we're going, it will be a rich experience for us all.

"And lastly Christine, I am more fortunate for your friendship than I can here express. There are many things we can't explain, many important things, but you and I share some affinity, some harmony, which I can't describe. If my flaws and disappointing weaknesses have lately been too apparent, I hope you will forgive me. But I just want to say to the other dear people here that she has, with her ineffable light, radiated hope upon me, over these months when there didn't always seem to be much hope. Thank you, Chris, and thank you all."

Now Rudi pushed himself up. "David, I will dispense wid all da tanks, for you know dat we have grown, against all odds, nearly as close as colleagues can. Perhaps it is dat we come from different cultures and so are not restricted by conventions. We exchange only d' essential tings. Da local cultural hang-ups get lost, swept under. I feel confident that we will find a way for you to make more films in da new year."

"I suspect, Rudi," David replied, "the demand for blind directors may be vastly overstated."

"David!" broke in Pat, "Hollywood's employed them for years, all following one another ad nauseam. But we will do better. We will translate your original vision into something vital and visible, and we will work with you when you're ready with a script."

"Absolutely!" seconded Rudi, and the others concurred with applause and cheers. I stole a glance at Marnie and Mandy. Through false smiles they peeked around. I wondered if inside they were crying out, or if they were wondering about their mom, who I hoped was with friends or family.

The week or so before they were to leave was not as busy. It seemed there really was an end to the film, and though David was pleased with its completion, he moved with noticeable aimlessness, which to some degree I absorbed as well. Much of the time he worked at home on Vestry Street, with Martina coming down to complete the burdensome paperwork. They will give up the 57th Street office, and this, I sensed, filled each with unspoken sadness. Several times Mandy came down, to visit and to help, but she and I never picked up our conversation.

At the office, Arliss asked me to work on several short articles over the week, before, late in the day, I usually returned to 22nd street to work on Eiley. Yet it felt as if I were lost there. The place seems as if it is a kind of halfway house, a temporary stop, neither home nor in any way connected. I sat at the desk, under some mantle of melancholy. Vestry Street, blocks south, seemed home to me.

David explained his disinclination to venture out as the normal fall-òff after a film, "My postpartum depression, after carrying it around for months . . . years really." Yet I think we both knew it was more. He needed real rest, before he faced the formidable uncertainty ahead. But we did not talk about it. When I tried, he veered away, saying we had exhausted the subject, or the subject had exhausted him. And so, for most evenings, I read to him, and we listened to music, holding each other silently.

Once, when we were propped up on pillows, when we'd talked about making love, but could not quite summon the spark, he wandered off, "What is this Janus-like, four-faced thing, a couple? Something merely biological, evolved to reproduce? Or is it two halves of a whole? What did Nature intend? . . . Or have we somehow gone off her page, into realms we're not equipped for, making it up on the fly? . . . Or do we travel some preordained path toward some evolutionary heights?

"Beginning as egg and sperm, do we not later long for that reunion? Does intercourse do it? Join us, raise us into some elevated state, or is that the role of abstinence?

"I dreamt that you and I traveled the world, along unbeaten paths, trying to reach back to some more elemental mode of living, where not only our skins, but souls, fuse.

"When we do make love, I wish I had more energy to explore and enjoy your every inch and fold and crevice. It still surprises me how little we know the landscapes of our bodies, our own and our lover's. How under-utilized is this life we're given . . . I want to burrow into your novel, and navel, and know everything you think about Eiley. There must be much you've not put in. I want to know what she thinks through the arc of her day. I want to live the life of the city with you, with you now as my eyes, describing in your rounded phrases all that we pass . . . I want to roam you and ream you, bore into you, enlarge you, not with child, but with life, as I feel you do me.

"How simple my attraction to you. Part of it is, as a wise lady wrote, inexplicable, like music. I feel you reach my innermost and highest selves, reflecting them at their best. I invite you in, increasingly deeper, as I dare to look myself . . . To find someone like this is a supreme joy, almost unimaginable, like the universe itself . . . What is this joy? And why is it here at all? . . . How can it be? How is it that there is such intense happiness, in a world that science tells us is all atoms and dark matter?"

December

Somewhere in the week's blur, their departure arrived. Saying goodbye at his house, I found myself both happy for him, and not wanting to let him go. My heart cried out, even as I knew this time together would help them.

Despite his blindness, and intermittent depression, for such it has seemed to be, the days since the screening have been quietly sublime. Our conversations have ridden whim and humor. I helped him pack, as did Marne and Mandy, coming down in the cold afternoons. Mandy, I think, accepts me now, having gained some understanding of the difficulties. But while Marnie shows no overt resentment, she responds to me with only a blank stare.

When he had telephoned for a cab to take the three of them out to Kennedy, we stood just inside his front door. I brought my cheek up to his chapped lips. His hands trembled as they pushed through my hair.

"Where shall we go, David, on our trip?"

"An island somewhere. I'll need a rest after two weeks with my dear daughters—all my transgressions laid bare."

"An archipelago in the far Pacific."

Although his lips stretched into a smile, he turned this way and that, to avoid further talk of this. "I hope Eiley finds her path," he murmured. "It's time she focused in."

"Well do I know. You'll be back before Christmas?"

"We think so. We've left it a little loose. It hardly seems like winter. Summer left only yesterday."

"Only thirteen shopping days."

"All days are shopping days. We all are shoppers."

"For some holy grail at discount. Send me a card."

Another smile, wry, and sent over my head. "Daily."

" . . . I think I hear your cab."

"I'll be picturing you . . . upstate, dancing . . . in bed."

"You must come to Maine next summer."

"I will. We have many trips ahead." A zephyr, however, some winter's breath, passed close by. I stretched toward him for a binding kiss. I did not mind his flaking skin, his underfed look, his mostly-closed eyes. Why was I letting this happen? My life's companion.

Outside, when we had locked his door, and I had led him to the curb—before I helped him bend carefully into the cab—we reached for a final embrace through our thick coats. The wind tried to pry us apart. My lips cracked in the instant that he pulled away. I guided his hand so that he would know where to duck. We wrestled his bag in awkwardly after him. I pushed the cab door closed, wondering at this help I gave. Stupidly, I tried to wave, twisting left and right to see, but could not find him through the window's reflection—this eerily repeated moment. Failing, I closed my eyes, as the cab leapt from the curb and whined down the block. I could not restrain a hand from reaching up, or mind from calling, 'Good trip,' before I shifted a leg against the wind, and stiffly turned away.

WINTER

December 22nd

Damp cold. Out of a featureless sky, a single postcard has fluttered down, from Mexico City, before they went south. Though busy, I've felt I'm simply waiting.

Memories mingle from the year: Father's slackening face, his lingering in bed, numbed by painkillers . . . Yet I cannot, do not want to, list all these images, the last conversations, his small cries.

The park piece sends me out, at least, into an overcast midday. Have not been here in months. All seems bare and sad. The other walkers are wrapped in their coats, faces averted, some striding, some barely moving, arms frozen at their sides. The last brown leaves pinwheel down upon their brethren. Squirrels nose under them, girdled against the ice and wind. The birds are gone, save for the unchanging pigeons. Another of Kirsten's proposals was to write up impressions of a homeless shelter. She must know she sends me back through days of failure.

In late afternoons, I've been returning to my brownstone, silent, still. I turn on the lights, cook a simple dinner, pasta, soup, or salad, and settle down, at the great desk—Dickensian, I console myself—there to try to chase down Eiley, her restless soul.

Clawing at its banks, three feet before them, the cold Delaware slides heavily by, its surface segmented into rotating plates of muddy pewter. Roy kicks at the frozen earth. "Man, everything here 's dead 'n' dying. Not a hint of the energy that surrounds us back in Oakland. I mean it's like I've stepped into some time-warp. Wouldn't be surprised to see some brontosaurus haul its ass out of this river, if it weren't so bitchin' cold."

"Come on, Roy, Colorado suffers its winters."

"But they're sharp and bright. Not like this."

Eiley's mouth twists with irritation. "The point is that they offered me the job. Now we have to decide what we're going to do."

"You've decided."

"You said you could work anywhere. Why not this place for a while? Your dream of Colorado is not going to disappear."

Roy turns his back on the river, shoves his hands deeper into his pockets. "I don't know, somethin' in me rebels. Somethin' cries out, it's death."

"And Oakland's inspiration?"

"Boulder is. But you see? You've already decided. At least at home, there's people 'round."

She looks away. "So you want me to turn them down?"

" . . . No, I can't say that."

"What then?"

"What we have. What's wrong with that?"

She waits, until their eyes meet, to show him her frustration.

He turns his head. "I know . . . for you, you should take it."

"Colorado can follow."

"I know, I know . . . yet somethin' in me cries against it."

"Thanks." Eiley moves away and looks out over the river. Ripples further section its surface. Surface segments seem to move independently, turning, merging, separating. Perturbations, she thinks. Without them, the patterns would repeat.

She does not want to separate from Roy, a deeper union than all the others . . . Makes no sense . . . How do some people manage to stick for years? The right fit, or resignation? . . . But she feels she's not ready to give up her

plan, not after the distance she's come, fleeing from her
mother's lost life—an intelligent woman who wandered into
one of her husband's traps . . . Eiley long ago promised
herself she'd never live like that. Now she wonders if this
promise has ballooned into obsession . . . or is it some hint
of what she'll need. . . .

Tried a draft in which she chooses not to take the editorship
by the Delaware, but then, reading it, saw she must.

Found my thoughts bumping back to David, wandering
through ancient ruins, each hand led by gazing daughters.

About to leave the office at end of day, thinking ahead to
developing Eiley's decision, was called back to my desk by one
more phone call, expecting it to be Arliss with a final editorial
suggestion. "Yes?"

"Christine?" A young woman's voice.

"Yes?"

"It's Mandy."

"You're back! I thought it was tomorrow or the next day."

"We came back early. Dad's sick. He's in the hospital." Her
voice cracked. "Can . . . can you come see him?"

Something cold sliced through me. "Of course. Where?"

"New York Hospital. York Avenue. Intensive care."

"God . . ."

Don't know how I got out of the building and found a cab. A
man, seeing my face, gave me his. The ride through rush hour
stuttered on forever. The driver tried, squeezing, shooting ahead
for every foot—till eventually he swerved to the curb, and I pushed
a bill into his hand and ran off. Inside, couldn't find the floor.
Several people steered me wrong, until I latched onto a nurse's
shoulder, pleading. She led me there, my head throbbing, the
corridors closing in.

Ahead, in a darkened alcove, I saw Mandy by a bed, standing,
head bowed. We, or rather I, embraced her awkwardly, briefly. She
steadied me as I turned to the bed.

He was there, sunken, sallow. His eyes were open but were

not blinking. I took his hand and leaned to him. "David, it's Christine."

His mouth moved faintly; a cheek tried to. I felt a breath expelled, and leaned closer, kissing his cold face. Bringing my ear to his mouth, was able to feel only the barest breath. Mandy accidentally bumped me as she slid closer. I saw IV lines disappearing under the blankets.

Someone approached, tapped my shoulder. I gripped David's shoulder, to not loose touch. Several hands gently peeled me away. I was led off a little, by a nurse and doctor.

"You're Ms. Howth?" asked the sympathetic nurse.

"Yes, what's . . . what's the . . . ?"

"The outlook, I'm afraid . . ." But the doctor's voice fell away, grew muddy.

"What?"

The doctor leaned closer. "I'm afraid the outlook's not good."

"Wha, what do you mean?"

"The cancer has spread, metastasized; it's pretty much everywhere."

"Cancer?"

"You weren't aware?"

"No . . . he never . . . said anything . . . No one did."

"I guess it seems only his doctor knew. He had lung cancer, which sometimes causes retinal deterioration—his blindness."

" . . . Oh God . . . Well . . . what can be done? What can you do?"

" . . . Nothing, I'm afraid."

"What? . . . What do you mean?"

The nurse took my arm. "Nothing except try to make him comfortable."

"What are you saying?"

"That it's a matter of hours."

"What?"

Two pairs of pale eyes were watching me. I tried to escape them, and turn back to him. I pulled, tried to duck away, but was restrained. "No! No! I don't understand. He'd gotten rest. He was putting on weight."

The doctor's voice came through my own. "His physician told us that he avoided most treatments that might've helped."

" . . . Why?"

"We're not sure. Apparently he was out of town a lot. Claimed to be too busy, after it was discovered."

"When was that?"

"Last Spring."

"Last Spring?" A wall, a wave of darkness overswept me, thrusting me down. Last spring? . . . I was turning; a hand went out, mine . . . floating . . . Nothing held me up, except other arms and hands. I was within their arms, leaning, fighting to get back, clawing. Mandy was there, looking down, hands clasped, face splotchy, moist. I ripped a tissue from my coat pocket and pushed it to her. Bending over him, I was searching, though my eyes were closing. Felt myself trying to reach him, trying to bring my cheek to his. Hands again were restraining me. I cried out and leaned more forcefully toward him, but his cheek held no warmth. I could barely detect his breath. Opening my eyes, I saw his were closed. I groped for his hand. I felt a faint reaction to my squeeze. He squeezes back! He moves! Someone cried, "David! David . . ." Hands once again were pulling, a chair was slipped under, I was falling back, onto it, knees folding, sinking—Someone was leaning past, a white coat brushed my brow, a voice whispered, "He's in a coma now." I bent over, pulled up my knees, pressed hands to eyes, shut out the light.

January

Lost weeks . . . have stretched on without shape or end. Cannot believe . . . that never did he make it clear. Hints, which I took for other things: ties to Kath, daughters, doubts, or demons . . . but never this. Believed he was paying and had paid enough.

Cast off daughters, all—adrift. Did their trip down through those ruins explode into a kind of hell, his wasting body a writhing terror alive before their eyes?

Saw them at the funeral: soft black velvet floating in a worsted sea. Their mother, Kath, I assumed, among them, on the other side: a ring of bowing heads supporting separate veils.

So many, in contrast to my father's paltry few.

Kirsten said take a month. I took a week, then went hurtling back, to escape the distended shriek. But thoughts, like beggars hands, float before my eyes . . . Does this end erase his work? Will it quickly fade from the minds of those who saw it, and by extension, from the general consciousness? He would say it's Nature's cycle. But then should he have given all up for his daughters, to have lived, possibly, for them? . . . And me? Or would that have been a different man? . . . Am I not the better candidate for such single focus? Having no one, but Luke, who depends on me. But then, other questions raise their plaintive heads.

I know what he gave me, and my work, through his own. And yet, I'd still prefer him alive, without his work, prefer him for who he was. Something clicked between us—maybe that we each saw the other as each wished to be seen.

Now Eiley waits to see what will be decided. I know I must take her off the shelf. Maybe it's time to see my craft, or guile, for what it is, a desperate living . . . to be tended only to the extent it's needed—really, when there's little choice.

Did he never trust me, never telling? Did he take me as his scribe, to record only the details he wanted known, or more, in moments of darkening despair? Was it scripted after first we met, or did it come upon him slowly as the end drew near? Was I one last reaching out? . . . These questions will be soon dispersed, with his matter. What might be said is that ours was a euphony I will not find again.

So, work is left. It gets me through the days: a means to pay the bills, a reason to hide behind my desks, or sometimes hobble out. I've read that description is love, and that work, maybe like virtue, is its own reward . . . Salvation may be aligning these things inside. On the other hand, I recognize that excessive inward focus leads inevitably to decay, or have I got it backward, once again? . . . To live instead, for the days, was his counsel. To fill them, to drink them dry, as one's lights demand. Both the way, and the rub.

Like aurora wavering in the northern sky, faint melodies have been whispering in my head, have sent me sifting for some words to sing: The Hobo's Lullaby, or something soft . . . don't know why. I usually hum them only to myself. But now, I think I might sing aloud, as I pull out my pages, in the faint chance that there's someone, like him, to hear.

THE END

Printed in the United States
1447500002B/164